TH
WINEMAKER'S
SECRET

ALSO BY CYNTHIA ELLINGSEN

The Lighthouse Keeper
The Whole Package
Marriage Matters

THE WINEMAKER'S SECRET

CYNTHIA ELLINGSEN

LAKE UNION
PUBLISHING

Published by Lake Union Publishing, Seattle

www.apub.com

Amazon, the Amazon logo, and Lake Union Publishing are trademarks of Amazon.com, Inc., or its affiliates.

ISBN-13: 9781503904538
ISBN-10: 1503904539

Cover design by Caroline Teagle Johnson

Printed in the United States of America

For my sister, Carolyn, with fond memories of our summers reading mysteries by the lake

Chapter One

The vineyard stretched across the bluff, its vines etched against the horizon in the muted light of the midsummer night. Laughter rang out across the main room of our family restaurant, Olives, as the party spilled out onto the patio, and wineglasses clinked in good cheer. My grandparents, holding hands in honor of their sixtieth wedding anniversary, stood next to the wrought iron railing overlooking Lake Michigan and the nearby town of Starlight Cove. In the distance, the lighthouse twinkled, its cheerful rhythm flashing against the water.

I let out a shaky breath. The speeches were just a few minutes away, and my parents had requested we all say a few words. My grandparents deserved to be celebrated for the wonderful family and business they'd built together, but the idea of public speaking made me want to go do inventory in the wine cellar.

"You okay?" Kelcee Whittaker, my best friend since grade school, gave me an encouraging smile. "I know you're nervous about this, Abby."

"I'm good." I adjusted the straps of my A-line dress. "My plan is to shock and awe." Taking in the crowd, I added, "Though that shock and awe might come from the moment I run for the door."

"You can't do that." Kelcee smoothed down a loose strand of my hair. "This is your big chance to show your grandfather you deserve your dream job."

Earlier that week, our operations manager had finally retired, but Pappy had passed on my application. He'd said he wanted the replacement to be someone "comfortable in the spotlight." I figured the best way to get him to reconsider me for the position was to knock it out of the park with my anniversary speech.

I planned to talk about the cherry tree that had prompted my grandparents to buy the vineyard. It was a sweet and sentimental story, important in our family history, and if I made it through without a panic attack, my grandparents would love it.

To take my mind off the stress of the speech, I took a gulp of chardonnay. Its buttery texture was smooth on my tongue and balanced with notes of apple and spice. It was young, only two years old, and one of our best chardonnays yet.

Kelcee leaned against the polished oak of the bar. "I wonder what your scandalous brother came up with for his speech."

"Dean?" I said, surprised. "Why?" He stood in the corner of the room, sporting black skinny jeans and a black T-shirt, like some too-cool-for-school rock star. The outfit irritated me. Maybe because, even though my brother was pushing thirty-five, he still dressed like a rebellious teenager.

She took a sip of cabernet franc. "No reason."

"He's trouble, Kelcee," I warned. "You know that."

Dean was also the best-looking Harrington, with his impish smile and wild black hair. He'd spent the past fifteen years doing who knows what in Chicago, and last week he'd come back. No warning, just rolled up the gravel drive on his Harley and sweet-talked my grandmother into giving him a room in the main house. Clearly, he was up to something—it was only a question of what.

I planned to figure it out and soon. The rest of us worked day and night to keep this place up and running, so I didn't appreciate Dean waltzing in like he'd never left. He assumed—in spite of everything—that he still had a prime place at the table, which bugged me to no end.

"Trust me on this one," I said. "You do not want to get involved with Dean."

"Relax." Kelcee rolled her eyes. "I do not have time for your criminal of a brother."

"He's not a criminal," I mumbled.

At least, he hadn't been for several years.

"Abby!" My mother beckoned me from across the dance floor. She looked radiant in a sequined turquoise dress and elaborate diamond necklace, her long auburn hair in an updo.

I set down my glass. "Duty calls."

The place was packed. I squeezed past cloth-covered cocktail tables dotted with plates of half-eaten appetizers and smiled at the familiar faces sipping from Harrington-branded wineglasses. My mother kissed my cheek when I made it to her. She smelled good, like red wine and roses.

"How do you think it's going?" she asked.

"Great," I said. "Perfect, actually."

Well, it would *be perfect, if it weren't for those darn speeches.*

Twinkling lights sparkled from the ceiling, and the scent of roses hung in the air. The start of the sunset streaked across the sky in hues of pink, yellow, and purple.

"So, I called you over to get your opinion," my mother said. "Mrs. Holt is hammered. Should we get her home?"

Mrs. Holt was in her late seventies and ran an herb garden just up the road. Her husband had died just a few years back. This party had to be difficult, watching a couple near her age celebrate so many years of marriage.

I spotted her on the dance floor. She shook her hips as if the string quartet was playing a salsa instead of Mozart. Still, her hair was perfectly in place and her party dress carefully thought out. I couldn't bear to ruin her fun.

"Let's leave it," I said. "We'll start serving her grape juice."

My mother drummed her fingers against her lips. "If she gets worse . . ."

"I know." I patted her arm. "I'll keep an eye on her."

My mother sailed off to greet a late arrival, sequins flashing with every step. Sometimes, I wanted to be as poised and glamorous as my mother, but I've always had more fun getting dirt under my nails in the fields than sitting still long enough for a manicure.

After heading back to the bar, I cleaned up stray napkins, refilled the Jordan almonds, and updated the cocktail staff on Mrs. Holt. I had just made my way back to Kelcee when our hospitality manager headed my way.

Rogers was one of my favorite employees. Kelcee thought he was a total grump, but really, he was a relic. Now in his late sixties, Rogers had been with Harrington Wines for over a decade.

He had a resonant voice with a hint of an upper-crust accent and was always meticulously groomed, with perfectly starched shirts and polished shoes. It was very possible the man ironed his socks. Really, though, it was Rogers's commanding expression that made people stand up and take notice. The vineyard, and perhaps the vines themselves, would crumble to the ground without him—I had no doubt about that.

"Good evening, ladies." He held out a tray of small, curved dessert glasses. "I thought you'd appreciate one of these."

"Ice wine." Gleefully, I reached for one.

Ice wine was my absolute favorite. It had originated in Germany in the eighteenth century, but it hadn't become popular in the States until the eighties. Still, my grandmother, who's German, had started making it during the very first days of the vineyard, and it had put us on the map.

If our family could claim ownership of a treasure beyond the vineyard, it would be our collection of ice wine. The wine was delicious and the vintage bottles, beautiful. They each had the Harrington Wines crest etched into the glass, an ornate *H* surrounded by cherry blossoms. Once Harrington Wines had become one of the top-ranked brands in northern Michigan, word had gotten out about our secret cellar of ice wine. The quality sometimes decreased with age, but that didn't matter. The acquisition of our vintage bottles brought in big money, whether collectors intended to drink them or not.

We had a case from each year we'd been open, starting in 1959. There were only eleven years missing, either because the grapes hadn't made it to frost or because the vines had caught rot and hadn't produced anything at all.

My grandparents valued the ice wine for different reasons. To them, each bottle represented each year of growing the vineyard and their family. Their most prized possessions were the vintage bottles from milestone years, like the year they were married; the year my dad was born; and then the years my brothers, my niece, and I were born. Opening a bottle was a sentimental occasion, and I could practically taste the warmth of our family memories with each sip.

"I love this." Kelcee tried the vidal blanc. "How do you get it so sweet?"

The wine geek in me lit up. "We pick the grapes the moment they freeze on the vine. The water inside freezes but not the sugar concentrate, so that gets pressed while the grapes are still frozen."

The ice wine harvest was hard, cold work, yet my grandparents always made it a celebration, with hot apple cider for the kids, mulled wine for the adults, and homemade apple strudel.

"Rogers is the only person on the planet who doesn't like it, and I'll never understand, since ice wine is liquid gold."

Rogers gave me a look, one eyebrow raised. Before he could respond, the sound system shrieked as the background music came to an abrupt halt.

Both of his eyebrows shot up. "Excuse me. Apparently, I have to educate someone on how to properly use a microphone." He swept off, leaving the scent of shoe polish and starched shirts in his wake.

I would have laughed, but the microphone comment could mean only one thing: it was speech time.

"Good evening, everyone." My father's voice boomed over the speakers. He stood next to my grandparents, who linked arms with him and my mother. My grandmother was short and plump, with a cheerful face, while my grandfather was tall, wiry, and often looked impatient, like he'd rather be out in the fields. "Our family would like to say a few words about the greatest couple of our time, Theo and Greta Harrington."

Kelcee handed me a tube of lip gloss. "You ready?"

I touched up my lips and nodded, embarrassed that my hands were shaking. I was thirty-two years old. How could I expect to run an entire vineyard if I was too scared to speak in front of people?

Quickly, I reread my creased note cards while my mother recited an homage to the power of family.

"Ich habe dich lieb," she finished, and the guests burst into applause.

"I heard a rumor we're supposed to give a speech?" a voice slurred next to my ear. "You look perfectly prepared, as always." Turning, I came face-to-face with Dean, who had been reading my note cards over my shoulder. A jaunty section of hair was styled over his forehead, and he gave me a goofy grin. "My idea is not nearly as charming as the cherry tree, but I plan to bring down the house with outrageous stories of our grandparents during their hippie days."

My stomach dropped as I noticed he held a glass of wine. My brother was a former cocaine addict, and his problem had nearly destroyed our family. It wasn't like we'd had a heart-to-heart since his return home, but it had been my understanding that he was sober. If he was drinking, there was a strong chance he was using again.

The very idea brought me back to a place in my mind I didn't like to revisit. Memories of a time my brother had been too skinny to fit in his clothes and his actions had been completely unpredictable. He'd once pulled a knife on my dad and hadn't remembered the next morning. Things like that had happened all the time, but my parents and grandparents had refused to give up on him, because he was family.

He turned to Kelcee. "So, what's cooking, Miss Whittaker? You still at your restaurant?"

She smiled at him. "Every day."

"I hope you're still making time to eat the roses."

I clenched my jaw. "*Smell* the roses. You don't eat them."

"Kelcee's a chef." He hooked his thumb in her direction. "She could whip up a good rose recipe if the occasion called for it."

Kelcee, the traitor, burst out laughing. I tuned them out as they played catch-up, and the microphone made its way to my eldest brother, Phillip. He gave a solid speech, then loped across the room, giving awkward high fives along the way.

"Where's my baby brother?" he shouted. "Dean, you're up!"

Dean and Kelcee were still chatting in hushed tones, so he missed the "baby brother" joke. The two were only a year apart, but Phillip had always gotten a kick out of the fact that he was the oldest. Either way, Dean looked baffled to have a mic thrust into his hand. Like some drunk disc jockey, he crooned, "I think there's someone we'd all rather hear from first. Abby?"

My mouth went drier than a vintage Chianti. I wasn't even close to ready. Like it mattered. The DJ pinned me under the spotlight, and four hundred eyes turned my way.

"Uh . . ." I fought off a wave of panic.

Show Pappy you can do it.

I drew in a deep breath. "I'd like to thank all of you, uh, for joining us tonight. Not only are my grandparents incredibly special people, but they have also built a wonderful legacy here in Starlight Cove."

Pausing, I looked around the room. Some people were listening and some having side conversations, but—most important—my grandfather was watching me with interest. Heartened, I continued, "To me, the strength of the winery represents the strength of my grandparents' love. That strength has given us all so much to celebrate."

"Here, here," someone cried.

"Here, here," I echoed. "And . . ."

Suddenly, my mind went blank. Silence stretched into infinity, and the light heated my face.

The cherry tree.

"The vineyard started the way many things do . . ."

Breathe, I thought. *Breathe.*

But it seemed like taking the time to breathe would bore everyone to tears, and I didn't want to forget what I was saying. So, I kept going, only taking in quick little gasps of air. My voice became weaker with each new word.

"It happened by accident," I said, gripping the mic. "My grandparents were out looking for the perfect piece of property for a cherry orchard when—"

Gulping in another quick breath of air, I tried to continue, but the syllables caught in my throat. At full volume on the mic, I started to stutter.

I couldn't believe it—I hadn't stuttered in years. When I was six, my mother had taken me to speech therapy, and I'd barely had a problem since. The speech therapist had warned my mother it could pop back up during stressful times. Now, it was like I was humiliating myself in show-and-tell all over again, unable to explain what it was I liked about my dolly.

A strong hand pressed against my back. "Give it up for my little sister," Dean roared, grabbing the microphone.

I trembled with embarrassment as I turned toward the bar. The daisy-scented perfume I had worn for the occasion had faded, and I smelled like sweat. So much for showing my grandfather I could handle the spotlight.

"It's okay." Quickly, Kelcee handed me a glass of water. "You survived."

"I blew it," I whispered. My legs were shaking so hard I probably looked like I was dancing.

Dean's voice cut through the room. "So, it's been a while since I've been home, although Harrington Wines runs in my blood. Literally, right?" He held up his wineglass, and everyone chuckled. "Sometimes, it's hard to believe the winery almost didn't happen. Did you know my grandparents wanted to start a cherry orchard instead?"

My mouth dropped open.

Dean's telling the story. He's giving my *speech!*

"Pappy and Oma were out looking at farmland when they spotted an ancient cherry tree. To their absolute disbelief, their initials were carved into the bark, next to a knot in the wood that—to this day—they swear looks like two wineglasses clinking together."

"It's a carving from the angels," Pappy shouted, and everyone laughed.

"Thanks to that angelic carving," Dean continued, "my grandparents started a vineyard. That cherry tree has lived long past expectation, and their business has thrived beyond expectation. Yes, they were scared to take the risk, but sometimes, when something great is on the line, it means letting go of fear. Here's to you, Pappy and Oma." He raised his glass. "Thank you for being brave enough to build this incredible life for all of us."

In the midst of thunderous applause, Dean made his way through the crowd and handed the mic to my mother. Then, he hugged my grandparents like a winning prizefighter.

"Unbelievable." I gripped the stem of my wineglass so tight I was afraid it might snap. "He stole my speech."

Kelcee gave me a sympathetic look. "It's a true story. Someone was bound to tell it."

Maybe. Even drunk, though, Dean had told it ten times better than I ever could have.

I shook my head. "Pappy looked like he actually believed I might say something good. He's never going to take me seriously, especially if I can't communicate with people. That's what the job's all about!"

"Abby, it seems to me . . . ," Kelcee started to say.

"What?"

"It seems you spend all this time trying to get your family to believe in you, but that will never happen, unless you believe in yourself."

Fantastic. One glass of wine, and my best friend suddenly had a psychology degree.

"What I believe"—I reached behind the bar for the bottle of chardonnay—"is that I'll have another drink."

Rogers appeared at the opposite end of the bar. He caught my eye with a familiar look that could only mean one thing: *emergency.* Of course, he was much too discreet to make that obvious to anyone else.

"Something's up." I set down the bottle. "See you in a minute." I hoped Mrs. Holt wasn't in trouble. I'd forgotten all about her, thanks to the stupid speeches. "What's going on?" I asked once I'd reached him.

He ushered me outside. "I need you to see something."

The evening air felt hot and dangerous. I practically tripped trying to keep up with him in my strappy heels as he strode across the gravel drive toward our storage buildings. Finally, he came to a halt in front of the ice wine cellar.

My stomach dropped as I realized the door was open and the keypad lock hung to the side.

"What happened?" I whispered.

Rogers dabbed his face with a handkerchief. "It appears we've been robbed."

Chapter Two

I rushed down the stone stairs into the cellar. The heat and humidity vanished into cool darkness. After flipping on the light, I froze.

The cellar was empty. Each temperature-controlled cooler assigned to protect nearly sixty years' worth of ice wine bottles—over five hundred total—sat vacant. The wine rack had been stripped. Eerily, other than the faded scent of fermentation, there was nothing to suggest the room had held anything at all.

I pressed my hand against the cold stone of the wall.

"When did you find this?"

"Ten minutes ago." Rogers stuffed his handkerchief into his front pocket without bothering to fold it, which meant he was just as upset as I was. "Your grandmother instructed we serve ten additional bottles. I came to get them and discovered this."

The distant pulse of music from the party echoed in the empty cellar. I pictured my grandparents dancing and laughing, oblivious to the hit we'd just taken.

"We need to call the police," I said.

The police chief, Henry, was a close family friend. He hadn't been able to make the party because he was on duty. I couldn't believe he was going to end up here anyway, in a completely different capacity.

"Of course. Yet when?" Rogers fretted. "This will be a public spectacle. The investigation would ruin the night."

Investigation.

I let out a slow breath.

Rogers was right: the grounds would be lit with red and blue flashing lights and invaded by the local news crews. My grandparents deserved a few more hours of happiness before having to deal with all of that.

"Oh, my dear girl." He paced back and forth. "This is a travesty."

"Oma's waiting on the bottles." My tone sounded much steadier than I felt inside. "She'll get suspicious if we don't pour. Let's use port. Just don't go near her, or she'll know. Once everyone—"

Outside, a loud engine sputtered.

"They're still here," I cried, certain an enormous getaway truck was about to make off with my inheritance. I raced up the stairs. Instead of a getaway truck, though, my grandfather's latest prop plane roared out of the red pole barn at the far end of the field.

Black exhaust lifted over the vines like a shroud. My grandfather cut to the right down the drive, heading toward the empty stretch of land where he kept a runway. The party guests stood outside, cheering him on.

"What on earth?" Rogers sputtered like the engine. "He shouldn't be doing this."

That had never stopped him before. Pappy had always loved aviation and spent his spare time and money fixing up small planes to fly over Starlight Cove. The doctor had recently recommended he give it a rest, since his eyesight wasn't what it used to be, but of course, my grandfather ignored him.

Pappy bounced the aircraft across the ground and lifted it up into the air. It banked, and the setting sun glinted off the propeller as he flew over the party. A white banner billowed out from behind that read **THEO LOVES GRETA**. From the cockpit, he gave my grandmother a thumbs-up.

I put my hand to my mouth and looked at Rogers. "Am I really seeing this?"

My grandfather was a grape farmer, not a charmer. His conversations centered around the weather, the vines, and his planes. This romantic gesture made my heart hurt even more to think someone had stolen such an important piece of my grandparents' history.

Pappy zoomed past once again, going higher. There was a strange rumble, and I squinted up at the sky. The plane dipped, and the murmur of the crowd stilled. Pappy pulled up, and I breathed a sigh of relief. Then, the engine sputtered out completely.

Silence settled through the air. The plane glided over the fields like a wounded bird and then dropped out of sight. Pieces of trellis flew up as it crashed through a canopy of vines. There was a resplendent boom followed by a puff of smoke. Someone screamed—it might have been me.

In high school, I had run track. I'd been faster than anyone, setting local records. Now I used that speed to barrel toward the old utility truck parked next to the main building.

The air inside the decrepit Dodge was heavy and smelled like dirt from the fields. I grabbed the keys from under the visor and cranked the ignition to life. I had just put the truck in drive when a man yanked open the door on the passenger side and jumped in.

"Go," he gasped. "I'm a doctor."

That was the best piece of news I'd heard all night.

I pushed the pedal to the floor as the sun dipped down below the horizon. Smoke rose up from the field like a signal, and I sped toward it.

Cranking the steering wheel, I pulled off the gravel and into our main riesling field. The vines were set wide enough apart to allow room for farming equipment, so the old Dodge easily fit through. It bounced over the ruts in the dirt, and I drove as fast as I could without losing the muffler, my eyes steady on the smoke from the plane.

The doctor rummaged around the glove box. He produced a first aid kit and pulled out bandages and protective gloves. Through the open windows, the scent of something acrid, like burned rubber, was distinct on the summer breeze. Clusters of grapes were dense around us.

The carnage of the aircraft loomed into sight. It had just missed hitting the ancient cherry tree. I gripped the steering wheel, staring at the scene in horror.

The doctor touched my shoulder. "I'm going to see if I can help."

I managed to nod, and he jumped out, the door clanking shut behind him. He had to climb over a row of vines to get to the wreck. The next thing I knew, I was out of the truck. The trellis cut into my legs, and I tumbled to the ground, practically choking on a mouthful of dirt. The doctor stood next to the plane, shaking his hand as though it had been burned. "He's not in there!"

A section of the front control panels had melted together, and smoke swelled from the debris. Coughing and squinting, I stood and scanned the field, spotting my grandfather sprawled out on the ground. I broke into a sprint and collapsed next to him.

His hands and forearms were red and raw. Blood gushed from a gash on the leathery skin of his forehead, but he was still breathing.

"Don't move him." The doctor was right next to me, kneeling down in the dirt. He opened Pappy's eyelids and waved a penlight in front of them.

I kissed my grandfather's forehead. The odor of smoke and oil transferred to my lips. The doctor took off his suit jacket and laid it over him as headlights jumped across the field.

I leapt up, waving frantically.

My family was packed into the back of a pickup truck, my father at the wheel. They piled out, helping my grandmother pick through the near darkness. My mother clung to my oldest brother, wailing.

"Is he breathing?" my father shouted.

"For now." Efficiently, the doctor wrapped the deepest cuts with gauze.

My grandmother approached and knelt next to her husband of sixty years. Cradling his hands, she moved her lips in a silent prayer. Sirens rang out in the distance, and I forced my mind to happier times: Pappy leading the harvest, cooking for our family at mealtime, and blushing sweetly when Phillip's seven-year-old daughter brought him flowers from the garden.

Nothing would be the same without him.

It could have been hours or minutes until the sirens got close and red lights bounced through our fields. Two fire trucks barreled toward the wreckage, followed by an ambulance. Paramedics rushed over. The doctor assisted them in stabilizing Pappy's neck and loading him onto the gurney.

My mother and Oma insisted on riding in the ambulance. The paramedics helped them into the back and shut the doors. Their sparkling party dresses looked out of place under the fluorescent interior lights.

The engine revved, and they sped away. The siren wailed and faded into the distance. There was a hiss as the firefighters neutralized the plane, and we all started coughing in the sudden rush of smoke.

Dean grabbed my arm. "You need to get away from this. It's not good for you."

"It's not good for anyone," I said, moving away from his grasp.

My family had always been overbearing about my health, because of the time I got sick as a child. Still, I didn't feel comfortable having Dean try to step back into that role. He'd been gone too long for that.

I pulled my father aside and told him about the robbery. It seemed insignificant now, compared to the crash. Still, as the words left my mouth, the reality flooded back.

My father took off his glasses. "My mother can't find out," was all he could manage to say. "Not now."

"I know." Through the thin cloud of smoke that hung over us, the stars were dim in the darkness.

Back when I had gotten sick, Dean had told me that when people died, they became stars. Of course, I'd believed him and was scared to go out alone at night for a year. Now, I wondered which constellation Pappy would choose to be a part of if he died.

The thought was too sad to consider.

"I'm not going to the hospital," I told my father. "I'll call Henry about the robbery. The sooner the police get involved, the better. Plus, we're slammed tomorrow—there are at least three bus tours and a wedding at sunset. Pappy would want things up and running."

My father shook his head. "He'd want you with him."

"I can't come, Dad," I whispered. "You know that."

I hadn't darkened the doorway of a hospital since I was eleven. I'd tried, once, when Phillip's baby was born. I'd only made it to the parking lot before driving away. The medicinal smell and stark lights would have brought back too many memories of being hooked to tubes and machinery, struggling to survive.

I stood in silence as my family headed for the hospital. As the firemen hosed down the plane, I noticed the water storage tanks on the fire trucks were enormous. The half-hysterical part of me wanted to ask them to water our vines.

A hand touched my shoulder. "You're shivering."

The doctor.

It struck me that he was handsome, with his dark curly hair and brown eyes. His face was smudged with dirt and his expression troubled. He held out his suit coat.

"Put this on."

It smelled like motor oil and smoke from Pappy, as well as notes of amber, cinnamon, and sage, probably from the doctor's cologne. The scent was comforting, like mulled wine in winter.

"Do you mind taking the truck back?" I asked. "The keys are in the ignition."

"Let me drive you back. You've been through a lot."

I gestured at the scene. "I need to talk to the emergency crews."

"This was a big shock," he said. "You should rest."

I let out a surprised sound, maybe a laugh. Rest? My family must have him on the payroll.

"Thank you for your help," I told him. "But I've got everything under control."

Turning, I went to go find the police.

Chapter Three

The first rays of sun crept through the window, and I snuggled into my sheets, lulled in that peaceful moment between sleep and memory. Then, images from the night before slammed through my head: my grandparents holding hands, the empty wine cellar, smoke rising from the field. I grabbed for my phone to see if my family had texted.

Mom: Pappy's in a coma in ICU. Release a statement to the workers.

A coma.

How was that even possible? Yesterday morning, my grandfather had been out in the fields, evaluating the experimental section of vines we had growing in gravel. He'd looked tanned, strong, and more energetic than most men pushing eighty. I couldn't imagine him resting on the couch, let alone a hospital bed.

Letting out a shaky breath, I read a text from my father.

Dad: You're in charge—check your email. Let's meet for breakfast to discuss a game plan.

We also had to discuss the ice wine. I did not look forward to telling him what the chief of police had had to say.

Henry had arrived at the site shaken about the crash. The second I'd told him about the robbery, he'd snapped into police mode, and we'd headed to the wine cellar in his cruiser. He had inspected every inch of the cellar and then had pummeled me with a million questions about the wine collection, our workers, and the last time I'd been in the room. Finally, he'd tapped his flashlight against the broken keypad.

"I hate to tell you this, kid. These typically don't release unless they lose their power source. Even though someone jacked this up, it still works."

I'd touched it, surprised to feel a small hum of electricity.

"Someone," he'd continued, "I'd guess one of your workers, wanted to make this look like a break-in. I'm willing to bet they used a key."

One of our workers?

Our sixty-acre vineyard had twenty-eight employees. The majority were part time or seasonal. Still, most had been with us for years. The thought of one of them stealing from us made me feel sick.

Peeling myself out of bed, I saw it was already six and padded down the hallway to the kitchen. Like the rest of my house, it was small, but it was mine. When I'd returned to the vineyard after the only summer I'd spent away from home, my first order of business had been finding a place to live. I hadn't wanted to move back into the main house with my parents, grandparents, Phillip, and his family. So, I'd convinced my grandparents to let me remodel the old gardener's cottage, the place where Dean and I used to have a playhouse. It was only nine hundred square feet, but what it lacked in space, it made up for in peace and quiet.

In the kitchen, I measured out enough espresso for a double shot. The coffee machine hissed and whirred, filling the room with a burned, earthy scent. The smell matched the smoke that still lingered in my hair.

I settled into a chair at the kitchen table. The space served as both my office and dining room. It was one of my favorite spots, because it offered a beautiful view of the vines and Lake Michigan. Biting into a chocolate doughnut, I turned on my computer and got to work.

My father had texted me the log-in information to access the operations files. Seeing them reminded me of the blunder I'd made with my speech the night before. The moment seemed even worse now, since it might have been my last chance to tell my grandfather how I felt about him.

Keep this place up and running. That will show him how you feel.

I studied the schedule. The day was packed with wine tastings, tours, reservations at the restaurant, and the wedding at sunset. Since my family was out, we needed extra hands to get everything done correctly and on time. I picked up the phone to call our staff, prepared to beg for help.

Turns out, I barely had to ask. Once our workers got over the surprise that we planned to stay open, they quickly agreed to come in. I had coverage for every missing member of my family and then some.

These are supposed to be the people who would steal from us?

The thought was impossible to process.

Once everything was in place, I called Rogers. He was in charge of one of our major tourist attractions, the tasting room, so he needed to know exactly what was going on.

"This could easily be a disaster of a day." I put him on speaker while sliding on a pair of white shorts and a purple polo shirt branded with the Harrington Wines logo. "I think we can pull it off, though."

"I am a bit surprised we're staying open." His tone made it clear he did not approve. "However, I understand if the vineyard cannot afford to lose additional revenue."

"The ice wine won't ruin us." I tied the laces on my shoes. "It's a lot of money, but it's insured. The biggest loss is the sentimentality."

"I wasn't speaking of the ice wine."

I paused. "What . . . then?"

The silence between us was uncomfortable. "I've heard rumors," he finally said, "that we aren't as solvent as we have been in the past."

I glanced in the hallway mirror before answering. There were dark circles under my eyes, and even my wild curls looked limp and tired, up in their typical ponytail. I was going to need a whole lot of coffee to make it through this day.

Yes, the winery had experienced setbacks. We had lost nearly every grape to drought a few years back, and to rot the next. The cost of sourcing grapes at the height of the season had made it impossible to turn a profit, but I'd never heard we were in trouble.

In fact, the only money talk I'd heard had happened at Sunday dinner a few weeks before. Phillip, who worked as our accountant, had asked Pappy for permission to perform an outside audit. Our grandfather used paper records for practically everything, and my brother had argued it was impossible to spot mistakes. Of course, my grandparents had refused.

"Everyone would know our business." My grandmother had looked horrified. "I might as well put a picture of my unmentionables in the *Town Crier*."

The fact that my grandmother had even mentioned her unmentionables was the biggest "no" of all time.

"Rogers, this is a farm." I grabbed my keys. "We're at the mercy of the insects and that great big yellow ball in the sky. As long as we produce enough to eat, drink, and be merry, we'll be just fine. I have to meet with my father. See you at nine."

Outside, the heat made me wince. The air smelled stale and dry, like the desert. One of the benefits of having a winery in Michigan was the cool days—our vines had about four weeks longer to flourish than those in arid places like California. I certainly didn't need to add "too much heat" to my list of worries.

Halfway to the utility truck, I spotted Dean strolling through the chambourcin field. He wore the same outfit from the night before and had pulled a baseball cap low over his eyes.

"Dean!" I shielded my eyes from the sun. "What are you doing?"

He didn't answer, and I jogged over. His clothes were rumpled and his eyes haunted. For a split second, I feared the worst.

"Is Pappy . . . ?" I couldn't finish the sentence.

Dean held up a cluster of grapes. "These are not in good shape."

Both relief and irritation shot through me. The cluster of chambourcin was, in fact, small and shriveled, but the grapes had a way to go before they became plump, dark skinned, and sweet. Their appearance was actually nature's way of discouraging the animals from eating them before they were ready, but I was not about to explain that to my absentee brother.

"Why aren't you at the hospital?" I asked.

"I couldn't just sit there." Dean pulled a grape off the bunch, popped it into his mouth, and spat it out. "Thought I'd come back. Help supervise."

Supervise?

I leveled him with a look. "You're welcome to be a set of spare hands. That's all we need now, thanks."

I stalked off toward the truck.

"Hey," he called. "I'm getting the impression you're not happy I'm back."

I turned and squinted at him in the sun. "Are you back? We haven't heard from you in years, so I'm not really sure what it is that you want."

Dean spread out his hands and grinned. "Isn't it obvious?"

Dread settled in the pit of my stomach.

Ever since we were kids, Dean had planned to run the vineyard. Based on the way he was drinking in the land that stretched from the coastline to the forest, he still thought that was a possibility. Heck, maybe it was.

Pappy had loved lecturing my brothers, not me, about rotating crops and heavy-duty farm equipment. He'd assumed I'd rather play dolls, no matter how many times I tried to jump in on the discussions. He had finally taken my interest seriously when I was eight years old and was the first to spot crown gall on one of our vines.

Still, Pappy had been pretty clear about the fact that he wanted my brothers to lead the charge, even after the horrific accident on-site that had made Dean turn to drugs. But Dean hadn't been involved with the vineyard in years. It infuriated me that he thought he could just show up and take over. Worse, that my family might very well let him.

"I've got to go," I said, heading for the truck.

"Abby, wait! You never answered my letter."

I winced against the sudden sting in my eyes.

Back when Dean had seemed to care about getting sober, he'd sent me an apology note. It had been part of a twelve-step program and had listed all the ways he had wronged me, including one hard truth I hadn't known about. That truth hadn't helped me forgive him—it'd only succeeded in breaking my heart.

"Water under the bridge," I called.

Blinking hard, I kept walking toward the truck.

~

Starlight Cove bustled with early-morning activity as I pulled into town. Locals and visitors strolled the sidewalks, drinking coffee and shopping at the early stalls open at the farmers market. Town was always so busy during the summer, but during the winter, our population was only forty-five hundred. It was nice to see downtown teeming with tourism, bringing energy to our old-fashioned streets.

The breakfast places were just opening their doors, perfuming the air with the scent of bacon and sausage. The pastel buildings that lined Main Street charmed me, like always, and so did the peaceful presence of the beach. I caught a glimpse of the midnight blue of Lake Michigan and the bright-red door of the lighthouse through the gaps in the buildings and took in a calming breath.

The lighthouse's sure, steady presence had helped me make it through the tumultuous years of Dean's addiction. There'd been countless nights I had stared out my bedroom window and watched the beam reflect across the water as I cried myself to sleep, terrified at the skinny, angry person my brother had become. The knowledge that the lighthouse had been there for over a hundred years gave me hope that, no matter the strength and fury of the storm, it could still be possible for my brother to find his way to safety.

Shaking off the thought, I let myself in through the back door of Kelcee's restaurant, Towboat. The kitchen was in happy chaos, with bacon smoking on the stove and eggs sizzling in the pan. Kelcee ladled batter onto a griddle, "getting crazy with the pancakes," as her teenage daughter, Sami, liked to say.

Ducking past the food runners, I headed into the cool cavern of the restaurant, breathing in the comforting scent of fresh coffee and real maple syrup. My dad hadn't arrived, so I read the specials off the board. There was an omelet that sounded good, with smoked salmon, chives, and cream cheese.

I had just put in my name for a table when a booming voice said, "A smoked-salmon omelet? Give me a good old-fashioned plate of pancakes any day of the week." Turning, I came face-to-face with Mayor Matty Brown.

Ugh.

Mayor Matty was short and portly with a white mustache that made him look older than his fifty years, which might have been the point. He had a voice like a megaphone and, rain or shine, sported a colorful suit with a matching bow tie. My grandmother and most of the upper crust of Starlight Cove found him "precious," but I wasn't sold.

"Abby." He pulled me into some sort of cheek-kiss side hug. "I was terribly sorry to hear about what happened last night. My wife and I had left not twenty minutes before and saw the fire trucks headed toward the peninsula. How is your grandfather now? I trust he's well?"

"He's in a coma." My voice cracked, and I felt embarrassed to let the mayor see me upset. Clearing my throat, I added, "So, no. Not really."

Mayor Matty paused to smile at a young couple in the waiting room. They must have been tourists, because they didn't leap forward for a selfie.

He turned back to me. "Perhaps I should pay him a visit. Your grandfather would say it was the best conversation we've ever had."

I smiled in spite of myself. Over the years, the mayor and my grandfather had butted heads on everything from land ordinances to liquor laws.

"This time," the mayor continued, "he's probably mad that I have no interest in that convoluted wine trail of his."

"The wine trail?" The humor drained right out of me. "That's my project."

There were five wineries in the area, and I believed a wine trail could build tourism and therefore revenue. Old Mission Peninsula in Traverse City had one, as did several other areas in Michigan. A trail would link the Starlight Cove wineries together and make for a more connected experience.

In my proposal, I had suggested visitors could collect a token at each winery and at the end, cash in their collection for a free, branded T-shirt. That would encourage tourists to stop by all of the wineries on the trail, plus it would put our name out there, since Harrington Wines would be the title sponsor of the event. I'd heard the project was buried in bureaucracy but hadn't known the mayor had no intention of letting it pass.

"Mr. Mayor, we're a tourist town rich with history." I gestured at the old-fashioned photos lining the waiting area. "That promotes tourism, and we need to find ways to build on that. The wine trail would attract—"

"The party crowd." He dropped his jovial tone. "Speaking of, I noticed your brother Dean is back in town."

I blinked. "Sorry, what?"

"Matty Brown." My father strode up. "Good to see you again, sir."

The mayor offered condolences regarding Pappy, gave me a quick nod, and waddled away like a walrus. I watched him go, still in disbelief at what he'd said about Dean. I might not have a positive opinion about my brother, but that didn't mean I wanted to hear someone else criticize him.

Kelcee's daughter sat us at a corner wooden booth with a perfect view of the lighthouse. The beach was right outside the window, and the seagulls pecked against the sand in the early-morning light.

The busboy served us coffee, as black and oily as the night.

"Mom said Pappy's in a coma?" I asked.

My father stirred creamer into his coffee. "Medically induced. The doctor saw some dangerous plaques on the brain scans. He's also in extreme pain from the burns and a few broken ribs."

I couldn't imagine how my father felt. Yes, I was close with my grandfather, but this was his dad. He had to be devastated.

"Is he going to make it?" I asked.

The words sounded strange, like a line from a movie.

My father's eyes met mine. "If force of will matters, he'll be up in no time."

Force of will.

My family always said that's exactly what had kept me alive.

I stared out at the water as my father updated me on the doctor's plans, more details about the coma, and theories about what had gone wrong with the plane. Once our food arrived, we discussed the logistics of the day. Finally, he got to the ice wine.

"What did Henry say?" he asked.

"He thinks it was an inside job."

My father frowned. "I can't imagine one of our people doing that. Stealing from us?"

"That's what I said." I took a bite of my omelet. The smoked salmon was perfect with the egg and cream cheese. I hoped the mayor saw me eating it. "Henry's going to start questioning people at lunch. I'm hoping they'll think it's related to the crash." The empty cellar flashed through my mind, and I set down my fork. "When should we tell the rest of the family?"

My father hesitated. "Not yet. Your mother wouldn't be able to keep it from your grandmother. Neither would Phillip."

"So, we'll wait."

"We'll wait." He took a drink of coffee and then pushed it away. "I have something additional to discuss with you. I heard you put your application in for operations manager."

A slow flush crept up my neck. "Dad, we don't have to talk about this right now."

"I'd like to talk about it." He studied me over the rim of his glasses. "Your mother said you were very upset."

"Pappy threw my application in the garbage." I didn't like complaining about my grandfather, given his current condition. On the other hand, it let me pretend life was back to normal. "I have photographic evidence."

Phillip had been working on a project in the main office when my grandparents had discussed setting up interviews. He'd texted me a picture of my résumé in the trash, along with the message "Fight harder."

My father squeezed the bridge of his nose. "Look, I'm impressed that you want to keep things running, and I think you'd be an outstanding replacement. When the time comes, I'll stand behind you. However"—he took off his glasses—"I need you to believe in your ability and to avoid getting caught up in other distractions."

"Like . . . ?"

"Dean."

I looked down at my plate.

Every year Dean had been gone, my family had worked overtime to get him back. My grandparents had begged him to come home for harvest, but he'd always made some excuse. My parents had gone to Chicago to visit him several times, and even Phillip had gone once or twice. I was the only one not interested in sharing phone calls, emails, and the hope that this time, he really was clean.

"You don't have to worry," I told my father. "Dean and I are adults."

"The two of you are also family," he insisted. "Let the past be the past."

Frustrated, I looked out at the lighthouse. "You don't know what he did to me, Dad."

"Well, he was a drug addict." My father's voice was frank. "I can't imagine it was anything good. I also can't imagine it was beyond the realm of forgiveness."

I squeezed my hands so tightly under the table that they hurt.

"No matter what, he's your brother," my father said. "He always will be."

A boat with a bright-white sail floated by on the lake. It painted a cheerful picture, along with the deep blue of the water and brilliant sunlight. My world felt so dark in comparison.

"Yeah," I mumbled. "I know."

My father made a move to stand up. "You ready?"

Quickly, I said, "One thing. Rogers made a strange comment. He heard we're in some sort of financial trouble?"

My father's eyebrows shot up. "Where did he hear that?" he asked, sinking back into his chair.

"You know he loves to gossip. Really, it could be from anyone." The dinner where Phillip had mentioned an outside audit jumped to mind. "Remember how Phillip wanted someone to look over our accounts? What was that all about?"

My father took a sip of water. "Your grandfather keeps records that make sense to him and your grandmother. It can be a challenge for anyone else to decipher them."

"Phillip must have found something," I pressed. "Why else would he bring it up?"

My father took off his glasses and rubbed his eyes. He looked exhausted, like he'd slept in a hospital chair all night.

"This is confidential," he finally said, putting his glasses back on.

My stomach tightened. "Okay." The chives from my omelet suddenly smelled too strong, and I pushed my plate to the edge of the table.

"Phillip thought he found a large loss in one of the books. However, he was unable to piece together the accounts well enough to substantiate the claim." My father fiddled with a sugar packet and then tossed it back into the holder. "For now, we have to operate under the assumption that things are fine. We'll take a closer look once Pappy's out of the woods."

It wasn't the answer I was hoping for. However, it explained where the rumor had started. Phillip couldn't keep a secret to save his life. He'd probably mentioned it to someone while drinking after hours in the tasting room, and the idea had grown wings and taken off.

If my father wasn't that concerned, though, it couldn't be that big of a deal. The vineyard was his legacy, even more so than mine. If something was wrong, he'd be the first to handle it.

The waiting area was crowded as we left. My father stopped at the stone steps that led out to Main Street, beneath the hanging light. He spent most of his time out in the fields with Pappy, and his skin looked weathered, especially in the fine lines around his eyes.

"I wish you would come to the hospital." He rested his hand on the railing. "I know you would rather not revisit the memories—"

"I can't," I said quickly. "I'm sorry."

The disappointment on his face cut through my heart, but I couldn't do it. There was no point in pretending otherwise. The fear of returning to the past, to a place that had caused me so much pain, was too strong.

He patted my shoulder. "I'll call you later."

I headed back toward the kitchen, waving at Kelcee on my way out. Sunlight reflected off the lake, and I fumbled for my sunglasses before staring blankly at the whitecaps on the water.

After getting into the truck, I drove back home.

The second I pulled into the drive, Raoul, one of my favorite field hands, flagged me down from the merlot field. Grabbing something from beneath the trellis, he strolled over, wearing an enormous straw hat that did little to combat the ever-present sunburn that colored his cheerful face.

"Hey." He leaned into the truck window, already smelling of sweat and soil. "This was half-hidden under the vines. I spotted it when I pulled in. Thought you'd be interested."

Raoul handed me an old box. It was about four by four inches, gunmetal green, and ragged with rust. It rattled as he passed it through the window, like there might be coins inside.

"It's gotta be treasure," he said. "Don't you think?"

The summer before, the whole town had been buzzing about a long-lost treasure from a shipwreck. The lost silver had become a hot topic. I was not about to believe any of it had been squirreled away in our fields, but the box was definitely intriguing.

"This was just sitting in the field?" I said, inspecting it more closely.

It had a small padlock holding it together. Even though the box was rusty, it didn't look dirty enough to have come from the ground. Still, it was possible it could have been turned up from the soil and rained on before anyone found it.

What could possibly be in there?

"It's pretty old," he said. "Looks like it fell off a truck or something."

The words struck me. There was a constant stream of UPS, utility, and maintenance trucks parading on and off our property. However, my mind went right to the robbery. The fact that there was something suspicious by the driveway could be significant.

"Did you tell anyone else about it?" I asked, with a glance out at the field.

"Nah. I saved it for you." Raoul stepped away from the window and patted the hood of the truck. "If it's treasure, I expect my cut."

"You're the best, Raoul."

He tipped his hat and headed back to work. I watched him go, grateful he was so honest.

Placing the box carefully on the scratchy front seat of the Dodge, I gunned the engine and headed up the drive, eager to learn what was inside.

Chapter Four

I stopped at the shed behind the main storage building for some tools to cut open the padlock. The cicadas and grasshoppers were singing their morning song. I loved the sound of the insects during the summer, as long as they stayed away from our vines.

Inside the shed, I grabbed a wrench, a pair of pliers, and some heavy-duty gloves. I had just pulled the light bulb string, blanketing the room in darkness, when footsteps crunched outside.

That's odd.

Our gardener didn't work on Saturdays. It was only eight thirty, and it hit me that no one knew where I was. It was a silly thought, since I never reported my whereabouts to anyone. Still, after the theft of the ice wine . . .

The hinges of the door creaked. I leapt backward as the enormous silhouette of a man filled the doorframe. The darkness clicked into light, and Wendell, our gardener, let out a startled shout.

"Good *gracious*!" He grabbed his chest. His hand was nearly brown with age spots and sun damage. "Miss Abby, what are you doing, lurking like that in the dark?"

Earlier, Wendell had volunteered to help out the field team. It hadn't dawned on me that he would show up early to get some gardening done too, but it should have. The sight of Wendell toiling away in his worn overalls to keep our landscape beautiful was as certain as the sun.

I held up my handful of tools. "I needed to take some things."

"Like ten years off my life?" Wendell mopped his damp forehead with a hanky. "How's Mr. Theo?"

I updated him, and Wendell muttered something about having the sense to keep his feet on the ground. "We're all praying for him." He gathered up his wheelbarrow and hedge clippers and headed out the door.

Back home, I keyed open the door and braced for a cool blast of air-conditioning. Instead, the house felt as suffocating inside as the tool shed.

Air's out.

It wasn't the first time. The cottage was one of the oldest buildings on the property, so something was always broken. It was all part of its rustic charm.

Taking a seat at the kitchen table, I pulled on the thick gardener's gloves, grabbed the wrench, and got to work. It only took four sharp twists for the lock to clatter to the floor. The same thrill of anticipation I got before trying a new wine rushed through me.

Inside, there was a small object wrapped tightly in a grimy piece of burlap. I handled the cloth carefully, allowing humidity and dust to pass through my fingertips. The cloth hid an intricately carved wooden box, like the puzzle boxes sold at the local art fair.

I reached for the latch but then drew back. The decoration carved into the wood—a small rose surrounded by a circle of petals—was eerily reminiscent of the crest for Harrington Wines. My heart started to pound.

This can't be coincidence.

Quickly, I opened the box.

It was empty and lined with worn black velvet, but I had heard something rattle inside. Determined to find it, I ran my finger along the fabric. There. Something hard was loose and trapped beneath it. My fingers worked the edges, and I extracted a brass key.

It was about two inches long and stamped with the letters *AIF*. It was impossible to tell if it was a hundred years old or a few decades. Either way, it wasn't a match for any of the locks at the vineyard. I rummaged around to see if there was anything else hidden away, but that was it.

Immediately, I called Henry. He picked up on the first ring.

"It's connected to the robbery," I said, once I'd updated him on the find. "The design on the latch looks a lot like our logo. I think—"

"Text me a picture."

I did, then chewed my fingernails, waiting for his response. Henry sounded more than a little impatient when he got back on the line.

"It's a rose," he barked. "Not an *H*. And the little petal thingies are different."

"Yes, but . . ." My throat started to tighten. "Okay, look at the pattern of the orb surrounding it. It's very similar to our design, and collectors find the strangest stuff. The symbol is so close to ours . . . it makes me think that the people who robbed us must have had this with them and—"

"Abby, have you slept?"

I gripped the key. "A little."

"Get some rest." His voice was uncharacteristically gentle. "Then, tell me if you think there is logic to what you're saying."

"But—"

"Kid, the last few hours have been a shock. Take a breath, and let me do my job. I'll be in later this morning to question the staff."

My neck was hot with embarrassment as we hung up.

I stared down at the box, running my finger over the symbol. Yes, the box might be a piece of trash that had nothing to do with anything. Sleep or no sleep, though, every instinct in me screamed it was connected. If I could find out what the key unlocked, maybe I'd have something substantial to report. Or maybe, I'd have nothing at all.

I sat back on my heels, thinking. How on earth could I figure out what the key even went to?

The Henderson brothers.

I'd grown up with the guys who owned Henderson Hardware. They knew everything about home repair but also hardware. If anyone could tell me what the mystery key was for, it would be them.

Besides that, visits to the shop were endlessly entertaining. The three Henderson brothers were all over six feet tall, with broad shoulders and rugged features. The store was always packed with women faking an interest in the latest nail gun or circular saw.

Unfortunately, I wouldn't have time to go today. There was too much going on. I slipped the key safely onto my key chain and headed for the front door.

Halfway there, I came to a sudden stop. The living room window—which I didn't use, because it didn't have a screen and let in too many bugs—was wide open. Two thoughts ran through my head at once: *(1) That's why it's so hot in here. (2) Someone's been in my house.*

Or was *still* in my house.

From the moment I'd set foot inside, I'd been so focused on the box I hadn't even looked around. Someone could have been right there in the living room. Or my bedroom. Was someone hiding in the closet, watching me?

"Hello?" I called.

No answer.

Racing to the kitchen, I dug through the drawers.

A few years back, a black bear had tormented the vineyard and surrounding farms, so Pappy had made us all carry bear spray. I'd read it could double as a can of mace. Gripping it tight, I quickly checked every closet in the living room and then crept down the hall toward the bedroom and peered in the door.

Sure enough, the closet door was cracked. Despite the heat, a chill ran through me.

Is someone there? Hiding in the darkness, waiting to strike?

My breath was tight, like it had been the previous night during my speech.

"Who's there?" I called in a shaky voice.

A floorboard creaked, and a surge of adrenaline cut through me. With a roar, I rushed forward and flung open the door. The closet was empty, except for my clothes, shoes, and half-full laundry basket. The only place left to look was the—

Whoosh.

Water rushed on in the bathroom across the hall, and my blood went ice cold.

I dropped the bravado and the bear spray and raced for my bedroom window. The screen popped out with a ping, and I scrambled down the wall. The thorns on the rosebushes lining the side of my house tore up my arms and legs as I scrambled away.

Our security detail picked up on the first ring.

"Gary," I gasped. "I—" Then, like the night before, the words caught in my throat.

"Abby?" Gary's voice was sharp. "What's wrong?"

I tried to speak and couldn't get anything out. The bypassing techniques I'd learned from my speech therapist had left my brain years ago. I was just about to panic when a familiar voice rang out behind me.

"Abby! Did you just jump out the window?"

I turned back to my house in disbelief. Dean hung out of my bedroom window, a grin splitting his face. He wasn't wearing a shirt, and his hair was wet.

"You did!" He burst into laughter. "You jumped out the window."

My fear dissipated into anger.

"Gary," I managed to say. "False alarm." I hung up without further explanation and stomped back toward my house. The screen from my bedroom window was on the rosebushes.

I glared up at my brother. "*What* are you doing in my house?"

"Taking a shower," he said, as if it were obvious. "I crashed in the bathtub right after you left to meet Dad."

"The *bath*tub?" I echoed.

"I was hot, the bathtub was cool . . ." He brushed the jaunty section of hair out of his eyes. "It was like sleeping on a waterbed instead of a Tempur-Pedic, but it did the job."

"You broke into my house."

He scoffed. "Back when this was our clubhouse, we always came through the living room window. Besides, what was I supposed to do? I don't remember you giving me a key."

I wiped off my sweating forehead with the back of my hand. My heart was pounding, and I was still scared out of my mind. Of course, my brother treated the situation like it was a big joke.

Fifteen years had passed since he'd left. Still, nothing had changed. I felt like a total fool—just like with the speeches. At least this time, there weren't two hundred people to witness it.

"You have five minutes to get out of my house," I told him. "Replace the screen, close the windows, and lock the front door behind you."

"Fine. You don't have to be so testy about it." He squinted at me. "Listen, I noticed some chocolate doughnuts on the counter . . ."

I didn't even respond.

Turning my back on him, I headed to work.

Chapter Five

The one thing that could always snap me out of a bad mood was the sight of our tasting room. It was my favorite building on-site—stately stone, ornamented with climbing ivy and black-framed windows. Red rosebushes lined the cobblestone path, and a small placard greeted guests:

IN VINO VERITAS.
HARRINGTON WINES, 1959

I also loved the soothing scent of the fresh oak floors, countertops, and wine racks. The wooden shelves lining the walls were stocked with endless bottles of wine, and merchandise was carefully displayed. The wall that faced the bluff had a large picture window and offered an incredible view of the vines against the backdrop of the lake.

Pushing open the door, I stopped. The typical aroma of oak was overpowered by the sweet scent of flowers. The countertops practically bloomed with floral arrangements in all shapes, sizes, and colors.

Rogers stood behind the bar polishing glasses, prepping for the onslaught of Saturday tours and tastings. "Isn't it wonderful?" He touched the petals of a nearby lilac cluster with affection. "They started arriving this morning, and it hasn't let up."

I walked over to the first bouquet and pulled out the card. It read:

Hey, you old codger. Thanks for teaching me to drink wine like a man. Now, hurry up and get better or I'll have to teach you about the healing properties of whiskey.

—Ward Conners

Ward owned the antique shop downtown. He and my grandfather had been good friends for years, and Pappy would get a kick out of his card. Setting it aside, I opened the next one, nestled in a bouquet of roses.

With love and respect. Wishing you well and praying for a swift recovery.

—The Jacobs Family

The Jacobs family had moved to northern Michigan from Napa about a decade ago to buy an abandoned winery. They weren't shy about asking for help, and my grandparents had spent countless hours teaching them how to build a successful vineyard in this climate. The Jacobses had been quick to become competition, and of course, they remained great friends and allies.

I reached for the next one, tucked into a spectacular arrangement of daisies.

Darling Theo and Greta,

The starlight in the cove has dimmed. Prayers for a swift recovery.

Lots of love, The Weatherlys

I blinked back tears. The Weatherlys had supported our vineyard from the beginning. Maeve Weatherly might look as proper as could be, but she loved nothing more than to sit on the porch at Olives, open a bottle of cabernet sauvignon, and swap outrageous stories with my grandmother. I could only imagine how upset Maeve was about the crash.

Quickly, I skimmed through some of the other notes and then considered the huge number of floral arrangements.

"Let's get these to Pappy as quickly as possible." I bit my lip, remembering the stark white walls of the hospital room when I was a child. I'd cherished every colorful bouquet, but there had been only so much space in the tiny rooms. "Actually, he'd need a separate wing to handle all of this. Let's pick a few favorites for him and distribute the rest to other patients."

Rogers nodded. "Quite thoughtful." He pulled a box out from under the bar and began to load them up.

"Wait," I said quickly. "Let's go through and make a list for thank-you notes first."

He held up a yellow pad. "Already done."

I picked up the notebook and hugged it close. "Thank you."

I considered the bounty of flowers and then the wrought iron clock on the wall. Billy, our bartender, would arrive any minute.

"How will we get these to the hospital?" I asked.

Rogers gave me a sympathetic look. "Let me worry about that."

I looked down at the wood grain of the bar, embarrassed to think my phobia was so transparent. Rogers had not been here when I was sick, but he knew my history. He must have guessed I was trying to avoid bad memories but was too tactful to bring it up. The kindness made my eyes sting with tears.

"Stop that, my dear." He passed me a napkin. "The only place we should ever cry is into a glass of wine, which means you still have a few hours to go."

Laughing, I helped him load up the flowers.

~

By the wedding at the end of the day, I was exhausted. There were so many details that kept the place operating that I barely had time to complete my own work, not to mention coordinate the police questioning and insurance adjusters. Running things on my own seemed crazy until I'd imagine telling Pappy all that I'd accomplished. Each time, that thought kept me moving forward.

The sun was setting as I pushed a cart full of sparkling-wine bottles through the gate of the garden on the bluff, the bottles clinking as they bounced over the cobblestone path. The wedding garden was another one of my favorite locations, with panoramic views of the vineyard, Starlight Cove, and the surrounding farms on the peninsula.

Even though I was exhausted, the day had gone without a hitch, with successful tour groups, tastings, and individual tours. Now, the bride and groom were out in our wedding field, about to say "I do." I had plenty of time to pour the sparkling wine into the glasses in the champagne pyramid and make sure everything was on target with our vendors.

The wedding coordinator, Hannah, waved at me. Her curly red hair was bright in the evening sun as she put the finishing touches on the decorations. I headed over, impressed as always with her work.

The tables were draped in white cloths with rose-tulle overlays, with an array of crystal wineglasses set beside colorful china. Sprigs of wildflowers and vines climbed from silver vases. The look was pure elegance and warmth, which the bride would love.

"This looks wonderful," I told her. "As always."

"Thank you." She fluffed a bloom of cherry blossoms. "These are especially lively today."

The cherry tree with my grandparents' initials carved into it flashed through my mind. I couldn't believe the plane had crashed so close to it. It was almost as if . . .

Pappy wanted to see it. One last time.

"Are you okay?" Hannah asked.

"Yes." The crash site was still there, like a crumpled and blackened tin can dumped in the field. "I wish the insurance adjusters could have taken that out today. The bride isn't going to want that in her pictures."

"No one worth their salt would complain. Other than that, the view is spectacular."

The wedding coordinator was right—the summer breeze smelled fresh and full of promise, while the fields looked lush and curvy in the low light. It was the perfect place to celebrate love.

Once the wedding guests began to make their way toward the garden, I poured myself an enormous glass of chardonnay and snuck off to the secret bench in the arbor on the hill.

The ice-cold wine burst with flavor in my mouth. The sensation made me think of the bag of grapes Pappy kept in the freezer. He liked to pop them in his mouth like bonbons, and eventually, everyone in the family had picked up the habit. The greatest faux pas in our family was taking the last grape.

Closing my eyes at the memory, I took another long drink.

"Is this seat taken?" a deep voice asked.

My heart skipped. It was the doctor. His dark hair curled around his ears in the heat, and he wore a light-blue linen suit. He stood outside the overhang of wisteria, holding two glasses of red wine. My mind jumped to the moment his gaze had held mine, right before he'd tried to save my grandfather.

"Hi." The sudden emotion in my voice embarrassed me.

I took a quick drink to hide it and gestured at the iron bench. He settled in. The summer breeze carried the same spicy scent from his jacket that I'd noticed the night before, and it hit me that I hadn't paid attention to the smell of a man for over three years.

"I'm Braden Pearce."

It hadn't even occurred to me that I didn't know his name. "Abby Harrington." I held out my hand. "I have to admit I'm kind of impressed to see you here two nights in a row."

Giving a lopsided smile, he said, "Don't be. If it weren't for my aunt, I'd be hiding out at home with a stack of medical journals. I've been her date the last two nights." Before I could ask for her name, he held up a wineglass. "I brought you this, but I see you're all stocked up."

"I'll take it." I balanced my chardonnay on the thick grass at my feet and reached for the red. "I love our pinot noir."

"How do you know what it is? You haven't even tasted it."

"The color." I held it up to the fading light. "It's like looking through a red lollipop instead of a stained glass window."

"Huh." He studied the glass. "I will never look at pinot noir the same again."

I could have gone on and on about the nose and the flavor profile too, but I didn't want to bore him. "Wine should supplement food and conversation," my grandmother always said. "Not serve as the main course."

I clinked my glass to his. "Cheers."

"Cheers."

"So, what do you think?" I asked, after a minute.

I worked in business development, but everyone in my family made the wine, so the grapes in the pinot noir had passed through my fingers in some capacity. During harvest, which took place in the fall, my family worked eighteen-hour days, seven days a week. So, every time someone I cared about tried one of our products, it mattered to me.

You just met. You can't care about him.

I did, though. Given what we'd shared, the doctor already felt like a friend. Heck, he'd practically earned himself a place in the family.

"It's delicious," he said. "Did you get some sleep?"

Why do people keep asking me that? I must look terrible.

"Not really." I studied the faded blush of the pinot noir. "Pappy's in a medically induced coma, so that's where that stands. Honestly, we wouldn't know which way is up without him, so . . ." I refused to finish the thought out loud. "Anyway. It meant a lot to have your help last night. Thank you."

Braden nodded, his profile strong and serious. "By all reports, your grandfather's a great man. Unfortunately, I never got a chance to introduce myself last night."

I ran my finger over the rim of the wineglass. Blackbirds chirped in the distance, and the green leaves on the vines seemed to glow in the golden light.

"He's my greatest influence." Then, because that sounded like the beginning of a school essay, I added, "He's just this incredibly tough person, you know? He's also a sweetheart. This one time, he—" I stopped. "You don't need to hear this."

Braden's dark eyes were kind. "I'd like to."

Turning to him, I said, "My favorite memory of Pappy was the day my brother Phillip brought his baby home from the hospital."

It had been late May, and the trees had been in bloom, filling the vineyard with the fragrant scent of cherries and the lazy hum of honeybees. My family had been gathered on the porch of the main house, holding **WELCOME HOME** banners and bunches of pink balloons.

"My grandfather didn't want anything to do with babies, and he was hard at work out in the fields. Or so we all thought. Phillip pulled up the driveway, going maybe two miles an hour. He and his wife fumbled with the car seat and carried it to the porch."

Braden gave me his half smile, as if to encourage me to go on.

"My brother said, 'I'd like to introduce you to our daughter, Ava.' There was this muffled cheer, and this giant pink teddy bear rushed out from behind the house. The baby burst into tears. My father must have been super on edge about protecting his new granddaughter, because he leapt off the porch, tackled the bear—"

"Oh!" Braden cried, as if watching a football game.

"—pinned its arms behind its back, and was about to throw it to the ground when we heard shouts from inside the gigantic pink head. These huge, furry pink hands lifted the head of the bear to reveal a red-faced and sweating Pappy."

Braden burst out laughing.

"It was ninety degrees, and he had been lying in wait to surprise the baby." I finished the pinot noir. "The funny thing about my grandfather is that he can be completely low key. Then he'll do something like that, or the thing with the banner last night."

"Was he lucid before they put him into the coma?" Braden asked.

I looked out at Lake Michigan to chase the images of the crash from my mind. "I don't know. I—"

Dean burst around the corner of the trellis. "We need to talk."

I jumped, practically kicking over the chardonnay. My brother was sunburned from helping out in the fields all day, with sweaty hair and streaks of dirt on his face. He looked like a vagrant—an angry one.

"Dean, you remember Braden." I used a lofty tone, hoping to make my brother's appearance seem like the most natural thing in the world. "He's the doctor who helped us out with Pappy last night."

I wanted to make sure Dean remembered, given his drunken state at the party. More than that, I hoped it would prevent him from saying something rude or embarrassing. There was no telling where my brother was at mentally these days, and I didn't want any surprises.

"Doc." Dean reached out and shook Braden's hand. "Thanks for your help, man." Then he raised his eyebrows. "So, I guess your work here is done."

"Hint taken." Braden caught my eye and winked. "Good to see you both." He grabbed our empty wineglasses and headed back to the wedding.

The moment he was out of earshot, Dean glared at me. "I thought you were in charge. The bride was down there freaking out on Rogers because the twinkly lights weren't on. What are you doing up here?"

"Wait, what?" The wedding coordinator was in charge of the reception, and it was not like her to let things slip. Jumping to my feet, I peered around the trellis.

Everything looked great. The twinkling lights were hung from wires draped over discreet stakes and lit like fireflies. The bride stood by a table, talking and laughing, looking as happy as could be.

I turned back to Dean. "We hold the lights until dusk, which happened about thirty seconds ago."

"Well, the bride was not happy. Something you would know if you were doing your job."

I stared at him in amazement. Dean didn't even work at the vineyard. This was so beyond the scope of acceptable behavior that I could barely process it.

"Are you high?" I blurted out.

Dean shot me a dark look. For a moment, he looked genuinely dangerous.

I held up my hands. "I'm only asking, because if you're not, I can't begin to imagine why you think it's okay to tell me what to do."

"I'm clean." His eyes locked on mine. "And that's the last time you're going to ask me that question."

I rubbed my sweating palms against my dress. "I'm going back to the party."

"Good," he said. "Maybe you could even try to run it, considering you told our family you were staying here to keep things under control. I bet they'd find it pretty interesting to hear the truth."

I came to a halt and turned to face him. Night had started to fall, and the shadows on his face looked dark and unfamiliar. I didn't know if he was high or drunk or just being a jerk. Either way, I'd had enough.

"Which is what?" I demanded. "I am *not* the wedding coordinator. So, don't run to Dad and waste his time with something completely irrelevant. The family needs to focus on Pappy right now, not whatever"—I gestured at the space between us—"whatever this is supposed to be about."

"That's rich." He kicked at a tuft of grass. "I don't see you focusing on Pappy."

My stomach clenched. "You haven't been a part of our family. So, don't you dare judge me."

There was plenty more to be said. I was so upset, though, I was afraid I would start to stutter.

The aftertaste of the wine was sour in my mouth as I made my way down the hill to the garden. The grass scratched at my feet through my sandals, and mosquitoes buzzed in my ears. Dean followed like a mountain lion stalking me from behind.

Dinner had been served, and forks clinked against the plates. Braden sat at a table by the lilac bushes. He chatted easily with a small group.

Rogers was over at the bar, restocking the wine bottles. I caught his eye. My fury must have been apparent, because he raised his eyebrows and headed right over.

Dean came to a halt next to me. "It's pretty obvious you have an issue with my presence." He didn't bother to lower his voice, so I pasted a fake smile on my face, hoping the wedding guests thought this was a normal conversation. "So, let me make something clear to you: I plan to be a part of the vineyard. Don't stand in my way."

His breath was hot on my face. It didn't smell like alcohol, which reinforced my belief he was using again. That would explain what he was doing home too. He probably couldn't pay his rent in Chicago.

Rogers watched him storm off. "Your brother seems to want to run this place. Shall I inform him that will never happen?"

I grunted. "Sorry the bride flipped out on you about the lights."

Rogers looked puzzled. "The lights?"

"Dean said . . ." My voice went dull. "Let me guess: there have been zero issues with the bride."

"She has been a glowing model of marital bliss." Rogers squinted at me. "I apologize if you were otherwise informed."

Soft jazz crooned from the overhead speakers. The grass was dry and faded beneath my feet. I was so tired that I could imagine curling up on it to sleep. The last twenty-four hours had taken their toll. Now, here was Dean, making up some story to have an excuse to act like a jerk.

Over the years, I'd wondered if the time Dean was on coke had really been as bad as I'd made it out to be in my mind. The dull ache in my stomach confirmed that it had been. I wished he'd never come back home.

"He hasn't changed a bit," I told Rogers.

Rogers adjusted his cuff links. "People don't change, my dear. Our ability to tolerate them might adjust with age. However, we should never expect a rosé to become a cabernet."

"You hate rosé."

Rogers tilted his head, watching the dance floor.

"So, you hate Dean," I said, working off the analogy.

"I don't know him." Rogers paused. "That said, I have heard the rumors, and the one thing that bothers me is that he chose to put himself in the hospital again and again due to his drug use. You didn't have a choice in getting sick. That strikes me as rather unfair."

"Life's not fair," I mumbled. "I think you taught me that."

Rogers gave a slight smile. "Then I've done my job. Speaking of . . ." He looked back toward the bar.

"Go." I wrapped my arms around myself, shivering in spite of the warm evening breeze. "Someone needs to keep this place from falling apart."

As Rogers headed back to work, his words rang in my head. I'd never thought about the fact that Dean's drug use was a choice, while my illness was not. It was a good point. Perhaps, on some level, that truth was part of the reason I had never been able to forgive him.

My father's words from breakfast came back to me. *I don't want to see you getting caught up in other distractions.*

I looked up at the clear sky, the stars twinkling like lights. Running the vineyard had been a challenge. So far, though, honoring my father's request to forgive my brother had been the most difficult thing of all.

Chapter Six

The next morning, running the vineyard became just as difficult as dealing with Dean. Everything seemed to go wrong. A storm from the middle of the night had dropped a tree right across the main drive, making it impossible for the first tour bus to get in. We resorted to shuttling the passengers up in the back of the Dodge. Then, our main guide called in sick, so Rogers had to give tours, which he hated. Dean nearly got into a fistfight with one of the field hands while they worked to remove the tree, and to top it off, the police chief continued interviewing our staff. That made everyone tense, even though they had no reason to suspect anything was going on.

My mother and Phillip came home to help in the early afternoon. I hugged them more tightly than usual when they walked into the tasting room. "I've never been happier to see anyone in my entire life."

There were dark circles under my mother's eyes. Still, she managed to look put together, dressed in a crisp white shirt, pale-blue linen pants, and a diamond tennis bracelet. Her lipstick left a powdered smudge on my skin as she kissed me.

"How are you holding up?" she asked.

Guests milled around us, waiting for the next tour. A small group took pictures, and Phillip offered to take a group photo of all of them.

"It's been wild. I'm glad we're open, though."

"Your grandmother is too." My mother squeezed my hands. "She said Pappy would be pleased."

I didn't know whether my mother was just saying that to be nice, but the compliment gave me the boost of adrenaline I needed.

"Then let's make it work." I straightened my shoulders. "Where do you want to be?"

Phillip stationed himself in the tasting room so my mother could catch up on emails and social media. I decided to find the field hand Dean had practically assaulted, to make sure everything was okay.

On the way, I bumped into Raoul. He was sweating and sun-burned. It was the first time I'd seen him since he'd passed me the box, and now he gave me a teasing grin.

"Are we rich?" He ducked under the eaves of the tasting room for some shade.

"You mean rich in the knowledge that we'll have to work for the rest of our lives? Then, yes. Absolutely."

He laughed, and I glanced around, half-afraid someone would over-hear. Even though the police chief had dismissed the box, I was still convinced it was somehow connected to the robbery.

"It was empty," I lied. "Pretty anticlimactic, huh?"

What was I supposed to say, though? *Hey, Raoul, I found a mystery key that I hoped would help solve a case, because, BTW, we got robbed, but we're not telling anyone, because the police chief thinks one of you did it?* Lying seemed much kinder.

Raoul scratched his head. "It felt heavy to me."

"No, I mean, it had another box in it." My shirt was already stick-ing to my back from humidity and nerves, even though I'd only been outside for three minutes. "Wooden. Old. Empty."

Could he tell I was lying?

"You can have it if you want." My throat tightened up. "Otherwise, I'll probably just pitch it."

"Nah." Chugging a bottle of water, he shrugged. "Not unless it's made of gold."

I wanted to make another joke, but the next words out of my mouth would surely stumble and catch. So, I gave him a quick smile and rushed away. I planned to go to Henderson Hardware first thing in the morning to see if one of the Hendersons could identify the purpose of the key. In the meantime, I could only hope it was worth the deception.

~

Once the day was done, my mother, Phillip, and I gathered at Olives for dinner with my brother's wife, Kate, and their seven-year-old daughter, Ava.

Typically, we sat at the long table on the back porch, breathing in the fresh summer air and drinking chilled chardonnay. Today, we sat in a low-lit booth indoors, which felt somber yet appropriate.

We discussed business while Ava colored. Once our food arrived, my mother looked around the restaurant and sighed. "It seems so strange to think the last time we were here, we were celebrating your grandparents' wedding anniversary."

Phillip took a bite of rigatoni. "No matter what happens, they have bragging rights. It's hard to believe anyone could stay married sixty years."

Kate laughed. "We'll get there."

"It is pretty impressive." I cut into my chicken parmesan. "My longest relationship was sixty seconds."

"That's not true." My mother opened a bottle of red table wine and passed it around. "We all thought you were going to marry that field hand you were sneaking around with. That relationship was rather significant."

My mouth dropped open. "You guys *knew* about that?"

Everyone at the table nodded, even little Ava.

"Wow." I ruffled her hair. "I guess secrets really are impossible to keep around here."

Three years ago, I'd gotten serious with a guy who worked for us. Jax. The very thought of him made my heart ache.

Jax and I had felt connected from the very first moment we'd seen one another. He'd been shirtless in the fields with a straw hat on his head, laughing with the field hands. I'd marched over, determined to help out with pruning. Next to him. For the entire afternoon.

At some point, I had mentioned my sink hadn't been working, and Jax had been quick to volunteer to check it out. He'd come over right after work, sneaking shy glances from under my cabinet. I'd ordered pizza as a thank-you, and we'd started drinking red wine. The next morning, we'd watched the sunrise from my bed.

Our relationship had been fast, intense, and absolutely perfect. There had been a few guys I'd dated over the years, but forever felt possible with Jax. It probably would have been, except he'd always dreamed of owning a vineyard in Chile. He was fascinated by the culture and of course, the wine.

By the end of the summer, he'd found an apprenticeship there and begged me to join him. I couldn't do it, though. The thought of traveling so far, leaving my family and our vineyard, was not a leap I'd been willing to take. Still, when I had time to sit with my thoughts, I sometimes wondered what my life would look like if I'd gone.

My mother waved a breadstick at me. "Why did you keep the relationship a secret?"

"Honestly?" I adjusted my napkin in my lap. "Because I was afraid Pappy would fire him. I can't believe he knew and let it happen. Oma must have laid down the law."

My mother nodded. "She believes in love."

~

After dinner, on the walk back to my house, I studied the stillness of the stars and considered my mother's words. *Love.* The sentiment was so simple and yet so hard to find.

My grandparents had not only found it—they'd made it last for years. Nothing could take it away, not even the theft of the ice wine. Still, if Pappy died, I knew more than anyone that my grandmother would need those memories.

"Some women cherish their wedding album," Oma had once said, cradling a bottle of ice wine from 1959, the year they were married. "This is what matters to me. The flavor of a year. When Pappy and I drink it together, that time comes rushing back."

I knew what she meant. Every time I took a sip of our 2009 cabernet, the vintage Jax and I had drunk that first night, the memory of him was so vivid. If I closed my eyes, I could actually feel his lips touch mine.

A star shot across the sky. I stood silent in the middle of the field, watching its promise glimmer and fade. Then I made a wish.

Please, I thought. *Please let my grandfather live. Let their love story last forever.*

Don't waste a wish on that nonsense, I could practically hear Pappy roar. *Spend it on the ice wine!*

Pappy would be furious to discover the ice wine was missing. I had to do something. But what?

The box with the rose on its latch was the only lead I had. It could not be coincidence that the box had cropped up the morning after the theft was discovered. No matter what the police chief seemed to think, I knew the two things had to be connected.

Tomorrow, I planned to prove it.

∼

Main Street was just waking up when I took the key to Henderson Hardware. The mist rolling off Lake Michigan brought with it the crisp smell of the freshwater lake, along with the vague scent of algae and fish. The air felt so different than it did on the peninsula—ripe and full of moisture, like the early-morning dew that nursed our vines.

The shopkeepers hosed off the front sidewalks and watered their flower boxes as I walked by. The Henderson brothers were not out front, and their door was still locked, so I tapped on the front window. The guys were always there an hour before they opened, rain or shine.

Carter Henderson came out of the back, wiping his hands on his jeans. He wore a fitted burgundy T-shirt that showed off his strong frame and brought out his freckles. When he saw me, he quickly unlocked the door.

"Abby, I'm so sorry about your grandfather." He pulled me into a brotherly hug. "How's he doing?"

"He's hanging in there. I can't believe it's already his third day in the hospital." It felt like no time had passed at all. "Your card was so sweet."

In high school, the Henderson brothers had lost their parents in a plane crash. Pappy's accident had probably brought up memories they wanted to avoid, yet they'd still sent a bouquet of wildflowers. Their note said they looked up to Pappy, both as a business owner and role model, and knew he'd pull through.

"We're rooting for him," Carter said.

I nodded. "I know."

"So." He cleared his throat. Then he gave me the teasing look I knew all too well. "Did you get another stamp on your passport, traveling all the way down here?"

I laughed. The townies always gave me a hard time for living so far out on the peninsula. It had been the same back when we were kids. They'd made fun of me and my brothers for taking the bus forty minutes to school. When it had snowed, we'd been the ones laughing, because we got to waltz into class late.

"Abby! I thought I heard someone of the female persuasion."

Cameron, probably my favorite Henderson brother, strutted out from the back of the store. He gave me the secret handshake we'd invented in gym class, then brushed a lock of curly hair out of his eyes.

"So, what brings you downtown? It's too early to fly south for the winter."

Carter burst out laughing. He and his brother punched each other with glee.

There was a shout from the back office, and Cody, the oldest, tore out of his office like a lion. "I told you two to unload the truck! What are—" Spotting me, he frowned. "Oh, hey, Abby." Folding his enormous arms, he leaned against the checkout counter. He had a tattoo of a cross on his forearm. "How's Pappy holding up?"

I gave them the update.

"He's as hearty as the soil he works on." Cameron smoothed his curly hair. "He'll be up and about in no time."

"Any idea what happened with the plane?" Cody demanded.

"NTSB said it was a mechanical issue. The engine stalled and died." I thought of Pappy tinkering on his planes late at night, under the blinding utility light he'd strung up in the pole barn. "They found a place where one of the wires was falling apart. Don't know how he missed it, but he did."

Cody stomped behind the counter and booted up their computer. "I heard you guys decided to stay open in spite of all this. Business must be booming."

I colored slightly, remembering the comment Rogers had made about solvency. I was glad the Hendersons had the opposite impression. Word couldn't get out that we were in trouble, because that could start all sorts of gossip we didn't need.

I gave a vehement nod. "We're always busy."

Cameron lounged in a small display of lawn chairs. "Now more than ever, I bet, since Carter's always at Olives, trying to wine and dine his *girl*friend."

Carter's freckles blended into his blush. He was dating Kailyn, a real estate agent who had been in our class, and they were the perfect match. She was bubbly and vivacious, which balanced out his tendency to be shy and awkward.

"So, what brought you in today?" Carter made a big show of getting down to business. "Do you need help on a project?"

It *was* getting close to time for them to open, so I decided to tease him about Kailyn another day. I pulled out the key and held it up.

"This was tucked away in a box. It doesn't go to anything at the winery, and I have no idea what it's for. Thoughts?"

Cody squinted at it. "It's junk." He pulled out a ream of receipt paper and popped open the receipt machine to reload. "Pitch it. No one likes a hoarder."

Disappointment flashed through me. Maybe there had been things of value in the box, and those were long gone. If the key was worthless, that would explain why it had been left behind.

"Hold up." Cameron hopped up from his lawn chair and held the key up to the window. The brass winked in the early-morning light. "Ignore the great wisdom of my older brother. You don't want to throw this away. It's the key to a safety-deposit box."

Carter crowded in, his freckled face lit with interest. "You think so?"

"I know so. It's from Starlight Cove Central, not the new bank." Cameron did an Egyptian-style dance, then pointed at Cody. "I believe my profound intelligence makes me employee of the month."

"Get that crap off the truck, and we'll talk." He headed back to his office. "Hang tough, Abby."

I gave Cameron a high five. "I don't know how you know these things."

"I'm a savant, minus the idiot." Loudly, he added, "That part went to Cody."

"Truck," Cody roared from his office.

Cameron scampered to the back, laughing. I tucked the key back into my purse and glanced up at the clock on the wall. The bank probably opened at eight thirty.

Carter, always the gentleman, walked me to the front door. "Let us know if you find anything good."

After stepping onto the sidewalk, I turned back. "Thanks again for the card. It meant a lot."

"Hey, we're all in this life together." His face got serious. "If you need anything, let us know."

I tried to thank him, but the words wouldn't come. Swallowing hard, I headed for the bank.

Chapter Seven

As I walked up the street, the haunting blue of Lake Michigan sparkled beyond the pastel-painted buildings that lined the road. Seagulls cried overhead as the lament of a barge called from the distance. I approached Starlight Cove Central and stood in silence, staring up at it.

The bank was so old it could have been formed with the sand dunes. The imposing structure lorded over the center of Main Street like a queen. The two stories were painted a faded white, and copper anchors lined the roof in honor of the storied history of our town's shipping heyday.

Inside, it was cool and quiet. Tellers sat behind brass cages that had to date back to the thirties, and quietly sifted through paperwork. The huge hands of a black clock ticked from the back wall. I gripped the key and gave the security guard a nervous smile.

Is this even legal? The key's not mine.

Earlier that morning, my father had texted that we had a meeting set up with the police chief at ten thirty to discuss the investigation. If the contents of the safety-deposit box seemed significant, I could share the information with him. Maybe that would keep me out of trouble. Either way, I was still hopeful it would give me some clue about the ice wine.

I approached the friendliest-looking teller. She wore a neat green suit and a bejeweled broach. Her name tag read SUSAN. "Hello, Abby." Setting down her paperwork, she smiled. "How are you feeling these days?"

I cringed.

Of course.

That's why Susan looked like a friendly face—she had been the class mother when I got sick in the fifth grade. She'd brought me a week's worth of homework to the hospital at a time, with the full assumption that I was not well enough to complete it. Most of the time, she was right.

"I'm much better," I said, like I had been ill last week rather than two decades ago.

"Good." She folded her hands. "How can I help?"

I held out the key. "This was passed down to me. Unfortunately, I don't have any other information, so I don't know what to do with it."

"It's one of ours." Her manicured nails hovered over the keyboard of her computer. "Let's start with the last name of the person who gave it to you."

My mouth went dry. "Ah . . ."

Deception was not my strong suit. Perhaps I should have told my brother what I'd found, since he practically had a degree in criminal activity. The very thought prompted me to be as honest as possible.

"It's from our estate, but it . . . okay, this sounds crazy. I'm not sure whose name it would be listed under."

Susan's fingers paused over the keys. "Did Theo pass away?"

"No," I said, quickly. "It's not from him."

"Good." Susan touched the cross on her gold necklace. "That would hurt my heart. Greta is in here all the time and could not be sweeter."

Leave it to my grandmother.

Our winery worked with the newer bank. Still, Oma had a relationship with every business in town. I hoped the teller had a confidentiality clause because otherwise, my secret key wouldn't stay secret for very long. That was the trouble with living in a small town—there was always someone with a story to tell. This time, that story happened to be mine.

"Hmm . . ." Susan clicked her tongue. "Nothing popped up. Who was the previous owner of the estate?"

"Wilcox." I wiped my hands on my shorts, reminding myself this was a necessary step in tracking down the ice wine.

"There are several boxes listed under Wilcox. However, they don't originate within the correct time period." She paused. "You said the key was passed down to you?"

"Yes." I fumbled with my purse. "I should go. I'll do more research and find out what box number it's supposed to be."

"That's not necessary. May I see the key?" I handed it to her, and she pointed out the letters along the top. "AIF is box 198." She typed something into her computer and nodded. "This box was paid on a hundred-year lease by G. B. in the late fifties. There is not . . ." She scanned the screen and clicked her tongue. "The box was rented prior to our approval list, so the contents are accessible by the key holder."

"Oh." I bit my lip. "Okay."

So far, this was working out better than I could have hoped.

Susan led me to brass doors leading into a vault and pressed a button on the edge. A buzzer went off as the doors opened. I followed her down the hall, my sandals slapping against the polished marble of the floors.

"Give me one sec to get the guard key." She unlocked an armored door. "I'll be right with you." Once she returned, she held out a clipboard. "Could you sign and date the log?"

The page was exclusively for Box 198. The only person who had ever signed it had done a great job masking their identity, if that was their intent, because their handwriting was nearly illegible. Peering at the date, I shivered.

August 20, 1959.

My grandparents had bought the vineyard in 1959. That was also when they had gotten married and made their first bottle of ice wine. If the box really was from some crazed collector, the contents could have something to do with the opening of the vineyard or my grandparents' wedding or anything, really.

Collectors could be intense. We'd once had a lady contact us because she was working on a collection of corks from Michigan wines. She'd heard my grandparents corked their wine from the first day of production and was willing to pay an outrageous price for one of the originals. The emails, phone calls, and visits did not stop until my grandparents finally agreed to sell her one.

"Follow me." Susan led me into a long room lined with tiny lockers. "One ninety-eight . . ." She inserted my key and the guard key into the box and turned them simultaneously.

I held my breath.

The door clicked open, and she took a step back.

"I'll let you remove the tray," she prompted when I just stood there.

"Oh!" I blushed. "Thanks."

My legs felt weak as I peered into the opening. A small manila envelope rested on a tray. I picked it up and was about to open it, when Susan said, "Let me get you set up in a private room."

The room was off the hallway in the vault, with an ancient wooden table and chair. It smelled like floor wax and money.

"Press the button if you need anything." She pointed to a small intercom system on the wall before shutting the door.

The only sound in the room was the hum of the air-conditioning. I studied the envelope for several moments. Then, before I could change my mind, I dumped its contents onto the table.

Clink.

A ring bounced across the wooden veneer. It was a simple gold band with a delicate floral pattern etched into the metal, most likely a wedding ring.

I held it for several moments, the weight heavy in my hand. I hardly expected it to tell me its story. Still, my grandmother always said the best way to understand a wine was to sit with it for a while, so I settled in.

The gold ring was dented and worn. It slid onto my pinky finger with ease, so it had once belonged to someone tiny, like my grandmother. She liked to say it was a great tragedy that my hands were too large to wear her rings, because I'd have to get them made into earrings or necklaces when she died. I scolded her for talking like that, and she just laughed.

"Death's a part of life, my dear," she said. "It's the ones who get left behind who suffer."

I took off the ring and looked for an inscription. There was a date inside the band, 12-7-56.

Why had it been hidden away for so long?

I took a quick picture. Something on the ring setting caught my eye as the phone flashed. It was hard to see with all of the wear, but one of the flowers seemed more intricate than the others.

Shining my flashlight close, I leaned in. The lines were thin sketches and nearly worn away. The design almost looked like a star.

I brought the flashlight as close as I could. The light finally hit it at the right angle, and the image became clear. I nearly dropped my phone.

It wasn't a star.

No. It can't . . .

I squeezed my eyes shut and then looked again. The carving was clear as could be. The thin lines formed a symbol of hate universal across the world. The ring that had seemed so pretty suddenly seemed strange and sinister.

It took a few moments to accept the reality of what I was seeing. I stared at the Nazi symbol for so long that my coffee got cold, and I wondered whether I needed to tell Susan I was all right. To be honest, I didn't quite know if I was.

The carving was not a scratch or a dent. It was a deliberate symbol.

Who would want that on their wedding ring? And why was this in a box with a crest reminiscent of the one on our ice wine?

I sat for so long that my neck got stiff. Finally, I slid the ring into the envelope and rang for Susan.

"Ready to sign out?" she asked.

The pen dragged across the page as I tried to decipher the original signature. The first letter almost looked like . . . yes. It was a *G*. The last name was nearly a scribble, but the first letter was definitely a *B*, which matched up with the owner of the box.

G. B. Who was . . . ?

I stopped. My grandmother's maiden name was Bauer. I squinted at the signature once again. Now that I knew what I was looking for, it was clear.

G. Bauer.

Oma must have brought the ring from Germany and hid it for someone. Family? A friend? I had no clue, especially since my grandmother refused to discuss the Nazi Party.

"It's ancient history," she argued, whenever the topic came up. "I should not have to talk about this simply because I am German."

Regardless, it was a hard topic to avoid.

One Thanksgiving, Phillip had returned from college for winter break. Drunk on rhetoric from World History 101 and a bottle of our latest table red, he'd argued that a discussion about the Nazi Party was relevant because it still existed. Oma had become incredibly agitated and had threatened to throw him out. I could see now how the topic would have upset her, especially if she'd had a connection to the person who owned the ring.

The box with the key had probably been hidden in the cellar along with the wine. The thieves must have dropped it, and I was beyond grateful Raoul had been the one to find it. Even though I didn't know the story behind the ring, I knew one thing for certain: it was a piece of history my grandmother would not want to claim.

Chapter Eight

"Abby!"

Main Street was starting to bustle as I walked back to the truck. The coffee shops were crowded, along with the breakfast cafés. Shading my eyes, I stopped and looked around.

Braden was a few doors down, standing under the pale-blue awning that belonged to Frannie's Frames. This time, we hugged like it was the most natural thing in the world. He smelled like soap and shaving cream, and I squinted at him in the sun.

"What are you up to?" I asked.

"Clerical tasks." His hair was still damp, and the way it fell emphasized his strong jawline. "Some credentials were broken during the move, so I had them reframed. Without the evidence, who would believe I'm a doctor?"

"I think you've made a pretty good case for it so far."

We smiled at each other.

"So, what are you doing downtown?" he asked.

I considered telling him about the theft and the mystery box. He seemed like someone who would have a logical suggestion about what to do next. At the same time, it was hardly something I could tell people.

"Errands," I lied.

He nodded. "Do you have a minute to see the new office?"

It was only ten to nine. Mondays were light for tours and tastings, and besides, the tasting room wouldn't even open until ten. I could afford to spare a few minutes, especially for the doctor who'd helped save my grandfather.

"Sure." I slid on my sunglasses. "I'd love to."

We chatted comfortably on the walk down Main Street and into the "business district," which was really just two side streets where offices mixed with charming old houses. It hit me that I'd never asked Braden what kind of doctor he was. The words were just about to leave my mouth when he stopped in front of Starlight Cove Pediatric.

"Here we are." He rubbed his hands together. "I bought the practice a few months ago. We're planning to reopen in two weeks."

I drew back. He was a pediatrician? Just my luck. I had spent more than my fair share of time in this very office. I never wanted to set foot in it again.

To be fair, the colorful Cape Cod looked completely different than it had when I was growing up. The gloomy gray exterior was now a bright blue with red shutters and a green door. It reminded me of something out of a kid's movie or a Lego collection. I nodded with fake enthusiasm, my throat too tight to speak.

Braden climbed up the steps and unlocked the door. "Let me know if you think the locals will like the changes."

I followed him up and peeked in, standing right outside the door. He really had done a lot of work. Like the exterior, the interior was completely different than I remembered.

Gone was the old green carpet that carried every disease that had passed through Starlight Cove. It had been replaced by a royal-blue rug splashed with yellow stars. The wooden walls were bright white, stenciled with colorful toy trains, zoo animals, and trees. Beanbags and sofas completed the cozy look.

Even though the initial look was completely different, there were still relics from the past. The lighting fixtures hadn't been touched, and I recognized the pane of glass covering the receptionist window. My memories were also firmly intact, so I was not about to walk through the front door.

"You coming?" Braden looked back over his shoulder.

I racked my brain for an excuse. "No, I can't. I . . . I'm allergic to the smell of new paint. My throat gets tight and . . ."

It was a total lie. It worked, though, because Braden came right back out.

Shutting the front door behind him, he gave me a half smile. "That's a bummer, but I'm glad you said something. You're much too old to be my first in-office patient. Would you like to sit out back?"

The area behind the office was a cool oasis with leafy green oaks, a small rose garden, and a covered porch. Braden ducked inside to make us coffee. When he came back out holding two mugs, its rich scent wafted toward me on the early-morning breeze.

"So, the contractors have been here for about a month." He handed me a mug and settled into the cushions of a blue-striped lawn chair. "The only thing remaining is furniture and tech. We should be ready to open the doors in about two weeks. In the meantime, I spend most of my time at the hospital, in the children's ward."

I raised my eyebrows. This was all hitting a little too close to home, and my nerves made my throat constrict. I was worried that if I tried to speak, I might stutter, like I did the night of the speech.

"The majority of the staff here stayed on, which was encouraging." Braden rubbed his hand against his chin. "My aunt warned me that the locals can be tightly knit. So far, though, everyone has been great. I—" He gave me a sheepish look. "I apologize. I'm talking your ear off."

Oh, why couldn't he be one of those self-centered guys perfectly happy to talk about himself? Then I wouldn't have to worry about embarrassing myself.

I gripped my mug. "That's fine." To my relief, the words came without any trouble. "The remodel looks great."

"Do you think the locals will like it?" he asked.

"Absolutely, it's so cozy. Sorry I didn't go in." Now that I was confident I could talk, the words tumbled out. "It's unfair, because I love the smell of fresh paint. It's like mud and bleach—"

"Mud and bleach?" He leaned forward and gave an eager nod. "You're right, now that you mention it. You have an incredible sense of smell."

"Occupational hazard." I took a shy sip of coffee. "Tasting notes everywhere I turn."

Blackbirds called in the still morning, and patches of sun fell across the grass.

"So, how did you end up taking over this place?" I asked, after a moment of silence.

A thoughtful look crossed his face. "I've been asking myself that a lot lately. I had a job in the children's ward at a hospital in Rhode Island that was fine. Plus, I was in a serious relationship that was also fine." He looked down at his coffee. "Then, this patient I was close to passed away. I realized life is a gift, and fine was no longer good enough. Aunt Patty called two days later and told me this place was for sale. I applied for a business loan the following week."

"That's impressive," I said.

He gave me a cautious look. "My ex didn't think so. She said I was having a midlife crisis. That was cause for concern, since I'm only thirty-five."

I laughed. "Well, running a business will shave a few years off your life." A stray rose petal rested on the chair, and I squished it between my fingers, filling the air with perfume.

Braden gave me his lopsided grin. "So, what's your role at the vineyard?"

"Business development. This one job opened up, though, and . . ."

The image of my brother jumped to mind, and I frowned.

"What?" he prodded.

"I really want the job," I admitted. "My father is going to fight for me to get it. My grandfather doesn't think I'm ready, though, and my brother, who hasn't even been in town since almost high school, has made things much more difficult than they need to be. I . . . sorry." I gave an embarrassed smile. "Now, I'm talking *your* ear off."

It was easy to do. Something about Braden made me want to confide in him.

"Not at all." He took a sip of coffee. "I imagine it must be difficult working with family."

"It's wild!" I turned to him. "The past plays into everything. A few weeks ago, Pappy told me I wouldn't be interested in the health effects of red wine because I don't like broccoli. I was like, Pappy—I hated broccoli when I was five years old!"

The memory cheered me. My grandfather could be infuriating. Still, he'd been a part of every stage and phase of my life. It made me happy to think of him that way, instead of in pain at the hospital.

"You never grow old working with family," I said.

"That's small-town life too, from what I hear." Braden set his mug on the glass top of the outdoor table. "No one forgets if you were the kid who embarrassed himself at school."

"It's true." I shrugged. "People don't forget."

The teller at the bank was the perfect example. To her, I would always be the girl who got sick at the petting zoo. Not to mention Dean. He hadn't lived here in years, but even the mayor knew his shortcomings.

"Speaking of work, I should go." I held out my mug. "Where should I put this?"

"I'll take it."

I followed him to the gate in the fence. The time had passed quickly. There was a decent amount of foot traffic on the sidewalk as tourists continued to head to Main Street to grab breakfast or for the more ambitious, a spot on the beach.

"Thanks for the coffee." I squinted up at him in the sun. "And the attempted tour."

"Hey, maybe I could come up to the vineyard tomorrow," he said as I headed out to the sidewalk. "See what a wine tasting is all about."

I stopped. "You've never been to a wine tasting? Braden, if you would have made that confession to Pappy, you wouldn't have had to dress his wounds. He would have leapt up and taken you to the tasting room on the spot."

Braden laughed. "I should work on my bedside manner." His dark eyes met mine. "I'll come tomorrow. See if you're around?"

I hesitated.

It was hard to tell if he was being friendly because he was new to town and we'd shared the experience with Pappy or if he was . . . flirting. I hadn't been involved with anyone since Jax had left for Chile. He and I still sent texts and emails, and sometimes it didn't feel like the relationship was over.

"Okay. Come on up," I said, careful to keep the invitation casual. "I'll have one of the bartenders hook you up. Thanks for the coffee."

Back on Main Street, I sat on a bench and let out a deep breath. I hoped the way I'd handled his tasting request hadn't come off as rude, but things with Braden could not go further than friendship. I liked him, but I was hardly in a place to explore something new, especially considering my current multitude of personal challenges.

You couldn't even walk into his office because you didn't want to face the memories.

I shuddered. Lately, the ghost of my illness had been looming too close to the surface. It felt like that was the case with so many problems from the past, when what I really needed to focus on was my future.

Chapter Nine

When I was eleven years old, I was in and out of the hospital for three months.

The illness came on suddenly, late October, while I played Monopoly with my brothers. Colorful leaves fluttered on the trees outside, we'd just eaten my grandmother's beef stroganoff, and my mother was in the kitchen, preparing hot chocolate with marshmallows. To top it off, I'd just rolled doubles and had nabbed the last of the green properties.

With one eye on Boardwalk, I wound up for the next roll. Out of nowhere, it felt like the room had caught fire. I'd never felt so hot in my life. Or so dizzy.

Dean elbowed me to try and mess up my roll. I tried to form words, but nothing would come. The dice flew out of my hand, and he turned to me, laughing hysterically.

"Doubles! That's your third—" His dark eyes went wide. "Abby? What's wrong?"

The next thing I knew, I was on the floor, surrounded by men wearing navy-blue shirts. My parents and grandparents hovered behind them with my brothers off to the side. Dean's face was scrunched up like he was crying, and I wanted to make fun of him but couldn't find the energy to speak. My eyes drifted shut once again. The next time they opened, I stared up at the low-lit tiles of a hospital ceiling.

My mother leapt to her feet. "Abby," she whispered, grabbing my hand.

It must have been the middle of the night, because she was the only one in the room. My tongue was thick and tasted like metal. I tried to sit up, and my arms wouldn't cooperate. It was like they were made of rubber.

"What happened?" I whispered.

My mother's eyes were rimmed with red. She had a big smile on her face, the one she used when she didn't want to scare us.

"You got sick," she said. "From the petting zoo."

I blinked, lying back against the pillow. "The petting zoo?"

The week prior, my class had gone on a field trip to a fall harvest fair an hour north of Starlight Cove. We'd giggled our way through a hayride, eaten caramel apples, and raced through a corn maze. I'd also spent a ton of time in the section with the petting zoo, because I was writing a report on sheep for my fifth-grade class.

"Kelcee's not sick," I said. "She wouldn't go in there."

Kelcee thought the petting zoo smelled and that the animals were filthy. Turned out, she was right. The animals were neglected and dirty, and the sheep made me sick.

"Several kids in the area have developed something called hemolytic uremic syndrome," my mother said. "So far, you have the worst of it. Do you remember when you got sick last weekend?"

Like I could forget. I'd had terrible diarrhea all weekend. Apparently, I'd contracted *E. coli* from the petting zoo. There had been a random outbreak across northern Michigan, and countless kids had gotten sick. The sickness had progressed into HUS, a blood condition that nearly killed me.

I looked around the hospital room. For the first time, I noticed my arms were stuck with IVs, and a machine echoed my heartbeat through the room. The rhythm increased audibly as I took everything in, getting more panicked by the moment.

Grabbing at the IVs, I tried to yank them out. "Mom, help," I begged. "Get these off me."

The room suddenly swarmed with nurses. The one with huge arms grabbed my wrists while another shoved the IV back into my wrist.

"It's okay," my mother pleaded. "Honey, it's okay."

My face burned with fever. A tear trickled down my cheek, and I turned my head so my mother wouldn't see. The pillow smelled sour, like an old gym shirt.

"I love you, honey." My mother's voice broke. "Everything will be all right."

Years later, my mother admitted she thought that would be the last time we would ever speak, because right afterward, my body went into septic shock, and my kidneys started to shut down. I remember a constant sense of panic in the room, traveling on a gurney down brightly lit hallways, and shivering with cold. I also remembered Dean at my side, gripping my hand so tightly it hurt.

"Me and Phillip are gonna give you Boardwalk," he kept telling me. "We haven't touched any of your properties. Get up, and we'll play. We've got the game right here."

Through a fog, I woke to see the Monopoly board set up on the hospital radiator, by the window. The trees outside were frosted with an early snow. The next time I looked, the game was gone, replaced by a bouquet of flowers.

It took me eight days to recover. A week later, I was back in the hospital for a kidney infection, followed by staph, and finally, pneumonia. The combination put me in and out of the hospital well into January in the new year.

When I first got sick, Dean stopped going to basketball practice to be with me. He made me silly mixtapes and brought notes from the kids at school, and we played endless games of war. He even switched bedrooms when I came home, so I could have the one with the bigger closet and the window that looked out over the vines.

The Tuesday before Christmas, I was back in the hospital with pneumonia, and everyone in the family came to visit. The fact that I got to pick what to watch on television was the only good thing about being there. *Rudolph the Red-Nosed Reindeer* was scheduled to play, and I didn't want to miss it.

"I'm tired," I said, because it was getting close to movie time. "I really should start thinking about going to bed."

There was little rest to be had at the hospital. Someone was always in and out of the room. The nurses were either checking vitals, drawing blood, or informing me a doctor was about to come in. If it wasn't that, it was the cleaning crew, the restocking crew, and once, a lady from some youth outreach program with a teddy bear who seemed disappointed that I wasn't younger.

"The queen has spoken!" Dean clapped his hands and stood by the door. He had started wearing his baseball cap backward, like some of the rough kids, which I didn't like. "It's time to go."

"Wait!" My grandmother let out a gasp. "The hospital left something on Abby's tray."

My parents stopped discussing business with Pappy, and Phillip put down his homework. Dean flopped down on the vinyl-covered chair in the corner.

"Sorry." He grinned at me. "I tried to get them out of your hair."

"It's okay." I reached for the tiny box on my tray. It was wrapped in silver paper and accessorized with a white lacy bow.

By now, I was used to getting presents nearly every day, so I didn't bother to feel the box and wonder what could be inside. Instead, I peeled off the paper, one eye on the television. My head pounded, like always. It seemed like the headaches were constant.

"Looks like jewelry," my mother sang, from her post on the edge of the bed. Her eyes were damp, and I was annoyed by the whole production.

I opened the box. Something heavy and gold fell onto the hospital bedsheets.

"Early Christmas." My father patted my arm. "We love you, honey."

My family fell silent, watching as I pulled the object from the sheets. The air seemed to leave my lungs. It was a bracelet, pure gold and dripping with the most beautiful charms I'd ever seen in my life. They glittered and winked under the fluorescent lights.

"Everyone picked out a charm." My grandmother hovered over the bed. "Guess who got what."

My mother took the remote control to the television. The talking snowman faded to black. I barely even noticed as I studied the bracelet, still in disbelief that something so decadent belonged to me.

"The gumball machine is from Grandma," I said slowly, "because we have bubble-blowing contests. Mom got me the heart. The lighthouse is from Dad, Pappy got the grapes—"

He let out a delighted guffaw, slapping his knee.

"The bucket of popcorn is from Phillip, because we watch movies together." My fingers fell on the final charm. It was a solid-gold Monopoly man. "This one's from Dean," I said, but choked up. "Even though he always cheats."

Everyone burst out laughing.

That night, the room was freezing. Still, I kept my left arm outside of the blankets so I could see the bracelet in the moonlight. My mother snored softly on a cot by the bed as I studied each charm. They were so detailed that I felt like my family was right there with me. For the first time in ages, my sense of comfort was greater than my fear.

I traced my fingers over the charms, then drifted off to sleep as the Monopoly man watched over me in the moonlight.

Chapter Ten

The sun warmed my shoulders as I walked down Main Street, happy to get as far away from the pediatrics office as possible. I checked my text messages on the way to the truck. There were a few from my dad with updates on Pappy's condition, which really hadn't changed. The final text was from Dean. I stopped under the awning for Chill Out, one of my favorite coffee shops, and gave the text my full attention.

> Saw Mom this morning. She agrees you need to find a spot for me to help out today.

With a sigh, I watched the families stroll the sidewalks of Main Street with beach bags and straw hats. Their children were dressed in colorful swim trunks and cover-ups, trying to trip each other with every giggling step. Back when Dean and I were kids, the idea of working together would have seemed like a fun adventure. Now, I didn't even want him around.

It was all well and good that my father wanted me to take on the main role in operations. Pappy could still say no, though. He'd be thrilled Dean wanted to be a part of things and could easily pass the job to him instead. Or if Pappy died . . . I closed my eyes, heartbroken to even have to consider that angle. If he died, my grandmother would definitely put Dean in charge, to honor the idea of Pappy's grandsons running the show.

That would be terrible for business. Dean had no experience, a bad attitude, and might still be on drugs. I didn't have the first clue what he was doing here.

Shadows fell across the sidewalk as a cloud crossed the sun. The thought I had worked so hard to fight back forced its way to the front of my mind.

What if Dean is responsible for the ice wine?

It was possible. Dean might feel entitled to it, in some way, and the wine was so valuable. What if he thought the benefits of the vineyard were his birthright, and he had come back to collect?

Depressing thoughts. Ones I couldn't share with anyone, especially not my family. Everyone was so darn happy to have him back. They would never believe he was capable of stealing from them. But he was a thief, with no regard for sentimentality—I knew that from personal experience.

My steps back to the truck were as heavy as my heart. There had to be more to my brother's homecoming than he was letting on. He hadn't been here in years, and now we were supposed to act like it was normal for him to show up with no explanation?

Was I really the only one who could see it?

Since I had to put Dean somewhere, I decided to let him manage the bar. The tours and tastings were scheduled in advance, and the staff was perfectly trained, because it all fell under Rogers's jurisdiction. There was little my brother could do to mess it up.

I figured Rogers would appreciate the opportunity to catch up on clerical work. However, when I met him at the tasting room and made the suggestion, he seemed hurt.

"You want Dean to do my job?" he asked.

"Of course not." I grabbed a bottle of window cleaner and wiped down the picture window until it sparkled. "I just have to put him somewhere, and this seemed like the safest place."

The cloth squeaked against the window in the silence that filled the room.

"You're always saying you would love time away to catch up on paperwork." I turned to look at him. "This is your big chance."

"Certainly." Rogers went back to sorting tasting menus, his posture stiff. "Family first."

I practically dropped the cloth. "Rogers, come on." I hadn't considered the possibility that he might feel as threatened by Dean as I did. "It's only for today."

Rogers stacked the tasting menus up on the counter without a word. Then, he pulled out a bottle of lemon oil. Pouring a healthy amount on a rag, he polished the wooden bar in silence. His shoulders were slightly slumped, and it hit me that he was starting to look old.

"Hey." I walked over and touched his arm. It felt strong under the starch of his shirt, in spite of his age. "You're the best we've got. That's why I'm putting him here, because it's organized. If you'd rather, I'll put him somewhere else."

Rogers set down the bottle of wood polish. "I prefer to keep my opinions to myself . . ."

I snorted. "No, you don't." Stepping behind the bar, I arranged the glasses necessary for tasting flights. "What's on your mind?"

"I thought your brother was a recovering addict. It would be cruel to put him in a bar, wouldn't it?"

I set down a glass. "He was drinking at the anniversary party. I mean . . . I don't know. This is a vineyard. If temptation is an issue, he shouldn't be here at all."

"Fair enough." Rogers folded the lemon-scented rag and tucked it beneath the sink. "However, the tasting room is our first point of contact with guests. Not to mention the allure of the cash drawer."

My eye fell on the register behind the bar. "I'm not worried about that. Stealing a few bucks really wouldn't be worth it."

Rogers met my eyes and looked away. A strong sense of discomfort settled between us. I wondered if he also suspected my brother was behind the theft of the ice wine.

"Well." He straightened his shirt. "I suppose I should prepare for a delightful day of clerical work." His eyes swept over the area behind the bar, as though frustrated to leave a job half-done. "Let me at least take out the recycling. No one bothered this weekend, and I've been tripping over this mess all morning." He hoisted up a box of empty bottles and carried them toward the back door, his posture extra straight.

"Rogers," I called.

He turned.

"I owe you one."

After giving a slight bow, he headed out the door.

I put the phone on speaker and gave Dean a call. He answered on the first ring.

"Get up and put on a uniform. You're in the tasting room today."

Long pause.

"Say that again?" Dean's voice was gruff and scratchy, like he was back in bed—or passed out in my bathtub.

I grabbed a box of recycling and carried it to the back door, raising my voice so he could hear me as I moved away from the phone. "You're in the tasting room."

Dean scoffed. "I'm not going to be a glorified *bar*tender."

I snapped up straight and raced back to the phone. "First of all, there is nothing wrong with being a bartender. I would jump at the chance to get a feel for how people like our products."

The back door clanked as Rogers returned.

"I want a real role," Dean was saying. "I'm not going to—"

"You're not the bartender—you're managing. Okay?" I snapped. "You're welcome."

I pressed end with a little more force than necessary. Then I looked at Rogers. "Unbe*liev*able."

Rogers shook his head. "The good news is that it's five o'clock somewhere."

Shaking my head, I grabbed another box of recycling and carried it to the back door.

$\sim$

Once my brother was set in his temporary role, I headed for my office. The offices were located in the warehouse, where we handled everything from quality control to filling bottles. There was little going on in terms of production, and since my entire family was out for the first time in the history of the vineyard, the space felt empty and almost eerie as I walked across the cement floor.

There were a few people hard at work, like our administrative assistant and the sales guy. The thing that made it sad was thinking about Pappy. If he wasn't in the fields, he was always up in his office, watching over everything from the crow's nest in the loft.

I stood next to the stairs for a moment, wondering if the scent of red wine and Altoids lingered on the aged vinyl of his desk chair. I almost went up but couldn't do it. The thought of seeing his desk stacked with its clutter of yellow pads, order printouts, and half-empty tins of mints was hardly a substitution for being by his side.

Instead, I settled into the desk in my office. The old-fashioned phone rang just as I'd finished sorting through label samples for our upcoming release. "Harrington Wines."

Kelcee's voice sang through the phone. "I know who's getting the mayor to put the kibosh on the wine trail."

I set down the sample I was holding. "Who?"

"Upper Mitten."

"Really?" I couldn't believe it.

Upper Mitten was a new winery that had been crowdfunded by a couple who attended business school out east. They had opened a new winery at the very end of the peninsula at the beginning of the summer, with a lot of fanfare about bringing "new life" to the wine community. Their vineyard served wine on tap, used silly names like Rock-Candy Riesling, and got a lot of publicity for attempting to invent a wine that tasted like cotton candy.

"The Germans did that years ago," my grandmother scoffed. "It's called trollinger."

The majority of the local vineyards felt the same disdain for the newcomer. It wasn't because we were unwelcoming; it was because Upper Mitten's whole shtick was so aggressive. The vineyards that had been here for decades had worked hard to make wine an inclusive experience.

Still, Upper Mitten's website, social media accounts, and marketing materials painted us as snobby and unapproachable. Their website actually said, *We're called Upper Mitten because we have the upper hand on inclusive customer service. With us, you don't need the secret handshake to drink the good stuff.* It made it sound like the rest of us served the swill to the tourists, which was not the case at all.

I'd figured they were just getting bad advice from a marketing person who worked remotely and didn't know the area, so I'd tried to introduce myself to the co-owner, Landon, at a networking luncheon. She'd been standing in the corner, sipping at sparkling water. The second I'd said, "Hi, I'm Abby Harrington, from Harrington Wines," she'd laughed. "Oh, wow. A real live dinosaur," she'd said and pushed past me to say hi to a girl who owned an ice cream shop.

It was so rude. I didn't want to have anything else to do with them, so I'd left them off the list of proposed wineries for the wine trail. I wasn't shocked to hear they didn't support a project that didn't include them. That said, it was surprising they'd managed to stop it altogether.

"How do you know that?" I asked, wrapping the rubber phone cord around my wrist.

"The owners had breakfast here," Kelcee said. "I was in the booth right behind them, going over the menu with a new waitress. They were practically gleeful about the fact that they got Mayor Matty to turn it down. They said you'd never be able to do it without his go-ahead."

"That's infuriating." I tightened the cord, watching my hand turn purple. Without approval from the mayor, we couldn't market the wine trail with the city's support or put up public signage to send people in the right direction. "Why would the mayor listen to them?"

"Get this." I could practically hear Kelcee lean forward. "He went to college with the father of one of the owners. They're fraternity brothers."

"*Fraternity* brothers?" I echoed.

"*Yes.*" She giggled. "Rumor has it, when the guy's dad came to town to have dinner with Mayor Matty, they both wore their pledge pins."

I snorted. "This conversation is completely over my head."

When people discussed college football, alma maters, and fraternities, I was the first to tune out, because I'd never gone to college. The idea of leaving home for such a long stretch had seemed scary, and besides, my future at the vineyard had been assured. It'd made more sense to spend time and money on the occasional industry event, like the years Phillip, my mother, and I attended the American Society for Enology and Viticulture National Conference.

"You need to talk to these people," Kelcee said. "Invite them to join the trail. They won't fight something that they're a part of."

"They insult the wine community every chance they get," I argued. "I don't want to partner with people like that. No one else will either."

"Abby, trust me on this." Kelcee's voice got serious. "They have Mayor Matty in their pocket. You need to get on their good side, or they will sabotage you at every turn."

Once we hung up, I drummed my fingers against the desk and stared out the window. My eyes fell on the empty cellar across the way.

Sabotage, huh?

I wondered just how far they would go.

Chapter Eleven

My cell phone rang a few minutes later. It was Raoul, fighting an emergency with the irrigation system in the western riesling field. The water pipe was old, and raccoons had broken through.

"We need all hands on deck." Raoul sounded frustrated. "The field's flooding."

Even though a flood wasn't an ideal situation, the vines wouldn't drown. The soil would help drain the water quickly enough that there would be little long-term impact on our grapes. Still, it wasn't like any of us had time to waste battling a flood, and it could create a problem if it got out of hand.

I headed up there, while trying to get ahold of Dean on his cell phone. The field looked like a pond. Our pump was working overtime while the workers bailed water into an enormous basin on one of the field trucks.

"We need another pump," Raoul called. He had scooped up bucket after bucket of water, lining them up behind him in the muck. "This is a mess."

"I'll call the Jacobses," I said.

With the phone tucked under my chin, I grabbed a bucket and got to work. The Jacobs family was more than willing to help, like always. They promised to get their pump to us in thirty minutes.

It only took twenty. The pump roared to life next to ours, and within minutes, the field looked less like a water park attraction and more like a vineyard. Raoul wiped his bandana across his sweating neck and gave me a high five.

"This isn't how I wanted to kick off the day."

"Could have been a lot worse," I said. "I'm glad you caught it when you did." My arms shook with exertion. I couldn't even count how many buckets of water I'd scooped. "I'll get in touch with the supply store and get the pipeline replaced."

"Good deal." Raoul offered me his water bottle, and I took a long drink. "So, listen." He beckoned me away from the group. "The police chief's been pulling people all morning for questioning. Mind if I ask what's going on?"

I hesitated.

Henry had been confident our staff would assume his questions had to do with the wreck. However, he could be pretty intimidating. I could see how a chat with him could leave even the most innocent person feeling on guard.

My response was careful. "Things are definitely not okay around here."

I'd already been dishonest with Raoul about the box, and I did not want to lie to him again. I was just as concerned as Raoul, but for different reasons, of course.

"Things won't be normal again until Pappy's out of the hospital," I said. "Henry's doing what he can. You know?"

The FaceTime ringer screeched from my phone.

Dean.

My stomach dropped. Why would my brother FaceTime? My immediate thought was that there had been a serious development with Pappy. "I have to get this."

Raoul nodded. "Just wanted to check in. Let me know if you need anything." Then he headed back to the group.

Wiping a damp hand across my forehead, I picked up the phone.

"Damn, girl." Dean leaned against the bar, a glass of red wine in hand. "You look like you slithered out of a swamp."

Relief shot through me, followed by irritation. "I'm working. Where have you been? We could have used a spare set of hands, which is what you claim you'd like to be."

"Didn't hear my phone." He gave a leisurely stretch. Gnats swarmed around my head, and I could only imagine the luxury of the cool, air-conditioned tasting room. "So," he said. "I've had to make my first executive decision as bar manager."

The sun was relentless. I tried to find some shade underneath our tallest trellis. There wasn't much, but it was better than nothing.

I plucked a green grape off the vine, the skin warm and smooth against my fingertips. "Which was what?"

"Billy the bartender's going home sick." My brother raised his eyebrows. "I need a replacement. You'll be the perfect fit."

Bartend? Not a chance. I was not about to miss the meeting with Henry because my brother was completely incompetent.

"You can bartend," I said, as though it was the most basic formula in the world. "Rogers can go back to managing."

Dean tsked. "I'm not TAM certified. Shall I tell Henry you'd ask one of your employees to break the law? Besides, you said you *look* for opportunities to be behind the bar. To interact with our guests to find out what they think of our product. I'm *handing* you the golden ticket." He lifted his glass. "You're welcome."

Before I could respond, he hung up on me.

∽

I thundered toward the tasting room.

The winery was a business, not some game. Dean might think his function was to give me a hard time, but I was about to set him straight. After pushing open the door, I came to a sudden stop.

Billy the bartender chatted happily with my brother behind the bar, looking healthier than ever. Spotting me, he burst into laughter. It took me a minute. Then I got it.

The whole thing was one big joke.

"Billy." I kept my shoulders straight as I crossed the room, then rested my hands against the polished wood of the bar. The scent of lemon oil was strong in the air. "You're fired."

Billy found that hilarious. "I didn't know you were such a sucker! I'd *never* leave you guys hanging. Remember the time I ate that sausage pizza my roommate left out for three days? That was rough, man, but I rallied."

Dean grinned. "He rallied."

I looked back and forth between the two of them.

"Look, Dean's the boss today." Billy grabbed a series of tasting bottles and set them out. "He says jump—I say how high." My brother handed Billy a twenty, which he held up. "Plus, he bribed me."

"Billy," I scolded. "You're better than that."

"Nah, I can be bought. You wouldn't believe what I'd do for a plate of chicken wings and a side of fries."

Dean burst out laughing. "You and me both, brother."

The two of them were so ridiculous I actually smiled.

"That's the spirit." Dean reached out and rumpled my hair.

Our eyes met. For a split second, it was like we were friends again. Until my father walked into the tasting room.

Dean's tone suddenly turned businesslike. "Hey, Billy. Give me a heads-up if you have any problems."

Before I could blink, Dean made a beeline for the office. I swore under my breath and raced to keep up. Rushing in, I said, "Dad and I have some things to—"

"It's okay," my father cut in. "He knows."

"What?" The air-conditioning gave me a sudden chill. "What do you mean he knows?"

The din from the tasting room went quiet as I shut the office door.

"Dean noticed we were questioning the workers," my father said. "He called and asked what was going on."

"I see."

Normally, I loved our meeting room. The small conference table was by a small sink and fridge, while plush couches, bookshelves, and dozens of racks of wine lined the other half of the room. The space was typically inviting, but thanks to my brother, it now felt claustrophobic.

"Look, it was obvious something's going on." Dean cracked his knuckles. "Henry's questioning everyone on-site. I had a quick talk with him. Imagine my surprise."

I took a seat at the table, my muscles already aching from the bailing work in the field. It was one thing if my brother actually was surprised. However, what if he knew perfectly well the wine was missing, because he was the one who took it?

My father pulled a chilled bottle of cherry wine from the small fridge and expertly dislodged the cork. The sweet scent filled the room. Holding it up, he gave us a wry look.

"Henry won't drink," he said. "However, your grandmother would disown me if I didn't offer."

I did my best to smile. "I'll get the glasses."

Oma had a simple rule: wine for every guest. It didn't matter if it was family, friend, or the furnace guy. She wanted everyone to associate Harrington Wines with warmth and hospitality, a creed that made me feel vaguely guilty about the situation with Upper Mitten.

I set out four wineglasses and poured a bowl of Gardetto's snack mix. My father and Dean were busy discussing the Detroit Tigers. Feeling left out, I poured a glass of wine and started to respond to work emails on my phone.

Henry rapped on the door a few minutes later. "How's everybody doing?" He ignored my father's offer of wine and took a seat. "So. We have a lead."

I set my phone down. "That's great news."

"Could be," he grunted. "An online seller tried to move a few cases. We set up a drop-off, but they must have got spooked, because they didn't show. Forensics determined the seller is located in northern Michigan, so the wine's still in the area."

Dean smoothed the jaunty section of hair that fell across his forehead. "You couldn't track them?"

"No, kid." Henry grabbed a handful of Gardetto's, and garlic wafted through the room. "The IP addresses pinged from location to location. Singapore was a biggie. Then it blipped through an internet café here. The place doesn't keep surveillance, or you'd be looking through the tapes and telling me who you recognize."

"We'd be looking through the digital files," my brother corrected.

Henry frowned. "Huh?"

"Digital files," Dean repeated. "Not tapes."

The air in the room got tense. My brother had a storied history with the police chief, since Dean had been nothing but trouble since he was thirteen. I had no doubt Henry had limited patience for his bullshit. Picking up my wine, I sat back in my chair and waited for the fireworks.

Unfortunately, my father interrupted the scene. "Think they'll try again?"

"That's what we're hoping." Henry crunched loudly on another handful of snacks. "We'll set up surveillance and go from there. Now, when I was talking to your employees, most of the staff assumed my questions were tied to the accident. Your bartender, Billy, seemed to think otherwise. He asked if the meeting was about the missing inventory."

My blood went cold. "Billy knew about the ice wine?"

Henry shook his head. "He asked about current inventory, stock missing from the bar. Said he'd reported it and that he was not the responsible party."

I looked at my father. "He hasn't reported anything."

I can be bought.

Could Billy be behind all this?

"Let me text Rogers." I pulled out my phone. "He would know."

Once Rogers arrived, his voice took on a note of disapproval at the question. "Indeed, Billy has mentioned sticky fingers at the height of the season. It happens when the tasting room gets crowded. People are drinking, inhibitions are down, and frankly, it's impossible to keep an eye on all of the merchandise."

"Hold up." Dean had straddled a chair at the end of the conference table. It squeaked as he leaned forward. "Why wasn't this brought to our attention?"

Rogers looked at my father. "It was handled." He adjusted his shirt-sleeves. "When this was presented to me, I reviewed the logs and identified minor inventory thefts of both alcohol and novelties. Minor theft is, unfortunately, to be expected."

"People are stealing," Dean said. "That's not expected—that's a police report."

Please. It wasn't like Dean spent his time writing love letters to the law. He'd done all sorts of terrible things when he was younger, like serving as the getaway driver for some deadbeat trying to rob a house. He was just lucky he'd never been caught.

"Dean," I said. "If we called Henry each time someone walked out the door with a corkscrew, a T-shirt, or even a bottle of wine, Starlight Cove would have to start advertising for additional candidates for the police force."

Henry snorted.

My father took off his glasses and polished the lenses. "Henry, do—"

"Hold on, Dad," Dean interrupted. "I'm concerned Billy felt the problem was worth mentioning to the police. Especially since that concern wasn't passed on."

"Ah, but it was." Rogers looked down his broad nose at my brother. "I reported it to your grandmother. She considered the loss irrelevant."

I had to sit on my hands to keep from applauding.

Well played, Rogers.

He had set a trap, and my brother had walked right into it.

Turning to my father, Rogers continued, "May I speak frankly?"

My father nodded. "Of course."

"Billy is a nice kid, even if he likes to complain. One of his favorite topics is the inventory logs. They're a mess. Handwritten, posted in several different locations . . ." Rogers glanced at me, and I nodded. "I understand his frustration, but when Greta and I reviewed the numbers—as much as we could read them—they did not indicate a significant loss. However, if Billy is still concerned, it should be looked into once again."

Dean grabbed himself a bottle of water from the mini fridge. "I'll do it."

I gripped the stem of my wineglass so tight I feared it would snap. "Phillip handles our numbers. He should review the logs."

My father shook his head. "He doesn't know about the robbery, and he can't keep a secret to save his life. I can't have my mother catch wind of this. Not now."

It was true, what my father said about Phillip. He was the one who'd told me Santa Claus wasn't real, that Mom dyed her hair, and that his wife preferred the pinot noir from the vineyard across the way. As much as I loved him, he really was incapable of keeping his mouth shut.

"Fine," I mumbled, like anyone at the table actually cared what I thought.

Rogers cleared his throat. "I would like to request . . ." He hesitated, then straightened his shoulders. "This may be bold. However, I would like to request you confirm what I've said with Greta. It won't tip her off about the ice wine, but I have been on this earth too long to waste time worrying about unnecessary suspicion."

My father smiled. "Duly noted."

Once Rogers left the room, Henry shut his notebook. "What's his story?"

"He's old and cranky." My father took off his glasses and rubbed his eyes once again. "Like the rest of us."

Henry grunted. "Speak for yourself."

"Rogers is a good employee," my father added. "He's been with us for years, and my parents have a lot of respect for him. However, he can be a gossip. He has his ear to the ground."

"That's good for us, actually," Dean said. "If we need a rat, he's our guy."

I glared at him. "Rogers is not a rat."

"He's got *fink* written all over him."

Henry got to his feet. "Keep me posted on the situation with the inventory. Whoever orchestrated the ice wine could have used that for practice. I'll have another chat with your bartender on my way out."

"Mind if I talk to him first?" Dean asked.

Henry hesitated. Then, to my absolute disbelief, he gave a sharp nod. "Fine."

The moment the door clicked shut, I hit the table in frustration. "Why wouldn't you leave the questions to the expert?"

Dean looked at me like I was an idiot. "No one's going to talk to a *cop*. Billy would think he was in trouble for something if Henry started in again. Whereas *I* am going to talk to him like a normal person. I bet you money I'll find out a lot more that way."

The plan actually made sense. Still, I couldn't stand the fact that Dean had his hand in everything. First the logs and now this. He was making himself indispensable within a matter of days, something I hadn't been able to pull off in a matter of years.

My father rested his chin on his hand. "The one thing that—" He stopped midsentence when the shades rattled in the breeze. "Shit." He rushed over to the window. Behind the shade nearest to us, the window was wide open. "The window was open?"

I jumped as he slammed his hand into the wall. Once, twice, three times. Then his shoulders slumped, and he stared outside.

Dean and I looked at each other. Quietly, I got to my feet.

I put away the empty wineglasses and washed the snack bowl, squeezing my hands to stop them from shaking. It was rare to see my father so upset, but in this case, it didn't surprise me.

The office was located at the far side of the tasting building. If someone wanted to know what Henry was doing here, it would have been a cinch to stand next to the window and find out. Once again, I thought of Raoul's comment and wondered how many of the workers knew something was up.

"Nothing we can do about it now." Dean got to his feet. "Except make a point to secure our meeting location in the future."

Secure our meeting location? Give me a break.

He put a hand on my father's shoulder. "How you holding up, Dad?"

My father adjusted his glasses and then shut the window. "We have a lead. It's a start."

Dean's voice was gentle. "I wasn't talking about that."

"I'm going to get back." He lowered the shade. "Your grandmother doesn't like to be alone for too long."

The words hung in the air. If my grandfather died, she wouldn't have a choice in the matter.

"Look, they can manage here without me." Dean gave my dad a hard pat on the back. "I'll come with you. All right?"

My father nodded. "I would appreciate that."

Tears of frustration clouded my vision. Mumbling an excuse, I left the room.

~

91

Outside, I blinked in the bright sunlight and took in several slow, deep breaths. The next tour was about to start, so guests were arriving in the driveway, kicking up white dust from the gravel. I moved out of their way, my hand pressed against the side of the building.

The fact that Dean was going to the hospital with my father made me so angry I could hardly see. This time, I was mad at myself. The need to see my grandfather was strong, but I couldn't get past the fear.

Just go. Now. Do it.

My feet wouldn't move toward the parking lot. They wouldn't budge. Memories of the nurses pinning me down and shoving needles in my arm, the machines beeping by my head, and that cold, clawing fear of death were too much. It was all in the past, yes, but memories got tricky when they came too close.

Rogers waved from across the drive. "Abigail." He beckoned for me to follow him up to the gardener's shed. He liked to hide back there and smoke. It was the only thing that did not match up with his fastidious demeanor.

We stood behind the brick building, the tall grass scratching my legs, as he shook out a menthol cigarette and lit it up. The butane lighter let off a quick burst of blue flame. There was the brief scent of burned mint, followed by smoke.

I thought of Henry saying, *What's his story?* It wouldn't have shocked me if my father had launched into the actual story, because my grandmother loved to tell how she and Rogers first met.

He had just moved to Starlight Cove and was working as a bartender at the Harbor Resort, a fancy hotel that had been in Starlight Cove for over a century. My grandmother had been trying to convince the bar manager to carry our pinot noir, but the manager had laughed in her face.

"Sweetheart, you'd do better to sell your grapes to the juice factories."

"He said it with a sneer," my grandmother recounted gleefully, every time she told the story. "Then Rogers showed up. I liked him immediately."

Rogers had liked her too. He had been curious about Michigan wine and had talked the bar manager into trying some. My grandmother had left with a sale and a new employee.

Rogers had only been at the vineyard for three weeks before he'd had to return to New York, because his mother was showing signs of dementia. She was from Croatia and barely spoke English, and he'd wanted to be there for her. When she'd passed away nearly a quarter of a century later, Rogers had gotten in touch with my grandparents and picked up right where he'd left off.

That was only ten years ago. Sometimes, though, it felt like he'd been here longer than any of us.

"I fear your father has lost his mind." Rogers leaned against the shed. "He is handing your brother, the least likely candidate, the keys to the kingdom. With all due respect, why are you letting this happen?"

It was rare that Rogers questioned my parents or grandparents, so when he did, I paid attention.

"Dad's not losing his mind; he's just stressed about everything that's happening." I sat on the ground, and the weeds pressed into the backs of my legs. Scratching them, I said, "He definitely trusts Dean more than he should, but in the end, it won't matter. My father's going to push for me to get the operations job. Who knows how long Dean will even stick around? Sometimes, I think he's here for the long haul, and other times, I feel like he'll be gone tomorrow."

"He's giving every impression that he's here to stay."

The thought brought to mind the ice wine. One of the few reasons I was willing to doubt Dean was involved was that he was still in town. If he had played a part, it would be a lot smarter to make this trip a quick visit and get out before anyone got suspicious.

"I appreciate the fact that your father is standing beside you." Rogers blew out a rush of smoke, his face deep in thought. "However, who's to say another position won't be invented for your brother? One with equal power?"

My posture stiffened. The idea of making decisions with my brother sounded exhausting.

"That would be . . . awful."

"Complicated, to say the least." Rogers finished his cigarette. Then he gave me a cautious look. "I noticed you stuttered during your speech the other night. Is it true you did that as a child?"

I rolled a piece of grass between my fingers. "Yep. It started in kindergarten and cropped back up after I was in the hospital. I got it under control pretty quickly, but now it's like it's coming back to haunt me."

"Look into it." His voice was gentle. "Your grandfather hates weakness in any form."

My eyes filled with tears.

Rogers looked alarmed. "Abigail, I—"

"It's not what you said; it's how you said it." I blinked, looking down at the grass. "Like Pappy will be back any minute to make me feel totally irrelevant again."

Rogers squished the butt of his cigarette between his fingers. "My dear, the only one who can make you feel irrelevant is you. However, he will be back. Death is such a boring solution. Your grandfather is a lot of things, but he's certainly not dull."

Our conversation rang in my ears all afternoon. Particularly the point about weakness. It was true that I was not as bold as I could be. If I wanted my brother to stop steamrolling me, I needed to change.

Unfortunately, I had no clue how to start.

I threw myself into cleaning the main cellar. It was a huge job, and I relished it. The opportunity to stand in the shadow of so many different varietals and vintages was exactly what I needed.

Positioning myself in the center of the room, I took in the history surrounding me. The bottles in this cellar only dated back about a decade, so I had worked on each and every one of them. There was nothing like that first taste, and the thrill of recognition when we spotted one that was special.

My grandmother always went quiet in a moment like that. I'd once asked why she wasn't cheering and hollering like everyone else.

"I am offering reverence." She'd buried her nose deep into the glass. "To me, good wine is like good art. I like to listen to what it is telling me."

I wondered what my grandmother would tell me if she knew I'd found the ring.

Even though I planned to leave the secret at the bank, the fact that the wooden box had been found in the field still nagged at me. I couldn't help but think it held a secret greater than just the ring. If I looked at it more closely, maybe it could still lead me to the ice wine.

Stop. You know *that's wishful thinking.*

Perhaps. But standing in this cellar, it hurt me to think such an enormous piece of our history was missing. The ice wine was so much more than something to drink or sell. It was a part of my life. It was hard to accept that it was gone.

I threw myself into cleaning, determined to drop the fantasy that I could figure out more than the police. I needed to forget the box, be patient, and hope for the best. It was the only way to keep from losing my mind.

My cell phone rang just as I was finishing up. Stepping outside into the humid afternoon, I picked up.

"Abby?" said a warm voice. "This is Dana Simpson from the chamber of commerce. Do you have a minute?"

"Hi, Dana." I wiped a hand across my sweating forehead. "It's nice to hear from you."

I suspected she was calling about the wine trail, even though it could be anything, really. Harrington Wines sponsored several events around town, so I heard from her quite a bit. Taking in a deep breath, I waited.

"I'm calling with difficult news." My heart sank. "The chamber met regarding your proposal for the wine trail."

"Oh?"

"The mayor does not feel it's the right time to move forward with the project. I'm so sorry, Abby. I know you put so much work into this."

I sank onto the top stoop of the concrete. It wasn't like I hadn't had ample warning from both Kelcee and the mayor, but I'd still hoped something would change. It was such a bummer to hear the news was official.

"May I ask why?" I asked, trying to keep my tone professional.

"The mayor said the list of proposed vineyards needed some work. He's willing to review it again in the future if you make some changes. That's all I know."

I couldn't believe it. Upper Mitten really had stopped the trail, even though it didn't deserve to be a part of it in the first place. Either way, my disappointment felt small and petty, given everything else my family was going through.

"Thanks for the update," I managed to say.

Her voice mirrored mine. "I wish I was calling with better news."

It hit me that Dana was local. I wondered if she was as bothered by the situation as me.

"Let us know if you decide to edit the proposal, and we can go from there."

"You know what?" I got to my feet. "I'll discuss the options with my family. For now, though, I'm going to say it's time to let this go."

There. I'd been bold, like Rogers had suggested.

It was a shame, considering how much time and energy I'd put into the project, but there were more important things to deal with right now. It was time to put my focus on them.

Chapter Twelve

It was late in the afternoon when I finished up with the cellar. I triple checked the lock on the door and then headed toward my office. Henry had spoken with our security team, and they had increased patrols around the vineyard. Still, I felt uneasy leaving all of that wine unattended. I was headed back to my office when Rogers texted.

You're needed in the tasting room.

Great. I hoped it wasn't someone with a blog eager to meet with a member of our family. That happened sometimes. The hours in the field and the cellar had put me in desperate need of a shower, and since we weren't selling soap, I was hardly an ideal representation of the brand.

After pulling my baseball cap out of my back pocket, I tugged it low over my eyes and headed over.

The last tour had just gotten out, and the tasting room was packed. Guests were lined up at the registers, and I stopped for a moment, surveying the room. Maybe our setup made stealing a temptation. There were baskets of trinkets everywhere and a large rack of wine right next to the door. Maybe we needed to think about moving it.

Immediately, I dismissed the thought. We couldn't nail down everything. That would hardly send a welcoming message. I had to assume the thefts were the exception, not the rule.

Rogers chatted up the customers with his usual flair while pointing out additional products to tuck away for the holidays. Spotting me, he raised his eyebrows and gestured toward the bar. I followed his gaze, and my mouth went dry. Braden stood there, talking with a young couple finishing up a tasting.

He wore a light-blue T-shirt, a fancy diving watch, and a pair of jeans that made me do a double take. His hair looked tousled with a small amount of gel, giving it a relaxed look. As if sensing my eyes on him, he turned my way and smiled.

"Hi." I headed over to him, hoping my baseball cap was successful at hiding my wild hair. "What are you doing here?"

He indicated the couple. They'd just finished a flight and were settling their check with Billy.

"I know I said I'd come for a tasting tomorrow, but . . ." He gave me the lopsided smile I was starting to really like. "They didn't need me at the hospital. I thought this would be a fun way to end the day."

Billy closed the cash register and turned to Braden. "I would totally hook you up, man. Can't, though. Our license to pour only goes until five."

"You can close out," I told him. "Once everyone's gone, I'll pour for him as a friend."

Billy gave me an unnecessary eyebrow wiggle. "Gotcha."

The look I gave him was stern. "This is the doctor who helped Pappy out the other night. He was probably too modest to mention it."

"Oh." Billy practically lunged forward to shake Braden's hand. "Hey, mad respect, man. Her grandfather . . ." He blew some air out of his cheeks. "Seriously. Thanks for helping."

I headed over to update Rogers, who also gave me an unnecessary smirk.

"Stop." I pulled off my cap and tried to fluff my hair. My curls felt like they had ballooned up to twice the size of my head. "This is just a thank-you for helping out."

Rogers patted my shoulder. "Whatever you need to tell yourself, my dear."

In the bathroom, I rinsed off my face and confirmed that my hair was hopeless. There was a bottle of grape-scented hand sanitizer under the sink, so in an act of desperation, I used it to take a quick army shower. I might smell like the harvest, but it was better than smelling like the fields.

The tasting room had cleared by the time I came back out, and Billy was pocketing his tips. Rogers tilted an imaginary hat at me, and they headed out together.

I looked at Braden. He looked at me.

Silence settled over the tasting room, and my throat got tight.

No. This is what I do. I am not going to get nervous here.

"All right." Stepping behind the bar, I pulled out two sets of wine flight glasses. "The first rule of a proper wine tasting: you can't drink alone."

"That's a relief." He settled in on a wooden barstool. "I was afraid I'd stumble all over my words."

Pfft. If he only knew.

He watched with interest as I polished the glasses, pulled some fresh cheese out of the fridge, and set it next to the basket that held the pretzel-like breadsticks. I poured us each a glass of water. Setting out a dump bucket, I gave him my most professional smile.

"Ready?" I held the sparkling white over his first flight glass.

He gave a serious nod. "Let's do it."

The golden liquid glittered in the low light of the room.

Braden put his nose into the wineglass and took in a deep breath. Taking the opportunity to get a good look at him, I noticed his nose was crooked in a few spots. The small imperfection made his appearance less intimidating.

He opened his eyes. "What? Am I doing it wrong?"

I leaned against the bar. "There is no 'wrong' when it comes to wine. There are ways to sample the nose that work better than others. In the end, it's what works for you."

"The textbook answer." He set down his glass and gave me a disconcerting stare. "Just so you know, I'm not here for the general tour."

The air in the room suddenly felt close and thick, like the sultry night settling outside.

He's flirting.

The knowledge made my movements slower and more focused.

I couldn't decide if I wanted to go down this path. There was already so much going on. Did I really want to add this to the mix? I didn't know. The only thing I did know was that I didn't want to see him walk out the door.

"Okay." I met his gaze. "I'll tell you the real deal."

I set aside our tasting glasses and pulled the Baccarat crystal off the top shelf. The glasses were antiques and incredibly beautiful. My grandmother and I used them every time we were alone in the bar.

"Six glasses?" Braden laughed, as I lined them up in front of him.

"We'll start with six," I said. "That should cover the basics."

For the first time, I felt confident. Stuttering was a distant threat, like a problem plaguing someone else.

I polished each piece of crystal until it glimmered, then poured a fresh glass of sparkling wine.

"The glass is where it all begins." I lifted the flute, and the bubbles seemed to dance in celebration. "The shape and size determine how well the ethanol vapors can escape. That creates a direct impact on what you smell, and what you smell determines what you taste."

Braden lifted the glass to his nose again.

"Wait," I said.

He lowered his drink.

"Before you smell the wine, look at it. The quality of the glass determines what you're going to see. For example, these are crystal. The glass is thin, and the design captures light in a way that's unique. It's like looking through a prism."

"Or a stained glass window."

I paused, touched that he remembered my comment at the wedding.

"Right." Clearing my throat, I continued, "Once you look, what do you see? To me, this looks like tiny stars dancing in a perfect golden sunset."

Braden groaned. "I'm going to fail at this."

I swatted at his arm. "You can't fail at wine. Except when our crops get sick, but that's a different story. What does it look like to you?"

"Beer. With bubbles."

I laughed. "I can see that. Now, you can smell—"

"Wait." Braden ran his free hand through his hair. "Don't we have to swirl it first? I can swirl like nobody's business." He demonstrated, sloshing the wine dangerously close to the rim.

I hid a smile. "The purpose of swirling is to release additional aromas. With sparkling wine, the bubbles bring the aroma to the surface for you."

"Humph." He settled more comfortably on the barstool. "So, sparkling wine is perfect for the lazy wine taster."

"I'll put that on our marketing materials."

The playful glint in his dark eyes was starting to make it hard to focus.

"Ready to smell?" I asked, brightly.

He brought the glass up to his nose.

"Now, put your nose all the way in," I said. "Don't be afraid to get it wet."

"I might be a novice, but I'm not stupid."

I burst out laughing. "I saw that in a movie once." He bit his lip, and I squeezed my stem more tightly. "Now, the ethanol vapors escape, and the aroma sets the stage for the flavor palette. The categories to describe the aromas are pretty scientific. I won't bore you—"

"I'm a doctor," he said. "Science is kind of my thing."

The wine nerd in me cheered.

"Well, we do want to drink at some point, so I'll just say you've probably heard wines described in weird ways. People might say it smells like flowers or pepper or even dirt."

"Aren't those people just saying that to have something to say?"

"Nope. Those smells really do exist. It has to do with minerals, phenols, and even bacteria. For example, it's possible to have a wine that smells like the earth. That said, it's a balancing act. You don't want too much of one thing. That's when you get into odors rather than smells." I paused. "Have your eyes glazed over yet?"

He held my gaze. "I'm mesmerized."

Blushing furiously, I said, "Okay, tell me what you smell."

He brought his nose close to the wine. "Something flowery. Like an old lady's perfume."

I giggled. "Me too. And . . ." I breathed in. "Sunshine. There's a freshness this grape seems to own."

Braden took another sniff. "It's odd, but I actually know what you're talking about."

It made me happy to think he understood.

"Okay. Now, bring a little bit of the wine into your mouth and roll it around your tongue. Then, open your mouth to taste the difference when you add even more oxygen. It will change from the beginning, the middle, and even the finish."

He lifted his glass. "Cheers."

I took a slow sip, watching. He did what I said, even closing his eyes as though to give more thought to what he was tasting. Then he opened his eyes and nodded.

"What do you think?" I asked, trying not to focus on the million different shades of brown in his eyes.

"It tastes how I imagine life to be at the vineyard. The spirit of this place. Effervescent and sweet. Still, it's complex." His eyes met mine. "Something worth coming back for."

A tiny tingle started in my stomach, and I wiped a bead of sweat off the glass. "I thought doctors were schooled in science, not poetry."

"We're schooled in a lot of things."

I cleared my throat, then took a sip of water. "Next up, we have the pinot noir . . ."

There was a lot to say about it. At the moment, though, the words *were* catching in my throat. Not because of a stutter, but because I was so attracted to this guy. Like that moment after the plane crash, when he'd handed me his coat. That act had made me feel safe. The same feeling returned every time I was around him.

We went through three more of the wines. The shared experience of rolling the wine in our mouths was a connection on a different level. It was sensual somehow, knowing we were both tuned into the same notes and flavors.

When I started to pour the cabernet, Braden brushed his fingers over the back of my hand. The move was subtle and sweet. Our eyes met, and he leaned across the counter and kissed me.

I started to resist, but the taste of his lips on mine was intoxicating. He took my hands and led me to the opening in the bar. Stepping out from behind it, I let him take me into his arms.

The kiss slowed and faded. Drawing back, I rested my chin on his shoulder as though it were the most natural thing in the world. Our fingers interlocked, and I smiled.

"I think that had the best tasting notes by far," he said.

I kissed him again.

"So, what's the next step?" He pulled me close. "Your professional recommendation?"

"My professional recommendation . . ." I thought for a moment. "Find the best bottle of cabernet, order dinner from Olives, and take it back to my place."

Braden's look gave me shivers. "I couldn't ask for a better night."

~

The heavenly aroma of leg of lamb and roasted vegetables perfumed my kitchen. I lit a candle, and we slowly made our way through the bottle of cabernet. Braden sniffed and swirled every few sips.

"I think you've become a tasting expert," I told him.

He grinned and took a bite of lamb. "Not to mention an advocate for your restaurant. This is delicious."

"Thanks." I popped a piece of roasted squash in my mouth. "It's kind of a joke in the family that we own an Italian restaurant since my grandmother is German." The ring from the safety-deposit box flashed through my mind. "Pappy is a spaghetti addict, so it had to be Italian. The restaurant exists to support his noodle addiction."

Braden's face got serious. "How was he, the last time you saw him?"

I ran my finger down the stem of my glass. "I . . . I haven't gone."

Braden blinked. "Really? Why?"

"It's been so busy around here, and . . ." I fiddled with my fork. "I'm scared to go into hospitals."

Braden suddenly seemed incredibly interested in his pasta.

I was mad at myself for bringing it up. "That must sound crazy to a doctor. I—"

"No." He dragged his fork across a section of sauce. "I couldn't set foot in a hospital for years."

"Yeah, right."

"No, really." He caught my gaze. "My sister died when I was thirteen."

My mouth went dry. "Oh." I reached for the remainder of my cabernet. "I'm so sorry. What happened?"

"Layla—her name was Layla—was born with a heart defect. She wasn't projected to live past that first year. Man, she was tough. Ever since she was little, she was always sick." He shook his head. "Pneumonia got her just after her eleventh birthday."

I closed my eyes. There were so many times I'd lain in bed, terrified each cough would be my last. The one thing that had helped me make it through that final phase was my charm bracelet. The heavy, shimmering reminder that no matter what, my family would be there until the end.

"She was my little sister. It . . ." He went quiet. Finally, he said, "It wasn't easy."

I reached for Braden's hand. "Were you close?"

"I don't know how she put up with me." He chuckled. "I used to steal her Barbies, take their heads off, and dye their hair green with markers. That sort of thing. She always got me back. Once she used nail polish to paint my Teenage Mutant Ninja Turtles hot pink."

"You were a good brother," I said.

The gold Monopoly man flashed through my mind, and I took a long drink of wine.

Braden's dark eyes caught mine. "Why are you scared to go into hospitals?"

I gave him a brief summary of the *E. coli* outbreak at the petting zoo and its resulting complications.

"I read about that!" He leaned forward. "That was big news. There were similar instances across the country before people developed an awareness. Hand sanitizer at petting zoos is practically a requirement now."

"It's obvious you're a doctor." I wadded up my napkin and put it on my plate. "Most people zone out the minute I start to talk about it. Were you always interested in medicine?"

"I think I became a doctor to take control of my fear," he admitted.

"So, I should become a doctor?"

"Nah." He took my hand. "Drinking wine all day is a much better deal."

"From a medical standpoint, red wine is good for your heart."

"See? You're practically a doctor. Healing the world one cabernet at a time."

Leaning in, he kissed me again. Things got heavy, and we both pulled away at the same time. We looked at each other, and I knew that if we touched again, we would move past the point of no return. Reluctantly, I got to my feet and started to clear the plates.

Braden jumped up to help. After looking around, he paused. "You don't have a dishwasher?"

"It's a tiny house. I have to do things the old-fashioned way."

He reached for the dish soap, and I shook my head.

"I'll do that later," I told him. "For now, we're going to finish the tasting."

I pulled a bottle of ice wine out of the fridge. The cool blast of air soothed my flushed face, and I lingered in the door a moment longer than necessary.

"Liquid gold." I held up the bottle. "You'll love this."

After dislodging the cork, I filled two dessert glasses. The sweet scent perfumed the kitchen. It hit me that I would have to start conserving my collection, a thought that was beyond depressing.

"What's wrong?" He held the tiny glass up to the light. "You suddenly seem quite serious."

Maybe it was the amount of wine I'd had, but the wedding ring from the safety-deposit box had been nagging at me all day. Keeping my trip to the bank a secret a second longer seemed impossible.

"If I tell you something, can I trust you won't tell anyone?"

Braden's face turned serious. "Of course. What is it?"

By the time I'd explained the robbery, the mystery box, and my trip to the bank, the ice wine was nearly gone, and we had moved on to espresso. He listened without interruption, his eyes getting big once or twice. I squeezed my hands, worried that I'd shared so much.

"I'm speechless." He finished his espresso. "It's impressive you're so calm about all of this."

I almost laughed out loud. "I might look calm. Inside, I'm freaking out."

Outside, night had fallen. Moths pinged against the window, trying to make their way to the light. I shut the shades, troubled I hadn't thought to do that in the beginning. It was doubtful someone was out there, watching me, but everything I'd told Braden served as a reminder to exercise caution.

"Hmm . . ." He brushed a crumb off the table. "Let's talk about the ring. I understand your reaction to the swastika, but perhaps you're jumping to conclusions. The symbol could have been something different altogether."

"It was definitely a swastika. I looked at it under a flashlight."

"Not the design, the meaning." He gave me that serious look I was starting to think of as his doctor face. "The swastika was a symbol of hope, I believe, before the Nazis put their stamp on it. Maybe it was on there to encourage a happy union."

I shook my head. "Doubtful. The date on it was from the fifties."

"Ah." He frowned. "That's different, then."

"It's all so strange. I just wish I could figure out . . ." My voice trailed off.

"What?" he prompted.

"You're going to think I'm crazy."

He flashed his lopsided grin. "I'm not a psychologist."

"Okay, here goes." I poured two final glasses of ice wine and told him my theory that the mystery box was somehow connected to the robbery. "The design on the latch of the wooden box has a symbol really close to this." I held out the bottle, running my finger over the family crest on the label. "It doesn't feel like coincidence."

"The box was found the night the wine went missing?"

"The next morning." I fidgeted with my glass. "One of our workers found it just off the driveway. It's almost like—"

"Someone wanted you to find it."

"Or ditched it. Maybe they found it hidden in the cellar, took what they wanted, and had no idea about the key." The sweet aroma of the ice wine wafted up from the bottom of my glass. The perfume warmed me, along with the comfort that Braden took me seriously. "The police chief basically told me I was being an idiot."

"I can't judge until I see the box."

"Be right back." I headed to my bedroom and pulled it out of the hiding spot under my bed.

On the way back to the kitchen, I stopped by the bathroom and gripped the edge of the cool porcelain sink, staring at my reflection. My hair was loose and wild around my shoulders and my cheeks flushed with wine. For the first time in days, I looked relaxed and almost happy.

There was a risk sharing this information with Braden. There was something about him that I'd trusted, though, ever since the moment he'd jumped into my truck. So, the fact that he was in my house, helping me work through this, made me feel more hopeful than I'd felt since Pappy's crash.

I returned to the kitchen and held out the box. "Ready to solve the puzzle?"

Chapter Thirteen

Braden studied the box as I hovered next to him. His hair, I noticed, smelled like spice and shampoo. I wanted to touch it, to see if it was as soft as it looked. Embarrassed, I moved away.

"So." I sat down. "What do you think?"

"It looks homemade."

The carving on the top was intricate but rustic. It was definitely homemade. And old.

"That's the symbol"—I pointed at the wooden latch on the box—"that's on the bottle of the ice wine." Then I motioned toward the bottle.

"They are similar. It could be significant or . . ." He paused, as though afraid to disappoint me.

"Say it."

"The symbol might be something common during that time. Chevron's so popular right now. You see it everywhere."

I burst out laughing. "Did you seriously just say that?"

Braden blushed. "My aunt owns a dress shop. I'm quoting her, word for word."

"Wait." My heart skipped a beat. "Aunt Patty is Patricia Wells?"

Patricia Wells owned an upscale clothing shop on Main Street. It had been in business for decades. When I was sick in the hospital, she'd sent me a pale-green silk robe as a get-well present that was much too elegant for someone my age. I had worn that thing until it fell apart and had never forgotten the kindness.

"Yep." He gave me his half smile, and the resemblance suddenly seemed obvious. "The one and only."

The room suddenly felt much too small. Patricia Wells had a kind heart, but she knew everybody. One slip of the tongue, and this could be all over town.

My panic must have been apparent because he put his hand on mine. "Don't worry. Doctors and lawyers are good at keeping secrets. I won't say a word."

"You can't." The relaxed vibe was gone. Words began to catch in my throat, and I squeezed my hands so tight they turned white. "Seriously."

Braden brushed a loose strand of hair away from my eyes. "Trust me."

I stared at him, willing the panic to subside. Finally, I whispered, "Okay."

Braden picked up the box. He ran his thumb over the black velvet stapled to the wood.

"Let's take this off," he said. "See if anything is underneath."

"Oh." I hadn't even thought of that. "Let me get some scissors."

"It should come off pretty easily." Braden tugged at the area near the staples. Sure enough, the fibers of the fabric released with one pull. Dust and a musty scent came and went as he removed the remainder of the velvet.

I pushed the crumpled mess aside and ran my flashlight over the wood. Nothing but a few black marks around the staples. Looking at him, I made a face. "Darn."

Moving to place the crumpled velvet back in the box, I stopped. There was . . . I squinted. There was a small symbol embedded into the smooth side of the fabric.

"Braden!" My voice shook with excitement. Quickly, I shined the flashlight at the symbol.

The velvet was stamped with a small bird with a cluster of grapes in its beak. A scroll that read *Feierabend* blazed across the center. The design looked like a family crest or maybe . . .

"Wait." Disappointment cut through me. "I think this is a brand symbol."

Braden squinted at me. "A what?"

"Brand symbol. Like a German Coke or Nike or something, stamped into the velvet to make it look fancy. The product was probably wrapped in this, and whoever made the box used the velvet to make it look nice."

Braden frowned. "I don't know. It seems like . . ." We both leaned in at the same time and bumped heads. Laughing, he continued, "You might be right. Either way, it could give us insight into the person who put this thing together."

Pulling out his phone, he tapped something in, then handed it to me.

He had Googled *Feierabend*. Several things popped up. Apparently, *Feierabend* was a German word meaning "the end of the workday." I clicked through the online images and scrolled down the page, hoping to spot the symbol once again.

Braden leaned over and saw it first. "There."

He pointed, and I clicked on the picture at the bottom of the page. I fully expected it to link through to a website.

Instead, it linked to an e-book available in English and German. I glanced at the table of contents written in English and let out a low whistle. "This can't be a coincidence."

Braden reached for the phone. "What is it?"

"Feierabend's a vineyard."

~

It took two minutes to move from the phone to my computer, where we downloaded the e-book, *A Concise History of Mittelrhein*. As the title suggested, the book offered a century's worth of coverage on Mittelrhein, a well-known wine region in Germany. Weingut Feierabend was a local vineyard.

Its chapter was accompanied by the same symbol imprinted in the black velvet. There were also several pictures of the vineyard itself. I scrolled through.

"The layout is really similar to ours."

"Especially that building." He pointed at a black-and-white photo.

The main building could have been our tasting room, with its stone walls, climbing ivy, and black-framed windows. The storage barns were also nearly identical to ours in size and scope. Even the entrance, with its circle of wildflowers and German flag, was reminiscent of the roundabout at the end of our drive.

"Perhaps your grandparents studied this vineyard." Braden peered at the screen. "When they were getting started. Is it really well known?"

"I've never heard of it."

I leaned forward and studied the remaining black-and-white photos. There was a picture of the original founders—the Braunsteins—as well as one of the Scholzes, a husband-and-wife team that had taken over the vineyard in the thirties. My eyes settled on the picture of them.

The Scholzes stood in front of a black storage shed in the middle of the vineyard, squinting and smiling in the bright sunlight. They looked proud and friendly.

I glanced at Braden, worried he might be getting bored. He didn't seem to be. His dark eyes were intent on the screen, and his lips moved slightly as he read through the text.

His finger moved to the track pad. "Can I scroll down?"

The next page made me wince.

There was an entire series of photographs of the Scholzes hobnobbing with highly decorated officials from the Nazi Party. The couple hosted a dinner party in the tasting room, stood next to a row of black cars alongside men with swastikas on their arms, and relaxed on a boat next to a group of smiling party members. They also celebrated at an event that looked like a wine festival.

Sure enough, Braden read the caption out loud. "The Nazi Party invented the wine festival in 1935, when the vineyards produced an oversupply of wine. Rather than allow the yield to go to waste, the vineyards created a massive party centered around the celebration of wine."

I gave Braden a wry look. "The Nazis invented the idea of a wine trail too. I learned that while I was doing research on how to start a trail in Starlight Cove."

"That's probably why all of this looks familiar." Braden reached for my hand and massaged it in a way that gave me shivers. "You probably saw this same information."

"Do you care if we read through it?" I asked. "I've only been looking at the pictures."

He laughed. "Sure."

Skimming the text, we learned the original owners were a Jewish family named Braunstein. They had received the farmland as a gift from their parents and developed it into a high-producing vineyard. Once the Third Reich came into power, they were no longer allowed to run their business. Shortly after, the Braunstein family sold the vineyard to the Scholzes.

"It sounds like they did it to survive," I said.

Braden's thoughts were darker. "Literally. Listen to this: 'Herr Scholz claimed close ties to a high-ranking official in the Nazi Party, and as a result, some felt the offer to acquire the failing vineyard was impossible for Herr Braunstein to turn down.'"

"That's terrible." I sat back in my chair. "Imagine working your whole life to build a business only to have someone take it away."

Braden continued reading. "'In the hands of the Scholzes, the vineyard flourished. It became a popular attraction for members of the Nazi Party. There were rumors that Hitler and Eva Braun twice attended dinner on-site.'"

Dread settled over me. "I'm starting to suspect the symbol on the ring has little to do with good luck."

I continued to read. "'Weingut Feierabend thrived long after the war. The Braunsteins returned and attempted to buy it back. The Scholzes refused to sell. Tragedy struck in 1950 when the main house caught fire, killing the Scholzes and leaving their ten-year-old daughter as the only survivor.'"

"Goodness," I mumbled. "The poor family."

We read the next part in silence.

> As the daughter was too young to manage a vineyard, her guardian sold it to the highest bidder. Today, Feierabend carries a storied history and sells the majority of their grapes to vineyards across Germany, producing only a limited amount of private label varietals.

I scrolled back to the picture of the young couple who had lost their lives in the fire. It had been taken at a family picnic with their daughter. The little girl wore a traditional German dress and dug in the dirt with a small metal shovel.

I felt a strange connection to the girl, probably because we'd both experienced trauma at a young age. It must have been terrible to lose both her parents and then her home. I leaned forward and zoomed in to take a closer look at her, and my blood nearly froze.

The little girl looked exactly like my grandmother.

"What's wrong?" Braden asked.

"I think I'm losing my mind." My hand hovered over the track pad. "This picture . . ."

"What?" he said when I didn't continue.

The little girl had the exact same face as my grandmother, down to the arch of her left eyebrow and the mole below her bottom lip. I would swear the little girl *was* Oma except that my grandmother had grown up on a farm, not a vineyard. Slowly, my eyes returned to the couple standing by the barn.

It hit me why the woman in the photograph looked so familiar: her face had a strong resemblance to my father.

I sat back in my chair again.

My grandmother always claimed to love the fact that my grandfather was a farmer because she, too, had come from farming stock. She had never once said the farm happened to be a vineyard. Of course, her passion for wine now made a great deal of sense. I just couldn't believe she hadn't shared her story.

Her parents were friends with Nazis! No wonder she didn't talk about it.

Or maybe I was being completely delusional. My grandmother's maiden name was Bauer, not Scholz. This could simply be a family that happened to look like my family.

People had doppelgangers all over the world. The fact that this photo and story happened to pop up while I was researching the name of vineyard found in a box on our property had to be a complete coincidence. Right?

Yeah, right.

Still, there had to be a logical explanation why my grandmother lied about her past. Perhaps it was too painful. After all, she'd lost her parents in a fire, the vineyard had been sold, and she'd had to live with a guardian.

That would explain the last name. She was probably adopted by her new family.

It also explained the wedding ring. It must have belonged to her mother, a relic that had survived the fire. It didn't explain why the date engraved on the wedding band was from the midfifties, but that was the least of my concerns.

Scrolling back up the page, I studied the picture of her parents. My great-grandparents. It was upsetting to think they'd had an affiliation with the Nazi Party. That wasn't something I wanted in our bloodline. Quickly, I minimized the screen.

"Well, that was a big waste of time." I got to my feet. My legs shook, and my throat felt tight.

"It was interesting, though. I didn't know a wine tasting would include a history lesson too." Braden rested his hands on my shoulders and made a move to kiss me.

I pulled back. "It's getting late."

"Oh." Confusion crossed his face, followed by embarrassment. "Sorry. You probably wanted to kick me out hours ago."

I tried to protest, and the words got stuck in my throat. He gathered our espresso cups and took them to the sink as an excruciating silence filled the room. For a second, it looked like he planned to wash the cups, but then he obviously decided the best course of action was to bolt.

Every part of me wanted to share the truth and confusion about what I'd discovered. I couldn't do it, though. It was too risky that the secret would get out, and I still didn't even know what it meant.

He walked to the front door. There I gave him a quick hug and a kiss on the cheek. The uncertainty he felt was clear in the stoop of his shoulders as he stepped out into the summer night.

I watched as he walked across the field, his form getting smaller in the moonlight. Stars lit the sky. It would have been such a perfect night if I could have focused on him instead of putting my nose where it didn't belong. Now I had no idea what to do.

My grandmother had lived a secret life. Surely, Pappy and my father knew her history. Probably my mother too, which meant everyone knew except me, Dean, and Phillip. Which was fair. Still . . . why did this information turn up in the fields the very night the ice wine went missing?

It felt intentional, and that scared me. Had someone discovered the truth about my grandmother's past? It shouldn't matter, because the connection to the Nazis was decades ago, and it wasn't her fault. Still, I could only imagine what people would say. The topic alone would do damage if it was linked to our vineyard.

The motor from Braden's car started up and echoed across the field. I knew I'd hurt him with the abrupt way I'd ended things. It was a shame, because I'd had fun with him—more fun than I'd had with a guy in ages.

On the other hand, I'd known from the start that it would be a challenge to get involved. My life was too complicated at the moment, and some days, I felt like my heart was wasting away at some vineyard in Chile. Still . . . I watched the red taillights head down the drive, remembering the taste of his lips on mine. Even though getting involved with him at this point would have been a mistake, it hurt to watch him go.

Shaking my head, I went back inside and brewed a small pot of decaf. It was late, but I planned to reread the chapter on my grandmother's vineyard. The small amount of caffeine would hardly matter—with or without it, I knew I wouldn't be able to sleep a wink.

Chapter Fourteen

Because of the ease with which Braden and I had found the information on Weingut Feierabend, I expected answers to pop like corks. Yet, after nearly two hours, I only managed to discover a few more things.

First, Weingut Feierabend was now called Weingut Sonnenschein. Like it said in the book, they produced grapes and sold small batches of private-label wine.

Second, I discovered a newspaper clipping buried within the files of a German library. It took me forever to find it since I didn't speak a word of German. The translate button eventually helped me prevail.

Unfortunately, I couldn't translate the article because it was on microfiche. I took a screenshot, determined to either type it into the translator or research a more efficient alternative. The second it popped up on my computer, though, I deleted it.

Keeping files about my family seemed like a dumb move. Especially since it was such a cinch to break into my house. Granted, it would take some serious spyware to crack my password, but still.

It's not the computer that makes you nervous. It's the fact that this secret exists at all.

True enough.

I rubbed my eyes and glanced at the tiny clock in the upper corner of my computer screen. It was nearly three in the morning; time to call it a night. Like it or not, this piece of history would still be there when the sun came up.

~

The next morning, I had to do rounds on the grapes. Each row needed to be checked for rot, bugs, and growth. It was mindless work and gave me more than enough time to think about what I'd discovered the night before.

The grapes on the vines passed through my fingers like worry stones as I tried to imagine what it would be like to carry such a secret. Weingut Feierabend had been such an incredible part of my grandmother's early life. The fact I knew nothing about it made me feel like I barely knew her at all.

On the other hand, she'd been just a child at the time. Her parents' death had been horrific, and the memories had to be incredibly painful. Maybe she just wanted to put it all behind her. That was something I could understand.

"Abby! Wait up."

I had moved on from the pinot noir and was headed into the section with vidal blanc when Jessica, our administrative assistant, came chasing after me. She was in her early twenties and looked adorable in a flowing purple patchwork dress with her hair done in two french braids woven through with ribbon. She carried a floral carpetbag, and its beadwork sparkled in the sun.

The care she'd taken with her appearance reminded me that I hadn't dressed in anything other than my uniform in days. The move was intentional, to honor Pappy. Everything he wore was Harrington branded. My grandmother had even sewn the label into the lining of his suit for the night of the party. Looking at Jessica, though, I longed to wear something loose and pretty to match a day like this.

"Can I talk to you?" Her voice had an upward lilt that I'd always liked. Everything she said sounded like a question.

"Sure." I bent the stalk of the grapes. It was firm and healthy. Marking it in my log, I said, "Let's walk and talk."

A stroll through the fields would clear my head. I'd been so focused on my grandmother and work I'd barely had time to notice it was a beautiful morning. In the distance, sailboats skimmed the water as birds soared overhead. There was a breeze off the lake, and the sweet fragrance of grapes filled the air.

"No, I . . ." She bit her nails. "Indoors? To be honest, I don't feel comfortable talking about this at all." Her wide eyes darted around as if she was afraid of something.

Or someone.

She took a few cautious steps back. "This was stupid. I—"

Quickly, I took her elbow. "Let's go to my house."

I drew the curtains at my cottage and offered to make eggs. We settled on licorice tea. While it brewed, I tried to get her to relax by asking for updates on her boyfriend, who worked with the Peace Corps. By the time we sat at the table, she seemed much calmer.

"So. What's going on?" I asked.

Jessica cradled the tea with both hands and blew on it. She wore several rings: sterling silver, opals, and some beaded. The rings reminded me of the one hiding in the safety-deposit box.

"I've . . . I've noticed that the police chief has been around a lot."

I sat up a little straighter. "Yes?"

"Some of us think his presence has more behind it than the plane crash."

I raised my eyebrows.

"I wasn't going to pay any attention to this," she continued, "because it's so weird. Since I don't know what's going on, though, it might matter."

"What might matter?" I asked, confused.

When we had first sat down, Jessica had slung her carpetbag over the edge of the chair. Now, she reached inside and pulled out a handful of turquoise cards. She tossed them onto the table like she couldn't be rid of them fast enough.

Each paper had a cryptic message handwritten in all caps:

WE KNOW THE TRUTH

WE WILL EXPOSE YOU

GET READY TO PAY

I drew back in shock. "What is this?"

"No clue." Jessica's pale-blue eyes were wide. "We've gotten one once a week for like, two months? I threw the first few away because I thought it was some weird prank. Now that the cops are hanging around . . . is it something else?"

I picked up one of the papers, a heavy piece of card stock, and studied it. It was almost like a part of something, like the lining of a fancy gift box or something you'd stick into a high-end invitation to keep it from bending in the mail.

"It's odd, that's for sure," I said. "It's probably a good idea to show it to the police."

The handwritten messages were so aggressive that there was no question that Henry needed to see them. What were they referencing? Had someone found out about Oma's past?

The connection her parents had had with the Nazis had little to do with her. Still, it wasn't the type of thing the locals would be quick to forgive. Our town relied on tourism. If the phrase "Nazi sympathizer" was connected to Harrington Wines, the backlash would be fierce.

Assuming this was even about that.

What else could it be about, though?

"Thank you for bringing this to my attention." I shuffled the turquoise papers like a deck of cards. "Let me know if we get any more, okay?"

"Abby, what's going on?" She tugged at her hemp choker. "This is a little scary."

"I'm sure it's nothing," I lied. "Somebody's always pulling pranks."

"This doesn't feel like a prank." Jessica stood up and grabbed her carpetbag. "I get it that your family is supertight, and we're just the workers. If we're in any danger, though, you're obligated to tell us."

"Just the workers?" I echoed. "Jessica, no one here is *just a worker.*"

It hurt my feelings to hear her even say that, because my family bent over backward to value our staff. We accommodated schedules, gave advancement opportunities, and did our best to make the vineyard a fun place to work. The tasting room was available to anyone who wanted to drink and socialize, my father spent hours with anyone who even mentioned an interest in learning how to make wine, and my grandparents had once paid for a field hand's medical bills when his wife had gotten sick.

The way Jessica talked, we handed out paychecks and said, "Good luck." Her comment also made it seem much more possible that someone working with us was behind all this. If our workers were actually angry with us, the theft could be about more than money.

At least that would let my brother off the hook.

Unless they were all in it together.

I ran my finger along the sharp edge of the turquoise paper. "I'll share this with the police. We will let you know immediately if they perceive this to be a threat. Thank you for bringing it to my attention."

Jessica left in a huff of patchouli. I studied the notes to see if I'd missed anything. They seemed to be pretty straightforward. Picking up the phone, I called Henry.

"Huh." His silence was gruff once I told him the situation. "Know what it's referencing?"

I swallowed hard. Sharing the information about my grandmother would be a major breach of trust. I couldn't tell him anything like that without talking to my family first.

"I don't want to guess."

Henry was silent for so long that I started to sweat. It was like he knew I was lying. Finally, he grunted.

"Forensics will check it out. I'll talk to the girl who found them."

"Okay." I hesitated. "Listen, will you tell her to keep things quiet? There's getting to be a lot for people to talk about around here, and we still haven't even told half my family that the ice wine is missing."

"You might want to do that, Abby." His tone softened, like he was stepping back into the role of family friend. "Word will get out soon."

He was right. It was just a matter of time before all eyes would be looking our way. The thought brought a now all-too-familiar tightness to my throat.

"Thanks for your help," I said. "I'll talk to you soon."

I hung up and stared down at the papers.

WE KNOW THE TRUTH

WE WILL EXPOSE YOU

GET READY TO PAY

The messages were frightening. I took pictures and texted them to my father. I knew he'd have questions. Unfortunately, I didn't have any answers.

Sure enough, my father texted a barrage of questions. Finally, I told him to call Jessica, because I didn't know anything else. I also hoped that hearing from him would help make her feel like we were taking her concerns seriously.

If we're in any danger, you're obligated to tell us.

Danger seemed like such a strong word. Still, no matter how much I wanted to ignore the threat, I couldn't get it out of my head. Someone was coming to get us—the question was why.

Chapter Fifteen

It was midafternoon when I finished rounds and gave the canopy over the grapes in the riesling field an affectionate pat.

"You're looking great," I told the plump bunches of fruit. "The sunshine seems to agree with you, and there's another good storm on the horizon. You'll get a nice drink. That's only fair, isn't it?"

"I'd say so," said a deep voice, and I practically jumped out of my skin.

Braden was walking toward me, carrying what appeared to be a bottle of iced green tea. His good looks were pronounced in the natural setting. More than that, I was once again struck by the warmth in his eyes.

"Thought you'd like something refreshing." He passed me the drink as if it were completely normal for him to be out here.

"What are you doing here?" I asked, delighted.

The memory of the night before rushed through me. The feeling of his arms around me, his lips on mine. Then, the fear that I had let him in too quickly and as a result, put my family's privacy at risk.

If I told Braden my concerns, I knew he would reassure me that he was not the type to gossip. Like when he'd said that doctors and lawyers were good at keeping secrets. The other part of me, though, the part that had discovered my grandmother had once lived a secret life, was too afraid to let someone so new into my family circle.

Braden smiled at me. "I wanted to stop by and say thank you for last night. The tasting far exceeded my expectations. I'm happy to tell that to the tourists, if you'd like me to."

I laughed but felt panicked inside. He was such a great guy. Someone who made me feel safe and vulnerable and all of the things that I really wasn't ready to feel right now.

"Well, I appreciate that." I took a sip from the bottle. It *was* green tea, with a hint of something fruity. "Is this pomegranate?"

"It was the closest thing to wine they had available."

I laughed. "It's delicious." I took another sip. "Thank you."

"You're welcome." He smiled that cute, lopsided grin. "I also came up here because I wanted to ask you in person if you'd like to have dinner tonight?"

The panic grew stronger. Yes, I wanted to have dinner with him. It had been ages since I'd enjoyed hanging out with someone so much. It just wasn't the right time.

"Sorry. I can't tonight." He looked ready to suggest an alternative, so I added, "I'd love to have dinner with you sometime. I need a little more time to get my head on straight, though. Things are so messed up right now."

He held up his hands. "I completely understand, no pressure at all."

The sun glinted off his watch, brightening his smile even more. For a second, I wanted nothing more than for him to talk me into it. To pull me into his arms and insist that we explore whatever was between us. Then I came to my senses.

It really wasn't a good time to get involved, especially not after what I'd discovered about my grandmother. I couldn't risk spilling the secret to someone I hardly knew for fear of the damage it could cause to my family. Dean had sparked plenty of small-town scandal over the years, but this was something different. The history of my grandmother's vineyard was dark and sinister, and not something that could get out.

"I really appreciate you stopping by." I avoided his gaze. "Unfortunately, I have to finish this up before lunch."

"Yes. Absolutely." He gestured at the field around us. "This is beautiful, by the way. Really incredible."

"Thanks." I took in the lush greenery. "I think that every day."

We smiled at each other. Then Braden gave me a wave and headed out. His exit felt better than it had the night before, when I'd been worried I'd offended him.

I plucked a handful of grapes from the vine and ate them in silence, watching him walk through the fields. Finally, I turned back to the vines.

"It's just you and me," I told the plants. "And I really couldn't tell you if I'm sorry about that or not."

~

I was out front working on our parking sign when my mother and Phillip pulled up in her white SUV.

The gold paint inside the black letters on the sign often went dull, so we touched it up a few times a season. The paint was slick and malleable under the brush and shimmered in the sun. The gold flecks made me think of my charm bracelet. I could still feel the soft surface of the gold pieces as they slipped through my fingers.

My bracelet had been stolen the summer I turned fourteen. I'd rarely had an occasion to wear it, so it was always in the exact same spot in my jewelry box. I'd discovered it was missing the night my parents were going to take me out to dinner to celebrate my straight As.

It had taken me years to catch up at school because of all the time I had spent in the hospital, and once I finally brought home good grades, the family had been excited to celebrate with dinner on Main Street. I'd opened my jewelry box, ready to slip on my bracelet, and instead, discovered it was missing.

I must have screamed, because both of my parents had come running.

"It's gone." I'd pointed at the jewelry box. "My bracelet."

My father had used a word that would have gotten me grounded. Then he'd added, "Valuables are supposed to be locked up, Abby. There have been too many strangers in this house."

A parade of workers had been in and out all hours of the day, because my grandparents were adding a sunroom. There were also always tourists that wandered into the main house, thinking it was part of the public grounds. Once it had hit me that my bracelet was really, truly gone, I'd burst into tears.

My mother had pulled me into a hug. "Maybe it's for the best. That bracelet held a lot of bad memories."

Not for me. The bracelet had helped to chase away those bad memories. Once it was gone, the bad memories had been the only thing I had left.

Don't think about it. There's no point.

The thought made me press my paintbrush harder than necessary against the sign.

The gravel crunched on the driveway, and I looked up. My mother and Phillip got out of her car. They carried bags of takeout from Burger Blast, the hamburger joint about twenty miles out of town.

"Looks good, Abby." Phillip admired the sign. "Here, I'll carry these up." He took the bags from my mother, who kissed me on the top of the head.

"We brought you a burger. Want to have something to eat?"

I considered the time. "Maybe. I was supposed to have lunch with Kelcee. I think I'm going to skip it, though. There's too much to do."

"No, go." My mother tucked her designer sunglasses into her shirt pocket. "Phillip and I are planning to eat and get right to work. Just text me what needs to be done."

"Mom, there's a ton—"

"Honey." She stopped me with a look. "This will all be here when you get back." She held out her hand for the brush. "Let me finish up."

It was a relief to pull up to Kelcee's. The charming two-story by the water was light blue with faded yellow shutters and always felt like home. To my delight, her brother, Kip, opened the door.

"Hey." He pulled me into a hug. "Long time, no see."

Kip had Kelcee's striking blue eyes and dark hair. He was one of the nicest people on the planet, and it was always great to see him. I was in the middle of updating him on Pappy when his fiancée walked into the living room and handed me a drink.

"Sangria." She gave me a conspiring grin. "It's made from red table wine from this Harrington vineyard place? Have you heard of it?"

I laughed. "It's good to see you, Dawn."

Like her fiancé, Dawn Conners happened to be both gorgeous and nice as could be. She had sun-kissed blonde hair and a poised, almost regal air about her. The previous summer, she'd moved to Starlight Cove to remodel the lighthouse and discover the truth behind an old family secret. Dawn might actually be a good resource for what I was going through.

"Come into the kitchen," Kelcee called. "It's ready."

The three of us strolled in.

"Every time I am here, I have serious kitchen envy," Dawn said, and I laughed.

Kelcee's kitchen was enormous, with massive wooden beams on the ceiling, professional-grade appliances, and a brick pizza oven. My favorite feature was the enormous island that doubled as a kitchen table. Copper pots hung overhead, perfectly positioned between a series of modern lights, and plenty of chairs sat around the counter for guests.

"Grab a seat," Kelcee called from the stove.

The air was ripe with the scent of roasted meat, onions, and basil. I peered over her shoulder to see she'd whipped up an elaborate fajita spread, complete with homemade tortillas and guacamole. It looked delicious.

I poured the sangria, Kip served up the guac, and Dawn filled glasses of water for everyone. Kelcee brought us fajitas with all the trimmings, and we all settled in around the counter.

"How's your grandfather doing?" Dawn asked.

"It's his fifth day in the hospital," I said. "It's not easy." I repeated the details I'd told Kip, and she shook her head.

"That must be hard. Your family seems close."

"Close doesn't describe it." Kip cheerfully crunched on a chip. "They're like the royals, living in their own little kingdom. They live up there together, guarding the walls of the castle."

Pfft. If that was the case, we needed better armor.

"How's the lighthouse?" I asked Dawn. "Are you still living there?"

"Yes!" Her face lit up. "We lived on Kip's houseboat this past winter but moved back in late spring. It's everything I ever wanted. Romantic, nostalgic, beautiful—"

"Our torrid romance or the lighthouse?" Kip cracked.

Dawn beamed at him. "Speaking of, have you asked her?"

Kip got serious, and he turned to me. "Dawn and I would like to get married at the vineyard next year."

"You would?" I got to my feet and hugged both of them tight. "We'd love that. When?"

"Next summer." Dawn pulled her purse off from the chair and took out a small bag of condiments. After selecting a travel-size packet of hot sauce, she shook it on her fajita. "We would actually love to get married—"

"*This* summer—" Kip clarified.

"But my parents will be out of town. So, we have to wait."

"They're headed for a dive in Greece," Kip explained, "so we could do it there, but—"

"Starlight Cove is home," Dawn finished.

They beamed at one another.

"Call me, and we'll get it set up." I smiled at Kip, so happy to see him happy. "We'll make it a dream wedding."

"Perfect." Kip took her hand. "Since she's my dream girl."

Kelcee and I glanced at each other and rolled our eyes.

Still, the love between the two was apparent. Just being around them flashed me back to the feeling I'd had in Braden's arms. Then I remembered all the reasons it wasn't the right time to get involved and focused on adding more cilantro to my fajita.

Dawn and I discussed wedding plans, and then Kelcee caught us up on the latest gossip from the restaurant. The sun shone in through the window, and the easy laughter of my friends made me relax for the first time in days. Suddenly, Kelcee banged her fork down.

"I almost forgot. Jerry Andrews is back in town. Can you believe it?"

The bite in my mouth went sharp, like I had added too much onion.

"That just killed my appetite," I said. "That guy is the last person I'd want to see."

Dawn tucked a lock of hair behind her ears. "Sorry, who?"

I stabbed at a piece of meat. "He was in class with my oldest brother, Phillip. Total piece of garbage. The type of kid who sped up when he saw a squirrel in the road."

Jerry Andrews was also the type who'd thought nothing of getting drunk before finals, driving ninety on the back roads, and introducing my brother to coke. I remembered him as a skinny teenager with bad skin, a rattail haircut, and the same worn heavy metal–band T-shirt.

Kip crunched down on a chip. "It's interesting he and Dean came back at the same time. I wonder if—"

"No." Kelcee shook her head. "They're not friends."

"How would you know?" Kip asked.

"I mean I can't picture it." She glanced at me, then dabbed sour cream onto her fajita. "Supposedly, he works as a barista at that weird internet café off the highway. It's a hookah lounge too, I guess."

I almost dropped my drink. "He works at the internet café?"

"Yeah." Kelcee frowned. "Honestly, I'm surprised it's still in business. Do people even use those places anymore?"

The taste of bile gathered in the back of my throat. It was one thing for my brother to have a past with someone like that. It was quite another to learn the guy worked at the very place where the person who'd stolen our ice wine had tried to unload it.

I pressed my water glass against my cheeks, which were suddenly flaming, and Kelcee gave me a worried look. "Abby, are you okay?"

I set down the glass and took in a few slow, deep breaths. "Yep."

She waited for me to say more. When I didn't, she got to her feet. "If it helps, I made flan." Clearing the plates from the table, she took them to the sink. "Any takers?"

Kip and Dawn raised their hands, and I managed to nod. They started talking about something they needed to fix on his houseboat while Kelcee dished up dessert.

While the bowls clinked in the background, I took a huge gulp of sangria, trying to push back the panic welling inside. The idea that my brother could have taken the ice wine was a real possibility. It made me sick to my stomach to think that way, but it was time to stop being so naive. In the past, he would have been first on the list of suspects.

I must have looked upset, because Dawn touched Kip's hand.

"Kip, we're being rude," she said. "Abby, tell us what else is going on in vineyard life."

To my absolute embarrassment, my eyes filled with tears.

Dawn took my hand. "You're worried about your grandfather, aren't you?"

"It's not that." I swiped at my eyes. "There's just . . . sorry. There's a lot going on in vineyard life. Too much to handle, really."

Kelcee handed out desserts. "Tell us," she said, her voice gentle.

In a monotone, I updated them on everything that had happened since the night of the anniversary party. Because Dawn now counted as family, I didn't hold back. I told them everything about the theft, the box in the field, the threatening notes, and finally, what I'd learned about my grandmother.

"That is unbelievable," Kelcee said, her blue eyes wide. "Your grandmother is one of the nicest people I know. I can't believe she was a part of that world in any capacity."

"I know." I started to pick up my spoon to try the flan but couldn't do it. Setting it back down, I stared at the pattern the caramel sauce made on the plate. "I'm so confused right now."

Part of me was tempted to share my suspicions about Dean, but I couldn't. He was still my brother, and it had always been so embarrassing to have my friends view him as the bad guy. Seeing Kip and Kelcee together reminded me of what it could have been like between Dean and me, if only things had been different.

Kip laid down his spoon, his handsome face serious. "Abby, what about the plane crash? Could that be connected somehow?"

The thought hadn't even occurred to me. "No. I mean . . . it was investigated. No one seemed suspicious."

"What caused it?" Dawn asked.

I explained about the faulty wire. Kip and Dawn exchanged glances. The idea that someone might have tried to hurt my grandfather was not something I wanted to wrap my mind around, but since Kip had brought it up, I had to admit that part of the report wasn't sitting well with me.

"Okay." I took a drink of sangria. "My grandfather is pretty meticulous. Incredibly meticulous. So, it *is* a little odd that he missed a wire that was falling apart. It's not like him."

"Bring it up with your dad." Kip's expression was somber. "See if he agrees."

"I can't imagine someone would try and hurt him. It's . . ." I shook my head, unable to continue. "It makes me wonder if it's all tied together, though. I'm convinced the wooden box is somehow connected to the theft of the ice wine."

Kelcee took a bite of flan. "Why?"

"Because the box was found the morning after the robbery, and the symbol carved into it is so similar to the one on our bottles. Of course, Henry thinks my theory is ridiculous."

"*Pfft*. Henry." Dawn rolled her eyes. "I seem to remember a time he doubted that I was chased by a man with a knife. Like I could mistake that for a friendly handshake."

As always, Kip was diplomatic. "He means well. He's just set in his ways."

"True," I said. "I'm just glad I was the one who ended up with the key to the safety-deposit box. Can you imagine if someone posted pictures of my grandmother's parents partying with the Nazis and linked it to Harrington Wines? *That* would be great for business."

Kelcee waved her spoon. "It was so long ago. No one would care."

"I disagree." Dawn's blue eyes looked troubled. "The shipwreck with my great-grandfather happened a hundred years ago. For the people around here, it could have been yesterday."

"Which is exactly why I have to figure this out before someone else does," I said.

Kip frowned. "Even if the ice wine is connected to the box, you need to let the police handle the robbery. It's what they do every day."

"I know, but—"

"It's personal. I get it." He took Dawn's hand. "But you never know what people are capable of. Things could get dangerous. It's not worth it."

I wanted to argue that it *was* worth it, but I understood what he was saying. The police knew what they were doing, and I didn't. The turquoise papers flashed through my mind. I certainly wouldn't know how to confront the psycho putting those out into the world.

With a sigh, I looked at Dawn. "I'm kind of jealous. You at least had the bonus of a treasure hunt when you tried to learn the truth about your family."

She shook her head. "It was the darkest time in my life. I'm sorry you have to go through this."

My throat tightened. "Yeah. Me too."

My flan was cracked and drooping in the warm afternoon. Picking up my spoon, I took a bite, and the burnt caramel was like a salve against my tongue.

"So, what should I do now?" I finally said.

"Research." Kip's voice was firm. "Document the things you know, and use logic to figure out the rest. I'd call the vineyard in Germany. See if you can find further history about the Scholzes and—"

"That's another thing. Scholz is not my grandmother's maiden name. I'm guessing she took the name of the family that took her in."

Dawn nodded. "I would also call the county clerk—or the German equivalent—in that town. It should be easy to research since so many people are into genealogy. They could give you information like when her parents died, when she was adopted, and things like that."

I fidgeted with my sangria glass. "I'd feel like such a snoop."

"You're not," Dawn insisted. "You're not snooping for sport. You're trying to help your family. There's a difference. Unfortunately, the box is probably the only freebie in terms of research that you'll get. My father always says lightning and cheap clocks rarely strike in the same place twice."

Kip chuckled. "Sound advice."

"Could you ask your parents?" Kelcee wondered.

I hesitated. "It's too risky. What if they don't know anything about it?"

Kelcee dragged her spoon through the leftover caramel on her plate. "Then it's your duty to step in."

Kip nodded. "Just be careful."

"The most important thing," Dawn said, "is to remember why you're doing it."

I pushed back my plate. "It sounds like I need to start digging."

Chapter Sixteen

It was dusk before I worked my way through my to-do list and called it a day. The time with my friends had helped make things feel less hopeless, and I looked forward to having the time to make the calls to Germany that Dawn and Kip had suggested.

As I walked down the path toward home, the air felt lush with the promise of rain, and in the distance, lightning lit the edge of the horizon. I relished the familiar stroll through the vines and the music of the cicadas chirping in the distance. Once I reached the path leading to my house, I stopped for a moment and closed my eyes, letting the sounds of the summer night drain the tension from my body.

"Are you *trying* to get jumped?" demanded a gruff voice.

I shrieked, and my eyes flew open.

Dean stepped out from behind my beloved apple tree. "Dad told me about the threats we've been getting. You *do* realize that someone a little unstable sent them, right? You can't just stand out here at night with your eyes closed."

I hated to admit it, but my brother was right. That said, I couldn't begin to imagine what *he* was doing here at this time of night.

"Did you break in again?" I asked, running my hands over the goose bumps on my upper arms.

Dean pulled a grape off the nearest vine and popped it into his mouth. "I was checking the irrigation pipes. I heard about the flood and wanted to make sure everything was secure."

It had been years since Dean and I had been friends. Somehow, I still knew when he was lying, and given my suspicions about the ice wine, the thought made me shiver. Quickly, I headed up the steps.

"I'm going to make dinner. It's been a long day."

"Great." He fell into step beside me. "What are we having?"

"Dean . . ."

"Abby." He swiped the key out of my hand and unlocked the front door. "I'm your brother. You're stuck with me." He gave me the silly smile I used to love. "And I do know how to boil water."

Even though I did not trust him, it was pretty clear he was not going to take no for an answer.

"Expect to be kicked out early."

He laughed. "I wouldn't expect anything less."

It turned out the only thing I had to eat were spaghetti noodles and a jar of arrabbiata sauce, so Dean got to show off his boiling-water skills after all. I sat at the kitchen table with my feet tucked under my legs, watching as he cooked.

"No vegetables?" he asked, after searching my fridge.

"Nope." I held up my glass of chardonnay. "But tons of fruit."

Dean turned me down when I offered him wine. He sipped at soda water instead. I wondered if he was trying to get back on the wagon.

"I don't buy vegetables," I told him. "They go bad too quickly when you're cooking for one. I steal salad from Olives."

"Thief." He strained the pasta in the sink, steam rising up around him. "Let's call and see if somebody will bring us parmesan cheese."

"I have that." I got to my feet and pulled a container out of the cupboard. "Here."

He gave it a suspicious look. "Doesn't cheese have to be kept cold?"

"Not according to Kelcee." I shrugged. "On the other hand, what does she know?"

Dean grinned. Then, he plated the spaghetti and sat down at the table with me. The spice went straight to my sinuses, and I sneezed.

"Gesundheit." He dug in. "Hope it's not too spicy."

Back when we were little, we used to compete to see who was better at eating foods that were stinky, sour, and spicy. I typically destroyed him on the first two, then he would crush me when it came to spice. Once he ate an entire jalapeño pepper without even breaking a sweat.

"Why are you cooking for one?" Dean asked. "Aren't you dating that doctor guy?"

I almost choked. "Braden?"

"He was here last night."

"How on earth do you know that?" I demanded. "Were you spying on me?"

"Didn't have to." Dean grinned. "My good friend Billy told me you let the good doctor stay for an after-hours tasting. You like him?"

I paused. Back in high school, we'd had these conversations all of the time. Dean was deep into alcohol and drugs by that point, but my girlfriends had been obsessed with him. They'd loved that he was a rebel. Of course, they weren't the ones who'd been terrified every night he'd snuck out of the house, waiting for the floorboards to finally creak the news that he'd made it back home alive.

"The doctor didn't stay over, if that's what you're asking." I spooned some more parmesan onto my plate. "Besides, we're not dating. I've known him less than a week."

It seemed strange to think it hadn't even been a week since the crash. It felt like so much had happened.

Still, I tensed, waiting for Dean to comment that it had been long enough for me to make it to the hospital, if I'd bothered. Instead, he hopped up to get us both napkins. Once he settled back into his chair, we ate in silence.

Dean finished his pasta and looked around. "It's strange being here. I remember when we first started sneaking in. It was all spider webs and rusty nails."

"And broken glass. Remember, we used it for—"

Dean burst out laughing. "Tattoos!"

I snorted into my wine. Like absolute idiots, we'd used the broken glass we found on the ground to slice tiny *x*'s in the tips of our pinky fingers, with a pledge to the clubhouse and its members. It was a wonder I hadn't started my career at the hospital with tetanus.

Dean waved his glass of water at me. "Phillip was so bitter. He couldn't believe we didn't invite him to be a member."

"Oh, please." I took a drink of wine. "Phillip never wanted to play with us. He was too busy trying to be old and cool. We were always the ones doing the fun stuff."

"There were some good times." Dean scraped the last of the sauce off his plate. He peeked in the pot on the table and gave me a questioning look.

"Go for it." I had only picked at mine. "I don't have much of an appetite."

Dean spooned up the rest of the spaghetti. "Why? What's up?"

For a split second, I considered telling him I knew his old friend was working at the internet café. It wouldn't do much good. If Dean was guilty, it would just tip him off. He'd probably leave town that very night.

"Nothing worth talking about." The reality of our relationship had returned with a thud. "Hey, when you talked to Billy, did you find out anything more about the missing inventory?"

"Barely." Dean scratched his neck. "What do you know about that guy?"

"Worked here the past three summers. Goes to college in Atlanta. Likes the Braves . . ."

"Is he into anything where he might need money?" Dean asked, glancing at me.

Anything where he might need money.

The question brought back the memory of the last time Dean and I had really spoken, back when we were still friends. It had been over a decade ago, during the one summer I'd spent away from home, taking an eight-week program for vintners in Sonoma.

Dean had already been in Chicago at that point, and his addiction had been bad. He'd kept me on the phone for hours the nights he felt scared or needy. The last week of summer, he'd called me from a pay phone at three in the morning California time, begging for money. I'd stretched the cord into the bathroom, scared the call would wake my boyfriend. He worked as a security guard at the vineyard and hated it that I was so close to my addict of a brother.

"You gotta help," Dean had sobbed as I begged him to calm down. "They're gonna kill me."

I'd promised to wire every penny I had. My boyfriend must have been listening at the door because he'd stormed in and ripped the phone from my hands.

"You piece of shit," he'd shouted into the receiver. "It'll go up your nose!"

He'd thrown the phone across the room, smashing it into pieces. I'd broken up with him on the spot, but it hadn't changed the fact that I had no way to get in touch with my brother. I'd spent the week in a panic and on the phone with my mother, convinced my brother was dead.

It turned out my ex had been right—Dean had used the money for drugs. He'd conned my parents into giving it to him, overdosed, and spent a week in the hospital. That was the last time any of us had heard from Dean for years, until the letters begging for forgiveness had started to arrive.

I set down my glass of wine. "Listen, I'm getting tired."

Dean glanced at the clock on the microwave. 8:04.

He frowned. "Let me at least do the dishes."

I sat in silence as he worked his way through the pile. The scene made me think of Braden's charming bewilderment that I didn't have a dishwasher.

Dean dried the last dish and put it away. Then he straddled a chair and gave me a frank look. "So, I heard what happened with the operations job."

My back stiffened. This was the last conversation I wanted to get into with him.

"Listen, I really am tired—"

I started to get to my feet.

Dean held up his hand. "Abs, hold on. It's cool that Dad's gonna fight for you. Still, you must be pretty pissed that Pappy skipped you over, right?"

I took a long drink of wine. "I'm not happy."

"You should be furious."

I looked at him in surprise. "What do you mean?"

The jaunty section of hair fell over his forehead, making it hard to see his eyes. "I mean, at this point the vineyard owes you something, you know?"

"Uh, no."

Dean stood and helped himself to the last can of Coke I had in the fridge. "Look, this place is a cash cow." He popped the tab and waved the can around. "Some shitty operations job is the last thing you should be worried about. One day, we'll own the whole thing."

My throat was tight. "Well, for now, I'm an employee. So, yes. I do think worrying about a job is appropriate."

He gave me a look like *yeah, right.*

"The vineyard is our inheritance," he said. "It's not unreasonable to demand a say in how it's run."

The spice from the arrabbiata burned in my throat. I couldn't believe Dean was so quick to include himself in the equation. I poured myself more wine and didn't answer.

"The way things are handled around here is a joke." Dean ran his hand through his dark hair. "Pappy still insists on paper records, which is just irresponsible, and these rumors about losing money? You have got to take back what's yours while you still can. I sure plan on it."

The flesh on my arms prickled. Everything from suspicions about the ice wine to the plane crash rushed through my head. Thoughts I didn't want to have.

Carefully, I wiped some red sauce off the table. "What do you mean?"

He slurped some Coke out of the can. "I mean I'm not just taking things at face value. Look, I might not stick around. I can't stand to see so many mistakes. I'll probably wait this whole Pappy thing out and then hit the road."

I closed my eyes. So, he was planning to leave. Right around the time the thief was trying to sell the bottles. It couldn't be coincidence. And he wouldn't—couldn't—have done something to sabotage the plane, could he? To speed up his "inheritance"?

Dean barked with sudden laughter.

I jumped, gripping the table. "What?" I asked, frightened to see his eyes were wild and manic.

"Being in here reminds me of so many things." He gestured at the interior of the kitchen. "Remember how we used to talk about our dreams?"

I got to my feet. "I'm going to bed."

"Abby, hold on." He reached out his hand, his face superintense. "Don't you remember? You used to hate it that Pappy didn't take you seriously. You planned to open your own place. To compete."

I hadn't thought of that in years. There was a time in my life when I had, indeed, planned to compete with my grandfather. Of course, that need had fallen away with time and maturity.

I walked my wineglass over to the sink. Dean had done a good job cleaning up. He'd even wiped down the interior of the stainless steel, something I rarely bothered to do.

"Would you still take on Pappy?" he asked. "If you had the money?"

I turned and met his eyes. "Would *you*? If you had the money?"

Dean gave me a guilty grin. "I hate to say it, sweetheart, but I don't have to. I'm a guy, so Pappy would be happy to have me by his side." He took another slurp of his Coke. "Besides, I wouldn't waste my money for something like that. I'd run away to a desert island and never look back." He dumped the can in the trash. "Thanks for dinner."

"We recycle pop cans." Irritated, I set it on the counter. "Ten cents a can."

"Ten cents, huh? Big money."

"It's not the money. It's the principle."

His eyes met mine. "Exactly." Turning, he headed to the living room and let himself out the front door.

I sank back down into a kitchen chair, the scent of garlic and orange dish soap still strong in the air. The conversation had left me shaken. Our dinner had almost been fun until he'd had a massive personality shift. It had to have been prompted by drugs even if I'd never seen him take anything.

Or maybe he had a personality disorder, thanks to the abuse he'd inflicted on himself in the past. Either way, I didn't want any part of it. The Dean I knew—the one who'd liked silly tattoos and ridiculous eating competitions—still existed in my memory.

This new guy was someone I didn't want to get to know.

Chapter Seventeen

For the first time in years, I woke up because of a nightmare. The sheets were damp and twisted in my hands, my breath came fast, and the room was much too quiet. I sat up, pulling my blankets close.

Something clanked in the living room, and I froze. Was someone in my house?

Holding my breath, I listened. The only sound was the air-conditioning as it whirred and complained. I flopped back against the pillow and let out a shaky breath, the doom of the dream still clawing at my mind.

It had taken place back in high school, and I'd stood in front of that guy Jerry's house. There'd been a chain across the front of the long dirt driveway and a black rottweiler in the front yard. In my dream, the dog had come running toward me, teeth flashing.

It bit me.

My body jerked a little as I remembered. Its teeth had made contact with my leg as I'd woken up. The dream was so real that I touched the outside of my right thigh to confirm I'd imagined the whole thing.

I pulled my blanket more tightly around me. The conversation from lunch with my friends rang through my head, along with the picture of Dean acting so erratic. Something nagged at me through the haze, and I couldn't quite put my finger on it.

It's the principle.

The comment Dean had made at dinner.

Maybe I'd been looking at the theft all wrong. The missing ice wine might not be about money at all, even though a seller could make a fortune from it. The missing ice wine might be about principle.

From the time my brothers and I were old enough to understand our family owned a vineyard, we'd been expected to be a part of it. Phillip and Dean, in particular. They were groomed to take on big roles. Phillip lived up to that, and later, so did I. Dean didn't, though, because he couldn't keep his nose clean.

I wondered if he resented that I had come so far, even though Pappy had barely expected me to achieve the basics. One would think he'd be a little more progressive, but jealousy did strange things to people. In fact, I'd spent so much time being jealous of him that it hadn't occurred to me that he could feel the same about me.

The way he'd talked at dinner—*at this point, the vineyard owes you something*—made his sense of entitlement clear. He might see himself as a victim, pushed aside from a legacy that had once centered around him. Why not steal our most important asset?

The thing about the plane crash, though . . . Dean wouldn't have done that. He and Pappy had always been close, even after Dean had left town. That didn't mean that one of his friends wasn't capable of doing something terrible, though, without telling him.

I'd had my suspicions about Dean's involvement since the very beginning. Given the fact that he was linked to the internet café, it was time to take action. This was all too serious to stand by in silence.

Turning to my side, I kept an eye on my open bedroom door. Shadows stretched down the hall. The strange fear that had come with the nightmare still lingered.

I kept my eyes trained on the shadows, half waiting for something to leap from the darkness and attack.

≈

Late the next afternoon, I arrived at the police station. The waiting room was empty, clean, and criminal-free. Heck, it almost looked cozy, with a pot of coffee brewing, Saturday afternoon television blaring, and a box of colorful doughnuts ready for the taking.

The guard at the front desk waved me back to Henry's office. The brightness of the station dimmed, and the floor tiles became yellow and faded. Halfway down the hallway, I wondered if it was too late to walk right back out.

No. You have to see this through.

If there was a chance this conversation could recover the ice wine, I needed to stand up for our legacy and get it done. Lifting my hand, I knocked on Henry's door.

"Come in," he barked.

The sun slanted through the blinds as he sifted through paperwork at his desk. He barely glanced up. After reaching for the jumbo-size Styrofoam cup of coffee by his right hand, he took a hearty gulp.

"I don't have any updates. So, I hope this is a social visit."

"It's not." I shut the door. It made a small bang, and I jumped. "Can I—"

"Sit," he barked.

The plastic chair in front of his desk felt about as comfortable as a witness stand. I adjusted my position a few times, trying to maintain some form of posture, which was impossible. It was like the chair was made to get people to confess to all sorts of sins.

Pushing aside his paperwork, Henry gave me his full attention. "What's up?"

I squeezed my hands tight. "I'm nervous about Dean."

146

"Nervous?" Henry's eyebrows shot up. "Why's that?"

I hesitated. Once I said the words, I wouldn't be able to take them back. Plus, they would make me the worst sister in the world. Still, if I didn't say anything, the thought would continue to haunt me.

"I think we need to consider the possibility"—I let out a breath—"that Dean had something to do with the theft of the ice wine."

This time, Henry did not react. Instead, he reached for his Styrofoam cup and took a long drink. The coffee smelled sharp and bitter from across the desk as he studied me over the rim.

"I don't have proof," I added quickly. "It's just that a few things stood out to me that I thought you should know." I updated him on Dean's connection to Jerry Andrews, the guy who worked at the internet café. Not to mention his strange comments at dinner. "Then, there's the question of whether or not someone tampered with the plane."

Henry rubbed his hand across his forehead. "Abby, the NTSB would have been all over that. Based on their report, I'm not concerned."

"There was a faulty wire," I said. "Pappy never would have let that happen. He checked his planes and checked them twice. He knew what he was doing."

"Accidents happen." Henry's tone was gentle. "People do make mistakes."

"Okay." I wasn't completely convinced, but his confidence made me feel better. "Then, speaking of mistakes, what about the stuff about Dean? It's been right there, staring us in the face."

Frowning, Henry picked up a small stone from his desk. It was a Petoskey stone, unique to northern Michigan, with faint circular marks that would become prominent if wet. He slid the stone back and forth between his fingers, like I used to do with the charms from my bracelet.

The longer Henry was silent, the more convinced I became that I was right and that the police department was already investigating my brother. My embarrassment was replaced by shame. Dean had already put my family through so much over the years. I couldn't believe he had done something like this too.

I was about to say something, maybe apologize on behalf of our family, when Henry finally spoke.

"What's your relationship with your brother these days? Close?"

I shook my head. "Not for quite some time."

Henry set down the stone. "You know, I never had brothers or sisters. I once thought that if I did, we would be the best of friends. In this line of work, though, I've seen families torn apart by everything from addiction to violence to simple misunderstandings."

Exactly.

Dean used to be my best friend. We used to share ice cream cones so we could try twice the flavors. Now, here I was at the police station, turning him in. If someone had told me back then that this would happen, I would have waited for the punchline.

"Things haven't been easy with him," I said. "Not for a very long time."

"I know." Henry went silent. Then he said, "I'm pretty confident Dean wasn't involved in the theft of the ice wine." He turned back to his paperwork.

Pretty confident?

I wrinkled my forehead.

Did that mean Henry was going to dismiss my concerns altogether?

The office suddenly seemed very small, as if the dry-erase board and the shades were closing in on me. Even the smell of the coffee seemed overpowering.

"Henry, I . . ." My stutter kicked in. The moment passed, thanks to a deep breath. "Dean hasn't been home in years. The moment he shows up, this happens?"

Henry drained his coffee and dropped the cup into the garbage. "I'll take your concerns into account." His tone was dismissive, just like it had been with the box.

Irritated, I said, "You know his past. He was an addict. He used to steal from everybody. Why wouldn't he do it again?"

Henry got to his feet and opened the shades. The bright sun made me wince. Turning from the window, he sighed. "You know, kid, there was a reason your brother got into trouble. It haunted him, that accident that happened in the fields."

The accident. I bit my lip, thinking back to another time I'd rather forget.

It had happened when Dean was fourteen, two years after I'd gotten out of the hospital. The vines had just been pruned, and Dean had been out with the field team responsible for pulling the canes from the canopies. It had been hard, aggressive work, but Dean had spent his time goofing off, like always. He'd messed around all afternoon, not listening to anyone. In the middle of telling a joke, he'd yanked hard on a cane without stopping to make sure the area behind him was clear. The cane had jerked back and hit a worker in the face. It had nearly taken out his eye, and even after emergency surgery, the worker could never see right again.

The incident had haunted my brother. He'd already been playing around with drinking and drugs at that point, but I'd often suspected that he'd fallen into harder stuff right around then, because he couldn't handle the guilt. Clearly, Henry thought so too.

"Dean's done some dumb things, but he's dealt with his issues. He's changed."

Rogers's words rang through my ears: *People don't change.*

I felt defeated. "You're not even going to look into it?"

"I said I'll follow up." His cool eyes settled on mine. "Although I want to be clear about one thing. The fact that I have to look into it at all is an insult to your brother and your family."

I glanced down at my hands. My nails were dirty, like always.

"Abigail, I'm not going to tell you how to feel." His tone softened. "My wife has taught me that's a dangerous move. But I will say this."

Henry paused until I looked at him.

"Family is forever. You can't escape where you come from and who you come from."

I'm not trying to escape my family! I'm trying to protect them.

I wanted to scream it at him. Instead, I stood. "I guess I shouldn't have said anything at all."

His gaze held a hint of disappointment. "Probably not."

Outside, I leaned against the rough grit of the brick building. I felt guilty and also incredibly angry. Yes, I looked like the worst sister in the world, but something was off.

Why was I the only one who could see it?

~

I walked down to the beach to clear my head.

It was a cloudy day. The boardwalk was cool under my feet and the breeze off Lake Michigan, chilly. The wind made so many caps on the water that it nearly looked like it was covered in ice. I watched as the waves turned from inky blue to frothy white and back again, changing with the wind.

The gulls cried overhead, and I took in a deep breath of the lake air. It felt so clean compared to the grit of Henry's office. In spite of the chilly afternoon, my skin felt hot with embarrassment. I could only imagine what Henry thought of me. I wondered if he'd take me seriously if he knew the whole story.

I had received Dean's apology letter in late August, three years ago. Jax had recently left for Chile. Every day, I'd taken five-mile runs to battle the heartache, and that morning, I had dared to stop at the mailbox in hopes of getting a letter from Chile. The mail typically came late in the day, and our administrative assistant picked it up on her way in, but I couldn't wait.

I had sifted through the stack, disappointed not to find a foreign postmark. Instead, there had been a collection of envelopes that looked exactly the same. There'd been seven total, in a neat stack, all post-marked from Chicago.

Dread had weighed me down as I'd walked back to the house. I'd barely spoken to my brother since the time he'd lied about needing money. I hadn't wanted it to be a feud; I'd just preferred to keep my distance. I hadn't wanted to open my heart back up to the heartache and worry.

Letting myself in through the kitchen, I'd set the mail on the station by the door and grabbed a water out of the fridge. Standing at the sink, I'd stared out at the vines and wondered why he was getting in touch and if the stunt would upset my parents. Knowing him, it was probably a fund drive, with Dean as the primary recipient.

Stop. He's your brother.

I'd sat down at the table and opened my letter.

Dear Abby,
I am writing to you today . . .

The structure had been a traditional form letter from an addiction recovery program. The first paragraph had jumped right into the ways Dean had wronged me. It was a laundry list of all the times he'd lied, manipulated, and betrayed my trust. It had gone on for so long I'd actually gone to the cupboard in the middle of reading it to get myself a protein bar. It had gone dry in my mouth as I'd gotten to the last part of the letter.

One of the greatest regrets I have in my life is a mistake you know nothing about. Abby, I stole your bracelet. I sold it and used the money to buy drugs. The memory makes me sick, because I will never forget the anguish in your eyes the night you realized it was missing. For this, I am deeply sorry and attempting to make amends. You'll find a check for $2000 attached to the back of this letter . . .

The protein bar all but forgotten, I'd gripped the edge of the table for so long that my muscles had gotten stiff. I hadn't moved until my mother had walked into the kitchen to make coffee. It was only then that I'd realized my damp clothes had gone clammy from the shock of my brother's confession.

"What is it?" My mother had pulled her silk robe tight and settled in next to me at the table.

I must have handed her the letter, but I don't remember doing it. The next thing I knew, she held me as I cried.

When Dean was deep into coke, he would come to get me late at night, desperate to talk. I'd follow him up to the roof of the main wine cellar, shivering in my pajamas, as the stars stretched in a glittering blanket over our heads and the vines lay like twisted labyrinths down below. Dean would perch on the edge of the roof, grinding his jaw or chomping on gum as he rattled off a litany of ways people had wronged him. He'd been out of high school for a year at that point, but his teachers and soccer coach were still at the top of the list.

I'd wanted to shake some sense into him, to tell him that the reason his teachers and coach had "turned on him" was because he'd practically failed out of school his senior year. To tell him to stop blaming everyone else for his problems and that he needed to get his life under control. In the beginning, though, I hadn't done that. I'd kept telling myself he had been there for me when I was sick, and he needed me to be there for him. But eventually, once he'd admitted to stealing from the till, the workers, and even the purse of one of our waitresses, I'd realized my silence wasn't doing him any favors. It had become my mission to help him get clean. I'd been convinced that, if I could be strong enough for the both of us, his attention would turn to something else, like getting into a good college or living up to his responsibilities at the vineyard.

There'd been so many times I thought I'd gotten through to him. He'd cry and promise to quit. He'd usually last a week, sometimes two. Then he would disappear again. He'd come home days later, dirty and haunted, claiming he'd gone on a fishing or camping trip. The last time he'd disappeared, he'd moved to Chicago with one of his deadbeat friends. So, I'd made myself available by phone, email, and the occasional weekend visit with my mother. I'd never given up on him, even when he'd cut me out of his life.

Until the letter had arrived.

The purpose of the letter had been to make amends. For me, it had had the opposite effect. It had showed me everything I had always believed about my relationship with him had been wrong.

That bracelet had meant so much to me during the worst time of my life. Dean had *known* what it meant to me, because I'd told him, numerous times. Yet, out of every piece of jewelry I owned, including a diamond tennis bracelet my grandparents had bought me, he'd robbed me of the one thing that was worth more than money.

It had been calculated and cruel. All the apologies in the world wouldn't change that, and they couldn't bring it back.

Now, it just seemed so ridiculous to me that my family, and even the police chief, thought Dean was this changed man. I wasn't under any illusions. When my brother was using, he didn't care who he hurt as long as he got what he needed.

Take back what's yours while you still can.

Yes, I felt guilty for trying to turn him in. Unfortunately, I had cause. As much as I wanted to let go of the past, it would have been downright criminal to ignore history.

Chapter Eighteen

The second I returned from the police station, my mother called me to her office. My hands immediately went damp with nerves. If Henry had called my parents to tell them about my report, I would have a hard time explaining myself.

The mosquitoes were out early, and I swatted them away as I walked to the offices. The chill of the evening made the smell of cement from the floor strong. Light shone down from the bird's nest, and I looked up at Pappy's office. For a split second, I imagined he'd recovered and my family planned to surprise me with the news.

Instead, I saw that Phillip was bent over a calculator and a stack of paperwork, putting together payroll. The sight shook me. Watching my grandfather do payroll was something I'd loved ever since I was a little girl. His expression was judicious as he looked over the numbers, eating peppermint candy and inputting information into this enormous calculator with a clattering receipt roll. I couldn't believe it was happening without him.

My mother greeted me with a kiss. "How are you?" She shut the door to her office and sat behind the desk. Her face was lined with concern. "Your father finally told us about the ice wine."

I sank into the chair across from her desk. "He did?"

"Yes." She pumped some hand lotion from the bottle on her desk, and the familiar scent of rose wafted toward me. "I'm so sorry you've had to deal with that on your own."

"He told Phillip too?" I asked.

"Yes. Everyone but Oma." Lowering her voice, she said, "Your father and I told Phillip she has a heart condition and the news would kill her."

"Oma has a heart condition?" I squawked.

"No!" My mother laughed. "She'll outlive every single one of us. However, we had to tell Phillip something to keep him from spilling the beans."

It was only a little white lie. Still, I wondered how many of those my parents had told over the years to keep the peace. Did they know about Oma's past?

My mother rummaged through the papers on her desk. "We also received another one of these." She held up a turquoise piece of paper. "Lovely, yes?"

TIME IS RUNNING OUT.

My stutter was instant. "Did . . . did you tell Henry?"

"Honey." She set down the paper and came out from behind the desk. "I thought the sound system was acting up during the speeches. You really did stutter, didn't you? How long has this been going on?"

Clumsily, I explained that the night of the speeches had started it all. "I was so nervous. It never occurred to me that, on some level, I might be afraid it would return, because I haven't stuttered in . . . well, it was a lifetime ago." I thought of my time in the hospital. Technically, that had been a lifetime ago too. "I guess time isn't the magic elixir we think it is."

"Time can be a tricky thing." My mother's pretty eyes were troubled. "You should go see a speech therapist before this becomes a real problem. Do you need me to call the office?"

I tried to say I wasn't a child, that I could handle it, but the words wouldn't come. Embarrassed, I took in a few deep breaths.

"No." My throat was tight. "I can."

Her perfectly made-up eyes studied me with concern. "Let me know if you need help."

I reached for the turquoise paper and held it up, determined to move the focus off of me. The type of paper was so strange. It wasn't from a notebook or a card, but it seemed to be part of something, like the bottom of a gift bag. "Did you . . . did you talk to Henry about this?"

"I texted him a picture." She examined the card stock. "He's going to send someone for it tomorrow. I just wish I knew what they were all about."

Fighting through my stutter, I said, "Mom, is there anything about Oma that might . . . I don't know. That you guys never told us?"

"Tons, probably." She squinted at me. "Anything specific you're wondering about?"

"Yeah." The words came easier now. "Things about her past. Her history."

My mother pulled a container of orange Tic Tacs out of her desk and shook one into her hand. "Is this because of Pappy? You know, I never knew much about my grandparents before they died, and I really regretted that. I only know the same tired stories you do about yours." She looked at me for a long moment. "Abby, come to the hospital. I'm sure Oma would be happy to tell you—"

"Hey, Mom." Phillip rapped on the door, his figure tired and lanky in the late afternoon. "Payroll's done. How do I do the checks?"

My mother got to her feet. "Did you try the printer?"

He rolled his eyes. "Every time I even thought about plugging it in, eighties music started to play."

My mother laughed, and the two headed over to the printing bay.

I considered my mother's reaction to my question. It seemed genuine. The odds were good my parents didn't know about my grandmother's other life, which was not the news I was looking for.

My eyes fell on the latest turquoise note.

TIME IS RUNNING OUT.

Something about the note was so sinister. Maybe the fact that I believed it.

~

My mother, Phillip, and I stayed late working. When we were ready to wrap up, they tried to convince me to join them at the main house for dinner. Phillip's wife had picked up pizzas, and my mother promised to open one of my favorite table reds.

I knew she wanted to talk more about the stuttering and try to convince me to come to the hospital, two topics I didn't want to deal with. She also mentioned Dean was on-site. I didn't know if could look him in the eye after my visit to the police station, so I decided it would be best to hide out in my cottage.

"I'm just going to head home," I decided as we stepped outside.

"Honey." She came to a halt in the gravel, her rose lotion perfuming the night air. "You have to eat."

"I know. I just . . ." My words caught again.

"You need rest." She gave a brisk nod. "However, I am going to get you the number for the speech therapist. There's no reason to let this get the best of you."

Phillip shoved his hands in his pockets and gave me a sympathetic look. "It's got to be so frustrating. You have to struggle to call me names."

I laughed. "It makes me think before I speak. Probably something I need to do anyway."

"Kate's always telling me the same thing," Phillip said. "Do you know how many trips to the dog house I could have saved myself over the years? I'm surprised she hasn't left me."

"Oh, come on," I scolded him. "She thinks you're the best thing since synthetic corks."

Phillip came to a halt in the middle of the driveway. "Take it back."

My mother and I burst out laughing.

"Keep an open mind, Phillip." She patted him on the shoulder. "One day, we might have to move to synthetics."

He rolled his eyes skyward. "God help us all."

The moon was up and hung low over the vines. The image was hauntingly beautiful. I was tempted to forget everything and join them for dinner, after all. It had been a while since I'd spent time with Phillip. Still, it felt wrong to take a seat at the family table mere hours after I'd tried to turn a member of my family over to the police.

Even in Dean's darkest hours, my parents had never given up on him. They'd sent him money, love, and support, no matter how many times he'd gone to court or put himself in the hospital. My mother would be heartbroken if she knew I still thought the worst of him.

"Have a good night," I called as they veered off to the main house.

The moment they were out of sight, Dean's warning about walking alone rang through my ears. Maybe it was because I was tired or because I felt guilty, but every sound suddenly seemed sinister. My phone buzzed in my pocket, and I almost ran into a trellis.

It was a text from Dean.

Come to the tasting room. We need to talk.

I stood stock-still in the moonlight.

Henry wouldn't have told Dean I reported him, would he? That had to be illegal. The police station was so small, though. Anyone could have seen me go there.

You're being paranoid.

I looked up at the moon. The night before, Dean had said he was going to study the inventory logs. Maybe it was about that.

I texted him back:

What's up? I'm headed home.

The comment bubble popped up longer than I liked. Finally, a message pinged through.

I can talk to you or Henry. Who's it going to be?

I stared down at my phone for a full minute, swatting away moths and mosquitoes. Did he mention Henry because he knew what I'd done?

Either way, it would be impossible to brush him off. He'd just break into my house if he really wanted to see me. Dread settling in the pit of my stomach, I agreed to meet.

~

The tasting room was dark, and the lights under the bar gave the room an eerie glow. I took a few tentative steps inside, half-ready to bolt.

"Dean?" I called.

Silence.

A prickle of fear went up my back.

My brother wouldn't . . . hurt me, would he? In high school, he'd attacked a few kids while he was high. That trend had probably continued out in the real world. Maybe it had been incredibly stupid to come to the tasting room alone.

I had just started to creep back toward the door when a voice next to my ear whispered, "Boo."

A floating face hovered at my shoulder, lit by a bright light.

I jumped straight up to the ceiling. Then, shouting and thrashing, I threw out my arms and struck in every possible direction until I made contact with a solid mass of flesh.

"Hey," Dean cried, laughing. "Stop hitting me."

His laughter stopped me short. Pulling back, I blinked and caught my breath. My brother flicked on the lights and retrieved his cell phone, which I'd knocked across the floor.

He pushed back a lock of hair and rubbed his arms. "Geez. You're an animal."

"You can't lurk in the dark, scaring people." I was almost dizzy with relief to see the face that had haunted me all day. "You're lucky I don't have a can of mace or something."

Dean gave me a serious look. "You probably need one."

I studied my brother. He wore the same skinny jeans he had on that first night and an oversize black hoodie. He hadn't shaved in a few days, and a smattering of dark stubble made him look rough around the edges.

"What did you need?" I asked. "I was about to call it a night."

"Follow me." Dean headed toward the office.

Even though I was relieved to see him and not some would-be assailant, I was not in a rush to trap myself in an office without an escape route. If Dean had stolen the ice wine, I doubted he had done it alone. He probably wouldn't do anything to hurt me, but I couldn't say the same about anyone else.

"Let me just text Mom." I fumbled for my phone. "I told her I might come for dinner."

Dean leaned against the office doorjamb and stared me down. "Are you scared of me?"

I stuttered out a denial.

"Sure, text Mom." His voice was bitter. "Tell her you're with your ex–drug addict of a brother, and you're afraid you might not make it out alive. Once you're done with that, we need to have a little chat."

He stalked into the office.

I let out a shaky breath.

The truth behind his words made me feel like a monster. He *was* my brother. It had been years since he'd given me a real reason not to trust him. Yet, I couldn't let go of the feeling that something was off.

Following him into the office, my eye went straight to the conference table. Inventory logs were spread out, along with various printouts. Dean didn't look up when I walked in. He just studied a stack of paper with intent concentration.

"I'm not scared of you." My voice was quiet. "That's not what this is about."

"Doesn't matter." He held up an inventory log. "What does matter is the fact that we have a serious problem. In the past year, the vineyard has lost roughly fifty cases of wine. That's six hundred bottles."

The sarcastic part of me wanted to say, "Thank you so much for doing the math." I was too shocked at the news, though. How could six hundred bottles be missing?

"That's impossible. Someone would have caught that." I reached for the logs and studied the pages. They were a handwritten hodgepodge. "Show me where you think you're seeing this."

Dean tried to explain, but it was impossible to see. So many different people had logged cases in and out. He was also talking too fast, like he was trying to sell me something.

I held up my hand. "If you want me to take this seriously, you're going to have to slow down and explain this to me like a child, because I don't see what you're saying at all."

He gave a rude snort. "Exactly. No one is meant to see the mistakes. I found them because I compared the logs to our production reports and tax records. This?" He slapped his hand against one of our record books. "It's a mirage."

Dean took it slow, explaining in detail the numbers with the aid of the few computerized reports, our tax records, and the inventory logs. Suddenly, I started to see what he was saying. There were mistakes that were small but deliberate, like an inaccurate starting point or the number one written to look like a seven.

"It's almost scary how clever this is."

Dean's dark eyes held mine. "Interesting choice of words." For a second, I got the impression he suspected me.

My shoulders tensed. "What's with the tone?"

"We talked about this last night." He scratched the stubble on his face. "This type of incompetence is unacceptable. How is it possible no one looked into this when Billy said it was a problem?"

"Oma told him not—"

Dean scoffed. "Only because she and Pappy can't stand for people to dig into their stuff." He held up the production reports. "Especially not a staff member they keep around out of pity."

"Stop. Rogers is one of our best—"

"I know you like him, Abby." Dean rubbed his nose, which I suddenly noticed was red. "Dad's right, though. He's old as shit."

"That's not what Dad said," I snapped.

It hit me that Dean might be jealous of the relationship I shared with Rogers. Or perhaps Rogers had been a little too obvious in his disapproval toward Dean.

Either way, the situation with the inventory was frightening. It was one thing to have an event, like a break-in. It was another to know that someone had siphoned out six hundred bottles, right under our noses.

"Anyone could have messed with the logs at any point." I tried to make rhyme or reason out of the jumble of numbers. "So, who did it?"

Dean shrugged. "You tell me."

"I'll call Henry," I said, getting to my feet.

"Hold up." My brother grabbed a water from the minifridge and took a long swig. "What about the money?"

I paused. "Money?"

"I heard we were having money issues."

The question caught me off guard.

"Why are you worried about the vineyard's financial situation?"

"It's our legacy. One would think you would care."

I gripped the wooden edges of the table. The money issue, if one even existed, was not something I was going to discuss with Dean.

"There's no issue. Not as far as I know."

Dean's face went dark. "Bullshit. I've heard people talking about it. Do you see how much is missing here?" He slapped the inventory logs. "Do you want that happening to our finances too?"

"The *vineyard's* finances."

I paced the length of the office. Walking past the window, I remembered how upset my father had been the last time we'd been here.

"Dad is not worried about the rumors," I said, turning to Dean. "Businesses lose money. For us, it sometimes comes from the restaurant and other times from production. Like when we had to bring in grapes because our demand was greater than our yield. If it ends up being excessive this year, it's because there was a loss. It doesn't have to mean someone is stealing."

My words sounded hollow, even to me. If someone really was stealing inventory, the odds were good they would find a way to steal money too.

Dean rubbed his nose. I must've cringed, because he stared me down. "I'm clean, Abby. I have been for a long time."

"Okay," I said, like I believed him.

He got to his feet. "I'm going to get permission from Dad to review our company bank accounts. Bills, deposits, withdrawals, all of it."

My spine stiffened. "I don't feel comfortable with that."

There was no need for Dean to have access to the vineyard's bank accounts. The fact that he'd gotten his hands on our tax records was invasive enough, but this was another thing entirely.

He shoved his hands into his sweatshirt. "Why? What are you trying to hide?"

"What?" My cheeks went hot. "Nothing. I—"

Dean peered at me. "Then why are you working so hard to act like nothing is wrong?"

I pressed my hands against the table. "Because thanks to you, I'm something of an expert at that."

There'd been so many times when we were in high school that I'd spent a ridiculous amount of time pretending things were all right. I'd acted like I thought it was funny that Dean passed out in class, picked fights after school, and hung out with the dangerous kids. That I wasn't terrified the time he broke his leg jumping off a roof, crashed my grandfather's sedan, or tried to get into a fistfight with a random guy in the tasting room.

"I'm good at pretending, but I'm not hiding a thing," I told him. "I just don't want you looking at our bank accounts. If Oma and Pappy knew, they would have a fit. Not to mention Phillip, because he's our accountant. Either way, I really *don't* know if there is a problem. I would be the first to tell Henry if I did."

"Yeah." He scoffed. "I have no doubt about that."

Our eyes met.

He knew I'd tried to turn him in. I had no idea how, but he did.

Well, whatever. I'd had good reason. I didn't trust Dean, and I probably never would.

Face flushed, I headed for the door. I half expected him to try and stop me. To my surprise, he didn't.

Maybe because he knew I was determined to stop him.

Chapter Nineteen

Since my mother didn't seem to know anything about my grandmother's past, I decided to get in touch with the government offices in Germany.

Monday morning, I set my clock for an hour earlier than usual and was up before the sun. Toasted bread and a cup of orange juice at hand, I settled in at the kitchen table with my cell phone. It felt like ages until I finally tracked down the country code and placed my first call.

The vineyard was at the top of my list. The phone rang three times, and just as I started to imagine the business was closed for the day, a woman picked up.

"Weingut Sonnenschein." For whatever reason, I imagined the woman with precise blonde hair and a white collared shirt.

"Hi." Cautiously, I said, "Do you speak English?"

"Indeed." Her response was quick and efficient. "How can I help?"

I explained I was doing research on the history of the vineyard. "What do you know about the original family? Back when you were Weingut Feierabend?" She went silent, and I rubbed my thumb over a bubble in the blue paint of the breakfast table. "I'm especially interested in the young girl who lost her parents in the fire."

"This happened many years ago." The woman made a clucking noise. "Two families owned the vineyard during that time period. Neither has been involved with the vineyard for many years."

"You guys don't keep a history or anything?" I asked, looking out my kitchen window at the expanse of vines. The history of Harrington Wines was a part of our tour. It surprised me that they would not have something similar.

"The history of that particular story does not serve our brand or purpose." Her voice was dismissive. "We barely sell to the public. We mainly supply grapes to the fruit-juice factories. Is there anything additional?"

It was clear she was ready to move on.

"No," I said. "Thank you—have a good day."

That was a blow. I'd expected the vineyard to be a fountain of knowledge. Instead, it was a fountain of . . . grape juice.

The next call was a little more difficult. I'd researched online how to obtain the records for births, marriages, and deaths. Various websites suggested I reach out to the German vital records office in the town where my grandmother had been born. The man answered on the third ring. He spoke English with a formal accent.

"Hi." I pulled up the photo of my grandmother as a little girl and traced my finger over it. "I'm doing some . . . genealogy research and seem to be stumped. Can you help?"

"My wife is a big believer." The man sounded like he was rolling his eyes. "She unearthed a connection to Frederick the Great. I think claiming royal lineage is simply an excuse to get out of the dishes, no?"

I laughed, in spite of my nerves. "Sounds like she's queen material."

"That's what she says. How can I help?"

"I'm trying to track down information on Greta Scholz. Her name seems to have changed . . . I believe she was adopted around age ten."

"Do you have email?" the man asked. "I will send you the proper forms. If the data may be released, it could take a bit of time to receive the information."

"Really?" I squawked. "It's kind of an emergency."

"Then I suggest you contact the embassy."

"No, it's . . ." I rubbed my palm against the table. "It's not exactly an emergency, per se—it's just . . . I kind of need to know now."

The man laughed. "You may be related to my wife, and therefore Frederick." He hesitated, and I held my breath. "Let me see what I can do."

While I waited, I sifted through the pictures at Weingut Feierabend. It was easy to imagine my grandmother as a child, skipping up the cobblestone paths.

The phone clicked, and for a second, I was afraid the clerk had hung up on me.

"Hello?" I gave the phone a nervous squeeze.

"Yes." The man's friendly voice came back over the line. Relieved, I grabbed a pen. "This should do. It's quite interesting. Greta Scholz, born May 28, 1940, married Olaf Fischer, born in September 1928, on December 7, 1956. F-I-S-C-H-E-R. He died December 2003."

I almost dropped the phone. My grandmother was married to someone else? And December 7 . . . that was the date on the wedding ring in the safety-deposit box.

A sick feeling filled my stomach. "When did they divorce?"

"This is why it's interesting." He sounded entertained, like the information made a good soap opera. "No divorce. However, two years after the marriage, Greta Fischer was listed as a missing person. That makes for some fun theories, eh? How are you related to her?"

My blood went cold.

"I'm . . ." I blinked, staring at her picture in disbelief. My grandmother was a missing person?

"No, I . . ." My voice caught. "I don't know her at all."

~

The news sent me straight to Kelcee's office in Towboat. It was before the breakfast crunch, so she had time to brew us cups of chamomile tea and settle in behind her desk. Once I'd finished explaining everything, her blue eyes were huge.

"This is wild," she breathed. "It sounds like she ran away. With your *grandfather*."

"I know. It's . . ." I took a sip of my tea, unable to form a clear thought. "I mean . . . if she was still married when my grandparents got married, is their marriage even legal? Olaf is dead now, but she wasn't divorced."

Kelcee's blue eyes looked troubled. "Do you think she told your grandfather? Got it resolved?"

I shook my head. "I doubt it, or the divorce would have been on the record, right?"

"Probably." Kelcee stacked some papers on her desk, while chewing on her lip. "You know, I'm more worried about the fact that she's listed as missing. You said her childhood name was Scholz. He was Fischer. What name did she use to get into the country? Not Fischer, or she would not be listed as missing."

My stomach went sour. I hadn't even thought about that.

"Bauer. That's the maiden name she always told us, and it's the name listed on her passport too."

I knew that for a fact because I'd been obsessed with my grandmother's passport when I was younger. It had seemed so worldly and exciting, with its colorful cover and official-looking stamp.

Kelcee looked pained. "So Bauer is a fake name."

"No." I shook my head. "That's not . . ." I didn't finish the thought, but my mind was racing.

It *was* possible. Very much so.

The Cold War had been in full effect during that time. False documentation had to have been a booming business. Kelcee was right—the only way my grandmother could have been listed as a missing person was because she'd left the country as Greta Bauer.

"She's not legal." The words were so shocking they came out in a whisper. Immediately, the threatening turquoise papers came to mind. "It's been years. She couldn't get into trouble for that now, could she?"

"No clue." Kelcee gave me a baffled look. "You should talk to a lawyer. You also need to consider . . ." She got that expression on her face I knew all too well. The one that meant she'd thought of something I would not like.

"What?" I asked, setting down my tea.

"If Pappy died, your grandmother would most likely inherit the vineyard. So—"

"It would get seized?" I cried.

Quickly, Kelcee looked it up online. "Okay, I don't think so. I think you're allowed to own property here even if you're not a legal citizen. I'm just skimming this, though, and it's the internet, so take that for what it's worth. I was going to say, if something happens to your grandfather, the will is written to a person who doesn't really exist."

I stared at her in disbelief. Losing Pappy was one thing. Could we lose the vineyard too?

"Talk to a lawyer," Kelcee repeated.

It was impossible to speak. I could barely think. I just sat there breathing in the sweet scent of the chamomile tea, trying to understand how my grandmother could have done something like this.

Kelcee put her hand on mine. "Tell me what you're thinking."

"I'm scared, and I'm furious." The words caught in my throat. "Oma has preached and preached about the importance of family. *Family first, family first.* Turns out it's all bullshit."

"I know your grandmother, Abby. Her family does come first."

"Not in this case."

She sighed. "I understand the need to process this. Once you do, protect your family. Talk to a lawyer, and get it figured out."

"I can't," I whispered. "If I start bringing people into this, the secret will get out."

"Based on the notes you guys are getting, the secret might already be out. This isn't the type of thing you want to mess around with. Handle it."

Handle it. Easier said than done.

~

I sat in the parking lot for a full five minutes before deciding what to do next. There was still a chance my mind was playing tricks on me. It had been years since I'd actually *seen* my grandmother's passport—I needed to examine it to be sure.

Hopefully, you're wrong about the fake name. You're tired, emotional . . . you probably got it wrong and there's some logical explanation for the fact that she ever used the name Bauer.

The thought made it possible to breathe properly for the first time that morning.

On the way back to the peninsula, I focused on the dense green trees along the side of the road, the pale-blue sky, and the white clouds as they wisped along the horizon. It was such a normal, natural sight that I felt hopeful, like this could still be a crisis of my own making.

The second I made it back to the vineyard, I headed for the main house like it was the most natural thing in the world. I hoped I wouldn't bump into anybody, which wasn't likely. The house was always bustling with activity.

Phillip's wife was making omelets in the kitchen off the main entry-way, filling the house with the scent of roasted onions, sausage, and bell peppers. Her daughter, Ava, danced along the smooth wooden floors next to the enormous staircase, trailing a collection of winter scarves behind her. The sight of her by the steps reminded me of all the times

Pappy had let us slide down the banister, timing us with his old stopwatch. He'd always given the winner a shiny silver dollar.

Dean had won almost every time.

"Morning." I poked my head into the kitchen.

Kate turned from the griddle, her face shiny from the heat. "Abby! Do you want some breakfast?"

"No, thanks. I'm good."

Absently, I flipped the pages of the family calendar hanging on the fridge. My mother put it together every year. This month had a picture of Pappy on the tractor with Ava in his lap, smiling like he didn't have a care in the world.

"I have to grab some paperwork." The lie made me nervous, and I tapped my fingers against the counter. "Anyone here?"

"Your mom left for the hospital, Phillip's taking a shower, and I haven't seen or heard from Dean." She gestured at the stove. "There's plenty to eat. I've got bread in the oven."

"Thanks, but really, I'm fine. I ate a few hours ago."

"Farmers." Smiling, she waved her spatula at me. "Always up with the sun."

Out in the hallway, I ruffled Ava's hair and took the stairs two at a time. Family photos hung on the wall of the long hallway leading to the bedrooms, their scenes as familiar as the aroma of my favorite wine.

I brushed my fingers across a picture of my grandparents. It had been taken at Christmas when my father was just a baby, in the main room with the atrium windows that overlooked the fields. My grandparents sat on the couch, my father in my grandmother's lap. Colorful Christmas lights bounced off her hair as snow fluttered outside. The picture was so perfect that my suspicions about my grandmother felt completely ridiculous.

Letting out a breath, I paused and listened. Phillip's electric razor buzzed in the distance. The door on the guest bedroom was shut. I crept down the hall and pushed open the door to my grandparents' room.

It was dark inside. The cream-colored brocade curtains were drawn, and the air felt stale since the room had been closed for so many days. The faded scent of my grandmother's Chanel No. 5 melded with the cologne my grandfather had worn at the party. The bottle of cologne still sat on the dresser, an emerald-green glass that probably dated back to the sixties.

The bed was made with the faded country quilt my grandmother loved so much. On her bedside table sat a bowl of pastel mints, a half-finished pastoral needlepoint, and a pair of reading glasses. My grandfather's side held an empty water glass and a stack of *Farmers' Almanacs*. No alarm clock—they both woke with the sun every morning. Instead, an old clock ticked away from the top of their dresser.

I crept toward their rolltop desk in the corner and lifted the lid. There were old pens, a calculator, and even a pencil sharpener. I sifted through a small stack of paperwork inside. It was relatively current, with details about last year's orders and crops. Setting it back down, I opened the bottom drawer and found more *Farmers' Almanacs*. The other drawers were full of photo albums. I set one on top of the bed in case someone walked into the room.

"I was feeling nostalgic," I'd say.

The fact that I was in the room alone at all felt wrong. Quickly, I opened the closet door and considered the boxes on the top shelf. It would take a step stool to get them down. Since I didn't know where Dean was, I decided to make that the last resort.

Instead, I headed for my grandmother's jewelry box. Rubies were her favorite, and her collection was extensive. I wondered whether it was safe to leave them unlocked and unguarded. It was something I'd bring up with my father. I pulled out the bottom drawer of the jewelry box and drew in a breath.

There was a collection of holiday brooches, like a pumpkin for Halloween and a wreath for Christmas, as well as a macaroni necklace one of us had made for her years ago. Underneath it all rested her driver's license, which she never used, and her old passport. Hands shaking, I opened it.

The photograph of my grandmother was striking. Her dark hair was poofed out in the style that had been so popular in the fifties, and she was much thinner than I had ever seen her. It hit me that she was just a young girl, with thick eyebrows and a haunted expression.

The lie was right there in black and white: Greta Lina Bauer.

Even though I had hoped for something different, I was not surprised. The thing that did surprise me was the thought of the girl in the photograph wearing a wedding ring engraved with a Nazi symbol. It didn't make sense. Maybe it had had something to do with why she'd run.

There was a sound in the hallway, and quickly I dumped the passport back into the box and leapt onto the bed with the photo album, waiting for someone to burst in. Finally, I got up and stole a look outside. The hallway was empty.

The family photos seemed to mock me as I walked by. They looked so perfect. Apparently, they did not tell the real story.

I need to research this Olaf guy.

My grandmother's first husband. Her real husband.

The words were startling in their implication.

You don't need to research anyone. You need to talk to your grandmother.

How, though? How could I possibly say, "Hey, Grandma, I know your husband might die, but out of curiosity, does he really even count as your husband since you were already married when you married him?"

The whole thing was such a mess.

My grandfather seemed to give me a warning look from inside the photos, as if to tell me to leave it alone.

That was understandable. The man had loved her for sixty years. He hardly needed to wake up from a coma to be hit with this news. Still, there was a chance he had known the entire time and had helped the woman he loved escape a bad situation.

Whatever the reason, it was quite the secret.

One I didn't like carrying on my own.

~

Sanitizing the floor and the tanks in the wine production room was always a painful task. Today, though, it was just what I needed. It was something physical to get my nervous energy out, and it would give me time to think.

I suited up in safety gear and pulled the chemicals out of storage. I was wheeling them across the gravel driveway in a large pushcart when Rogers flagged me down. He looked dapper in a pair of navy linen pants, a matching sport coat, and a white shirt.

He's old as shit.

Dean's rude comment rushed through my mind. Yes, Rogers was in his late sixties, but that hardly counted as old. Besides, he had earned his level of responsibility at the vineyard, unlike Dean, who expected to waltz in and run the place.

"Morning." I adjusted the goggles hanging around my neck. "You look nice."

"Ah." Rogers adjusted his sport coat. "I rather can't believe I'm saying this. Dean sent me on an errand that proved fruitful."

"Dean sent you on an *errand?*"

"A sales call." Rogers adjusted his cuffs. "I placed our red table wine in The Forest."

"Rogers, that's great!"

The vineyard had been trying to get an order from The Forest for months. It was a new, high-end fusion restaurant, open exclusively for the tourist season. The restaurant had originally planned to carry wines from Italy and California exclusively, so the fact that Rogers had gotten us in was a big deal.

"Ross has been trying for months," I said, speaking of our sales guy. "How did you do it?"

"I told them that tourists want to experience the full flavor of Michigan." Rogers sniffed. "That means having the option to order a local product. Then I reminded them that we recommend dining options to over a hundred tourists every week, so it might serve them to be on that list."

"Good for you!" I gave him a high five. "That's such good news."

There had been so many negatives lately that it was nice to be reminded of our purpose. The grapes, the wine, and the local flavor. Our sales guy wouldn't care that Rogers was the one who had finally gotten our wine in, as long as we had a presence.

"I can't believe I'm saying this either, but did you share the good news with Dean yet?" I asked.

Rogers's face switched to disapproval. "I'll leave that delightful task to you. Speaking of, what's the latest with the inventory issue? Wasn't he going to look into it?"

I updated him, and Rogers looked startled. "Abby, I can assure you, I—"

"It's not your fault," I said. "You reported it to Oma. That was the best you could do. Given the fact that our records are a complete mess, there is no way you could have known."

Rogers glanced at the tasting room and sighed. "Still. I'm sorry you have to deal with all of this. Our biggest problem a month ago was getting everyone to agree on the design of the new labels."

I brushed a grasshopper off the handle of the cart. "The good old days."

The thing I didn't want to tell Rogers was that, in the light of day, I wondered how much of the big discovery about the missing inventory was true. What if Dean had made it all up? Back when he was a drug addict, he'd been so good at manipulating situations to work in his favor. He could have faked the mistakes in the logs to make himself look good. It wouldn't have been that hard.

The inventory logs were handwritten. Dean could have planted certain details to build his case. He'd look like a hero, my family would hand him the keys to the kingdom, and he would be free to rob us blind.

Of course, I didn't dare share that theory with Rogers. He already had a terrible opinion of Dean. I didn't need to fan the flames, especially since there was still a chance my brother really had found a mistake while we had missed it.

I stared out at the fields. "This whole thing is a mess. Which is exactly why I'm going to hole myself up in the production room and clean with toxic chemicals until I can't think."

Rogers patted me on the back. "That's the type of commitment we like to see around here."

I pushed the cart across the gravel. It was not an easy task. Still, compared to everything else going on, it was a walk in the park.

Chapter Twenty

There was a knock at the front door of my cottage. Dean, no doubt. It seemed the more I tried to get away from him, the more determined he was to get in my space.

I stomped to the front door, wondering why I had never installed a peephole or a side window that could just let me know who was out there so I could go ahead and pretend to not be home.

"Who is it?" I used my grumpiest voice.

There was a silence. Then a small thump, like whoever was standing there had leaned into the door. "It's me."

My entire body flashed hot and cold. *Jax.* The sound of his voice was as familiar as the taste of my favorite wine.

Quickly, I undid the locks and threw open the door. The sun came out from behind a cloud and cast a blinding white light over his silhouette. For a second, I thought I'd died or something, and this was heaven.

Jax's high forehead and strong nose were browned from the sun, the deep lines in his forehead framed by shaggy black hair. His shoulders were as wide as I remembered and seemed to promise pure survival if we were stranded in the woods, on an island, or even in a restaurant with slow service. His gaze held mine as we stood in silence. Then a stupid grin stretched across my face.

"What are you doing here?" I asked.

"You mean, what am I doing there when you're here?" he asked.

We stared at each other.

Then he charged forward, and his lips crashed into mine.

∼

His familiar scent permeated my bedroom when I walked in with two mugs of steaming hot coffee. This was our ritual, since Jax drank coffee like water. He pulled himself up from the sheets and looped one strong arm over my pillow.

Settled into the crook, I breathed in his sweat and reveled in the feeling of his arm against my skin. He passed me my mug, and we both took long drinks, gazing at each other over the rims.

"I've been here so often in my mind." He traced his thumb over my cheekbone. "The beauty in Chile is indescribable. The mountains hover in the background of the fields with colors like a Monet. It's still never compared to you."

It had been three years, so I had forgotten how he spouted poetry instead of words. It was as effective as ever.

"Pretend I'm saying the exact same thing back to you," I said, giving a lazy stretch, "but the color of the horizon here is a Manet."

He laughed, the sound as raw and rugged as his arms. I settled into his arms and sighed. It was so strange to think that a few days ago, I'd been kissing Braden, and now I was here.

The disappointment on Braden's face before he'd walked out the door flashed through my mind. What would he think if he saw me now?

Like that even mattered. I barely knew him, and Jax was the love of my life. It still felt like a dream to have him back.

"So, what happened?" I asked, tracing my finger across his jawline. "I thought you were gone for good."

"My grandmother's dying." When I gasped, he added, "It's okay. She's ninety-five. The decline was quick. It's for the best."

"You should be with her," I scolded. "Not here with me."

It was kind of a hypocritical thing to say, considering my grandfather was in a hospital less than an hour away, and I still hadn't seen him. I could only imagine what Jax would say about that. He'd never bought into the idea of fear. He believed life was mind over matter, a quality I'd always admired.

"I know," he said. "I'm headed back tomorrow."

Disappointment cut through me. "Tomorrow?"

His family lived in a suburb of Toronto, in Canada. It was at least a seven-hour drive.

"You'll see me again." Jax laced his fingers with mine. "I'm not leaving without you this time."

My heart started to pound.

"Jax, I can't—"

"You can." The look he gave me was so intense I shivered. "I have enough saved up to buy our own vineyard in Chile. It will be small, to start, but it's a piece of property with room to expand. The culture is incredible, the wine's even better, and it would be ours. Don't say you haven't thought about it."

I had thought about it. So many times, before he'd left and after. I'd spent too much time thinking what a fool I'd been to let him go, but that didn't change the fact that I was rooted here, like one of the vines.

"You know I can't do that." My voice sounded weak. "My family's here."

"Your family's in here," he said, putting my hand on his chest. "That's what I want it to be between us. Forever."

I held my breath. Was this leading to a proposal?

"What do you mean by that?" I said carefully.

He set my coffee cup on the table. Rolling on top of me, Jax cradled my face in his hands. "You know what I mean."

Before he'd left, Jax and I had talked in detail about getting married. We'd planned to do it here at the vineyard. His father would officiate, and Ava would serve as the flower girl. The main cake would be three tiers of buttercream and the groom's cake, vegan. He wanted matching tattoos on our fingers instead of rings.

"Nope," I'd always said. "Real rings are a must. Including an engagement ring."

The idea of a ring had meant so much to me. Even though we'd talked about the future, I'd wanted something concrete. Now, a ring didn't seem to matter so much. After all, we'd been apart for three years, and now that we were back together, it felt like no time had passed at all.

Did a proposal really matter?

"Chile is amazing," Jax said, his eyes holding mine. "I brought an entire carload of wine for you, so you'll know what life will be like. You'll be able to taste it."

Our lips melded, and images of mountains played against the backdrop of my mind. We'd been here before. This time, though, it felt different.

I'm not leaving without you, he'd said.

The intensity of that statement startled me, along with my feelings about it.

I don't want you to leave without me.

I never wanted to be apart from him again.

~

The next morning, I woke to an empty bed.

At first, I panicked, worried Jax had left without saying goodbye. Ridiculous, perhaps, considering talk about the future had continued through the night. Still, Jax had always been elusive.

There'd been times he would disappear for days without warning. I'd find a note or get a voice mail message with details of this plan or that to rough it in the woods, join his buddies on a hiking trip, or spend time fishing out on Lake Michigan. He never invited me, mainly because I wasn't cut out for extremes. There'd been this one girl, though, Lydia, who'd hung out with his group of friends like a groupie. She was an adrenaline junkie, like him, and I'd been convinced she had a thing for Jax.

"It doesn't matter if she does!" Bringing her up had always sent him over the edge. "What is the real issue here?"

The real issue was the fact that sometimes I worried I didn't fit in with his lifestyle. That disconnect had made it hard for me to believe we could last forever and had prevented me from following him to Chile without a commitment. Now, looking at the empty bed, those feelings returned, and I wondered what I'd been thinking, jumping back in so quickly the night before. Getting up, I padded out to the living room and stopped.

Jax sat in the center of the floor, meditating. I watched him in silence, relieved that he was still here and impressed at his discipline to be still. At least, until a snore escaped his lips. I giggled, and his eyes flew open.

"Looks like you were deep in thought," I said.

Yawning, he beckoned me over. "Some temptress kept me up all night."

We kissed, but since he was leaving, this time it felt less about anticipation and more about decision-making.

"You okay to drive?" I asked, for lack of anything better to say.

"I'll get some coffee." He got to his feet and stretched, then looked out the window. The sun was just starting to come up, its golden rays stretched over the canopy of the vines. "I forgot how beautiful it is here."

"When are you coming back?" I asked.

"After the funeral, once she passes. I'll head back down."

I wanted to offer to go with him. Of course, I couldn't do that.

I'd explained it all to him the night before. As expected, he'd lectured me about letting fear control my life. The conversation had been annoying to me, because I didn't want to waste our time on my shortcomings. Eventually, we'd returned to discussing and drinking the wine he'd brought, before heading to bed.

"Either way," he said, "my ticket back to Chile is booked for the end of the month."

I ran my hand over the rough fabric on the back of my favorite armchair, feeling it prickle against my skin. "I thought you said you wouldn't go without me."

"Abigail, my caveman days are over. I'm not going to drag you onto the plane by your hair." He walked over and kissed my nose. "Besides, not every volcano is ready to explode."

What does that even mean?

Resting my hand on the table, I looked at him.

"I'll keep that in mind."

~

I was in a dark mood when I made it to my office and drank a large cup of coffee, trying to shake the feeling.

Really, I should have been happy. I'd missed Jax for years, and now he was everywhere. His scent was in my hair, I could feel him every time I moved my body, and his words—some more poetic than others—echoed in my head. Still, I felt annoyed.

He was gone. What did it matter if he had big plans for what our future looked like? Nothing made those plans different from last time.

You're just protecting yourself. It hurt so much when he left.

That wasn't it, though. It was that comment he'd made about volcanoes, like I wasn't fiery enough for him. As if the fact that I didn't want to uproot my life to do what he wanted was a character flaw in me. Finally, I picked up my phone and called him.

"Some volcanoes aren't ready to explode?" I demanded. "That's the dumbest thing I've ever heard. Look, if you want me to move to Chile, that would require a proposal. I don't remember hearing one."

The silence on the other end of the line made me wonder if I'd dialed the wrong number. Then his throaty laugh echoed across the distance.

"You told me you needed a ring," he said. "Otherwise, you would have heard a proposal."

I stood stock-still in the middle of my office. The air seemed thin, like I was standing on top of a mountain. Images of our future together flashed through my head.

Jax. The vineyard. Chile.

"I can't get you a ring, though," he said. "I don't have any money."

I leaned against the desk to support my shaking legs. "You have enough money to buy a vineyard. So, I'd say you have enough money to buy a ring."

"I have enough money to buy a vineyard because I haven't bought a ring."

I'd have to learn Spanish. Maybe Raoul would teach me. I couldn't go until after harvest, after Pappy was better, and . . .

What was I thinking? I couldn't go to Chile.

"I'll forget the ring if you forget Chile," I said. "We could buy a vineyard here."

There was an agonizing minute of silence. Finally, he spoke, a smile in his voice.

"When I come back we'll look at some. Okay?"

My mouth dropped open. Then, my heart soared. The entire time we'd dated, Jax had refused to consider anything but Chile. If he would stay here, it was a done deal. We could finally be together.

"That's more than okay," I managed to whisper. "It's perfect."

Suddenly, the future seemed full of possibility.

⌒

Two days later, I sipped at a coffee and tried to focus on the emails cluttering my inbox. I had made a pretty good dent when the text icon on my computer lit up.

I hadn't heard from Jax since our call, other than a thumbs-up emoji when I texted to see if he had arrived safely. My heart was still on fire, though. Images of growing our own vines, developing our own wine, and building a vineyard kept playing in my mind. I hoped the text was from him, but no, it was Rogers:

You might want to take a look at this.

The link led to a blog. It sounded like trouble the moment I read the first few words.

Small Fish in a Stale Pond

By: Charlie Winters, co-owner Upper Mitten

The coffee went sour in my mouth. Slowly, I began to read.

Opening a winery is a dream come true for me and my wife. We had visions of creating an innovative space that would open a dialogue about the complex consumer relationship with wine. The reality of our adventure has turned into a competition with Goliath, an old-school winery that runs our small community and does not want to let the outsiders in . . .

The blog went on to tell the story of how Upper Mitten had felt ostracized by the locals from the day they'd rolled into town, thanks to the "local elitism" instigated by a certain powerhouse winery and a proposed wine trail where they were one of the only exclusions. He never mentioned us by name. Still, the description left no question who he was talking about.

The article was ridiculous. It made it sound like we were in a battle to undermine the underdog when we'd never even been to their vineyard.

Maybe that was the problem. We didn't bother to bring over a plate of cookies.

I typed in and deleted a response at least three different times. Finally, I decided my mother was better suited to comment, as she handled our PR. I sent her the link, and ten minutes later, my father stormed into my office.

"Dad!" It was a relief to see him on the property. We needed to discuss inventory and countless other business matters. "I wanted to show you—"

"We need to have a little chat." Pulling a chair up to his desk, he took out his phone. "What is this?"

His screen was lit with the blog from Upper Mitten. It had been shared several times. Of course, our name was in the comments, along with various stories of bad customer service. The complaints were minor and probably reflected less than 1 percent of our guests, but they definitely made us look bad.

I held up my hands. "Upper Mitten didn't seem like a good fit for the wine trail, so I didn't include them. That's it."

"That's not it." He pulled up some particularly inflammatory comments. "Look at this response. Somebody suggested a boycott."

My mouth dropped open. "No one would suggest that. I bet Upper Mitten opened up a fake account and posted that!"

My father ran his hand over his face. "Either way. They got the idea out there. People love to root for the underdog. We don't need this right now."

"No kidding," I muttered. Especially with the threat of my grandmother's secret past hanging over us.

My father studied me over the rim of his glasses. "Figure this out, or I'll have to rethink my position on operations. Building relationships is a big part of the job, and I need to know you're capable of that."

I opened my mouth to protest, but my father had already stormed out of the room.

Capable?

Yanking the keys to the truck off the hook on the wall, I headed outside. It was time to talk to these people, face-to-face.

~

Upper Mitten winery was located on the farthest point of the peninsula. For decades, the property had been an unsuccessful blueberry farm managed by a family that had spent the majority of their time down south. It hadn't been a surprise to anyone when the farm went into foreclosure. Pappy had considered buying the property to expand. Thank goodness, my grandmother had talked sense into him.

"It would be confusing for guests," she'd argued. "The locations are too far apart."

We'd all agreed, but as I drove up the sleek paved driveway leading to the winery, I could see why my grandfather had made the suggestion.

The point was surrounded by water. The vines caught the cool breeze from all sides in a way ours did not, which would create some interesting growing conditions. Plus, the scenery was idyllic.

Even with such a perfect setting, the parking lot had few cars in it, which seemed odd. Our lot was currently packed with tourists.

Maybe they were struggling to get people in the door. The location might offer interesting weather conditions, but it also made for a longer drive, and it looked like a lot of the tourists didn't bother. Hmm. That could be behind Upper Mitten's desire to paint itself as an underdog. It was hard to buy into that, though, considering the money that had gone into the place.

The main building's design was pretty outlandish: a cross between a fast-food joint and the glass pyramid outside the Louvre. It would be interesting to see how the window panes stood up to our brutal winters. I also didn't envy their heating bill.

Charlie, the co-owner who had written the blog, yanked weeds out front. I recognized him from his picture, a Nordic-looking guy in his early thirties with a wiry red beard and a head full of curly hair. The air smelled like the clove he was smoking.

"Hi." I squinted at him in the sun. "I'm Abby Harrington, from Harrington Wines. Do you have a few minutes to chat?"

Charlie eyed me for a moment before tossing the butt of his clove into a bucket. "It's cooler inside."

I hoped to at least see a couple of people bellied up to the bar for a tasting, but the place was empty. The scent of coffee permeated the air from a large coffee bar set up in the corner. There was also a section of arcade games and a merchandise area featuring irreverent T-shirts with quotes like **I LIKE WINING**. In the corner, there were large televisions and tables set up with wine taps. It looked like a great spot to catch a game.

The articles I'd read about Upper Mitten had made me think the vibe would be obnoxious. Different for the sake of being different. Instead, it seemed like a really fun place to hang out, other than the fact that no one was there.

"Do you have a tour out?" I asked.

Maybe the tour parking was in the back and I'd missed the sign.

Charlie gave me a cold look and stepped behind a bar. He ignored my question and poured something fizzy, saying, "Have a seat."

I sat on a barstool. It was 1950s style, with a tight vinyl cushion in a sparkly red. "This is nice. It's different."

"Different isn't good around here."

He certainly wasn't making this easy.

"No, I mean . . ." For a split second, I was afraid I was about to stutter. I tapped my fingers against the edge of the bar, and the moment passed. "Different as in cool."

"Here's our sparkling white." Charlie slid the drink across the bar.

"Thanks. Did you produce the grapes here?" I asked, trying to find common ground.

He eyed me over the rim of his glass. "Nope."

That was the end of the information.

"We outsource our grapes sometimes too. To keep up with volume."

Quickly, I picked up the drink and took a sip. It was a little sour. Incredibly sour, actually.

"Does it rock your world?" he asked, his voice dry.

I hesitated.

It was so important to keep the peace. I was there to extend an olive branch, so it wouldn't be smart to criticize their products. That said, my grandmother had taught me that, when it came to wine, honesty was the best policy. Clearly, she hadn't adopted that philosophy in other areas of her life.

"No one has the same palate," she liked to lecture. "True vintners will never begrudge the truth."

I gave him a friendly smile. "It's not for me."

The back door opened, and Landon, the co-owner who'd called me a dinosaur, rushed in. She wore a pair of plaid shorts and an eighties-style rock and roll T-shirt, along with a collection of leather bracelets. Her hair was unkempt in a way that appeared to require a lot of product.

"Got your text," she told her husband. "Couldn't miss it."

I assumed "it" was me.

Great. This was superfun.

"She hates our sparkling wine," he said, leaning his elbows on the bar.

Landon practically sneered at me. "What's the problem?"

I could only imagine the entire exchange added to their blog. My father was going to kill me.

Pulling the drink close, I said, "Look, I'm not in the business of judging wine. I'm in the business of making it. It would be great if we could talk about—"

"Come on. Harrington Wines is quite the legend." Landon swiped my glass and held it up to the light. It looked almost cloudy. "It would be helpful to have some advice."

Did she mean that? It wasn't like business was booming. Maybe the problem had little to do with location and everything to do with their wine.

"Okay." I sighed. "If it would help."

They leaned forward as I took another sip. It was one of the worst wines I'd ever tasted. No alcohol, weak flavor, and its viscosity was almost . . . thick.

"It's too tannin forward for a sparkling wine," I said. "The minerals are overpowering, and there's no alcohol."

Charlie tugged at his beard. "Tasting notes?"

"Grapefruit and sparkling water," I said, my voice dull.

The row of blue LED lights lining the bar started flashing like crazy, and I looked around in confusion.

"Right on!" Charlie yanked a bottle of Pellegrino and a carton of grapefruit juice out from below the counter and held them up. "You nailed it. This is how we start all of our tastings. You wouldn't believe the lofty terms people use to describe grapefruit and sparkling water because they think that's what they *should* be doing. We tell them to trust their instincts and speak the truth, man. The emperor isn't wearing any clothes."

He reached out and offered a fist bump. Feeling awkward, I took it.

Resting my hands against the sleek bar, I said, "That's tricky."

It was also kind of rotten. I couldn't imagine paying for a tasting to end up feeling stupid.

"What if someone's allergic to citrus?" I asked.

Landon pulled her hair up into a band. "We have a warning posted in the tasting catalog." She crossed her arms. "So, why are you here?"

"The blog." Even though the very thought of what they'd written irritated me, I kept an even tone and forged on. "You're right, your winery was not included in my original proposal, and I apologize. You weren't officially open yet when I submitted it. If you'd like to be involved, I would be happy to add your name."

The excuse was weak, as the winery had been under construction for nearly a year, and their PR blitz had started months before their doors opened. Still, one could argue it was fair to wait to include them until their wine was available. From their expressions, though, they weren't buying it.

"We're not big on bullshit," Landon said.

The back of my neck turned warm. "What do you mean?"

"I mean, the wine trail isn't going to happen without us." She gave a smug smile. "Pretending you want us onboard isn't going to change that."

"Look, you're a new winery. You're not busy. You would get a lot further with the backing of—"

"Excuse me." Landon's dark eyes flashed. "*We're* solvent. Our investors have made it possible for us to survive for quite some time to come. We don't need to bow down to some self-designated king whose coffer is running dry."

I stared at the couple in disbelief. They'd heard something about our finances too?

Charlie gave a serious nod. "Let's talk when it's time for a buyout."

These people were truly unbelievable. Like we'd ever let them take over our vineyard. Still, the fact that they would even suggest it made me want to smash their perfect glass walls into a million pieces.

Landon must have sensed my rage, because she stalked across the room and held open the door. "We're not interested in the wine trail.

So, you can take this whole song and dance where it belongs—out the door."

"If you're not interested in the wine trail," I said, "why did you post that blog?"

Landon smirked. "Publicity, my dear."

"That's horrible." The words caught in my throat. "You can't . . ."

I wanted to tell them off. Explain that these types of tricks had no place here. That the culture was about the tradition of the harvest and the appreciation for wine and its rituals. To share the importance of letting someone enjoy a tasting, instead of making them feel foolish. I couldn't say a thing, though, because my words were stuck.

Pushing past Landon, I headed to the Dodge. My face had to be as red as the flowers lining the sidewalk.

So much for making friends. If anything, I now knew the face of the enemy.

Chapter Twenty-One

It was time to let go of the idea of having a local wine trail, at least with Harrington Wines at the helm, because those horrible people were going to do everything possible to stand in the way. It was a shame because their vineyard was beautiful, the tasting room innovative, and the wine . . . well, I had no clue, since the only thing I'd gotten was grapefruit juice.

The visit replayed in my head like a bad movie the entire fifteen-minute drive down the peninsula. Finally, I picked up my phone and called my dad.

"How did it go?" he asked.

As much as I wanted to scream and cry about how bad the visit had been, he was my boss. I needed to act like a professional. It was the only way he would ever take me seriously.

"They're pretty angry. I apologized and invited them to join the trail. They seemed gleeful at the opportunity to turn us down and said they posted the blog for publicity."

My father sighed. "See if you can come up with anything that would get through to them. Oma loves to tell me this community was built on compromise, not conflict. Let's find the compromise."

I gritted my teeth. "I'll figure it out."

We hung up, and I gripped the steering wheel even tighter. I had no idea what to do to resolve things. It made me question whether I really was capable of being the operations manager.

From the second the job had become available, I'd been so determined it was the right path. Now, I couldn't help but wonder whether I was ready or whether it even mattered. It would, if Jax and I stayed. If we didn't . . .

I shook my head. That wasn't worth thinking about, because I was not about to run away. Either way, my grandfather had said he wanted someone capable of handling the spotlight. I took that to mean an ability to speak in public. Perhaps what he really meant was someone capable of cleaning up public messes . . . or someone with enough tact to avoid them in the first place.

The wine trail was such a good idea. It had the ability to strengthen the wine industry and increase tourism. Unfortunately, I'd picked a fight with the one bad seed that could ruin the batch.

The whole situation was the type of thing my grandmother and I would have discussed late into the night, sitting at the kitchen table and drinking wine. We would have analyzed the problem from every angle, if only for the opportunity to be together and have another drink. I missed her.

And Pappy too.

The moment I let the thought in, I couldn't let it go.

Everything made me think of him. The lake in front of me, the small plane crossing the sky, and his tin of peppermint Altoids in the console. I missed traveling to Main Street with him to get twist cones, practicing amateur photography at the sand dunes, and dropping off wine samples all over town.

I couldn't imagine losing my grandfather. Never getting another smile or hearing one of his diatribes or strolling together through the fields. It meant losing one of the people who mattered to me the most.

And I would have missed the chance to say goodbye.

The Henderson brothers would give anything to see their parents one last time. What was I thinking, refusing to go?

I'd wasted so much time focusing on the wrong things. The situation with my grandmother, the ice wine, the idea that someone could have sabotaged the plane . . . anything to stop me from thinking about the fact that the very person who led our family was on the brink of death in a hospital bed.

The entryway for Harrington Wines was just ahead. I could turn right and return to the vineyard or go straight and see my grandfather.

I hesitated for only a moment. Then I drove right by.

~

The trip to the hospital was a blur. I was so focused on what it would be like to see Pappy that I didn't make time to think about what I was doing. It was only when I pulled into the shade under a tree in the parking lot that I took a cautious look around.

The exterior of the hospital had not been renovated since I was a child. It was exactly the same: a six-story building made of sandy brown stone and reflective windows. The landscaping was bleak, with tiny trees and a handful of depressing bushes at the entrance.

A vague fear gripped my stomach. The phantom sting of the IVs came rushing back. Rubbing my arms, I remembered how cold it was inside and regretted not bringing a sweater.

Who cares? The thing that matters is Pappy.

I got out of the truck and headed for the main entrance. A man on the path in front of me wore a white windbreaker that looked like a parachute. I focused on the strings hanging off the back and imagined we were tandem jumpers. The image forced me to follow him through the front door.

The medicinal smell cut through my nostrils as the fluorescent lights buzzed overhead. The old, tired gift shop was to my right, selling the same assortment of balloons, flowers, and novelties from two decades ago. A purple bear rested in the window, practically saluting me with a balloon on a stick.

Dean had once bought me one just like it.

I took in a deep breath and tried to focus. This was not about me; it was about my grandfather. That reminder got me halfway down the hallway. Then the elevator doors pinged open, and a man wheeling an antibiotic drip stepped out.

Back when I was sick with HUS, the blood transfusions had been endless. The nurses had tried to do them at night so I would sleep instead of pay attention to what was happening to me. They had hung a bag covered in foil next to my bed and told me not to snoop.

At first, I'd followed directions, but curiosity had gotten the best of me. I'd turned on the lights, pushed aside the foil, and stared in horror to realize the bag was filled with blood. It was attached to a tube that transported it into my body.

It had taken three nurses and a sharp shot of sedation to keep me in that bed.

Now, the sight of the bag holding the man's antibiotic drip took me right back to that time. The elevator doors seemed to recede, and my legs gave way. I grabbed at a decorative table to keep from falling.

"Ma'am, are you all right?" A woman in a white coat caught my arm. "Let me call you a wheelchair."

I wanted to tell her no, but the word choked in my throat.

A large woman in teddy bear scrubs was exiting the elevator. The doctor waved her over, and she came running. I tried to duck, terrified she was going to jab me with a needle.

"No." I jerked away. "Please."

The nurse's hands closed around my arm. I shrieked and pushed the two women with all my might. The doctor's face changed from worry to fear.

"Security," she called, drawing back.

The guard left his post at the front door and came running toward me.

"Wait!" A familiar voice rang down the hall. "She's with me."

To my absolute horror, Braden was at my side. I don't know how much he'd witnessed. His dark eyes were worried as he grabbed my hands, and he shook them gently, trying to get me to look him in the eye.

"Abby. I need you to breathe. *Breathe.*"

What was he doing there? Vaguely, I remembered he'd said something about spending his time in the children's ward. It was just my luck he'd happened to take his lunch just in time to witness this.

Using every ounce of strength, I shook him off and ran for the door. The wind caught it and trapped me inside. I pushed with all my might, Braden calling after me.

Fresh air filled my lungs. Racing across the asphalt, I prayed he wouldn't follow. The truck was over a hundred degrees inside. Still, as I turned it on, I didn't waste time with the windows—I hit the gas and peeled out.

Staring straight ahead, I gripped the steering wheel as hard as I could. It took twenty minutes for me to think about anything but the road in front of me. My teeth were clenched so tight they were practically locked together.

There's something really wrong with me.

It was bad enough my mother was telling me to see a speech therapist. Now it was pretty clear I needed a real therapist too.

Even though I'd made a point to avoid the hospital, I hadn't known my fear ran that deep. I had just had a *public* meltdown. The security guard could have hauled me off to the mental ward without a second look.

Hands shaking, I picked up the phone and called Jax. He picked up right away. My voice shook as I detailed the experience. Finally, he spoke.

"I'm waiting for the punch line."

I paused. "What do you mean?"

"I mean I just stepped out of my grandmother's wake to hear some long, drawn-out story about how you're afraid to go into a hospital."

His grandmother died?

"Jax, when did this happen?" I asked.

"Two hours after I got home."

The shadows in the trees outside the window got deeper. I couldn't believe he hadn't called me. Our last conversation had been about marriage, so shouldn't he have told me this?

"It was intense." His voice was rough with emotion. "My brother and I took off. Went cliff diving."

The explanation baffled me. Yes, people handled grief in different ways. It was just that I'd forgotten how frustrating his disappearing act could be.

"Are you okay?" I asked.

"Yeah. I need to get back in there, though."

"Of course," I said, quickly. "Give my love to your family."

It bothered me he hadn't called. He must have wanted to handle his grief on his own, but to me, that approach seemed so isolating. It also made me feel ridiculous for trying to express what I'd just been through.

In the context of the loss of his grandmother, my problem *was* ridiculous. Of course, I never would have brought it up if I'd known his grandmother had died. How was I supposed to know, though, if he didn't tell me?

Is this really the person I want to marry?

Marriage was something I wanted to do one time. I wanted to be with someone who pushed me to be the best version of myself. Jax and I had a deep connection, but it seemed there were a lot of stumbling blocks in our way.

No relationship is perfect, though, I told myself. *It takes time . . . and maturity.*

Something that, maybe, I needed to work on.

I caught sight of my reflection in the car mirror. My eyes were rimmed in red, my hair was flying all over the place, and my typically cheerful expression was shrouded in exhaustion. I was a mess.

It was ironic, because for years, I'd taken pride in the fact that I had my life together. My brother was the drug addict and the criminal, while I was a completely normal person. However, it was becoming clear that I had never been closer to falling apart. I needed to make some changes in my life and fast, because at this point, I felt barely equipped to get by.

Chapter Twenty-Two

I called the outpatient clinic for the speech pathologist first thing the next morning. They had a cancellation late that afternoon. I finished up what needed to be done at work, delegated the rest, and headed over.

The clinic was located only a few buildings down from Braden's new office. I hunched my shoulders to appear smaller, as if he'd duck his head out at that very minute.

Pushing open the door to the speech clinic, I took a look around. The waiting room was small and clean, with a handful of patients, gray tiled floors, and magazines I would never read. I had just taken a seat when my phone buzzed.

It was from my dad:

The doctors are going to wake up Pappy.

My heart skipped a beat. Then a foolish grin spread across my face. It had been almost two weeks. If they were going to wake him, that had to mean they thought he was going to be all right. I fired off an entire series of happy emojis. To my surprise, my father sent one back.

I picked up the phone and called him. "This is good news, right?" I kept my voice low, so as not to irritate the other people waiting. There was an older lady working on a knitting project and a teenager watching something on her phone.

"It's great news." My dad sounded more upbeat than he had in ages. "They still don't like the plaques in his brain, but this is a strong next step. His hands and arms are healing nicely, and they'll be able to manage the pain with a drip. They're doing it tomorrow afternoon. Can you be there?"

I was quiet for so long that he said, "Abby?"

In a rush, I confessed to what had happened in the lobby of the hospital. It was humiliating, but he needed to know I'd tried. Especially since this whole ordeal might soon be over.

"I'm sorry you went through that." His voice was quiet. "Look, we're trying to get your grandmother to go home and get some rest tonight. We know she won't get a wink of sleep once he's up, and she's exhausted."

I sat up straight. "That would be great. Will you text me if she decides to come?"

It would be the perfect opportunity to ask her about the past. I had no idea if I would be bold enough to tell her what I'd found, but at least I could ask some of the right questions.

"I will. Either way, I'll give her your love."

"Thanks, Dad." My voice caught. "I'm so happy to hear this."

Once we hung up, the gray walls of the waiting room suddenly seemed much brighter, the lights almost cheerful. My grandfather was going to make it. In spite of the problems that remained, that was the one thing that really mattered.

"Abigail Harrington?" called a woman from the hallway.

"Yes." Quickly, I got to my feet and followed her.

The room she led me to reminded me of a schoolroom. It had a large desk, cabinets along one wall, and a chair that looked comfortable. There were no windows.

Settling into the comfortable chair, I answered her questions without stuttering. Then she stepped out, and a man in a pressed pair of khakis and a button-up shirt walked in. He was middle-aged, with blond hair, a good tan, and pale lips. For some reason, I imagined him spending weekends sailing with his dog.

"I'm Dr. Crawford." He shook my hand. "Thanks for coming in."

He took a seat behind the desk and reviewed my paperwork in silence. Finally, he looked up and smiled.

"Tell me what's going on."

The request was so casual it was like he wanted to discuss vacation plans.

I told him about my grandparents' anniversary party, the way I'd panicked during the speech, and the follow-up episodes. Of course, I didn't stutter a bit with him.

"Hmm." He steepled his hands. "Any stressors these days? Anything unusual going on?"

I almost laughed out loud. "Let's see. My grandfather was in a plane crash, we were robbed, and I'm trying to get a job that might go to my brother instead, despite the fact that he's an ex–drug addict. I'm also scared to visit my grandfather in the hospital, because I spent a ton of time there as a kid, so—"

"So, nothing a warm bath and a glass of wine couldn't cure," he said, and we both laughed.

Then I looked down at my hands. "Pretty hopeless, huh?"

"Life happens." He tapped his desk twice with his pen. "That hardly makes you hopeless. Tell me what took you to the hospital when you were younger."

Dr. Crawford took notes as I talked, asking me to elaborate on certain memories. We probably spent thirty minutes on the past. I had to force myself to stop talking, which was quite ironic, considering what had brought me into the office in the first place.

Finally, he closed his folder, got to his feet, and moved to the area with the table. There was a microphone-and-recorder setup, along with a big blue notebook. Based on my prior experience, I knew the notebook was filled with speech exercises.

Dr. Crawford gestured at the setup. "Ready to make all this a thing of the past?"

I sat down so quickly I practically knocked over the chair. "You have no idea."

~

The exercises brought up all sorts of emotions I wasn't ready to deal with. Fear from the past, the shock of my grandfather's accident, and the shame that had come with my brother's escapades. Still, I made it through and left with a handful of tricks and a follow-up appointment. It would hardly solve everything, but for the first time in ages, I felt like I was moving in the right direction.

I stopped at one of my favorite lakes on the way home to calm my nerves. Ducks swam by, and frogs croaked from the lily pads. It took about forty minutes of staring out at the water for me to finally breathe normally.

Once it started to get dark and mosquitoes hummed in my ear, I headed back to the truck. My phone buzzed as I was climbing in.

Dad: Oma's staying at the hospital tonight.

I was disappointed, but it made sense. She hadn't left his side yet. Why start now?

Back home, I poured a generous glass of chardonnay and sat at the kitchen table, staring straight ahead. The wine worked its magic, so I turned on my computer and got to work. When my stomach growled,

I realized how late it was and forced myself to get up to find something to eat.

Banging open kitchen cupboards, I realized I was out of food. I'd been too busy to go to the store, and I couldn't even scrape up a can of soup or frozen macaroni and cheese. The pizza delivery places never delivered after ten since we were so far out, so that left me with only one option—Olives.

Earlier that day, I'd noticed the salad special was fresh burrata with pancetta, sliced tomatoes, and basil. That, coupled with bread, olive oil, and a hearty cabernet, sounded like the perfect meal.

I walked across the fields as quickly as I could. The night was overcast and the stars faded. The memory of the robbery and the threatening notes made the shadows seem longer. My nerves were on edge again by the time I rushed up the restaurant's front steps.

Pulling out my keys, I stopped. Olives closed at nine. The lights were all out in the main room, but there was a light on in the kitchen.

The hairs on the back of my neck stood up. The last one to leave was typically our dishwasher. Even he was usually out by ten o'clock at the latest, and it was ten fifteen.

Don't freak yourself out. He could still be working.

Still, I queued up security's number on my cell phone and unlocked the side door as quietly as possible. Standing stock-still in the darkness, I listened.

The only sound was the chirp of crickets outside and the jingle of my keys.

Using the low light on my phone, I wove through the tables. Something banged in the kitchen, and I jumped. My finger pressed the button to call security just as a woman's laugh rang out from the back. Quickly, I hit cancel.

Did our dishwasher sneak a girl in?

I thought he was married with two kids and hardly the devious type. Still, ever since the theft, it had been hard to tell whether to trust our workers.

Letting out a breath, I pushed open the kitchen door. I was prepared for pretty much anything other than what waited for me.

Dean was at the stove holding a spatula. Kelcee stood next to him, wearing her lucky jeans and a low-cut tank top. She touched his arm while laughing at something he said. Reaching out, he brushed a lock of hair behind her ear.

I watched in horror as the two looked at each other with adoration. The steam of the pan rose up between them. My brother leaned forward, and my best friend closed her eyes in anticipation.

"You can stop right there," I blurted out. "This is *not* going to happen!"

Kelcee's eyes flew open, and she jumped backward.

Dean barely blinked. "What are you doing here, Abby?"

"What am *I* doing here?" I surveyed the kitchen.

There was an entire assortment of chopped vegetables set out, along with strips of chicken. Apparently, stir-fry was on the menu.

"First of all, the restaurant is closed. You have no business cooking in here." To my surprise, my words came out smoothly. "There happens to be a little something called public health regulations. If anyone in this room should know that, it should be *you*." I finally locked eyes with Kelcee, who looked appropriately guilty. "So, I suggest you take your little romantic interlude and have it somewhere else. Or, better yet, that you don't have it at all."

I slammed out of the kitchen in a huff.

So much for dinner. I couldn't believe Kelcee was sneaking around with my brother. Was anyone honest anymore?

Footsteps crunched after me on the gravel. Dean. I practically took off running.

"Abby. *Abby*, stop!" His voice was furious. "I've had about enough of your attitude."

"My *attitude*?" I whirled on him. "I've had about enough of *you*. Why Kelcee? She's been through enough with men."

"I would never hurt her. Kelcee is . . ."

Dean shoved his hands in his pockets and shrugged. With his tousled black hair and skinny jeans, he looked like a rock star trying to find the lyrics to a new love song. If his track record with women hadn't been so shameful, I might have bought it.

"Kelcee is my best friend," I finished for him. "And she has worked really hard to get where she is in life. I don't want you to screw it up."

"Why would I screw it up?" he demanded.

"Because that's what you do. You make a mess, and then you leave."

In the light of the moon, Dean looked hurt and angry, all at once. "Why do you have so little faith in me?"

"Please." I brushed away a mosquito. "I haven't seen you in years. You said the other night you probably weren't sticking around. You . . ." For some stupid reason, my eyes stung with tears. Turning away, I headed for the path to my house.

"I tried to make amends with you," he called. "You were the only person who didn't respond to my letter. You didn't even cash my check."

The letter.

Everyone in my family had been so quick to forgive him. They had all sat around the dining room table, reading their letters out loud like it was story hour by the fire. I'd refused to participate.

My mother had pleaded with me to forgive him. "He's trying to heal."

"So am I," I'd told her.

Now, I gave him an icy glare. "Do you know what . . ." My stutter kicked in. It took a moment, but I finally managed to say, "Do you know what that bracelet meant to me?"

Pain crossed his face. "Yes. At the time, though, I was in too deep to care."

"Well, I'm too tired to care." Frustrated, I brushed loose a vine blocking the path. "Besides, your letter wasn't even a complete apology. You left out something pretty significant."

He furrowed his brow. "What?"

With a scoff, I headed down the path.

"Abby." Dean jogged up and grabbed my arm. "Talk to me. Please."

I kept walking, my breath coming fast. Finally, the path opened into the clearing by my house. Dean was still behind me. Fighting back tears, I turned to him.

"Do you remember one of the last times we talked?" I said. "Really talked?"

Dean's face went dark. For a flicker of a moment, his eyes met mine. It was obvious he knew exactly what I was talking about, but he didn't answer. Instead, he brushed a cobweb off his sweatshirt, while the muscle in his jaw pulsed.

Drop it. Let the past be the past.

I couldn't, though. I'd been too angry for too long.

"You called me in the middle of the night. You *lied*." My voice shook, and the words were tight in my throat. "You said some guys were after you. I was going to empty my bank account for you, give you every dime I worked so hard for that summer, because I was a total sucker. And you knew it."

Dean looked up at the moon. "You gave up on me. You hung up the phone."

"No, I didn't," I practically shouted. "My stupid boyfriend broke the phone, because he was sick of you taking advantage of me! The next thing I knew, you had overdosed and were back in the hospital. Surprise, surprise." I stormed off again.

We made it to the front of my house. There was a wooden bench beneath the apple tree, and Dean took a seat. The muscle in his jaw pulsed harder as he stared at the ground. I was half-tempted to go inside, but I couldn't walk away from the fury that had burned in my heart for so many years.

"Dean, I broke up with that guy that very night," I said. "Because he was a total jerk, but also because I believed in you. I believed you were in danger." My voice cracked, but I fought back the tears. "I believed that if I didn't help you, something terrible would happen. Instead, I learned a big lesson: that jerk was right."

The words got caught in a stutter, and Dean looked down at the ground. Impatiently, I brushed away a tear. It was frustrating to cry over something that had happened so long ago, but the fear, the hurt, and the betrayal were still there, as fresh as if it had just happened.

"I should have thanked him for teaching me to not be such a sucker," I finally managed to say.

"I didn't lie to you."

"Oh, give it up," I practically shouted, then headed for my front door. I was not about to let him stand there and lie yet again.

Dean jumped in front of me, blocking my way.

"Please move," I said. "I don't want anything more to do with you."

"I didn't lie to you," he insisted. "I lied to Mom and Dad."

Something in his voice made me pause.

"What do you mean?" I asked.

"Will you sit?" he asked, gesturing at the bench.

I brushed away another mosquito, tempted to walk away. Finally, I sat. The paint on the bench was chipped, and it scratched the skin on the back of my legs.

Dean sat next to me. "I wasn't in the hospital for an overdose. I . . ." His voice broke, and he turned to look at me. "Do you even want to hear this?"

No, but I needed closure on that night. It had destroyed my faith in my brother, long before the confession in the letter had ended our relationship altogether.

"Go for it," I muttered. "I'd love to see how much you're still willing to lie to my face."

Dean turned away, clenching his fists. Fireflies flashed in the field behind him like falling stars. Letting out a breath, he turned back to face me.

"It was the worst night of my life." His voice was low. "I called you back at least ten times before I could finally accept the fact that you, the one person I trusted more than anyone, had finally given up on me too. I deserved it. I knew that, but it didn't make it any easier." He looked up at the sky. "I was halfway back to this girl's apartment I'd crashed at when a car pulled up next to me."

Suddenly, I wasn't so sure I wanted to hear this.

"It was a black SUV," he continued. "Bass pumping like a death march. I started to run. The doors clicked open, and footsteps pounded on the sidewalk behind me." My brother's tone went flat, his eyes distant. "I don't know how many of them there were. Four, maybe. One had a metal pipe." He lifted up the jaunty piece of hair that had bugged me so much, and I put my hand to my mouth. A red scar stretched from the center of his forehead up and through his hairline, just past his ear. "They split my head open like a melon, broke six ribs, and left me for dead."

I swallowed hard. "Dean, I—"

"Don't worry." He gave a bitter laugh. "They never asked if I had their money."

I pressed my palms to my knees to stop them from shaking. "Why didn't you tell us what really happened?"

"I figured it was best to keep the people I loved far away." He shrugged. "Besides, I got what was coming to me."

"That's not true."

"Maybe." His eyes met mine. "But the things we think aren't always true."

Crickets chirped from the woods, and I looked down at my hands.

His version of that night shocked me. I had been so scared, so convinced something terrible had happened that I had barely slept for a week. I couldn't believe that my fear had not only been right but that I'd never had the chance to help him.

Shaking my head, I got to my feet. "You should have told me."

"You deserved some time away."

A cloud covered the moon, and the night suddenly felt dark and silent as a tomb.

So many years wasted.

I wanted to be mad that Dean hadn't told me the truth, that he'd made that decision for me. On the other hand, the fear and anxiety that had come from trying to talk him out of his addiction had been so exhausting. Maybe he'd done me a favor by forcing me to take a step back, but that didn't make the truth any easier to face.

Dean looked at me for a long moment, his dark eyes as familiar as my own. I couldn't believe he'd gone through all that, alone. I couldn't have stopped his addiction, but at least he would have known I was there for him, like he had always been for me. If only he'd told me, things could have been so different. Before I could change my mind, I took a few tentative steps forward and gave him a hug.

His shoulders stiffened, but then he hugged me back. We held each other in silence, the weight of so many years still heavy between us. I looked out at the shadows of the vineyard, my heart full of regret.

He stepped away and gave me a wry smile. "Were you coming to the restaurant to steal salad?"

I nodded. "The burrata."

He gestured at the path. "Kelcee probably busted out of there a half hour ago."

"She wouldn't do that." I thought of the way she'd looked at Dean the night of the speeches. It was obvious she cared about him. "I bet she's hungry, though. Why don't you go back and finish up dinner?"

Dean shoved his hands in his pockets. "I'm sorry, Abby. About so many things."

"Yeah. Me too." The words were thick in my throat. I was afraid to say more, not for fear I'd stutter, but because I was afraid I would burst into tears.

My brother and I looked at each other for a long moment. Then he gave me some sort of salute. "We'll talk later." Turning, he headed down the path.

I sank back onto the bench and looked up at the stars. The moon hovered behind a cloud and for the moment, the stars were bright. Still, it was impossible to see it because my hands continued to shake from Dean's description of that night.

I'd been angry with my brother for so long. Now, I was mad at myself. How could I have been so shortsighted? It had taken almost nothing for me to think the worst about someone I loved because I was too scared to give him another chance.

I even tried to turn him in.

Putting my head in my hands, I regretted my visit to Henry more than ever. I was so grateful he had given me a lecture instead of an investigation.

There had barely been a day when I hadn't thought about Dean in some way or another. If only I had picked up the phone and tried to fix things, our relationship could have been so different.

He's here now, though.

It was a second chance, to put aside the past and focus on the present.

The fireflies flashed again, and I felt something shift inside of me. It was like the tightness in my chest, the scared feeling that sometimes made it hard to breathe, finally let go. My heart felt lighter. For the first time in as long as I could remember, it seemed like there could be a chance to save the relationship between my brother and me. It didn't change the fact that he'd stolen from me, lied to me, and caused more heartache than I cared to remember. But knowing the truth about that night made it seem possible for me to forgive him, something I'd thought I'd never be able to do.

Chapter Twenty-Three

Kelcee texted me first thing in the morning.

U free for a hike early afternoon? The bluffs?

I was brewing an espresso when the message came through. Steam rose from the machine, heating my face. Taking a step back, I tried to determine the best way to respond to Kelcee's message. To be honest, I felt betrayed by her, but I didn't know if it was because she was involved with my brother or because she'd hidden that fact from me. Maybe it was a little bit of both.

Kelcee and I had sought each other's opinion on the men in our lives ever since the third grade, after I'd developed an ill-thought-out crush on Casey Winthrop. He'd had a Spiderman cake for his birthday, and I was so obsessed with the blue-and-red frosting that I'd mistaken my culinary cravings for true love.

Kelcee had been horrified and had tried to talk sense into me at recess. "Gross! He makes fun of reading. He's weird."

Still, I'd flounced up to sit with him at lunch the next day, mainly because I'd hoped he'd bring leftover birthday cake. Sure enough, there'd been a huge piece crammed in his Spiderman lunch box, but he'd refused to share it with anyone. I'd eyed the smear of blue frosting around his mouth and secretly vowed never to kiss him, even if forced into an arranged marriage.

From that moment on, Kelcee's dating advice had earned a front-row seat in my life, and my input had always been important to her. Except when it came to my brother, apparently.

I took a sip of espresso, wincing at its bitterness. The thick liquid settled on my tongue, and I took my time making a piece of toast, debating how to respond.

My phone chimed again.

Kelcee: Two o'clock work?

I looked at the schedule on my phone. That was right when Pappy was scheduled to come out of the coma. If I couldn't be with my family, Kelcee was the next best thing, even if I was mad at her. Finally, I sent a response.

I'll be there under duress.

Her answer was immediate.

Quit being a baby. See you then.

~

Once I got to work, there was plenty to take my mind off my brother's relationship with my best friend, as the Starlight Cove wine festival was quickly approaching. It was a small annual event that took place in the main park downtown. Jazz quartets played as tourists sampled the regional wineries, and we were typically the title sponsor. It hit me that I needed to double-check to make sure our permit approvals had been submitted to the city, something my grandmother typically handled with the help of our administrative assistant.

When I went to see Jessica, she was hard at work in her tiny office. Folk music blasted from her computer, and her hair was up in pigtails. In a complete sidestep from her typical crystals and hemp jewelry, she wore a gold necklace with a diamond pendant hanging from the center.

"Jessica, that's beautiful," I said, pointing.

She slid it beneath her neckline. "Oh. Yeah, it's . . . I hope it's not weird I wore it to work. I have somewhere to be after, so—"

"You should wear what you want," I said, confused at her reaction.

It dawned on me that I knew very little about Jessica's personal life. Or the personal lives of most of our staff, which went back to the comment Jessica had made that one day, about putting our family first. We probably did need to take steps to get to know our workers better, if we wanted to claim a close relationship with them. Bridging that gap would make it to the top of my list of goals if my father could get past the conflict with Upper Mitten and continue to push for me to have the main role in operations.

I'd revisited Upper Mitten's publicity-seeking blog that morning, and thank goodness, the sharing trend was over. The next internet cause had taken hold, so hopefully we were off the hook for a while. Pulling a chair up to Jessica's desk, I gave her a friendly smile.

"So, what was the occasion?" I gestured at the necklace. "Was it from your boyfriend?"

Her neck flushed a deep shade of pink. "Uh . . . no. My parents. Christmas."

For some reason, I didn't believe her.

"Jess, did you and your boyfriend break up?" I asked gently.

The wide-eyed look she gave me was so deer-in-headlights that I got my answer.

"I'm so sorry," I said quickly. Suddenly, this getting-to-know-you session didn't seem like the best idea. "There's probably some HR law against me asking you that type of thing, anyway. So, listen. Can I get your help with the prep for the wine festival?"

Jessica gave an efficient nod and pulled up the information on her computer, clearly thrilled to move away from my line of questioning. It turned out the due date for the permits was practically here, so it was a good thing it hadn't slipped through the cracks. We got to work on the paperwork, and once everything was complete, I got to my feet.

"Thanks for all your help." I smoothed my hair, which had already gone fluffy in the heat. "I'm going to go hunt down an iced coffee."

I was halfway out the door when Phillip walked in with an armful of mail.

"Abby, good. You're here." Dumping the mail on Jessica's desk, he said, "I was about to head over to the hospital but wanted to bring this by. We got another one."

He held up a piece of turquoise paper.

My stomach dropped as I read the message:

THE DAY OF RECKONING HAS COME.

"These get weirder and weirder," I said, reaching for it.

"Should we be worried?" Phillip scratched his chin. "It sounds like they're about to do something."

I studied the note. There weren't any markings or impressions to give us a hint where it had come from, no matter what angle I studied it from. "Let's see if Henry can get a patrol car up here. Or we can double our security."

Phillip nodded. "Sounds good. I've got to head out. Kate and Ava are waiting in the car."

My shoulders slumped. I felt so guilty knowing that Phillip's entire family would be there to greet Pappy when he awoke.

"Tell him I love him." I had to fight to keep the tremor out of my voice. Letting out a breath, I turned to Jess. "Thanks again for your help. I'm going to go deal with this."

Jessica chewed at her nails. "Henry told me if I was worried not to come to work."

At this point, I wouldn't blame her. *The day of reckoning?* Clearly, whoever was behind this was ready to unleash their fury. It felt so surreal that I didn't feel nearly as frightened as maybe I should have.

"Do what you need to do to feel safe," I agreed. "No one will fault you for that."

Jessica fiddled with the pendant on her necklace. "I talked to Billy about it, and he said if anyone was in danger, it was him, since he was the first line of defense. I'm hidden away back here in the office."

The idea of our freewheeling bartender offering counsel to Jessica almost made me laugh out loud, in spite of the topic. Billy was a bartender, though, which meant he was well schooled in the skill of offering advice.

"Leave it to Billy," I said. Then, something about her comment registered. "Wait. Does everyone on staff know about this?"

I hated to think an issue like this was on the gossip circuit, especially when the news should have come from us. It was probably time I sent out a memo to the staff.

"Oh." Jessica slid the diamond pendant back and forth on the chain. "No. I only told him because he saw me talking to Henry, and I was a little shaken up, so he gave me a drink and—"

I held up my hand. "Not a big deal. I'll inform the staff this afternoon to be on the lookout for anything strange. It looks like it's time to start taking this seriously."

Heading back to my office, I studied the turquoise paper pinched between my fingers and thought of Billy's words.

The first line of defense.

It was an interesting way to view things.

Especially since I had no idea where to watch for the attack.

∽

Midmorning, Rogers called and asked me to come to the tasting room. I'd just finished drafting the memo informing and warning the staff about the notes and had sent it to both Henry and my father for approval. There were piles of paperwork still waiting for me, and I didn't feel like stepping out into the muggy sunshine unless it was necessary.

"Is it urgent?" I took a gulp of iced coffee. "I'm right in the middle of some things."

His answer was cryptic. "I'd say it warrants your attention."

Sweating in the humidity, I hustled over there, convinced every bottle we owned had now come up missing. The scent of oak and wine was ripe as I walked in, the heat of the summer day lingering on my skin. The tasting room was busy, with a good number of guests shopping and waiting for the next tour to start. I longed to sit at the bar and linger over an ice-cold glass of chardonnay with them.

Billy greeted me with a goofy smile. "You received a delivery."

I surveyed the room, looking for Rogers. "What? The new wine labels?"

The latest samples were set to arrive today or tomorrow. Rogers knew I was eager to see them, but really, that could have waited.

Billy wiggled his eyebrows. "If they're made out of petals and pollen, I guess."

"Wait. Flowers?" I was completely confused. "For me?"

Jax and I had barely talked since the conversation after his grandmother died. Part of me felt like I should be upset about it. On the other hand, it was pretty typical. He would get in touch when he was ready, and things would be exactly the same between us.

Flowers, though.

Odd. He was more of a pick 'em himself type of guy.

Rogers walked out from the stockroom with an armful of T-shirts. Spotting me, he set them behind the cash register and breezed over. Clearing his throat, he pointed at the end of the bar.

"Those arrived for you." He raised his eyebrows. "It looks like you have made quite an impression."

An enormous bouquet of tropical flowers took up the entire width of the counter. Their perfume scented the air like our Meritage, one of our most floral wines. I picked through the blooms for a card, but there wasn't one. Then, my eyes surveyed the tasting room, a blush already heating my face. What if Rogers and Billy were making such a big deal out of this because Jax was here, waiting to jump out and propose?

"You guys." I squeezed my hands. "Is someone—?"

Billy handed me a small package. "This came with it. I hope it's chocolates, because I skipped breakfast and I'm starving."

Quickly, I opened the long, thin box. It was . . . a stethoscope. Neatly wrapped in white parchment paper. Confused, I fumbled with the gold-embossed card resting inside.

It read:

Here's a little something to keep close to your heart for your next visit to your grandfather. May it give you strength and courage. All the best, Braden

I stared at the gift in disbelief. Ever since the call with Jax, I had felt more ashamed than ever about my fear of the hospital. But this . . . this didn't make me feel ashamed. It made me feel understood. It had to be one of the sweetest, most thoughtful presents anyone had ever given to me.

Billy peered at the package and let out a disappointed grunt. "Please tell me that's chocolate art. Not an actual stethoscope."

I brought the circular metal part toward Billy's chest. "Let's see if it works."

"You'll just hear my stomach growl." He pointed at Rogers. "This is the guy to examine. See if he even has a heart."

Rogers crossed his arms with a huff.

"Rogers has one of the biggest hearts around." I smiled at him. "He just likes to keep it well hidden."

Rogers colored slightly and turned away. "The pot and the kettle," he muttered and headed off to take care of business.

~

I sat in my office and held the stethoscope in my hands. The bell end was cool to the touch, and the contraption smelled like plastic and metal. Pressing it against my chest, I slid in the ear tips and listened to my heart.

Thump thump. Thump thump.

Up until now, the sound had always made me think of the beeping of the heart monitor in my hospital room. Now, it reminded me of the roar and the rhythm of our bottling equipment, filling bottle after bottle of wine. It made me think of thunder and rainstorms and life.

The moment Braden had grabbed my hands at the hospital and told me to breathe rushed through my mind, but quickly I pushed the thought aside. Braden's gift touched my heart, but it didn't change the fact that I was in love with someone else.

Picking up the phone, I called Braden. It went straight to voice mail.

"Hey, it's Abby. I wanted to say thank you so much for the beautiful flowers and the stethoscope. Definitely one of the most unique gifts I've received, but . . ." I dropped the bravado. "Braden, it was really thoughtful. I have to let you know, though, that I'm not in a place to continue what we started. I just wanted to say thank you. That was really, really sweet."

I hung up and set the phone aside, surprised at the rhythm thundering through my chest. Maybe I should have said more, but Braden didn't need the details about Jax and me. I wasn't available to pursue a relationship, and that was that. Still, I felt sad, somehow.

Two hours later, a text came through.

Braden:

Glad you liked it. Enjoy your day.

I stared down at my phone. The text seemed a little abrupt, but what did I expect?

Quickly, I sent him a thumbs-up emoji and got back to work.

~

Early afternoon, I climbed into the truck and pulled onto the highway to meet up with Kelcee. It had already been a long day, with call after call from the staff regarding the memo. My phone buzzed in my pocket again, and I picked up, ready to give the same speech:

We are taking the threat seriously. The police are sending a patrol car to remain on-site 24-7. Anyone who sees anything suspicious should report it immediately . . .

"They're postponing bringing him out of the coma."

My father's voice rang through the phone, thick with disappointment.

"Postponing?" The word made my stomach drop. "Why?"

If they were planning to postpone, something had to be wrong.

We can't lose him. How could I sleep at night, knowing I missed the chance to say goodbye?

"There are still some strange plaques on his brain." I rolled up the window so I could hear my father better. He sounded defeated. "The doctors think it's wise to take a little more time, just to be safe."

"But they think he'll be okay?" I said.

"They don't know."

"Dad." The word came out a whisper. The cab was hot with the window up and the smell of peppermint strong from my grandfather's tin in the console.

"I know." He cleared his throat again, and we sat in silence. Finally, he said, "What's the update on your end?"

The route to the bluffs where Kelcee and I were meeting was halfway to town, so I had plenty of time to fill him in on work. It felt unimportant, compared to what was happening with my grandfather, but I relayed the staff's response to the memo, as well as plans for a wedding that evening, the upcoming wine festival, and production news. Before we hung up, I squeezed the phone tight.

"Let me know if anything changes with Pappy," I said. "Please."

Outside the truck, the parking lot was cool from the shade of trees, and the air smelled fresh, like wet moss. It was pretty empty, for the height of tourism season, but there were a few families heading into the path that led through the woods. I walked over to the edge of the bluff and took in the view.

The town of Starlight Cove sat at my feet like something out of a picture-perfect postcard. The white spire of the main church rose up over the water, the pastel buildings on Main Street created a romantic tableau against the sky, and the lighthouse stood in stoic silence. Behind me, the cool canopy of the forest was rich with the thick foliage of summer, and I let out a deep breath, trying to reconcile the fact that Pappy might not ever see a view like this again.

"Hey," Kelcee called.

Turning, I spotted her waiting by the path. She wore a pair of black running shorts and a tank top wet with sweat, so she'd probably arrived early to jog. Sipping from a water bottle, she lifted her hand in greeting as I headed her way.

I didn't have it in me to be angry. Instead, I pulled my hair back in a ponytail, slid my sunglasses on top of my head, and hugged her.

"I heard about your grandfather," she said. "I'm so sorry."

We headed into the forest in silence. It was a paved trail that meandered past a small creek. Birds chirped in rhythm with the hum of the afternoon insects, and finally she turned to look at me.

"You okay?" she asked.

"I don't know," I said, watching a dragonfly dart across the water. "The fact that the doctors were the ones who put Pappy in the coma in the first place always brought me this sense of comfort, because I figured that meant they could wake him up at any time. Since that's not true, I don't know what to think."

"Dean says they're just being cautious," she said. "They don't want to bring him out until they're sure. He seems to think it will be okay."

I squeezed my hands. "That's good to know."

Dean wasn't exactly an optimist, so her words reassured me. I half wished I could talk to him, but even after our heart-to-heart, I wasn't quite sure where we stood.

Kelcee took a sip from her water bottle. "I should have told you about him. I'm sorry."

The breeze picked up, and the light drifting down from between the trees skittered across the path like a squirrel.

"How long has it been going on?" I asked.

"Oh, since you were in the hospital." My feet came to an abrupt halt. Kelcee stopped too and brushed her hair back from her eyes. For a split second, the teenage version of my best friend, the one with bangs and a popped-up collar on her Polo shirt, looked over at me. "Do you even want to hear this?"

Feeling numb, I nodded.

"Back when you got sick, Dean and I were both so scared, and we gravitated toward each other. It wasn't romantic at first." She took off her sunglasses, the blue of her eyes as vibrant as the lake. "He was just my best friend when you couldn't be."

I took a long drink from my water bottle and started walking again, trying to process what she was saying. I had known the two were friends but always assumed it was brotherly, the way it was for me and Kip.

"Things didn't get serious until that accident Dean caused at the vineyard," she said, following me. "Remember how he disappeared?"

Like it was yesterday. My mother had paced the hallways for two days straight, while my father and Pappy had searched every inch of the fields and beyond, looking for him. My grandmother had been the only one who'd seemed convinced he was safe and that he would come back when he was ready to face what had happened.

"He was with me," Kelcee said, looking guiltier than ever. "I snuck him up to the attic, and he stayed there for two days, while I tried to convince him that it was okay to go back home."

Kelcee had grown up in one of the old, beautiful Victorian homes that rested on the bluff overlooking Starlight Cove. The home was so large it was practically a mansion, so it would have been simple for Dean to stay there undetected. I just couldn't believe she had never told me.

"I know," she said, as if reading my mind. "But it was impossible to tell you what I felt for him. He was your brother, and I was only fourteen, so would you really have believed me if I said we were in love? It wasn't like we had some relationship where we sat together at lunch and went to school dances. He was not an easy guy to deal with."

That was the understatement of the century. I could only imagine how hard a romantic relationship with Dean would have been. The broken promises. The erratic behavior. I was surprised Kelcee had put up with it at all.

I stopped at the edge of the stream and stared out at the moving water. Finally, I picked up a stone and tossed it in. "How did you two reconnect?"

Kelcee took another long drink from her water bottle. "Social media. It wasn't anything serious. Just hey, how are you? I didn't know he had come back until the party for your grandparents." We turned away from the creek in silence. "I plan to see what happens. Nothing is forever."

The sentiment made me feel protective of Dean. It had been so long since I'd had that emotion that my eyes pricked with tears. Kelcee noticed and gave me another guilty look.

"I should have said something."

"It's not you." The salt of the tears mixed with the sweat on my face. "It's just everything adding up. Like all of these memories are falling on me at once."

Nothing is forever. Is that really true?

It was starting to feel like it. My grandfather would be lucky to have tomorrow, which was something I could barely stand to consider, and even though I'd reconciled with Dean, our relationship would never be the same. Then there was Jax. If we were going to move forward, it had to last forever, or what was the point? Kelcee and I took a pathway out of the woods and sat on a bench at the edge of the bluff, one that looked out at the water.

"Memories are one thing," she said. "But you can't live in the past. Since Dean's a big part of that, I will say this: He was a shitty brother for years, but he's a really, really good guy. You need to see him for who he is now, not who he was back then."

"I know." I ran my hand over the rough wood of the bench. "I'm going to try."

We sat in silence, then she looked at her watch. "I have to head out. I'm supposed to go fishing with Sami and Kip. Do you want to come?"

"I've got to get back to work. There's a wedding at sunset." The sun sparkled over the lake, and I gestured at it. "I think I'll stay here a few minutes. Clear my head."

Kelcee took off her sunglasses. "You okay with all this? I mean, me and Dean?"

I nodded. "Yes. I'm . . . I'm happy for you."

She leaned down and gave me a quick hug. "Call me if anything changes with Pappy."

"I will."

The wind had picked up, and as I watched, it shaped the white grains of sand on the beach into ripples that would smooth with time. With a sigh, I leaned back on the bench.

It was hard to believe my brother and best friend had been sneaking around since we were kids. It's something I would not have seen coming, not in a million years. Stranger still was that, in spite of the ways they'd changed, they seemed like a perfect match. I couldn't help wondering if that was true about me and Jax.

It felt odd questioning our relationship. It was just . . . we'd barely talked. I needed to know that if I planned for this to be forever, he would be there. Not be out scaling mountains or skinning a boar with his bare hands or whatever.

Taking out my phone, I called. He picked up on the first ring.

"I'm on the road," he said, before I could speak. "I'll be there tomorrow."

Joy rushed through me, followed by an almost panicked sense of relief.

"Really?" I whispered.

He paused. "Are you crying?"

"No," I lied, blinking back another round of tears. On the beach below, the ripples in the sand changed as the wind blew. "Bad reception. I'm up on the bluffs."

"Well, it's time for us to make some plans," he said. "It's been long enough."

"You don't know how happy I am to hear you say that," I told him. By the time we hung up, I couldn't hold back the tears. My life had felt so out of control that the idea of returning to the familiar comfort of my relationship with Jax filled me with relief. The timing felt ideal, like it was meant to be. Getting to my feet, I ran my hands over my shorts and brushed off the sand.

You can't live in the past.

Kelcee's words rang through my head, and I stood at the edge of the bluff, looking down. The wind had picked up, and the waves were high. They crashed against the shore, churning the sand in the shallows and changing the landscape of the beach.

I wasn't living in the past. Finally, I was planning for the future. Yes, it was scary and confusing, but it was time. Living in the past made about as much sense as trying to force the view in front of me to stay exactly the same.

Chapter Twenty-Four

My heart skipped five beats when I saw Jax's car kicking up dust on the way up the drive. I ran out to meet him, a smile stretched across my face.

"Hey, gorgeous," he said.

We kissed through the driver's side window, and I breathed him in. He smelled like the wind. I leaned in, letting my cheek rest against his.

"I missed you." His beard was back, but carefully trimmed with a mustache and goatee. "I'm so sorry about your grandmother."

"She's playing pinochle and drinking manhattans somewhere. How's your grandfather? Any change?"

I shook my head and pulled back. "No, unfortunately."

He started to open the door, and I rested my hand on the edge of the window. "Actually, I was hoping we could go on an adventure." Since he'd already driven for hours, I said, "Let me drive."

True to form, Jax didn't try to guess where we were going. He settled into the passenger's seat and shut his eyes. He was asleep by the time we pulled out of the vineyard. I drove about twenty minutes north of the peninsula, and he woke when I cut the engine.

"Man, I knocked out." He rubbed his eyes and looked around. "Where are we?"

I had parked at the top of a small hill with a view of untouched farmland. The fields were bright green with wild purple clover and sur-rounded by fir trees on three sides. It was even more pastoral than it had looked in the pictures.

"Let's go check it out," I said.

He gave me a sideways look, followed by a slight smile, like he knew exactly what we were doing here.

The first time I set my foot on the grass felt significant, like it was the start of something. Turning to him, I let out a hopeful breath.

"So . . . I went to school with a girl who's a real estate agent, and I asked her to send me some options for farmland. There were a ton. But there was something about this that struck me. I think this should be our vineyard."

Jax raised his eyebrows. His eyes still looked tired, but they were so beautiful, like the different shades of wood in an oak barrel.

"Our vineyard?" he echoed.

In my fantasy, this was the part where he scooped me up into his arms and agreed that Chile was much too far away. In reality, I knew it was going to be a much harder sell. So, when he cleared his throat and shoved his hands into the pockets of his cargo shorts, I pressed on.

"It's twenty acres," I said, pointing, "which is a good start, and Kailyn—she's the real estate agent—said the land across the road is unused. They might want to sell eventually too. The price on this one is right, though, because it's an estate sale and—"

I could hardly believe it when Jax actually did scoop me up in his arms. His lips pressed against my hair, and I let out a breath I hadn't realized I was holding.

"Abigail, I love it," he said. "It's perfect."

"Really? You think so?" My heart soared. I turned my head, and we kissed, a long, lingering kiss that seemed to answer the question for him. It was such a perfect moment that the years we'd been apart seemed to melt away. "I can't believe it." I beamed at him. "We're going to have our own vineyard!"

"Not *just* a vineyard." His tone turned mysterious, and he set me down. "Here, let's have a drink. I want to talk to you about something."

I watched the broad expanse of his shoulders as he pulled a bottle of Chilean wine out of the back seat. He laid a ratty blanket on the ground, and we settled in. I took a long drink of a bold red, straight from the bottle.

Handing it back to him, I said, "Tell me what you're thinking."

Jax sat cross-legged, and he rubbed his hands against his calves. "I think it's great, and if we can get enough people, we may as well just buy the land across the street too."

There were grasshoppers everywhere, and a green one landed on my knee. It scrambled to find footing before it gave up and jumped away.

"We *might* be able to get investors," I said cautiously. "It would be a hard sell, but it might be possible because of my family. That said, investors could—"

"Not investors." He picked a piece of clover and stuck it between his lips. "I'm picturing a co-op with some of my buddies. Get this: a winery in conjunction with a cannabis farm. Once marijuana is legal, we'll be ahead of the game."

"Hold on." There were two major problems with what he'd said but only one that mattered at the moment. "You want to start a vineyard with your buddies? It's supposed to be you and me."

The first prickles of disappointment started in my stomach, and I pushed them away, convinced I wasn't hearing him correctly.

"The more people we get, the more workers we'll have." Jax smoothed back his thick hair. "It would be like a big family."

"Um . . . you do know that my family owns the biggest winery in the area, right?" Without an ounce of irony, I added, "If you want a big family vineyard, you're looking at it."

He gave me a wry look. "Funny."

"I'm not trying to be funny." I ran my hand over the rough fibers of the blanket. "If that's what you want, that's what we'll do. We don't have to reinvent the wheel."

Jax didn't answer, and I lay back, staring at the sky. Confusion rushed through me like the clouds rolling by. Jax's warm body pressed against mine, and he chewed in silence on the clover.

"You really want this to only be us?" he asked.

He knew I did.

Turning, I met his eyes. "It sounds like you don't."

He let out such a long and loud sigh that I could smell the wine on his breath. "It's not that I don't want it to be us, it's just . . . look, you want me to stay here in the States. That's not exciting to me. The co-op is. It would have lots of ideas, new blood, things would always be happening . . . I mean, that's how it is where I'm at now in Chile, and it lights me up."

"Running a place together wouldn't?"

"Not really." He shrugged. "That's not a reflection of how I feel about you—it's just . . . the place I'm at now makes me happy. I'd want to bring that same energy here."

At my silence, he took my hand and traced it with his fingers.

The gesture made my heart ache, because even as his skin touched mine, the moment felt like the start of a memory. Something to freeze-frame to look back on as one of the last times we really touched.

Stop thinking like that. You love him. You can make this work.

I thought back to the first moment I'd seen him. When our eyes met, it had felt like coming home. Was it still possible to get back to that place?

The silence that settled over us seemed to last forever. He sat up, took a drink from the bottle, and offered it to me. This time, I shook my head. I didn't like Chilean wine. At least, not the ones he'd picked out.

The first few sips were delicious. They made me think it was the best wine I'd ever had, until it became unbalanced. I never knew what to expect, and I had no guarantee it would ever be simple enough for me to understand.

Like Jax.

Once, our relationship had been so passionate and romantic. We'd spent hours talking about our dreams, but I must not have been listening. Jax had gone to Chile for a reason—he craved excitement.

I didn't.

In the past few weeks, I'd had more excitement than ever, and it wasn't how I wanted to live. Sure, I could encourage Jax to do the co-op, and I could stay at my family's vineyard, but it wouldn't work for long. Eventually, we would resent each other, because it wasn't the life either of us wanted to invest in.

You can't live in the past. Turning to him, I gave him a sad smile. His dark eyes met mine, and even though I tried to fight it, a tear trickled down my cheek.

"Why are you crying?" he asked, brushing it away.

"My grandfather always says a vine is only as strong as the soil you grow it in, and I think . . . " Struggling to keep control of my voice, I looked at him. "Jax, you and I don't want to grow in the same place. I was so happy to have you back, especially right now, but I think we need to accept we want different things and move on."

"Abigail." He squeezed my hands. "We can't go from talking about marriage to ending things. I get it. You're scared. That's been your narrative for a while now, and I'm telling you, it's time to let go of all of that. Relationships cause hurt. They cause heartache. If you try to close yourself off, because you don't want to risk all that, you'll miss out on the opportunity to love."

The funny thing was, I didn't relate his words to my relationship with him at all, but to my relationship with my brother. I had wasted too much time moving away from Dean, for fear I'd get hurt. I wasn't going to do that anymore.

"Abigail?" Jax squeezed my hand. "Tell me what you're thinking."

"I'm thinking about family." I held his hand tight in mine. "How easy it is to hurt the ones you love the most." The wide expanse of green stretched out around us. In another life and at another time, this plot of land could have been the start of something great. "Jax, you have dreamed about Chile ever since I first met you. If you stayed here, you would hate me. Not right away, but eventually, because this isn't the life that's right for you. I wish it was, but . . ." Gently, I dropped his hands. "It *is* true that some volcanoes aren't ready to explode, Jax. But some of us are perfectly happy being hills."

He took another sip of wine in silence. With a sigh, he got to his feet. I stood, too, and he pulled me up, then into a hug. I held him as tight as I could before finally letting him go.

That night, I stood in the kitchen and ate frozen grapes straight from the storage bag, letting the cool air of the freezer soothe my swollen eyes.

The ride back to the vineyard had been silent. I could feel the both of us second-guessing my decision. There'd been a moment he'd cleared his throat, as if about to make a proclamation. Then, a chipmunk had darted in front of the car, and he'd had to swerve to miss it, which had put his focus back on the road.

When we'd pulled up in front of the tasting room, he hadn't gotten out. I'd been relieved, because I hadn't known if I could say goodbye twice.

Instead, he'd leaned out the window and given me a rueful smile. "You'll always be one of my favorite years."

I squeezed my hands tight. "You too."

Now, I shut the freezer and stood at the window, biting down on my last grape. The chill numbed my teeth, but I loved the flavor. They tasted just like home.

"Hey." Phillip called first thing Monday morning, his voice urgent. "Could you help me out? Kate's got a doctor's appointment in Ann Arbor late this afternoon. I completely forgot about it, and I need someone to watch Ava." His voice went low. "It's her five-year, so I really have to be there. Mom's going to take over tonight, because we'd like to stay over, but can you watch her today?"

"Of course," I said, immediately dismissing the to-do list sitting on the desk in front of me. "I'll head up to the house."

My brother's wife was a breast cancer survivor. It had been caught early, and they'd used the most aggressive treatment available. Even though she had been in the clear for years, the five-year marker was a huge milestone. My brother definitely needed to go.

Ava was already in full action by the time I made it up to the house. She wore button-up pajamas and a pair of purple rain boots. Her bubble machine was on, and she danced through the floating apparitions to music from the Disney Channel.

I hugged her tight. "Hi, Buttercup."

"Hi, Dandelion," she said, squeezing me back.

We'd made up the names one night when I was reading her bedtime stories. There'd been a picture of a dandelion ready to be blown off the stem. She'd giggled and said it looked like me. I'd pointed at the picture of the yellow buttercups and said they were so sweet—they looked like her—and the names had stuck.

"What do you want to do today?" I asked, swiping a minimuffin from a plate on the side table.

"Hey!" She stopped in the middle of her dance routine. "I was saving the blueberry."

Quickly, I looked at the muffin in my hand. "This is cranberry." I chewed the bite in my mouth to be sure. "With orange."

"Good." Ava grabbed the blueberry one. "Let's go play in the fields."

Phillip and Kate poked their heads in right on time to hear her request.

"Why does it not surprise me that she wants to do that with you?" Kate laughed, giving me a hug. "Thank you."

"There's nothing I'd rather do than hang out with this one," I said honestly. It would be such a relief to have something happy to take my mind off ending things with Jax. "And I'm thrilled for you. This is a big deal."

Once her parents were out the door, Ava gave me a big grin. "You ready?"

"Hold on." I took in a deep, dramatic breath as if to gear up for a day of fun. She giggled, and I said, "Okay, let's do it."

The morning was a whirlwind.

Moments before racing to the fields, she decided to change into a princess dress, and we played a quick round of Queen of the Castle on a large rock behind the house. Then we chased each other through the chambourcin field, dug up worms in the mud, and stalked a monarch butterfly for at least a half hour. The sun was hot, and finally she begged me to spray her with the garden hose in back of the house.

Turning on the nozzle, I winced at the icy water. "We're only doing this for a second."

I gave her a quick mist, and instantly she burst into tears and ran into the house.

Feeling like the worst aunt ever, I chased after her.

"Buttercup, wait," I called. "I'm sorry! Don't track mud in the house."

The princess dress was marooned like a casualty of a shipwreck in the main hallway. The sound of snuffles led me upstairs to Ava's bedroom, where she was wrapped in a huge terry cloth robe and sprawled out on her bed. Shivers racked her body.

"Honey, I'm so sorry." I felt so guilty. "I shouldn't have agreed to that."

Goodness, she knew how to put on a performance. The water had only been on her less than ten seconds. Suddenly, it hit me that her face was bright red, in spite of the sunscreen I had so carefully applied.

Touching her forehead, I sucked in my breath. She was burning up.

"Ava," I breathed. "Hold on."

The thermometer was in the childproofed section of her bathroom closet, along with a collection of medicine. I grabbed a bottle of Children's Tylenol and the dosing chart, certain she had a fever and wondering when it had started. She'd acted perfectly normal all day.

The thermometer read such a high temp that I shook it and tried again, convinced it was wrong. Nope. 104. In the middle of summer, out of nowhere. Plus, her parents were across the state for the night.

Dread settled over me.

Rushing to the bathroom, I ran a cold bath and tried to call Phillip. No answer. Same with my parents. Close to panic, I dialed Braden.

"Hey." He sounded surprised. "Did you change your mind about dinner?"

I explained the situation, and his tone turned professional.

"I'll be right there."

～

Ava had a double ear infection brought on by a summer cold.

Braden spotted it within moments of his arrival and called in a prescription for an antibiotic to the pharmacy downtown. I sent Jessica to pick it up, and while we waited, Braden stuck around to monitor Ava's temperature. It had gone down thanks to the Tylenol, some cold compresses, and a cherry popsicle.

It was clear he had a way with kids, making her laugh in spite of the agony of her ears. I liked seeing that side of him.

Once Ava's antibiotics arrived and she fell asleep, we stepped out into the hallway.

"I can't thank you enough."

Braden smiled at me. "No problem. Keep her hydrated and cool. The antibiotics will take a while to work their magic, so the biggest hurdle is that fever."

I leaned against the hallway wall. It was the first time I had taken a moment to breathe since noticing she was warm.

"We played all morning. The fact that she was sick completely escaped me. I feel terrible."

"Don't." He shook his head. "Kids are great at hiding their illnesses if there is something better to do than be sick in bed. I imagine that, for her, it was playing with you."

Every time I was with my niece, it made me wonder if I would ever be lucky enough to meet the right person and have a family of my own. I wondered if Braden felt like that, working with kids every day. He would definitely make a good father.

"What?" he asked.

I flushed slightly, afraid I'd spoken out loud.

"Nothing." My eyes fell on a photograph of my grandfather just over his left shoulder. "I'm just trying to figure out how many more members of my family you're going to have to help until—"

"You agree to have dinner with me again?"

Part of me was tempted to go. I enjoyed his company, and really, what would it hurt?

"I was kidding," Braden said, at my silence. "No pressure. For real."

"It's just . . . timing."

He studied me for a moment. "Take the time you need, Abby. I'll always be available. For friendship, at least."

The thought made me sad, somehow. For now, though, it was the only type of relationship that made sense.

That night, I took a bottle of chardonnay to the arbor. I knew it probably wasn't safe to sit up there alone, but it was well worth the risk. The stars were out, and the crickets chirped like a symphony. It was the type of night that made me miss my grandmother.

My grandmother and I had spent countless evenings sitting on the bench overlooking the vineyard. Most nights we'd drink wine, some nights we wouldn't, but we'd always talk. It felt too quiet without her.

Taking a long drink, I looked out over the shadow of the water. The melancholy view matched the thoughts plaguing my mind. My grandfather, as always, hovered at the fringe of everything. He'd been in the hospital for over two weeks, which was much too long.

"I knew I'd find you here," said a gruff voice.

My wine sloshed over the rim and soaked the front of my shirt. While fumbling for my cell, I realized it was Dean, sneaking up on me again. It took a moment for my eyes to adjust, and once they did, I couldn't believe what I was seeing. He was with my grandmother, holding her arm and a flashlight.

"Oma!" I scrambled to my feet. "What are you doing here?"

Before she could answer, I hugged her tight. Everything about her reminded me of home, from the rough texture of her gray hair to the powdery scent of her skin. I was so happy to see her that I was practically bouncing up and down.

"Did you smell the chardonnay all the way from the hospital?" I teased.

My grandmother laughed. The sound was different than before the crash. It was almost bewildered, like she too was surprised to be back home.

"They're planning to move forward with Pappy tomorrow." Dean smiled. "The nurses insisted she come home to rest, and I brought her up here, because this little spitfire thought the best way to rejuvenate was with a little bit of scenery and a whole lot of wine." He handed me the flashlight and an empty glass. "Have at it."

He headed back down the hill before I could thank him.

For the first time in years, the exchange between me and Dean had felt normal. The thought made my chest tighten with emotion. Turning to my grandmother, I gave her a big smile.

"How is Pappy?" I asked.

My grandmother poured herself a glass of wine and settled in on the bench. "Why should I tell you?"

Fiddling with the stem of the glass, I said, "I'm sorry I haven't been there. I've thought about both of you every day. I can't imagine what it must be like."

My grandmother swatted away a mosquito. "Sitting with your grandfather while he is in a coma is like waiting to see if my heart will ever beat on its own again." Since she was tired, her accent was more pronounced than usual. I had to fight to focus on what she was saying and not the things I knew about her. "I have willed my heart to beat, but there are moments I forget to do this, and that's when I remember. It is not up to me."

Beyond the hill, the lighthouse flashed in its particular rhythm, and I swallowed over a lump in my throat. It was obvious my grandmother loved Pappy. So, why had she spent so many years living a lie?

I wondered what would happen if I laid it all on the table. Told her what I'd found and asked to hear her side of the story. The night was beautiful, the stars were out, and I could smell the familiar scent of the Coty face powder she had used since long before I was born. It seemed impossible that her history could be as dark as I'd been thinking.

I took a long sip of wine. The chardonnay was buttery on my tongue, and I finally dared to start asking questions.

"When you first met Pappy, was it love at first sight?"

"Oh, yes." Her voice brightened at the memory. "I thought he was a movie star. I was such a plain girl, selling flowers at the market. He sat in a bierstube with his friends all afternoon. They were American and backpacking through Europe, which I found incredibly romantic and quite bold, given the times. When I stood at the bus stop to go, he came to talk to me. I had ten roses left in my bucket, and he bought every one. Then he gave them to me."

I took another long drink for courage. "Were the flowers from your parents' farm?"

"I sold them for my guardian." Her answer was short. "This is how I earned my keep."

The wine went sour on my tongue. "Was your guardian a family friend?"

He had to have been her first husband.

My grandmother reached down and fumbled around for the bottle of wine. She poured more wine into her glass and ignored my question. "Your grandfather, he asked me to dinner. I knew this would cause trouble. My village was a thirty-minute bus drive away. I was not allowed out after dark, but I went to dinner." Her dark eyes danced as they met mine. "Your grandfather bought me schnitzel. I fell in love."

I wrinkled my nose. "I would have dumped him."

Oma chuckled. "Then I have not taught you well." She patted my knee. "That night, I knew I would be with him for the rest of my life."

Love at first sight. Could that be the reason she'd taken such an incredible risk? Or had she seen him as a way out of what had to have been a bad situation?

"How did you know?" I asked.

"I saw in him my future. The winery, your father. That when he left Germany, I would leave with him."

I looked down at my wine. In the low light of the moon, the cool liquid glistened.

Tell her. Tell her what you found.

Turning to her, I opened my mouth to speak, but my stutter stopped me. Frustrated, I took a breath and tried one of the bypassing techniques I'd learned. That didn't work either. The words refused to come.

"You're struggling." Oma rested her hand on mine. "My dear, I know a little about love. Here's my advice: if you would give him your last drink of wine when there is no more to spare, he is the one you have been looking for." She clinked her glass to mine. "To true love. May it find you, just as it found me."

The conversation my grandmother thought we were having was so different from the conversation I wanted to have, but at the same time, I was happy the words wouldn't come. She'd been through so much. It allowed me one more night of pretending things could stay the same.

Maybe that wouldn't last long, if the day of reckoning truly had come. But at the moment, I didn't want to force the truth. I wanted to pour the wine and enjoy the bit of happiness we still had left, because time kept marching on, and tomorrow, this night would be nothing but a memory.

Chapter Twenty-Five

I bolted awake from a dead sleep at the sound of pounding on my door. It was dark outside, and I stared at the ceiling, a dull headache fogging my brain. I'd stayed in the arbor with my grandmother until well after ten. Then we'd headed to the tasting room, opened a bottle of red, and continued sharing memories about Pappy.

My grandmother had spent a lot of time talking about the vineyard. The way they'd built it up from nothing, battling everything from vine rot to tax legislation and worker shortages along the way. I had told her about the struggles Upper Mitten was having and how they had taken it out on us.

"We will help them," she'd said.

I must not have explained it properly.

"Oma, no. They're awful." I'd shuddered. "They deserve—"

Her wrinkled hand had slapped mine. "No one deserves to suffer. If we can do good in this world, we must. We will find a way to help them."

The topic had soon been lost in a story of the first year at the vineyard. With her dry delivery, she'd had me laughing hysterically at a terrible tale about drought, pests, and the time Pappy had ripped the vines out of the ground, declaring they would plant corn instead.

"I said, 'Fine, we will use it to make whiskey,'" she'd joked, opening another bottle.

It had been one of the best nights I'd had in ages.

The pounding on the door started again. After leaping out of bed, I stumbled for the front door.

"Who is it?" I called, resting my hand against my head.

"Me." Dean's voice was ragged. "Open the door."

I looked at the clock on the wall, completely confused. It was four o'clock in the morning. It wasn't harvest, and unless we'd been hit with another robbery, I couldn't begin to imagine what he was doing here.

The chain rattled as I threw open the door. "Dean, do you know what—"

"Pappy's bleeding on the brain." His face was tight. "They're doing immediate emergency surgery. Dad already picked up Oma. I'm in charge of you."

"That's impossible." I gripped the edge of the door. "You said tomorrow was—"

"Abby." My brother's face was lined with such raw pain that I knew it was not only possible, but that it could be the end. "Get dressed."

"Okay," I said. "But he is going to be fine. It's good that they caught it. They'll fix it, and he'll be better than he was before."

My hands would not stop shaking. I pulled on khaki shorts, a branded Polo shirt, and sneakers while saying a silent prayer for Pappy to pull through. Dean took one look at my outfit and went back to my room to grab a sweatshirt.

"Take this." His voice was gentle. "It's cold in there."

Darkness loomed over the vines. We started to walk up the path in silence, the ruts uneven under my feet. The memory of the hospital flashed through my brain, and I stopped.

"I have to go back to the house."

"Not a chance." Dean blocked the path. "You are coming if I have to physically pick you up and carry you to the truck."

Too numb to argue, I said, "I just need to get one thing. Please."

Dean stared me down. Finally, he moved aside.

Back inside, my house felt safe, warm, and familiar. I wondered what would happen if I locked the front door, crawled back into bed, and pulled the sheets over my eyes. I already knew the answer: my brother would break the window.

"Let's go," he shouted. "Right now!"

Rushing to the top drawer of my dresser, I pulled out the box Braden had given me. Taking out the stethoscope, I tucked it into the pocket of my shorts and headed back out to the field.

It was so early the birds hadn't even started to sing. My mouth tasted like old wine. I hoped Dean didn't ask what I'd gone back for, because I wasn't about to tell him. Even I didn't believe a stethoscope would make a difference when I tried to walk back through the hospital doors.

Dean drove much too fast. The one time I let my eyes to drift to the speedometer, it read eighty. I wondered if it was fear of not getting to Pappy in time or if he always drove like that, like someone was chasing him in the night.

We rode in silence. There were few cars, and I stared blankly at the woods, hoping a deer wouldn't dart out in front of us.

I put my hand against my forehead, remembering my grandmother the night before. She'd sat on a barstool, her head thrown back in laughter at the memory of my grandfather on their wedding night. The silver fillings in her molars had flashed, and for a moment, she'd looked so young. The picture of her as a girl at the vineyard blurred through my mind like the scenery that sped past outside the window, and I sat up straight.

Dean glanced over. "You okay?"

The world seemed to spin and whirl in front of me. I let out some sort of a grunt and gripped at the door handle.

"Abby?" He had one eye on the road and the other on me.

"Can you pull over?" I managed to say. "I think I'm going to throw up."

~

Twenty minutes later, we stood at the front doors of the hospital. The wooden bar across the handle resembled a barricade, warning me to stay out. I stood on the sidewalk, chewing my lip like a piece of bubblegum.

Dean pushed past me and opened the doors. He must have realized I was no longer next to him, because he turned. "We've got ten minutes until the surgery. Come on."

I dug my hand deep into my shorts and gripped the cool disc of the stethoscope. Even though every part of my body was shaking, I managed to walk through the double doors. This time, the gift shop was dark.

Somehow, my legs carried me to the elevator. It was small and the door a faded yellow. The gears cranked as it crept down to us.

Dean put his hand on my back. "Hang tough." His voice was gentle. "You're going even if I have to drag you."

Thanks to my brother, I made it up to Pappy's room. I expected a flurry of activity from the hospital staff, but the room was silent. For a split second, I wondered if this was a cruel trick designed to get me there until I realized my family stood at the bed, praying over him.

He was asleep, his head thrown back. His skin was waxy and pale, which I'd never seen, since he had spent his life in the sun. He also looked thin in the patterned white hospital gown, and the muscles in his arms seemed depleted.

Dean led me to the bed, and we knelt down with the rest of the family. My mother gripped my hand, tears streaming down her face. I closed my eyes and took deep breaths, trying to stay calm.

There was a sudden sound as a flurry of hospital attendants blew into the room. My father got to his feet. A nurse in green scrubs put her hand on his shoulder.

"We need to take him."

My mother started to cry. She kissed Pappy's bandaged hands, and my grandmother did the same. I hung back, feeling like an outsider, and they started to roll him out of the room.

"Wait," I tried to cry, but the words wouldn't come.

Dean grabbed the bed. "Hold on. Abby?"

I made my way to my grandfather and kissed him on the cheek. "I love you," I managed to say, stuttering each word through my tears.

My grandmother squeezed my hand. Then I rushed out of the room, down the stairs, and back outside. The sky was patchy with the start of dawn.

Climbing up into the cab, I clenched my fists tightly together and took in several short breaths. Memories of Pappy rushed through my head. I focused on the first time we'd ever shared a glass of wine.

It had been a few days after my eighteenth birthday, and I had just finished working my shift in the tasting room. The night had been quiet, other than the cicadas settling in the cool evening air and the gravel in the parking lot crunching under my feet. Pappy had burst down the path from the main cellar, clutching a white container in his hand. His eyes were bright and his teeth purple, which meant he'd been tapping the barrels to see where they were at in the aging process.

"Where's that genius son of mine?" he'd shouted at me. "Have you seen him?"

"Not since breakfast," I'd called.

Pappy had started to turn back, but then he'd stopped and squinted at me. "You know what? You'll do. Come here."

Next thing I knew, my grandfather and I were sitting on the steps outside of the tasting room with two glasses. By some miracle, not one of our workers or family members came by, so I got to sit and listen to a private lecture on the aging process while drinking my very first glass of merlot. When Pappy had stopped talking, I'd begged him to keep going and to pour me another.

"I can tell you're my granddaughter," he'd said, and the pride in his voice had been unmistakable.

The memory made me burst into loud, painful sobs that echoed across the interior of the cab. I cried until there were no tears or tissues left, and I had to wipe my nose on my sleeve like a child. Exhausted, I rested my head against the window and fell asleep.

~

A few hours later, Dean brought out pizza slices and bottles of water. He climbed into the driver's seat and handed me a paper plate. "Breakfast of champions."

"Thanks."

I downed the bottle of water, and we ate in silence.

"He's still in surgery." Dean popped his crust in his mouth. "Do you want to go back?"

"Inside? No."

"I mean, do you want to go home? I'll take you."

I dragged my finger through an orange streak of grease on the plate. "Do you ever think about it?" I asked. "The time I got sick?"

Dean wadded up his paper plate. "I spent ten years of my life trying not to think about it." He glanced at me. "I don't remember too much. The beginning, sure. But once you went back into the hospital for pneumonia, Mom and Dad started telling Phillip and me that it could be the end. It was too much. I had a drink every time I came to visit."

My eyes widened. "You were thirteen."

"I was terrified." The muscle in his jaw pulsed. "No one knew. Not even you."

When I was in the hospital, Dean had always brought a quick joke or a smile. I never would have made it without him. It was a shock, though, to realize that support had cost him so much.

"The fact that you were always there meant everything to me." I squeezed my water bottle so hard the plastic made a popping sound. "The times you weren't, I pretended . . ."

His eyes met mine when I paused. "What?"

There was no point in bringing up the charm. How I'd used to pretend it was him, those last few days, watching over me.

"Nothing."

He popped open a Coke and offered it to me first. I shook my head, and he took a drink.

"I messed up," he finally said. "I know that. There's nothing I can do to change it."

The meeting with Henry haunted me. I couldn't believe I'd tried to turn my brother in.

"I've messed up too." I looked at him. "When it came to you."

He looked away. "Yeah?"

"Yeah."

I grabbed our trash and got out of the truck. There was a green garbage can by the sidewalk. I stuffed our paper plates on top of coffee cups and old newspapers. After taking one last look at the hospital, I headed back to the truck.

"Thank you for bringing me here." I climbed back in. "Most of all, thank you for taking me home."

Dean fired up the truck, and we roared out of the parking lot. The hospital hovered in the rearview mirror until it faded into a blur.

Chapter Twenty-Six

Once Dean and I made it back to the vineyard, we worked in silence in my office. He reviewed financial information using my computer while I finalized details for our role in the wine festival. It would have been a strangely peaceful morning with my brother, if it hadn't been for the silent fear that hovered over us.

My phone rang. "Dad." Immediately, I put him on speaker. "Dad, hi."

"Hi, honey." I glanced at Dean, unsure from our father's tone whether things were good or bad. Then he started to chuckle. "Pappy's awake!"

Dean's relief mirrored my own. "Dad, that's so great," he said. "How's he doing?"

"Well . . ." My father laughed. "He's in ICU, and he might have to stay there, because he winked at a nurse, and your grandmother might kill him."

I burst out laughing. Dean scooped me up in his arms, cheering, and we danced around the office in glee. Rogers must have been in the building, because he rushed in at the noise and came to a dead halt. I could tell he was shocked to see me celebrating with Dean.

"It's about my grandfather." I waved him over for a hug. "They did surgery, and he's in the ICU, but he's fine. He's going to be fine, right, Dad?"

"He has a long way to go." My father sounded cautious but downright jubilant, if the combination were possible. "But yes. The doctors anticipate a full recovery."

I hugged Rogers, who responded in his typical stiff-armed fashion.

"That is such great news, Dad." Dean fist pumped the air. "Keep us posted."

Dean and I beamed at each other when I hung up. Then I jumped up and down again.

"I knew he'd pull through."

Turning to Rogers, Dean held up his hand. Even though it clearly pained him, Rogers gave my brother a high five. Rogers then caught my eye and murmured, "Do you have a minute?"

"Business or personal?" I pulled sparkling wine glasses from the cupboard and set them on the table.

Rogers straightened his cuffs. "Business, of course."

"Sure, grab a seat." I poured three full glasses. Sliding one to Rogers, I said, "Dean, get over here. Let's toast first."

Dean stopped. "Shoot." He fumbled for his phone. "I've got to get this. Go ahead. I don't know how long this will take."

The office door clanked shut behind him, and I held up my glass, beaming. "To Pappy."

"To Pappy," Rogers echoed. "I knew he'd pull through."

I updated him on the night with my grandmother and the sudden trip to the hospital. My mood was as bright as the bubbles fizzing up the glass. It took me a few moments, but I finally noticed Rogers was not nearly as happy.

"What is it?" I asked. "What did you want to talk about?"

Rogers set his empty glass next to Dean's full one. It looked like my brother was not going to make it back for a while, so I divided it up between me and Rogers.

"I don't know how to say this . . ."

"Go ahead." I air toasted him. "Nothing can upset me today."

"I've heard rumors of big purchases." His dark eyes were full of disapproval. "From members of our staff."

"Oh." I was confused. "What, you think we're paying them too much?"

Rogers just looked at me. Then I got it.

The ice wine. The inventory. The theft.

"Who?" My tone went flat. "And what?"

"Billy the bartender has purchased a very new and very fancy truck." Rogers ticked it off on his fingers. "Our cook and gardener recently put a down payment on a house on a lake, and Raoul is planning to ask for three months off after harvest. He and his wife are taking a trip around the world. A cruise, I believe."

My mouth fell open. "You're kidding."

"Unfortunately, I am not." Rogers cleared his throat. "Your family has been generous with the hourly wage. That said, *I* don't own a BMW."

My eyes fell on the picture window in my office. It looked dingy in the early-morning light. Getting to my feet, I pulled out a container of Windex and cleaned it with a fury, the smell of ammonia practically cutting my nostrils.

"So, only four of our twenty-eight employees are acting like they've won the lottery?" I demanded, turning back to Rogers.

His forehead furrowed with displeasure. "Four is not enough?"

I wadded up the dirty paper towel and tossed it in the trash. "Thank you for telling me. I'll pass the information along. Actually, we might be dealing with five." In a low tone, I told him about Jessica's diamond pendant and how she'd acted so strange about it.

"Now that you mention it . . ." Rogers furrowed his brow.

"What?" I pressed.

"Billy and Jessica have been spending time together." His voice carried a heavy weight of disapproval. "She's gotten into the habit of showing up after her shift and joining him for a glass of wine before he closes out for the night."

My eyes widened. "Do you think he bought her the necklace?"

He adjusted his shirt sleeves. "It is a little suspect, as cubic zirconia is closer to Billy's price range."

I felt guilty for talking like this. "Is that fair? Maybe . . ."

"Fair? Up until two weeks ago, Billy drove a car with a muffler falling off and lived on his friend's couch. The first week of the season, he had to borrow a pair of khaki shorts to meet uniform." Rogers raised an eyebrow. "I don't find it judgmental to say it would be quite odd for him to have the means to gift a diamond necklace. Especially considering he just bought a truck."

Perhaps Jessica's story was true and the gift was from her parents. I didn't want to blame Billy.

"He seems like such a nice guy," I mumbled. "I hate thinking this way."

"I do as well. It's simply something to be aware of." Rogers gave a weighty sigh and walked to the door. There, he paused. "It seemed you and Dean were getting along quite nicely. Was it the news about your grandfather?"

"We've come to an understanding."

The admission made me feel guilty somehow. Probably because I'd spent so much time complaining about him.

"It's fine," I said. "I promise." Sitting back down at the table, I reached for my phone. "I'm going to share the information you gave me with Henry. About the fact that everyone around here suddenly seems to be rolling in it."

Rogers shook his head. "I'm not sure that's a good idea."

"Why?" I demanded. "It's worth looking into."

He hesitated. "I don't want the staff to feel uncomfortable. Tensions are already high. This could only add to it."

The words were true. On the other hand . . .

"I get that," I said. "But I really do think we need to look at everything right now."

Rogers sighed. Finally, he nodded. "I guess it's better to be safe than sorry."

❧

Henry's response was pragmatic. "So what? Every single one of these people could have saved their pennies."

"Come on." I leaned against the desk. "They all happened to save their pennies at once?"

Rogers winced. Pointing at his watch, he indicated he had somewhere to be and headed out.

"Send me their work history and pay stubs," Henry said. "We'll look into it. Hey, how's your grandfather?" At the update, he let out a pleased grunt. "Good. I'll look forward to issuing him a citation for reckless flying as soon as humanly possible."

Dean returned to the office ten minutes later, drinking a Coke. I updated him, and he straddled a chair.

"I'm with the big chief on that one. We can't fault people for buying new stuff. Billy could have saved for that thing for years."

"That's what Henry said."

"Guess he's my soul mate."

I smiled. It had been a while since I'd been around Dean's sense of humor. I'd missed it.

After bundling up some paperwork for the festival, I placed it in a folder. "I'm going to have Jessica take this downtown. I don't think I can look at anyone in the chamber of commerce right now." I pointed at the Coke can. "Please don't spill that on my computer."

Dean scoffed. "Says the girl who drinks wine right next to the keyboard."

We grinned at each other.

This new relationship between us was tentative but fun. We'd missed out on so many years together, but now I could imagine what it might be like to have my brother back. For the first time, I hoped he planned to stick around.

Chapter Twenty-Seven

There was plenty of work to do in preparation for the wine festival, so it ended up being another late night.

Once I finally wrapped it up, I noticed the lights were on in the tasting room and went to investigate. A small group of staff members was in there, drinking, which was nice to see.

The tradition had been started by my grandparents. They were of the mind-set that anyone who worked for us should have the right to get to know our products at their leisure. At any given moment, one of our workers could end up sharing a drink with Pappy or my grandmother, which seemed to make everyone happy.

Our security officer was stationed in the tasting room at night when he was not out patrolling the grounds, so it wasn't a security issue. However, given recent events, I couldn't help but wonder what message the open bar policy gave to our workers. Maybe that inclusive mind-set gave the impression that our wine was there for the taking.

It was a topic I planned to discuss with my father, but I'd have to tread lightly. Even though he never hung out with the staff, he was not one for bucking tradition. Plus, it would be a hard rule to change unless we offered an equally attractive alternative.

"Hello, boss," Billy called, and I headed over. He sat with the small group at the bar, which was a departure from his typical role behind it.

There was a girl sitting by Billy, and I could have sworn he'd had his hand on her back, but he dropped it as I walked over. The girl turned. It was Jessica. Seeing her with Billy brought me right back to the conversation Rogers and I had had, about whether or not Billy might have bought her the necklace.

And where he would have gotten the money to do that.

Stop.

The voice in my head was firm. It wasn't fair to put Jessica on a list of suspects because she wore a nice necklace. Or because she was interested in Billy, who made a career out of being personable and charming.

"Hi, guys." I gave everyone a half wave. "How's everyone holding up?"

"Excellent." Billy grinned at me. "Phillip is going to bring us in a sample of the new cabernet sauvignon. *We* couldn't care less, but he's all excited about it."

My mouth dropped open. "I can't believe he didn't call me."

The cabernet was our next wine in line for bottling. It had aged for three years, and right before the anniversary party, we had practically begged our father to let us see where it was at. Phillip had first dibs on sampling the wines because he'd started as a vintner before moving over to finance, so it made sense he got to try it first, but I was surprised he hadn't called.

I perched on the barstool next to everyone and got caught up in a debate about the benefits of organic vegetables versus regular ones. Jessica's family owned an organic farm in the lower part of the state, and some of our workers were strong believers. However, Billy still had to be convinced.

"I think it's a bunch of bunk," he said. "A piece of lettuce is a piece of lettuce. I want to stay as far away from it as possible regardless of what kind of fertilizer it's grown in."

Jessica slugged him, and everyone laughed.

Phillip arrived then, carrying a plastic container full of wine and chatting with Rogers. When he spotted me, a grin broke across his face. "Wow, that was quick. I just texted you."

My phone buzzed in my pocket at that very moment, and I felt relieved. I didn't like the idea that Phillip could have left me out of something so important.

Rogers stepped behind the bar and pulled out seven glasses, then joined the group as Phillip poured a small sample for each of the staff members. Everyone reached for it eagerly. Then Phillip poured samples for me and him, leaving plenty of extra in the jug.

"Speech," Billy cried. "Speech!"

Phillip thought for a moment, his eyes scrunched up behind his glasses. "Benjamin Franklin said, 'In wine there is wisdom, in beer there is freedom, in water there is bacteria.' At least, Mr. Ben said that on our social media."

I laughed. Half of the quotes my mother put on our social media were from the internet and, most likely, misattributed. We teased her about it all the time.

Everyone raised their glasses and toasted. Then we all put our noses in the glass, inhaled the rich cherry and blackberry aromas of the young cabernet, and slowly took a drink. The crop from a few years back had been particularly promising, and the wine did not disappoint. It practically burst in my mouth and gave a grand, almost vanilla-laced finish.

Rogers and I looked at each other. He raised his eyebrows, and I could practically read his mind. *One of our best ever.*

Jon, a seasoned field hand, let out a low whistle. "I'm taking credit. I'm sure I was on cabernet duty for this."

"I take no credit," Billy sang. "But I'll drink it."

Jessica laughed uproariously and even touched his arm.

The scent of fresh berries was ripe in the air, and I could see Phillip was about to dole out additional samples, when Dean came storming into the tasting room.

"I need to talk to you two." He pointed at me and Phillip, ignoring everyone else. He slammed into the conference room without a word.

The rudeness surprised me, but I had a feeling it was deliberate. Clearly, Dean felt we were a little too accommodating with our staff.

"The king has spoken," Phillip teased, heading out from behind the bar. He hesitated, and I could tell he was tempted to leave the plastic jug on the counter for everyone to finish off, but he changed his mind and grabbed it.

As I got up, I noticed Billy and Jessica exchange glances. I didn't know if it was about the wine, the way Dean had acted, or their secret relationship, but something about it felt off. Their budding relationship was definitely something I wanted to discuss with Rogers.

"Any idea what this is all about?" Phillip asked as we walked over to the room. He glanced at his watch. "I have to get back to the family, or Kate's going to disown me."

"I hope it's nothing, but it seems like every time we turn around, it's something."

We walked in to find Dean camped out at the conference room table.

"Cat's out of the bag," he said.

Holding up his phone, he displayed a headline from the local paper's website.

Harrington Wines Heist in the Hundreds of Thousands

"No," I breathed.

The article was online and would run in the print edition in the morning. The odds were good people had already caught wind of it. That meant a lot of unwanted attention, but it also meant my grandmother would find out. She was pretty sequestered, but all it would take was one well-meaning nurse expressing condolences or looking for gossip, and she would find out the terrible, awful truth.

"Did you text Dad?" I asked.

Dean nodded. "He's trying to decide whether or not we should tell Oma or roll the dice."

Phillip grabbed wineglasses from the shelf by the sink, shaking his head. "We can't tell her. It would set off her heart condition."

I still couldn't believe our parents had lied to Phillip about that. Dean must have felt the same, because he glanced at me. For whatever reason, it struck us as funny at the same time, and we burst out laughing.

Disbelief colored Phillip's face. "What on earth is funny about that?"

I tried to answer but only succeeded in laughing harder, which made Dean let out a series of loud snorts.

"Are you guys being serious right now?" Phillip looked down at his uniform. "Kate keeps telling me I need to replace these shorts. Is it my . . ." He felt his zipper with a concerned expression, and Dean and I just lost it.

Dean laughed so hard he hit the table with his hand again and again. Just watching him made me giggle even harder. Phillip gaped at the two of us. Every time I tried to stop laughing, I would look over at Dean, and he would mimic Phillip checking his fly, and we would both lose it all over again.

Phillip finally started to get annoyed, which was a funny sight in itself, since he never lost his cool. But once he started pacing and glaring, Dean and I pulled it together.

"I'm sorry, man," Dean said. "It's been that kind of day. Look, Oma doesn't have—"

I widened my eyes at him. It was one thing to regress to the days when we'd ganged up on Phillip but quite another to admit our parents had lied to him because they thought he couldn't keep a secret. Thank goodness, Dean got the message.

"Oma doesn't need to hear it from us," Dean finished. "It'll get to her soon enough."

Phillip nodded. "Exactly." He plopped down at the table and held up the jug of cabernet. "There's only one way to deal with this mess. Drink."

"Is that from the barrels?" Dean asked, interested. He pulled the container close and took a deep breath. "I can't do it. I've been eating zinc all day, because I thought I was getting a cold, so I won't be able to taste it."

"I would pretend to be sorry about that." Phillip topped off two glasses. "However, it means more for me and Abby." He raised his eyebrows. "Let's drink. Quickly, though. I've got to be back home by ten."

~

The three of us hung out in the main office until Phillip had to leave. It was the first time we had hung out together in nearly two decades, and no one wanted it to end. We swapped stories about childhood, our parents, and even confessed to when we'd taken our first drink.

"Seventeen," I said. "That summer I worked in the tasting room for the first time. I sneaked some of the riesling."

"Thirteen." Dean ran his hands through his dark hair. "I thought wine tasted like moldy prunes. I stuck to cider for a long time after that."

We turned to Phillip. He grinned like a carved pumpkin, his teeth purple from the wine. He finished off his sample glass and set it down with a bang.

"Eight." There was a note of triumph in his voice.

"Eight!" I grabbed the arms of the chair. "That's not true. That's way too young."

"Yeah, I call bullshit," Dean scoffed. "I was the one with the addiction problem. What are you talking about, eight?"

Phillip shrugged his lanky shoulders. "Pappy had a glass of red on the table in the library, and I thought it was grape juice. I knew my mistake the second I tried it but kept going because it was so darn good. I puked three hours later, and Mom thought I had the flu."

I shook my head, baffled. "You think you know a person."

"I also have a tattoo that says wild man."

My mouth dropped open.

"Are you serious?" Dean demanded. "I think we need to see that."

Phillip got to his feet. "You guys will fall for anything. I had my first drink when I was eighteen, you morons. And you can see my tattoo when you kiss my ass." Tapping his watch, he sang, "Good night."

"'Night, Phillip," I called.

"Wild man," Dean repeated, when he'd left the room.

Once again, we looked at each other and burst out laughing. This time, I laughed until I cried.

~

Back at home, the silence in my house made me feel lonely, so I decided to work. It was for the best—my email backlog went for days.

My fingers clacked against the keyboard, and the silence became peaceful. I made a cup of cinnamon tea and opened the window by the kitchen table. Moths attacked the screen with such a vengeance I could hear the pulsing flutter of their wings.

The emails were mostly typical, with questions about our products, tour requests, and queries from would-be brides about booking the vineyard for a wedding. Then I landed on one that was somewhat unusual.

> Thank you so much for taking time to read this. I
> am a local artist, and I've started a business creat-
> ing sculptures out of old bottles. I know it's a long

shot, but if your vineyard has any extra bottles that you're planning on recycling, could I have them instead? I would offer to pay, except I am the epitome of the starving artist—ha ha. Thank you for your consideration, and I look forward to hearing from you. Sadie

Out of curiosity, I clicked through to the girl's Etsy page to see her work. The sculptures were beautiful, elaborate creations where metal design work framed and showcased the wine bottle it encompassed.

The recycling comment made it clear the girl had done her research. Recycle pickup was the next morning, so we would have a ton of bottles to donate. It was just a matter of sorting them out of the bin, which sounded like a good way to get some fresh air before tackling the emails that still remained.

Grabbing my keys, I stepped out into the summer night. The vines looked like etched silver in the moonlight. The crickets chirped as I walked down the path, listening to the crunch of my feet against the dirt.

I heard the telltale clink of bottles being moved to recycling behind the tasting room. Rogers was probably doing last-minute cleanup. Sure enough, when I crept around the corner, he was still hard at work, loading the recycling into the back of one of our utility trucks.

I tapped him on the shoulder. "Surprise."

He let out a shout and whirled on me like a ninja. I barely jumped back in time to miss his swing, and then I burst out laughing. Even though it shouldn't have been, it was pretty entertaining to see him panic.

"I didn't know you were scared of the dark," I teased.

He straightened his shirt, his ears flushed under the outdoor lights. "I'm simply prepared to protect myself, given recent events."

I laughed, trying to imagine Rogers taking down a criminal.

He brushed off his hands. "I thought you called it a night."

I told him about the email from the artist seeking bottles. Rogers-style, he looked slightly irritated. "So, we are simply going to *give* this woman bottles to use for financial gain?"

"It's not like we weren't going to throw them away. Besides, it will be good advertising." The truck was nearly loaded, and I gave him an apologetic look. "I'm sorry you did all this work just to have me pull everything off."

"No rest for the weary." He sighed. "Where would you me like to store her bounty?"

"I'll help. It's a beautiful night, and my house was a little too quiet."

Hopping into the truck, I considered the assortment of items to be recycled. Rogers had broken down boxes, so there was a pile of cardboard neatly arranged on the left. Then there was the collection of general items, neatly sorted into bins. The bottles were off to the right, stacked in the remaining boxes.

"Let's do ten boxes," I decided. "She'll have enough bottles for the rest of her life. Can I pass them down to you?"

He nodded, and I grabbed one closest to the end of the truck. "Geez." I almost dropped it, surprised at its weight. "I am out of shape," I admitted. "These things are heavy."

"It's how I keep my girlish figure," Rogers joked.

The next few boxes were lighter, which was a relief. We were seven boxes deep when it hit me that if we were going to use this for advertising potential, I should give her a decent variety. Of course, that meant more sorting.

It was getting late, and I felt guilty keeping Rogers there.

"You really don't have to help with this." I knelt down on the hard aluminum of the truck bed. "I'm going to sort through to make sure I get her some pinot noir bottles, and I love the label on the cab—"

The words died on my lips. Beneath a stack of empty bottles sat a neat line of full bottles that were still unopened.

"Rogers," I breathed. "Look at this."

He hoisted himself into the truck bed. As he looked into the box, his eyebrows shot up. "That's how they're doing it," he muttered. "This is how they're stealing our inventory." He looked back toward the tasting room as though the guilty party might still be in there.

"No." I didn't want to believe it, based on one box. "Maybe this was an accident."

I dug through a couple more. There were only empty bottles, and I started to feel better. Then I remembered the weight of the first box I'd unloaded.

I hopped out of the truck and found it. Sure enough, it had six full bottles covered by a collection of empties.

"It's the perfect plan." My voice was dull. "The wine is just sitting by the road waiting for recycling. Whoever's doing it picks it up in the middle of the night. I can't believe we've been so stupid."

Rogers looked so angry steam practically rose from his perfectly pressed shirt. "The patrol car is on-site because of the hate mail," he said. "Let's stake him out at the end of the driveway. The thief will come to collect the bottles, and that will be that."

The thought that this could soon be over gave me a rush of adrenaline. As much as it hurt me to think that someone on staff was stealing from us, it was no longer possible to dispute. Now I could hardly wait to find out who it was.

"Let's get 'em," I said and picked up my phone.

~

I was practically giddy at the thought of putting an end to all of this and wanted to wait at the entryway of the vineyard myself. Both Rogers and the plainclothes officer talked me out of it.

"That's irresponsible and dangerous," Rogers said, as the radio crackled with various reports from the open windows of the police car. "I have no doubt a confrontation like that would be the end of you."

"You have little faith in *my* ninja skills?" Neither Rogers nor the officer smiled, and I rolled my eyes. Swatting away mosquitoes, I said, "Fine. But if you catch someone, please let me talk to them before you take them in."

"No promises." The officer nodded at me. "But I'll see what I can do."

Rogers and I watched as the officer drove down the driveway without headlights. He planned to park near the entryway behind a cluster of trees. I squeezed my hands in anticipation.

"You okay?" Rogers asked.

"Thrilled." I rubbed my hands over my upper arms. They had goose bumps in the cool summer night. "We're going to get them. The thing that sucks is that this proves it's someone here, and that really bothers me."

"I agree." Rogers looked pale in the light of the moon. It was low over the fields and made the vines look strange and twisted. "However, you never know why people do the things they do."

"I don't care." My fists clenched. "I'm not planning on being empathetic."

"However, you should plan to be safe," he warned. "Don't go down and try to interfere—"

"I won't," I insisted.

He raised an eyebrow. "However, do let me know what happens."

I walked back to my house, wondering where we'd gone so wrong. Unlocking my door, I logged on to my computer to email Sadie, the girl from Etsy, about the stash of bottles.

> Hi Sadie, Your work is beautiful! We'd be happy to share with you. There are plenty in recycling today, so you'll be able to take as much as you want. Come to the tasting room and ask for me, and I'll get you set up. Cheers, Abby

I lay down on the couch with a blanket and the television remote control, determined to be ready to bolt out the door the second the thief was caught. Eventually, I drifted off to sleep.

The officer called at six thirty the next morning.

"I've got her."

Chapter Twenty-Eight

I jumped off the couch and raced for the Dodge. The sun had just started to rise, and a deceptively calm hue rested over the vineyard. Dust kicked up in the rearview mirror as I floored the truck down the drive, a thousand different thoughts running through my head.

The main thought was, *Which worker had been stealing from us?*

When Officer Williams had called, I'd been half-asleep. Now I couldn't believe I hadn't asked for her name.

We only had about ten women who worked for us. The only one I could imagine stealing from us was, unfortunately, Jessica. I had my fingers crossed tight that she and Billy were also the ones who had taken the ice wine and that it would be a quick recovery.

Officer Williams waited at the bottom of the drive. A lone figure sat in the back seat of his car, but I couldn't see her face in the dim light. I jumped out, slammed the door of the truck, and steeled myself. When I got to the rear of the car, I stopped short.

I'd never seen the girl before in my life. She was a petite blonde in her early twenties with pink streaks in her hair, piercings covering each earlobe, and wide blue eyes rimmed in red. She looked tearful but baffled, like she couldn't believe she'd gotten herself into this situation.

I felt a flash of pity but quickly fought it back. She had to be someone's girlfriend, and they'd sent her to do their dirty work. Leaning my head into the window, I glared.

"You know, my grandparents started this place with nothing." My voice shook with anger, but there was no chance I was going to stutter. There was too much I wanted to say. "They built it from scratch and, with hard work, made it what it is today. The thing that makes me sick is that you think it's okay to tear down what other people worked so hard to create, to take something that isn't yours. I'm glad you got caught, and yes, I can guarantee we're going to press charges."

The girl's eyes filled with fresh tears. "I wasn't stealing! Abby told me I could take them."

How dumb was this girl, using my name?

"You're looking at Abby," I said. "So, nice try, but I've never seen you before in my life."

"We emailed," she cried. "You told me you had bottles for me in recycling."

I froze. "What?"

This couldn't be . . .

"I make sculptures using bottles?" she pleaded. "You said you had boxes I could use for my art projects. I thought you meant to just grab them before the recycling trucks did."

It was Sadie, the girl from Etsy. She had completely misread my email, and now we had the wrong person in a squad car.

"I'm so sorry," I managed to say. "I think there's been some miscommunication."

Officer Williams had sat in silence up until this point. Now he glanced at me in the rearview mirror. "Everything okay?"

I rested my hands against the edge of the car-door window. There had been several moments in my life when I'd felt foolish, but this one took the cake.

"There's been a mistake," I mumbled. "This is not who we're looking for."

Officer Williams practically leapt out of the front seat to help the poor girl out of the back of the car. I rushed to her side and cringed, noting he'd cuffed her. Once he undid the bracelets, she rubbed her wrists and let out a shaky sob.

"What kind of people are you?" She seemed to stand as tall as her five-foot frame would allow, pink hair wild in the morning breeze. "Do you really arrest anyone who tries to repurpose your trash?"

I wanted to hug her but doubted she would let me. Officer Williams gave me her purse since I was closer to her, so I settled for handing her that. It was a recycled cigar box with a bedazzled dog chain attached.

"I am so, so sorry." I dug my shoes into the gravel drive, trying to ground myself so I didn't stutter. "We've . . . we've had some thefts. You just walked into the wrong place at the wrong time."

Her red-rimmed eyes darted toward her old red sports car as if plotting a getaway. Through the open window, I saw the car had fluffy purple seat covers, a boom box sitting on the front seat, and a collection of cassette tapes. I could imagine her singing to old music on the way here, thinking she was about to score big, only to have one of the worst scares of her life.

"I cannot tell you how sorry I am," I told her. "Please let me make it up to you. I really do have tons of boxes of bottles for you, but they're up at the tasting room. Let's get you those and send you downtown for a nice breakfast. And we'll get you a case of wine."

Sadie's face lit up. "Really? That's cool." She looked around, rubbing her wrists. "This was wild. I wonder if any of my friends drove by. They'll know my car. I'm going to get some questions."

I looked out at the road. Since we were located at the beginning of the peninsula, a consistent amount of traffic passed by in the mornings. Even now, more than one driver looked over at the police lights with curiosity.

"Shit," I breathed.

So much for being discreet. If the person who actually did plan to steal from us had been anywhere near here in the past thirty minutes, our cover was blown. Considering the recycle trucks were due to arrive any minute, the odds were good.

"I bet we missed them," I told Officer Williams.

He took off his hat and wiped his forehead. "I should book her on obstruction of justice," he muttered.

Sadie must have heard, because her eyes widened.

"He's kidding." I patted her on the back. "Follow me up. I've got a ton of good bottles for you, and I'll give you some of our best wine."

I hopped in the truck and headed up the drive.

Chapter Twenty-Nine

Sadie was all smiles by the time we loaded up her car. She was thrilled at the variety of bottles I'd set aside for her, not to mention that I'd decided to give her two cases of free wine. The invitation to have breakfast at Towboat on our account didn't hurt either.

"This was bananas." Her slim hand shook mine. "My first experience in a police car."

I laughed. "Hopefully your last. Again, I'm really sorry."

"Nah, it's okay." She gave me an impish grin, heading for her car. "This will be a story to tell my grandkids, right? I'll bring you by one of the sculptures when it's ready."

"See ya." I waved as she pulled out from behind the building.

Even though the encounter had wreaked havoc on our plan to catch the person stealing our inventory, I liked Sadie. If her art looked half as good as it did in the pictures she had online, I planned to offer to let her sell some in our gift shop. It was the type of unique takeaway our visitors would love.

It was almost nine, time for our weekly staff meeting. I imagined Rogers was already inside, wielding the box of doughnuts he always picked up for the occasion and wondering why I hadn't texted him about what had happened with the recycling. I was just about to head in when Sadie poked her head back around the building.

"I'm blocked in." She looked panicked again. "I can't be on the news. My parents would disown me."

"What are you talking about?" I followed her around the corner of the building, and my mouth dropped open.

Every news crew from Starlight Cove and three counties beyond was parked in front of the tasting room. The cameramen were gathering B-roll as the reporters chatted with one another. I pressed my fingers against the ridge between my eyes.

"Could this day get any worse?" I mumbled.

"You're not the one who started it in handcuffs." Sadie rubbed her wrists. "Seriously. I get stage fright. I can't talk to—"

"They're not here for you." That, I could guarantee. "I'll have them let you out."

Had my mother called a news conference in response to the blog post about the ice wine? I hadn't checked my phone since early this morning but hadn't felt it vibrate either. I waved the news vans aside to help Sadie pull out, then approached the nearest group of reports.

"Hey, guys." I recognized some of them from television and others from the night of the plane crash. "It's been a busy morning. What's going on?"

Gillian G. Smith, the lead reporter on the most popular station in town, gave me a sympathetic look. "We're hoping for a statement."

It wasn't going to be from me. Speaking on camera made me much too nervous. On the night of the crash, the reporters had insisted on talking to someone. I'd had Rogers do it, but I knew he wasn't comfortable with the spotlight either.

"I'm a bit behind this morning," I said. "First, what's this all about?"

I didn't want to blow our cover by mistake. It would be ridiculous to blurt out something about the ice wine only to learn they were here to discuss the wine festival or even a high-profile wedding.

"There was a blog posted about the ice wine." Gillian Smith's eyes lit up. "Is it true the entire collection was stolen?"

I gave her a friendly smile. "Let me make one quick call."

A group of the field hands was filing into the tasting room for the meeting. They gaped at the news trucks before slipping inside. I walked around the back of the building and stood in the shade of the eaves. Pacing back and forth, I called my mother. She answered on the first ring.

"They don't waste any time." She clicked her tongue. "Don't worry—I'm almost there. I was coming in to put out a statement on the wire. Tell them to give me ten minutes. If they can't wait, I'll email them the official statement. That's the best we can do."

Taking in a breath of the morning air, I headed back over to the newscasters. They gathered around, and I passed along the message.

"Now, I do have a staff meeting to get to," I finished. "So, thanks for waiting and—"

Gillian stepped forward. "Real quick. I know this is a delicate topic, but I would like to hear your feelings on the situation."

"I feel bad for my grandparents." Now that I had spoken to my mother, I felt comfortable giving a small sound bite to the reporters. "This vineyard is their life's work, and the ice wine is very special to them. I'm sure they'll want it returned as soon as possible."

"I can only imagine." Gillian's heavily made-up eyes were sympathetic. "But I meant the situation with your brother Dean."

"Dean?" I squinted at her. "What about him?"

The reporters exchanged glances. Walter, the one with a straw hat and an old-school camera around his neck, cleared his throat.

"Dean was brought in for questioning about the theft," he said in his gravelly voice. "Early this morning."

"What?" I whispered.

Walter puffed out his chest, as if pleased to share the story. "Yeah. Someone placed an anonymous tip that he tried to sell the wine. The police apprehended him about a half hour ago, when we were arriving."

My mouth went dry. I had been behind the tasting room with Sadie and missed the whole thing. I couldn't believe Henry hadn't called me before doing something like that.

"Do you have a comment?" Gillian asked.

"Yes. They're making a big mistake," I managed to say, then practically ran to the safety of the tasting room.

~

The staff stood around drinking coffee and eating doughnuts. Rogers was waiting at the bar, the agenda printed out and ready to go. My entire body felt numb as I took my spot next to him, the paper shaking in my hand.

"Who was stealing the bottles?" he murmured. "I drove past but didn't recognize her."

"It's a long story. I—" The words on the agenda blurred in front of my eyes. It was hard to focus on anything because my mind was still trying to process the fact that Dean had been arrested.

"Is it why the news crews are here?" Rogers asked, gesturing at the picture window. Our front lawn was crawling with reporters, and I felt ill.

"No." I wiped my forehead with the back of my hand. "They're here about the ice wine."

He raised an eyebrow. "Shall we tell the staff?"

There was powdered sugar on the bar from doughnuts, and I used the paper to brush it off. "Should we do what?"

He gave me a funny look. "Would you like me to communicate the information to the staff?"

I watched as the news crew waited for my mother. I needed to text her about Dean but could hardly think. The one thought that kept going through my mind was that his arrest was my fault.

I'd made a huge mistake making those accusations to Henry. No matter what anyone said, I knew Dean was not behind the robbery.

"Can you run the meeting?" I asked Rogers, handing him the paper. "I need to make a call. I'll be here for questions at the end."

Ducking my head, I hurried to the office. There was a strange hush in the room, and I wondered if anyone had seen my brother taken away in handcuffs. I also couldn't help but wonder if someone in this room had called him in.

There was no longer a question that someone on-site was stealing inventory. They were probably involved in the ice wine too. Whoever had called in the tip must have figured Dean would serve as a good scapegoat, thanks to his past.

The office was quiet and smelled like cranberries from a scented potpourri plug-in. I yanked it out of the wall and sank into the desk chair. The soft leather cradled me like a hug, and I picked up the phone to call my mother.

"What?" she cried. "I'll call Henry right now."

The line went dead. Just then, blue and red lights pulled up outside the window.

Dean.

They must have realized they'd made a mistake and brought him back.

I leapt to my feet and rushed out of the office. Rogers had been talking about the wine festival, but he came to an abrupt halt as Henry walked in, without my brother. The staff started to murmur.

"Keep talking," I told Rogers, sweeping past him toward Henry. "What is going on?" I demanded in a furious whisper.

Henry's eyes cased the room. My staff put on a good show of listening to Rogers, but I could tell their attention was on us.

Henry leaned in close enough for me to smell the coffee on his breath. "Guess I owe you an apology."

"For what?" I demanded.

"Ignoring your concerns about Dean."

The room seemed to spin around me.

"Henry, no," I insisted. "I was wrong. This is a bullshit tip. He did not do this."

"Someone claimed Dean tried to sell them a case of the ice wine. One of the ones from the early seventies. Our undercover units also saw him at the internet café a few days ago, with a kid who has a rap. This isn't looking good for him."

Random images flashed through my head: Laughing in the clubhouse with Dean when we were little. Playing Monopoly. Hours on the phone while he was trying to get clean. The disgust on my ex-boyfriend's face after he threw the phone across the room. The letter where Dean confessed to taking my charm bracelet. Finally, the hunted look on his face as he told me what had happened the night he was jumped.

Dean had changed. Yes, it had taken me too long to see it, but that was my fault, not his. I wasn't about to let him be accused of something he did not do.

"No," I insisted. "Someone is trying to get you to look in the wrong direction."

Quickly, I surveyed our staff, trying to spot who was capable of doing this.

Raoul sat on a chair sipping a coffee. His cap was pulled low over his eyes, but his tanned face was lined with sympathy. Wendell and his wife sat in the back row, shooting suspicious looks at Henry. Billy was over at the doughnut box getting a refill. He looked like he'd woken up ten minutes ago, with his hair sticking up in ten different directions. Jessica had her hands folded in her lap, but she was wide eyed and watching me. It was impossible to tell who was guilty, if any of them.

Henry cleared his throat. "Either way, we have to hold him while we look into it. I stopped by to let you all know I'm sorry I didn't get to talk to you first."

"My mother's here." I spotted her car roaring up the drive. "Why don't you tell it to her?"

I stalked over to Rogers, who was in the middle of going over plans for the wine festival.

"I need to talk to them," I interrupted. In a low voice, I added, "Someone is trying to pin this on Dean. He was brought in for questioning a few hours ago."

Rogers's mouth dropped open. "Dean was arrested?" His voice boomed across the room.

Several employees exchanged glances, as if they had seen this coming. Rage flashed through me.

Turning to the group, I said, "My brother had nothing to do with this." The words were biting and fast. "So, if I hear of anyone discussing this on social media or with the press, you will be subject to immediate dismissal. Consider this your only warning."

Henry stood by the door, holding his hat. His cool eyes watched our staff, as if he were trying to gauge their reaction.

I glared at him. "Thank you, everyone. That's all."

Stalking off, I slammed the office door as hard as I could. Once safe inside, I fell against the wall and burst into tears. I couldn't believe any of this was real.

Chapter Thirty

The next few hours were some of the worst of my life.

My mother and I hid in the main house by the phone, waiting to hear from Dean. It felt like the old days, back when he was out partying and we were worried he wouldn't make it home alive.

"I can't believe Henry did this." My mother slammed the kitchen cupboard. Turning, she pushed her gold bracelets up her arms and glared at me. "He was at our wedding. What kind of man claims to be a friend and allows something like this to happen?"

"I don't know," I said. "All I know is that it's not Dean's fault."

My mother busied herself with a side of ham and some Swiss cheese. There were dark circles under her eyes that I hadn't noticed earlier. She must have gone to the bathroom to cry at some point, perhaps after the news conference, and smeared her mascara in the process.

Her silence built. Then she stalked over to the fridge, pulled out a jar of pickles, and slammed it on the counter. It was a wonder the jar didn't shatter. Turning to me, she crossed her arms.

"So, you've finally deigned to forgive him?" she demanded.

"What?" I said, surprised.

"You heard me." My mother returned to making lunch, practically throwing food onto our plates. "From the moment he came back, you've treated him like an enemy. Your father said you were barely speaking. Well, I won't tolerate that." She thrust a plate at me. "He's your brother, Abigail. I will not stand for you to . . ."

The words sputtered, and my mother burst into tears. Her shoulders slumped, and she covered her face with her hands. I leapt to my feet and pulled her into a hug.

"It's okay, Mom," I whispered. "He's going to be okay."

Her thin body shook with sobs. "He won't stay here. Not after this."

My face pressed against her shoulder and the silky fabric of her white shirt. I couldn't even count how many times my mother and I had held each other just like this, crying over Dean. She pulled back and turned to the counter, her shoulders trembling.

"He might stay," I tried. "Once this is all over . . ."

"No." She shook her head. "He's not going to stay in a place where people refuse to stop judging him based on his past. I should have known it wouldn't work. I've spent my whole life trying to hang on to him. This time . . ." Her eyes were damp with tears. "For a moment, I really thought I could have him back."

I thought of the dinner Dean and I had shared at the stone cottage, reminiscing about the good old days in the clubhouse.

"Yeah." Reaching out, I touched her hand. "For a second, I thought the same thing."

~

Two hours later, my mother and I were seated in the study, hard at work on our laptops. Work was the only thing we could do to keep from going crazy. The wine festival was that weekend, and there was still plenty that needed to be done.

My mother's phone buzzed. "That must be Henry." Immediately, she put it on speaker.

"Carol? It's Dana Simpson from the chamber of commerce. How are you?"

My mother gave me a disappointed look and kicked her stockinged feet onto the ottoman. "Depends how much time you have. How can I help?"

I darkened my screen and shut my computer. Was the chamber going to kick us out of the wine festival because of the news about Dean? They had done things like that before. The last thing our town liked was a scandal.

"I wanted to reach out before making any big changes," Dana said, "out of respect for the fact that you're the title sponsor of the event."

My jaw clenched, and my mother got to her feet.

"What do you mean, changes?" She brushed her fingers over the family photos lining the mantel of the fireplace.

There was one with Pappy and Dean on his tractor. They both had long pieces of grass sticking out of their mouths. Dean was about ten years old, shirtless, and grinning from ear to ear.

"Upper Mitten winery did not turn their paperwork in on time," Dana continued. "Their booth was going to be next to you, but we now have an extra space. Would you like it, or should we move everything in closer?"

My mother gave me a surprised look.

The opportunity to have additional real estate at the wine festival was a big deal. The lines were always long and the space crowded. There was plenty we could do with additional space, like set up an extra tasting area to make the experience more comfortable for guests.

I was just about to give my mother an enthusiastic nod, when my grandmother's words ran through my head: *No one deserves to suffer.*

"Dana, it's Abby," I said. "Did Upper Mitten want to participate?"

"They were disappointed." I could practically hear her shrug. "Rules are rules, though. If you don't have a tasting permit on file and approved, you can't sample your product."

"What if . . ." I paced the room. "Dana, could we sample their products for them?"

My mother drew back. "What?" she mouthed.

I held up my finger, willing her to hear me out.

"I . . . I suppose." Dana sounded baffled. "Technically, you're allowed to sample whatever you want, so—"

"We'd like to do that," I said, giving my mother a questioning look. She shrugged. "If they'll allow it. Let me contact them, and I'll call you back in thirty."

My mother pressed end. "What was that all about?"

"Oma and I had a long talk the other night. Long story short, she wants to help them out. I'm not convinced they deserve it, but I will say this: The level of anger they had over being left off a wine trail was pretty intense. To me, that indicates they care about their winery. I think they need help and don't know how to ask for it."

A small smile played at the corners of my mother's lips. "I'm impressed, Abby."

"Well, don't be quite yet." I picked up my phone. "They might say something stupid, I'll hang up on them, and then we'll be right back where we started."

I opened my computer and pulled up Upper Mitten's number. After hesitating for only a moment, I called them.

"You want to do *what*?" Landon demanded.

I repeated the offer.

Landon was quiet for so long I thought she'd hung up on me. Then she came back on the line, her voice quiet. "That's . . . that's really cool. Thank you."

"No problem." The relief in her voice made it clear we were doing the right thing. "Drop off some cases tonight, along with sample cards and maybe a gift basket or something to raffle off. Hopefully, this will help get your name out there."

Once we were off the phone, my mother gave me a thumbs-up. "Now can I be impressed?"

I flushed and looked down at my computer. It felt a lot better helping the new winery than begrudging the fact that they were here.

"Let's hope their wine isn't that good," I said. "Because I have to admit, their winery is pretty impressive."

My mother laughed, and we settled back in to work.

~

Henry called a half hour later. Once again, my mother picked up right away.

"I'm hoping you're calling with good news." Her voice was thick with disdain.

If Henry noticed, he didn't acknowledge it. "We've released him. There's no evidence. The whole thing could have been a prank. We do have to keep him on the radar, but I am pretty confident he's not involved."

My mother's eyes met mine. She looked relieved. It hit me that, in spite of our insistence that Dean could not be guilty, it was hard not to question whether history could be repeating itself.

"Where is my son?" she asked.

"He took off." Henry sounded apologetic. "Carol, you know I—"

"You're just doing your job," she said. "But I'm a mother, Henry. So now I have to do mine." With that, she hung up on him.

My mouth dropped open. "Mom. He's the chief of police."

"He'll forgive me. And if he doesn't . . ." She raised an eyebrow. "I'll talk to his wife."

The next call was to Dean, who didn't answer. That wasn't a surprise, but still, my mother looked as pained as she had in the kitchen.

"Give him some time, Mom," I said. "He'll come around."

"Sure." She looked down at her hands. "That's what I've been telling myself for years."

Chapter Thirty-One

The sun had just come up by the time Rogers and I loaded the truck for the wine festival. We planned to close the vineyard for the day, because based on previous experience, we knew anyone interested in wine would spend the day downtown. The security guard and the field workers would remain on-site, but otherwise, our entire staff, including the ones who worked at the restaurant, planned to meet us there.

Rogers gave a disdainful look at the cab of the truck before hoisting himself inside. "This is cruel and unusual."

"The truck or the hour?" I asked.

I was already two espressos deep and nervous about the festival. Typically, it was one of my favorite events because we always bumped into a million people. It was nice after the seclusion of the vineyard, but today I dreaded the inevitable questions about the ice wine and my brother.

No one had heard from him since he'd been released, not even Kelcee. His motorcycle was gone, but his things were still in the guest bedroom. I wondered where he was staying and hoped it wasn't with any of his friends from high school. That could only lead to trouble.

"What's on your mind?" Rogers asked.

The headlights bounced along the highway, and I opened the window to let in the early-morning breeze. "Upper Mitten," I lied. "That's the one thing that is going to make today tolerable."

Their administrative assistant had dropped off several cases of wine, a beautiful gift basket, and an apology. I'd told the assistant we were the ones who were sorry, for not welcoming them into the fold when we should have. Then my mother, Rogers, and I had opened their wine to see what they were all about. Their semidry riesling was pretty impressive, and the others weren't bad.

The shops in Starlight Cove were still dark when we drove into the downtown area, the gas lamps along the sidewalk still flickering in the light of dawn. The buildings passed by in a pastel blur as we drove through town and into the roped-off parking section near the main park by the water. It was already crowded, and we immediately found ourselves greeting old friends.

By the time the tent, portable fridge, and sampling items were set up, the air was fragrant with exhaust from the food trucks. Everything from egg-and-sausage sandwiches to gyros was available, and my stomach rumbled. The moment the gates opened, we would work nonstop until close, so I decided to grab something while I still could.

"Do you want food?" I asked Rogers. "I'm going to get egg-and-cheese sandwiches for the crew."

Even though I still had no idea which one of our workers was stealing from us, I had decided to stop suspecting everyone. I didn't want to spend the day giving the stink eye to people who did not deserve it. Besides, my mother and I had a trick up our sleeves.

We'd hired a security contractor to install cameras while everyone was off-site for the festival. It was something we'd talked about doing for years. Whether we could actually catch anyone stealing was up for debate, but at this point, we were willing to try.

I crossed the soft grass of the park to get to Kelcee's portable kitchen. She stepped out from behind the counter, and we ducked off to the side.

"Any news?" Her blue eyes were wide and worried.

I shook my head. "No. His bike is gone, but his things are still at the house."

She sighed and looked out at the lake, her dark hair blowing in the breeze. "I haven't heard from him." Her voice was as heavy as my heart. "I'm worried. Why would he just take off like that?"

I drew back. "You don't think he did it, do you?"

Her eyes locked on to mine. "If you're really asking me that, we aren't friends."

She looked so protective I nearly choked up. "Sounds like he's found a good girl. I'll let you know if I hear anything. You do the same."

The doors to the festival opened soon after the last crumb from the sandwiches was gone. The day blurred by as I sampled products, answered questions about the heist, and tried to build interest in Upper Mitten. I saw pretty much everyone in town, including the speech therapist (he was a chardonnay drinker), the Hendersons, and even Aunt Patty.

"Braden's planning to come later." She winked at me while cashing a ticket in for a glass of sparkling white. "Thank you so much for all you've done to welcome him to town."

Billy was standing next to me and made some sort of noise, maybe a snort. He caught my eye and wiggled his eyebrows.

"Of course," I told Patty, after shooting a look at Billy. "We really appreciate all he did that night to help Pappy."

"Well, I hope you get to see him today. I *know* he would be happy to see you." She winked again before sailing away into the crowd.

I pointed at Billy. "Not one word."

He smirked like a champion and got back to work.

Sure enough, I spotted Braden later that afternoon. He was toward the back of the line while I was busy sampling with a group. My heart caught at the sight of him. He lifted his hand and waved, but that was it.

"Cold." Billy looked confused. "Everything okay with that?"

That's what you asked for, I told myself. *You can't be upset.*

"We're just friends, Billy."

Still, I slung the wine a little faster and didn't smile as big as I had before.

Things started to slow down around two, when the crowds had worked their way through all of the booths and people had begun to migrate to Main Street for a late lunch. It was the time we always held our drawing, in an effort to keep the remaining crowd engaged. This year, we were giving away a wine tour for a party of ten, followed by dinner at Olives.

"You ready to emcee?" I asked Billy.

He wore his baseball cap backward, like Dean used to do. "I was born with a mic in my hand," he said, giving me a bright-white smile.

Billy grabbed the box where people had been dropping tickets all day. It wasn't necessary to be present to win, but if the winner was on-site, they received an additional bottle of wine. He tucked the box under his arm and climbed up onto a stool.

"Ladies and gentlemen." Billy put on a goofy voice that caught the attention of everyone in the area. He shook the box with glee. "It's time to step up for our big drawing—"

"Wait!" I had almost forgotten the gift basket from Upper Mitten. Someone had tucked it beneath the tasting table, and I fumbled to pull it out, dropping it in the process. Three bottles of wine clinked to the grass, along with a package of cured salami, a box of crackers, and a bar of chocolate that looked decidedly soft in the heat. The decorative tissue paper from the bottom, along with a thousand pieces of squiggly white and turquoise confetti, followed in a big, messy heap.

Luckily, no one had seen me drop it except Billy, who choked back a laugh.

"First," he said, "we are going to start with a beautiful prize from a new local winery that we hope you will go and see in person, Upper Mitten . . ."

I scrambled to reassemble the box, grabbing the tissue paper to shove back in the bottom. Suddenly, I stopped. There was a small piece of turquoise paper wedged into the base of the gift basket. It was a heavy piece of card stock that they must have used for decoration.

And to write hate mail.

Setting my jaw, I got to my feet. "We're not giving this piece of crap away," I muttered to Billy.

"Huh?" The freckles across his nose wrinkled as he squinted at me. "You ruin it or something?"

"Or something," I agreed.

Turning to Rogers, I held up the piece of turquoise paper. His eyebrows nearly lifted off his head. Mumbling some excuse to the others, I rushed away from the tent with the whole mess in my hands.

I knew Henry was on-site, keeping order for the festival. I stopped a few feet away from our tent, the sun beating down on the back of my neck. The park was much too crowded to try and carry the basket over to him, and I didn't want to risk having it knocked out of my arms. I took it to the parking lot, picked up my phone, and called him.

He answered on the third ring. Once he heard what I had to say, he grunted.

"I'll have a unit bring them in."

I stared down at the mess in my hands, completely baffled that Upper Mitten had agreed to accept our help when they were the ones sending us hate mail all this time.

Keep your enemies closer . . .

Clearly, that was exactly what they had decided to do.

~

The Compass was a bar next to the beach, just off Main Street. It was one of those dark-and-moody type places, with wooden walls and small round windows that looked out at the water to make it feel like you were sitting on a ship. Since most people were still at the festival, it was easy to find a little table in the back, so I could take a moment and regroup.

The waitress had a sleek ponytail and freckles. Probably a college girl who came up to work for the summer, because I didn't recognize her and she didn't recognize me.

"What can I get you?" she asked.

"Um . . ." I picked up the drinks menu, at a loss since they didn't serve wine. "That looks good." I pointed at a picture of a frothy pink vodka drink with whipped cream on top.

"Oh, I love those." The waitress giggled. "Dangerously drinkable. Anything to eat?"

"No, thanks."

I hadn't had anything to eat since that morning, but I was too upset to be hungry. It was so embarrassing to think I'd rushed to help Upper Mitten and they were laughing at us the whole time. We should have just taken their spot at the festival and called it a day.

The festival.

Quickly, I texted Rogers where I was. Even though things were wrapping up, there were still at least three hours of work left to do. I promised I'd be back in a few minutes, but he let me off the hook altogether.

We'll handle it. Take some time—but let me know what happens to them. I hope it starts with JAIL.

I couldn't help but laugh.

The waitress set down my drink, which was huge, and she must have thought I was laughing at it, because she said, "Right? My boyfriend and I usually split one, even though he'd never admit it."

Boyfriend.

Jax would never have deigned to drink this. He would have insisted on a craft beer at a place like this and pushed me into having the same thing.

"This looks great." I dipped my straw into the whipped cream. "Thank you."

The lake was a deep blue outside the window, and after I'd taken a few sips of the drink, the rage coursing through me started to subside. Even though I felt duped by Charlie and Landon, it was nice to know they were the ones behind it all because that meant the threats to expose us had nothing to do with my grandmother's past. Instead, Upper Mitten just wanted everyone to think we were this big bad bully, which is why they'd put out that stupid blog. It was a relief to be done with it.

The ice in the drink gave me an ice cream headache. Quickly, I pressed my tongue up against the roof of my mouth to warm it up. The strawberry drink was already half-gone but super-refreshing, so I signaled to the waitress for another. She looked a little surprised but nodded.

That's what happens when you're raised at a winery, I planned to tell her. *Alcohol tolerance.*

There was hardly any alcohol, though. The thing went down like a smoothie. If anything, I'd walk out of there with a sugar buzz.

The phone rang as she set down my second. It was my parents. Judging by the noise in the background, they had me on speakerphone at the hospital.

"Henry briefed us on Upper Mitten." My mother was furious. "I can't believe it. We were trying to help them!"

"You know, I think they're just immature." Now that I'd started to cool down, the whole thing almost struck me as funny. I filled my parents in on the details of what had happened the day I went for a tasting. Once I'd told them the whole story, I added, "They seem like they have a lot to learn."

"Hmm." Surprisingly, my dad sounded amused. "Maybe we'll have to teach them."

People had started to file into the bar, and I wondered if I should give up my table or order another drink. I was actually starting to feel a little light headed, so I probably needed to find something to eat and get back to work. Even though Rogers had said they would handle it, there was no reason I couldn't help.

"Hey, let's talk about this later," I told my parents. "I'm still downtown, and it's getting a little loud."

We hung up, and I signaled to close out. I pulled out some cash, trying to add a good tip. But I could not get my brain to do simple math.

I must have looked helpless, because the waitress returned. "Everything good?"

"Yeah. I can't add at the moment. How much alcohol are"—I cleared my throat—"is in these?"

"Two shots of vodka in each drink. 'Course, Teddy's back there today." She gestured at the bar, where a tall guy was working. "He's a heavy pour. Boss gets on him all the time."

I tried to thank her but could barely talk. It suddenly felt incredibly important to get out of there before any of the locals showed up. Quickly, I shoved some cash at her and headed for the door.

Braden was walking in as I headed out.

"The doctor," I cried, delighted to see his half smile. He might have been with a group of people, but I didn't stop to think about that. Instead, I grabbed his arm and pulled him to the sidewalk.

"Braden, I am so glad to see you." I flopped onto a nearby bench. Loudly, I whispered, "I think I'm suffering from a self-induced medical emergency."

He looked concerned. "What is it?"

"Braden." I held up my hands. "I think I'm drunk."

~

Nearly a loaf of bread, several glasses of water, and a very strong cup of coffee later, I could finally form a rational thought.

"You saved me," I said, stretching out on a lawn chair. "Again."

Braden looked over from his chair and grinned. "Feeling better?"

We were sitting in the backyard of his practice. Thank goodness it was so close, because he'd nearly had to carry me. By now, my buzz had faded into a dull headache, but thanks to the water, I didn't feel sick. Just embarrassed.

"I'm so sorry I took you away from your friends."

"Not at all." He set down the golf magazine he'd been flipping through. "It's good to see you."

"Like this?" I laughed.

"No. Just . . . in general." He rolled up the magazine and pointed it at me. "I'm getting the sense this doesn't happen to you very often. Getting drunk."

"This was a total accident." I took another sip of water. The saccharine taste of strawberry still lingered on my tongue. "Looks like I need to stick to wine."

It was getting late, and the mosquitoes were coming out. The second I brushed one away, Braden got up to light a citronella candle. Shaking my head, I settled against the pillow of my lawn chair.

"You are such a great guy, Braden."

His eyes met mine. "But . . ."

"Look, I really like you." The quiet words surprised me. Clearly, I was not as sober as I'd thought. "It's just . . . things have been pure chaos. I haven't been in a place to start something, and to be perfectly honest, I ended something."

Telling him about Jax was the last on my list of things to say, but now that the words were out, I hit him with the full story.

"This was the guy I thought I was going to marry. I realized that at some point, he'd become an idea of what my future would be. But what we had should have been left in the past."

Braden squinted up at the sky. "I would say where do we go from here, but I think I already know your answer. You need time."

"I'm sorry," I said.

He crossed his arms behind his head. "For what? Living your life?"

For helping me in spite of it all. For trying to understand me at a time when I barely understand myself.

"I loved the stethoscope," I said. "It meant a lot to me."

"Yeah?"

"Yeah."

The flame of the candle flickered in the breeze, and Braden got to his feet.

"If you're feeling better, I should drive you home." He looked at his watch. "I actually have dinner plans."

I felt ashamed for hoping the dinner was with Aunt Patty.

"Someone from the winery will still be in town to drive me," I said. "I'll be fine."

My heart was heavy as we walked to the gate. Down the block, jazz music crooned from a neighbor's outdoor speakers. It was a perfect summer night. I regretted the fact that Braden and I couldn't spend it together, grilling a steak and talking on the back porch.

"Thanks," I said. "For your medical expertise."

He rested his hand on the fence post. "I'll bill you."

We smiled at each other, and I headed down the block. I turned back to wave, but Braden was already gone.

Chapter Thirty-Two

My father, my mother, Phillip, and I sat in the conference room, a bottle of cherry wine open and several glasses set out across the table. The mood in the room was tense as we waited for the owners of Upper Mitten to arrive. My father drummed his fingers on the table, then looked at me.

"You sure you're up for this?" he asked.

I squeezed my hands tight under the table. There was a risk that I would stutter, and I knew my parents were worried about that. Not because they would be embarrassed, but because they would feel my disappointment at not being able to communicate as clearly as I would want to. Still, I had to try.

There was a low greeting from the tasting room, and Rogers poked his head in the door.

"I have Charlie and Landon for you."

My father gave me a questioning look, and I nodded. "I've got this."

"Let them in," he told Rogers.

My family sat in silence as Charlie's Nordic frame slunk through the door, followed by his wife. This time, she looked decidedly less smug, fidgeting with an arm full of bracelets as they walked in.

My father stood and shook their hands. Once everyone was settled in, he looked at me. "Abby?"

I drummed my fingers against the table and focused on a speech strategy that could help me get through this. Taking deep breaths, I waited to feel confident. Finally, I cleared my throat.

"We'd like to thank the two of you for agreeing to meet with us."

Charlie ducked his head. He looked unkempt, like the last few hours had been too much for even his beard pomade to handle.

"We have decided not to press charges for the situation with the notes," I said.

Landon's face brightened. "Oh, thank you so much." Her voice was hoarse, as if she'd been crying. "Thank you. We wanted to take it all back when you offered to help us, but by then, it was too late."

"What did you hope to accomplish?" I asked. "By sending them?"

The couple looked at each other. Finally, Landon spoke. "I don't know. It was all so stupid. We thought it would freak you out, and maybe you would shut down or something until you felt safe again." Her voice was small. "It sounds so petty, saying it out loud. It's just really hard to compete with you."

I looked at my father, and he gave me an encouraging smile. "You guys," I said, feeling more confident with every clear word. "Everyone on the peninsula is technically in competition, but we're also in business together. We had a field flood recently, and one of the other vineyards stepped in to help. We're a tight-knit bunch. We help each other out whenever the opportunity comes up. That's why we invited you to share our booth at the wine festival, even when you missed your opportunity to participate."

Landon nodded furiously. I could tell she was desperate to comment but was not about to interrupt, which I appreciated.

"Over the years, the other vineyards have loaned us their equipment, their workers, and their enthusiasm. We do the same for them." Charlie and Landon exchanged frustrated glances, and once again, I felt guilty about the situation with the wine trail. For a second, I thought it was going to trip me up, so I tapped my hands against the table, using one of the stress-release exercises the speech therapist had taught me. The moment passed, and I said, "We excluded you in the beginning, because you tried to divide the community. In your marketing materials, you insinuated the way we interact with our guests is snooty and wrong."

Phillip grunted. Taking off his glasses, he cleaned them with extra fury.

"You're welcome to market your products however you see fit," I continued. "However, we would like to request that before you continue to make those assumptions, you take the time to attend the tastings and take the tours offered by the other wineries. It might surprise you to see how welcoming we can be."

Speech complete, I folded my hands. It was a relief to make it through without stuttering, and I sat a little taller knowing I was capable of taking control.

My mother slid an envelope forward, her gold bracelets clinking against the table. "This is a schedule of each tour and tasting offered at each winery on the peninsula, as well as complimentary passes to each one. When you go, please introduce yourself to the owners. They'll want to meet you."

"Not because of the notes," I said quickly, noticing Landon's panicked look. "Nobody knows. In fact, it's not the type of thing people around here need to know. We just wanted to take a moment to start over and let you know that we plan to view this as a learning experience and move on."

Landon shook her head. "I mean, why would you do all that?" Her shaggy hair flopped into her eyes as she glanced around the table. "We were awful."

The thing my grandmother had said flashed through my head, about the time Pappy had threatened to plant corn instead of following their dreams. "We're doing it because my grandparents faced some big challenges when they started this place. They almost gave up. The people you see sitting around this table were lucky enough to be born into something that was well underway."

My father cleared his throat. "That's not to say we haven't faced challenge after challenge on our own. However, we'd like the opportunity to lend a helping hand."

"And to apologize," I added. "Look, I know I made a huge mistake leaving you off the wine trail. It was rude. It didn't warrant a full-fledged creepy-note attack, but I get it, and I'm sorry."

Landon and Charlie looked at each other. Then Charlie jumped to his feet and vigorously shook hands with everyone around the table. "We can't thank you enough. This was truly a lesson learned."

My mother laughed. "Good. Then let's have a toast to celebrate. Abby?" She pushed a bottle of our cherry wine across the table.

"Let's drink." I filled the glasses, the liquid pink and shimmering in the low light. "Here's to new friendships."

We all took a sip, and Charlie's face puckered.

My father glared at him. "What's the problem, son? You don't like our wine?"

Landon let out a strangled sound. "No, it's just . . ."

The couple looked absolutely baffled. Then, suddenly, Charlie burst out laughing. His face turned red enough to match his beard, and he fanned at his mouth.

"Any tasting notes stand out?" I asked innocently.

"Tart cherry, tap water, and Tabasco," Charlie roared.

Everyone in my family started laughing too, punctuated by Landon's sharp giggles. My father pulled a bottle of cabernet franc from under the table as my mother whisked the glasses away. I passed around the real drinks, and we toasted once again.

"To growth and development," my father said.

I smiled at him. "Cheers to that."

~

The walk across the vineyard back to my house finally felt peaceful, now that the ordeal with the notes was over. It was a relief to know I'd imagined the threat against my grandmother and that her story would remain in the past. It was also good that we'd made some new friends along the way.

Long after my parents had left, Phillip and I had stuck around talking with Landon and Charlie. It had been fun hearing their ideas for the vineyard and figuring out ways to help. Phillip had been especially intrigued by the big-screen TVs. He'd made plans to get a group of friends over there to watch the soccer playoffs as soon as my grandfather was well.

It was long past time for a real dinner, so I made a plate of almonds, cherries, Brie, and crackers. The bottle of semidry riesling I'd been eager to dip into was cooling in the fridge, and I poured myself a glass. I settled back against the cushions of the couch, picked up the remote control, and debated whether to watch a movie or something quick and mindless.

I had just cued up an episode of *Family Feud* when there was a knock at the door.

The wooden floors were cool against my bare feet, and out the window, the late sunset cast a golden hue over the vines. I decided that once I ate, I would head up to the arbor to watch the moon rise and clear my head.

"Who is it?" I asked, resting my hand on the knob.

The brief moment of silence stretched long enough for me to grip the stem of my glass. The threat of the notes was over, but the thief was still on the loose. I'd just started to back away from the door when a gruff voice said, "It's Dean."

Relief rushed through me. Flipping the lock, I threw open the door. "Where have you been? Mom's been so worried."

His face looked drawn and tired. "Can I come in?" His dark eyes darted past me, as if making sure no one was there.

Once inside, he picked up the bottle of riesling and studied the label.

"Do you want a glass?" I asked.

He shook his head, setting it back down. "Nah."

"It's good. Rieslings are normally so sweet, but this one is balanced. It's impressive."

Dean took a seat on the sofa. "You don't have to sell me on our wines."

"Habit." Perching next to him, I met his eyes. "I'm so sorry that happened. You okay?"

Dean glanced at the television. The game show was well underway, with families squared off. The one wearing matching T-shirts gave the right answer, and they leapt up and down, hugging each other like the best of friends.

My brother turned to me. "I wanted to say goodbye."

My stomach dropped, and I set down my wineglass. "You're leaving?"

As recently as a week ago, I would have been thrilled at the news. Now I was disappointed. For a moment, I had actually thought he was going to stick around.

Our mother would be crushed.

"Chicago?" I asked.

He nodded. "My old boss got in touch. Needs my help on some projects."

"Does Kelcee know?" I asked.

"I'm seeing her after this."

I took a sip of the riesling. There were notes of green apple. Dean and I used to eat sour-apple suckers and play war in the clubhouse. It seemed strange that those days felt like yesterday, given the time that had passed.

Looking down at my hands, I said, "Dean, I wish—"

"It's my fault." His voice was quiet. "I don't blame you in the slightest."

It was my fault too. I could have tried harder. I could have offered forgiveness, helped him reacclimate to the vineyard. I could have, *should* have, been his sister.

"Will you be back?" In a rush, I added, "I hope you'll come back."

He gave me a wry look. "I try not to lie too much these days." Getting to his feet, he reached into his pocket. "I got you something." A small package landed on the table. It was wrapped in red tissue paper and tied with the twine we used on gift baskets in the tasting room.

"Open it later," he said when I reached for it.

I got to my feet and studied him. The same old fear I'd felt since he'd started using drugs cut through me, the fear that I would never see him again. Leaning forward, I gave him an awkward hug. He smelled like motor oil, and even though my arms were around him, I could already feel the distance between us.

"Take care of yourself," I said.

"You too."

We looked at each other for a long moment. Then Dean lifted his hand and headed out the door.

I collapsed on the couch, not surprised to feel tears prick the back of my eyes. For a quick moment, I'd had the opportunity to rebuild the relationship that had once meant everything to me. Because I was too stubborn and too selfish, I'd let the chance pass me by.

Picking up the package, I held on to it through the remainder of *Family Feud*, drinking to get up the courage to see what he'd given me. Finally, I felt bold enough to unwrap the tissue.

Inside there was a note and a small black box. I opened the note first.

It's amazing what you can find if you look hard enough.

What did Dean find? Did this have something to do with Oma? I opened the box and dug through more tissue paper. There was something hard beneath it. The thin paper peeled back, and my stomach dropped.

I blinked. "This can't be . . ."

It was.

My gold charm bracelet.

The one I had clung to during those long and scary days at the hospital, the one I had pictured in my memory, again and again. With shaking hands, I picked it up, the gold heavy in my hands.

The sensation of holding it reminded me of a few years ago, the time I'd visited Starlight Cove Elementary. The hallways had always seemed so big, but they suddenly looked tiny, like the desks and the lockers. Likewise, the bracelet and its charms were much smaller than I remembered, but the details sparked emotions that felt frozen in a time capsule.

The lighthouse, the grapes, the gumball machine . . . they were all there. Finally, my eyes settled on the Monopoly man. His hat was dented, but his suit was still a perfect fit, and his face was the same as I remembered.

"Hey, old friend." Gently, I tapped him on the hat.

The memories from a time the bracelet had meant everything to me floated through the air like ether. I couldn't grab on to them. The bracelet was finally in my hands, but it didn't whisk me away to fix the past. It was part of the here and now. For the first time in ages, that didn't feel like such a bad place to be.

Chapter Thirty-Three

Late the next morning, I stood at the bar in the tasting room, the charm bracelet firmly attached to my wrist. We had received a shipment from UPS, and when I walked in to pick it up, I noticed Jessica once again hanging out at the bar with Billy. The moment she spotted me, she turned away as if they hadn't been talking.

"What did I miss?" I asked brightly.

Jessica's eyes were made up with black eyeliner and gold gemstones, like she was some sort of princess. The look irritated me for some reason. Maybe it was because it made her seem slick in a way she hadn't before.

"More to the point," I said, meeting her eyes. "Jess, what are you doing in here?"

There were two older couples doing an early tasting at the bar, so I was careful to keep my voice casual. However, the look on her face made it clear she knew I had my eye on her.

"She needed her phone charger back." Billy tossed a rag from one hand to another. "I borrowed it at the meeting, and it's been jammed behind the bar ever since." He grinned at her. "Sorry if it's sticky."

I looked back and forth between the two of them. It struck me that Jessica's lips looked swollen and red. If the two were dating, it really was possible that . . .

"Is this true?" cried a voice.

I turned to the door, and my stomach sank. It was my grandmother. Based on the horrified look on her face, I had no doubt she'd heard the news about the ice wine.

"Hi, Oma," I said, hoping the interaction seemed normal to the guests finishing their wine flight. "You guys, this is my grandmother. One of the founders of the vineyard."

The guests nodded and smiled at her.

"Is it true?" she demanded, completely ignoring them. Her voice echoed across the room.

"Excuse me, please." I shot Billy a *distract them, please* look.

"I have something you two might be interested in." Billy pulled a bottle of dessert wine off the shelf, along with two small glasses. "This will change your life."

Rushing up to my grandmother, I took her elbow and led her out the door. The insects complained in the heat of the morning, and the sun was blinding. Once my eyes adjusted, I saw my grandmother was near tears.

"Take me to see it." Her voice was ragged. "The wine cellar."

"Oma, no," I pleaded. "It's not going to make a difference."

"I will go myself, then." She walked up the gravel drive toward the storage sheds, her burgundy dress swishing with each purposeful step.

It wasn't hard to believe she knew. To be honest, it was hard to believe it had taken this long for her to find out. Letting out a breath, I followed her down to the cellar.

She stood stock-still, put her hand to her mouth, and sank onto the steps.

"No." Her head swayed from side to side. "No."

"I'm sorry, Oma."

I took her hands. She looked at me, her dark eyes clouded with age and heartache. "It's my fault. This is because I am a stupid, stupid woman."

"What do you mean?" I dared ask.

She sniffled. "I have made mistakes in my life that will ruin us."

"I know." The words were out before I could stop them. "I saw the ring."

She snapped her neck toward me, her eyes bugged with rage. "You?" she gasped. She leapt to her feet, nearly falling off the cellar steps. "You do not deserve to be a part of this family!"

Before I knew what was happening, my grandmother rushed forward and pummeled me with her fists. Over and over, swearing at me in English and German. Yelping, I covered my face with my hands.

My lips stung and oozed warm salt. My grandmother had split my lip. Before I could even process this, she came at me again, fists flailing.

"Oma, stop!" I grabbed her hands and fought to hold her away from me. "The box with the key was in the fields after the robbery. I didn't *try* to find it."

She froze, her eyes small slits. "After the robbery?"

"Yes." Since she looked like the fight had left her, I put my hand up to my lip. It pulsed with pain all the way up to my nose. Blood trickled out of the side, and I pressed my hand against it, trying to stop the bleeding. I couldn't believe my grandmother had just punched me in the face.

"Why did you hit me?" I cried.

She squinted at me in the dim light. "Come." Taking my other hand, she tucked it under her arm. "There is much to be said."

∽

My grandmother snuck me through the front door of the main house and took me up to her bedroom before anyone could see us. She tsked and fussed over my lip, dabbing it with iodine and insisting I use a cold compress. The care she took was her way of apologizing, and when she finally paused, the wet cotton ball against my skin, I reached up and touched her hand. She sat next to me on the love seat and fixed me with a frank gaze.

"The box was hidden in the ice wine cellar," she said. "It was buried beneath the storage area for 1959. Only someone who removed every single one of those bottles could have found it."

"I'm glad it ended up in the right hands," I said.

"What do you mean by that?" she said carefully. "How much do you know?"

I met her gaze. "Everything but why you did it."

She looked away. There was a long silence broken only by the ticking from the old clock on the dresser. "You must think I do not love your grandfather."

"That's not true." The words sounded strange as they fought past the swelling in my lip. "I know you do."

Her eyes wandered over her bedroom, as though she were taking in all the years spent there together. "I married my first husband when I was sixteen." I made a face, and she shook her head. "There was no choice. My parents were dead. They had been for quite some time."

"They owned a vineyard," I dared to say.

Oma frowned. "You know this?"

"Weingut Feierabend. I found the brand symbol on the back of the velvet cloth inside the wooden box, which led me to it."

She leaned forward. "Do you still have the box?"

I nodded, and she pressed her hands to her chest.

"It was made by my father," she said. "He was gifted at wood carving. It once sat on the tasting room counter at Weingut Feierabend as decoration. As a young girl, I had to stand on my tiptoes to see it."

"Our crest was inspired by the design on the latch," I said. "Right?"

Her dark eyes met mine, full of hesitation. I could tell she was worried about sharing the history she'd fought so hard to bury but knew there was little choice.

"Yes," she finally said. "The box is precious to me, one of the few things I have left of my parents."

"Your mother, she looks just like Dad."

Oma smiled. "She was so beautiful. My father too."

"They were friends with Nazis?" I asked.

My grandmother's face clouded. She ran her hands along the armrest of the couch. The fabric was green-and-gold brocade; it was as rich and lush as all of her decorations.

"My father grew up with one of the Nazi Party leaders in the area. His name was Krauss Fischer. They had always been such good friends, and with time, Krauss moved higher and higher up the ranks." She placed a pillow behind her back, as if settling in for a long story. "My father had always been a farmer, but his dream was to own a winery. His family was not rich. Then, one day, Krauss picked him up in his fancy black roadster and drove him to a vineyard in Mittelrhein. It belonged to a Jewish family."

Her expression became distant.

"The owners were not allowed to work, because they were Jewish, but this particular family ignored the rules and continued to produce and sell wine. The day Krauss picked him up in the roadster, my father sat in the car, watching in disbelief, as Krauss arrested the owner and seized the property. The family was taken away and my father handed the keys.

"My father did not tell my mother the true story for some time. They had been there for three months when someone else told her. The fight was the first of many."

"How old were you?" I asked.

My grandmother wrinkled her brow. "They acquired the vineyard in 1938, and I was born in 1940. It was a hard time for my mother. She felt they should return the vineyard to the original owners. My father was much more pragmatic: returning the vineyard was impossible, due to the laws at the time, so why let the opportunity go to waste?"

I stared down at a small patch of sun fighting to make its way through the curtains. Dust floated through it.

"The years went on," my grandmother continued. "Krauss used the vineyard as his own personal playground. He brought high-ranking officials. They spent money hand over fist. It gave my father the capital to open a restaurant, buy cars, and experiment with wine. He loved wine, you see, and spent every moment producing it or drinking it.

"The vineyard was everything to him, and with time, it became one of the most successful in the region. Everyone knew that it had the full support of the Nazi Party, and at that time, many people respected that, as mistaken as they were. Even once the war was over, those who survived used it as a meeting place to discuss their glory days.

"It seemed like everything was swept under the rug until 1950, when the daughter of the original owners returned. She tried to prove the vineyard had been seized, as it was. But by that time, my father felt it was his. He cited the deed of sale the previous owner had signed. The poor woman had no proof that her father had not been a willing participant. However, everyone knew the truth, especially my mother. One month later, the main house caught fire. I was the only survivor."

"That's terrible."

I pushed the cold compress into my face, trying to numb the emotions coursing through me.

"Krauss told me the daughter came back for revenge," she continued. "That the fire was arson. Of course, I later learned it was caused by a faulty fireplace. It didn't matter either way." My grandmother closed her eyes. "Krauss became my guardian, and once I was old enough, I was forced to marry his son. I hated everything about them. Especially their ideology."

"They were—"

"Nazis." She practically spat out the word. "The only thing that made it bearable was the knowledge of what my mother had done." For the first time, Oma smiled. "My mother helped the Jews escape the country during the war."

My mouth dropped open. "What?" The pictures of the high-ranking officials at the vineyard ran through my mind. "How?"

"There was an abandoned horse barn on the far edge of the property. It was falling down, so no one ever went there. She housed families there. I discovered this information in a journal that survived the fire. It was tucked away in the lining of a trunk, and I destroyed it before Krauss could take it from me, which was the smartest thing I could have done." Oma gave a slight shudder. "My mother was so brave, you see. She helped five families escape."

"That's incredible." I'd heard of things like that. It was remarkable to think my great-grandmother had actually done them.

"Yes." Oma's eyes grew distant. "My mother would hate to know I had to spend my life with those people. She would be so disappointed in me."

"It wasn't your choice."

"I could have fought them, like she did." Oma's voice was dull. "The war was over, but they still committed unspeakable acts. My complicity was as horrific as their crimes."

"Why did you keep the ring?" I asked. "Why didn't you just melt it for the gold?"

She folded her hands. "It belonged to my mother. Krauss liked the fact that it was free, of course, so he gave it to his son when it was time to marry me. Olaf carved the date of our marriage along with the Nazi symbol into the ring. Once I escaped, it was much too risky to take it to a jeweler to have the symbol removed."

I met her eyes. "Did you love Grandpa? Or was he just a way out?"

"It was love at first sight. But he does not know about this." Oma reached out and brushed a gentle finger over my bruised face. "Yet someone other than you has discovered my secret, and they plan to take all of this."

"All of what?"

"The vineyard." Oma gestured in the direction of the window. "They want money. Or they will ruin us."

"The ice wine," I whispered.

"Perhaps. But money." She tapped her knuckles on her knees. "Lots and lots of money."

It finally hit me.

The missing money.

"You're the one stealing," I breathed.

Oma's shoulders slumped. "You know of this too?"

I put my head in my hands and squeezed it hard, as though that could help me process all of this. "Who's blackmailing you?" I demanded. "And how much have you given them?"

"I do not know."

"How much?" I took her hand. "It's okay. How much?"

"Nearly two hundred thousand now."

I dropped her hand. "We *have* to tell Henry."

"No." Her answer was immediate. "The scandal would be too great. Our family . . . and I do not know what would happen to me."

"Because you faked your papers."

She patted my leg. "You always were the smart one."

I picked up the cold compress and pressed it to my face. "Oma, we need to ask for help."

"Henry would not help. He would report me. He is a friend, but he is also a pit bull."

I sat back against the green brocade of the couch. Henry very well could tell my grandmother that, although he loved and cared for her, the law came first. That's how he was.

"Could we tell Pappy?" I asked.

"I am nearly eighty years old. Why now, when I never told him the truth of who I have been? If it had simply been the issue of my first marriage, he would know. Of course, I did not trust him with the information when we left Germany. I was afraid he would fight Olaf. That man was violent and without a fear of consequence. He could have killed Theo without blinking an eye."

"He was violent with you?" I asked.

My grandmother sniffed. "He found reasons to punish me nearly every day. It was not safe to leave. I had to change my name and go where he would not find me."

"Could he be the one blackmailing you?" I asked. Then I remembered. "Never mind. He's dead."

My grandmother shivered. "He is?"

"I checked his records. How about one of his children? We could see if he had children. I'm sure the vineyard seems like a money pot to anyone on the outside."

"Ah." Her dark eyes were solemn. "That could be possible."

The gravity of what she'd said was still sinking in. I couldn't imagine the fear and heartache of being scared of someone you were forced to live with, especially at such a young age. When I was seventeen, I'd been terrified Dean would get drunk and wrap a car around a tree, but that was nothing compared to what she'd gone through.

I chewed on my fingernail. "How long have you been giving money to this person? And how do they ask for it?"

"Nearly three years." She spread her hands out. "I receive a letter in the mail. In the beginning, it had instructions on where to leave the money, but no more, as it is always the same." Before I could ask, she said, "I'm to pretend to feed the ducks at Starlight Point Park. The money is in the bread bag. I throw the bag away, and I leave."

"You've never stayed?" I was aghast. "To see who came to get it out of the trash?"

She gave a sharp shake of her head. "The instructions are clear. I would be reported."

"Oma . . ." I groaned. "This is so wrong. We need help! First of all, the letter is coming through the mail, so that has to be some sort of federal offense, right? Then, the blackmail . . ." My eyes fell on Pappy's cologne on the dresser. "What if we told Pappy the truth, got you a lawyer to figure out immigration, and then found a way to nail this guy? Or girl."

"The risk is too great." Her eyes were genuinely afraid. "What if I am forced to leave? Or if I am put in prison? I cannot live without Theo, and what would that do to him?"

There was a very strong possibility that my grandmother would be in serious trouble. But what was the alternative?

"We have to do something," I insisted. "I'm not going to let someone take the vineyard from us because we are too afraid to stand up to them. Plus, you think the same person is responsible for stealing the ice wine, don't you?"

My grandmother pressed her lips together.

"You said no secrets," I reminded her.

She folded her hands. "I think this person has become quite bold."

"Then it's time to take them down. When do you expect to hear from them again?"

"I already have." Her voice was small. "They sent me a letter right before the anniversary party. The drop-off is today."

"Okay." I nodded. "I'll be there."

"No." My grandmother's eyes widened. "You mustn't. Let us think this through together, and perhaps . . . perhaps when your grandfather is well, I will enlist his help. I will not do anything until then, and neither will you." I didn't respond, and she gripped my hand. "Promise me."

I got to my feet and opened the curtains. In the late-afternoon light, the fields were green, gold, and picture perfect against the lake.

I couldn't imagine allowing someone to keep chipping away at our property, if there was anything I could do to stop them.

My grandmother had every reason to be afraid, but this couldn't go on.

I didn't want to lie to her, but she owed me one. Walking back over to her, I squeezed her hand. "I promise."

Chapter Thirty-Four

My grandmother wanted to shower and change before going to the bank.

I rushed away from the main house, pretending I had to run an errand for work. My lip pulsed and ached in the heat of the afternoon. Ducking under a tree away from the tasting room, I called Kelcee.

The night before, she hadn't answered her phone, probably because she was upset about Dean. Now her voice was thick and stuffy, like she had a cold.

"Are you okay?" I asked, and she burst into tears.

I pressed my hand into the rough bark of the tree, listening as she detailed the "efficient" way Dean had ended things.

"I get it. I'd leave too," she sniffled. "No one is ever going to let him live down his past. Not around here. It's not fair."

Once she'd assured me she would be okay, I updated her on the situation with my grandmother. I kept my voice low, in a hushed whisper, and looked over my shoulder at least five times to make sure no one had snuck up on me.

Kelcee let out a low whistle once I'd finished. "Looks like Dean left at the right time. He would go ballistic if he knew someone was doing this to your grandmother."

"I plan to do that for him."

"Well, you'll need to borrow my car. She'll be less likely to notice you that way. I mean, you're planning to follow her, right?"

I wrapped my arms around myself. "I figured you'd try to talk me out of it."

"Not a chance," she scoffed. "Whoever is behind this is messing with your family and your business. You need to take them down. If she's headed to the bank, you need to be there the second she gets out."

"See you in thirty," I said and pressed end.

Finding parking on Main Street during the day was practically impossible. Somehow, I got lucky and found a spot seven spaces away from the bank.

Kelcee's old Tahoe was tan and about as nondescript as a car could possibly be. Still, to be safe, I wore a blonde wig she still had from Halloween, a pink ball cap, and a pair of glasses without lenses. I felt ridiculous leaving Kelcee's house in the costume, but once I got behind the wheel, I didn't feel that out of place.

The wig was hot but oddly realistic. I hunched over my phone, pretending to text. My grandmother, or anyone else strolling the street, would have to look twice to know it was me.

I'd sat there about twenty minutes when my grandmother's old Cadillac made its way down Main Street and pulled into the parking lot. Moments later, she came out of the side alley and walked through the front door.

Ten minutes later, she came out gripping her black leather purse and giving a furtive look around. I ducked down low in my seat and waited for her car to exit the driveway. Then I followed her from six cars back.

My grandmother had always been a menace behind the wheel, which made following her a challenge. Somehow, I managed to keep her in sight without blowing my cover. There were a few times she looked in the rearview mirror of the old Cadillac but didn't spot me.

She pulled off the highway into Starlight Point Park. I followed as slowly as I dared. The moment I could pull off, I did, taking a spot next to the countless tourists.

My grandmother got out with a bag of bread and walked up to a well-populated lake along the trees. She tossed a few pieces of bread to the ducks. Then she walked to the trash can and dumped the bread bag in, presumably with the bankroll of cash inside.

It pained me to think of how many times she'd done this. Each time, I'm sure she'd felt immense guilt to betray her family in an effort to run from the past. My grandfather would have helped, if she only would have let him in. But given her experience with her previous husband, it was understandable she didn't trust how he would react.

My grandmother stood at the edge of a bluff and stared out at the water long enough to make me nervous. I gripped the steering wheel, watching.

She wouldn't do anything crazy, would she?

To my horror, she took a step forward and teetered dangerously close to the drop-off. I was just about to leap out of the truck when a group of nearby children burst into giggles. My grandmother turned to look at them. Then she squared her shoulders, tightened the straps on her sun hat, and headed back to her car.

I steeled myself for a stakeout, more determined than ever to catch the responsible party. Kelcee was right: whoever was doing this to my family needed to pay.

～

Three hours later, the bread bag was still in the trash.

I'd sat there long enough to watch the gas needle on the SUV dip, and as a result, I'd cut the engine. It was a hot day, and even with the lake breeze, I longed for the air-conditioning.

"Come on." I drummed my fingers against the steering wheel. "Where are you?"

My head was starting to hurt from the dull ache in my lip, not to mention the tension, heat, and hunger. I hadn't eaten since breakfast, and it was a little past two. The park didn't close until ten. I probably should have thought to bring a sandwich.

One hour later, I opened Kelcee's glove box and started rooting around. Nothing. Finally, I hopped out and looked in the trunk.

Jackpot.

Kelcee wasn't a big "prep for emergencies" type, but Kip was always looking out for her. In the cargo area, there was a full pack of water bottles, a box of Power Bars, a solar radio, and a thermal blanket. I grabbed a bottle of water and two Power Bars and settled back into the front seat.

Rogers texted once I'd polished off the first bar: Are you out for the day?

Guilt cut through me.

I was so upset about my conversation with Oma that I hadn't even thought to let him know I was leaving. That said, things were off these days, and he would understand.

Don't know. Is everything all right?

I took another bite of the Power Bar, relishing in the waxy texture. The phone lit up.

Everything is under control. Let me know if you need to talk. I heard your grandmother learned of the ice wine.

My eyes sparked with unexpected tears. It took me a few minutes, but I finally managed to respond.

You're ruining your reputation as a diva, Rogers. Be careful, or I might start to suspect you have a heart.

He sent me a gasping emoji, and I laughed.

When this was all over, I planned to talk to the family about giving him a promotion or recognition of some sort. The same went for so many of our employees. Even though we hadn't rooted out the bad apple, the majority of our staff loved the vineyard as much as we did. I intended to make sure they got their due credit and felt that our vineyard was worthy of loyalty, so nothing like this would ever happen again.

I settled back in the leather seats and finished the rest of the first water bottle, my eyes trained on the trash can.

It was going to be a long day.

~

The Power Bars lost their luster, and I was desperate to use the bathroom. I was starting to think the thief wouldn't come until after dark, which would create a problem. I'd have to park the SUV behind some trees so it couldn't be spotted and then hope not to get busted by park security.

Frustrated, I grabbed a handful of change from the console, adjusted my wig, and headed for the bathrooms. There were vending machines lined up outside. After using the bathroom as quickly as possible, I kept one eye on the trash while investing Kelcee's meter money in a Snickers bar, two bags of fruit chews, and a package of blueberry Pop-Tarts.

The snacks kept me sane until late. No one had come but mosquitoes, and cars were starting to clear out of the lot. I was just about to pull the truck behind a cluster of trees when a maintenance truck pulled up to the trash.

"No," I whispered. "What are they doing?"

There were two men, about my age. One unhooked the clear garbage bag and tossed it into the back of the truck while the other replaced the liner. Then they grabbed some equipment and began cleaning up the loose water bottles, wrappers, and napkins that littered the grounds.

"Ma'am," said a voice near my ear.

I jumped so high I almost hit my wig on the ceiling.

A security guard stood at the door of the SUV. He had pale-blue eyes and a weary smile.

"Park closes at ten."

"Oh." I pretended to double-check the time on my phone. "Okay." *Shit.*

I stalled as the security guard finished his rounds of the parking lot. He sat in his car, watching and waiting for the space to clear out. It would have been impossible to pull behind the trees at this point. Besides, the money was in the maintenance truck.

Maybe they're involved. Maybe they hand off the bag to someone.

The thought gave me a burst of much-needed adrenaline.

I pulled out of the drive and went down the hill, the view of the nearby sand dunes bright and beautiful through the trees. At the end of the hill, I pulled over and waited.

Ten minutes later, the maintenance men zoomed down the drive and onto the highway. I waited for three cars to pass and pulled out after them. Heart pounding, I followed them.

I followed them for three other parks and eighteen miles out to a remote location off the main highway. I turned off the headlights and loitered by the side of the road, watching as the team moved the waste into a dumpster outside one of the main buildings. They made no attempt to search it.

One of the guys lit a cigarette, and they chatted for a few moments. Then they headed off to their separate cars and drove away. Finally, when I was sure no one was around, I turned the headlights back on, pulled down the drive, and parked behind a weeping willow tree. The branches covered my truck, and I cut the engine.

I rolled down the windows and waited.

The sound of the crickets chirping in the night and the croak of frogs from a nearby stream or lake soothed my frazzled nerves.

The money was still in the dumpster—I had no doubt. The plan was eerily similar to the way the wine bottles were being transferred out of the vineyard. Could this also be coming from someone who worked for us?

I closed my eyes, trying to picture everyone's faces. I couldn't imagine anyone blackmailing my grandmother . . . it seemed impossible. And yet, it had been happening for years.

Three years, to be exact.

Who had been at the vineyard for more than three years?

Most people. It was impossible to pin down the likely suspects.

I drummed my fingers against the window ledge, nervous to be out alone. My plan was to take a video to serve as evidence and then present it to Henry without telling him exactly what we were being blackmailed for. Utility lights around the building would make it possible for me to get a clear picture.

The mosquitoes started to come into the car, and I used the can of bug spray sitting in the door. The scent was sharp, and it smelled like artificial pine in the small space of the truck.

My stomach growled, and once again, I regretted not taking the time to grab something to eat before doing this. Proof I didn't have a clue what I was doing and probably shouldn't be here at all.

Forget the danger factor—what if none of this added up? What if someone had grabbed the money out of the trash can when I wasn't looking. I had walked away once to go to the bathroom. What if I'd missed it? I could sit here in the car getting eaten alive all night and not discover anything at all.

I tapped my fingers against the steering wheel and listened to the bugs in the woods. Time passed, and I started to get drowsy. I might have even drifted off for a moment, but I bolted awake at the telltale crunch of tires on gravel.

I sat up straight.

Just as quickly, I ducked back down. The truck was well hidden behind the tree, but what if the headlights of the incoming car somehow revealed me? I was trapped with no way out.

I'd have no choice but to floor it, crash through the tree, and tear down the gravel drive. But at the moment, I was so filled with rage at the thought of coming face to face with the person who had been blackmailing my grandmother that I could hardly see.

A black BMW with tinted windows drove up next to the dumpster. The door opened, and my heart nearly stopped. I couldn't believe who was inside.

Chapter Thirty-Five

Rogers stepped out dressed in a black tracksuit. His hair looked damp, as if he had just taken a shower. For once, he didn't look like the perfectly dressed butler in his work uniform and polished shoes. He seemed relaxed and smug in a way I had never seen.

How could I have been so stupid?

I'd trusted him. I'd confided in him. And I'd let him lead me in the wrong direction again and again and again.

There'd been so many moments he'd encouraged me to question the people I cared about. He'd repeatedly planted the seed of doubt regarding my brother, and later, our workers. I must have looked like a puppet on a string, calling Henry to report members of our staff every time Rogers made the suggestion.

Your family has been generous with the hourly wage, but I don't own a BMW.

How many words out of his mouth had been a lie?

All this time, I'd thought he was my friend. I'd been so wrong. He was a monster.

Rogers had blackmailed my grandmother and, without question, stolen the ice wine. The smart move would have been to pick up the phone and call Henry, but I was too angry. Instead, I leapt out of the truck and rushed through the leaves.

I wanted to punch, hit, and kick him until the disbelief and confusion stopped. Instead, I let loose a tirade of rage, screaming at him as loud as I could, my voice echoing through the trees. The expression on his face went from startled to horrified.

"You stupid, stupid girl," he cried. "What are you doing here?"

"What are *you* doing here?" I shouted. "I trusted you. My *family* trusted you, and this whole time you were a stuffed-up piece of lying shit. I hate you. I *hate* you. You are going to rot in prison, you—"

"Contain yourself." Rogers rushed forward and grabbed my arm. His grip cut into my skin, and I winced. "It was not supposed to be like this. Don't you understand you are the only one I care about? You shouldn't be here!" His eyes were scared dark slits, and he smelled like menthol and aftershave.

I glared at him. "Let go of my arm."

He did, and we stared at one another. Bugs flurried overhead in the yellow night-lights, and I swatted them away. Finally, a smirk settled on the corner of his lips.

"Don't you dare laugh at me," I hissed.

"Oh, my dear girl." Rogers leaned against his car and pulled a cigarette out of his pack. He lit it and took in a deep breath. "I would never laugh at you. I'm laughing at how absolutely cruel life can be." He suddenly looked tired, the natural circles under his eyes dark in the night.

My heart was pounding so fast I could barely breathe. I watched him in silence, taken aback that he seemed as upset as I was.

A twig cracked in the forest, and we both jumped. I squeezed my arms tight against my body to stop them from shaking, unsure how to proceed. There'd been so many times, so many situations where I had turned to this man for help and for support. Now I realized I didn't know him at all.

Rogers looked up at the sky. I did the same, disbelief and rage still coursing through me. The canopy of trees blanketed the view of the night. The yellow night-lights hanging from the back of the building were bright in comparison to the stars.

"You were a part of our family," I finally said, my voice echoing in the still night. "How could you do this?"

"Do you know what type of person your grandmother is? The things she has done?"

So, he knew.

"Yes." I looked at him. "But it was a long time ago, and it had nothing to do with you."

"It had everything to do with me." Smoke rose around his face in a cloud. "You see, my grandparents were the proud owners of a vineyard once too. It was called Weingut Feierabend."

The ground under my feet was made of asphalt, but in that moment, I could have been falling through air. I fought for my footing.

"That's impossible."

"My dear girl, things are not impossible simply because we do not want them to be so."

"No, but . . ." My mind was reeling. "You said your mother was from Croatia."

He gave me a look.

Of course.

Rogers had lied. To hide his true heritage from my grandmother. Because he was a terrible, sneaky man.

"My grandparents," he continued, "like yours, built their vineyard up from nothing. It was very successful for a time, and they had a good life with three children—the oldest was my mother, but they also had twin boys. Everything was perfect until the evil of the world came to call like rot." He rubbed the ember of his cigarette between his thumb and forefinger, watching the ashes fall to the ground. "The vineyard was stolen from them, but they couldn't let it go. They remained in

Germany—perhaps foolishly—in hopes of claiming it at a later time. Of course, they were placed in concentration camps." He lifted his chin. "My mother was the only survivor."

I put my hand to my mouth. "Oh, Rogers. I'm so sorry."

"Yes, it is rather horrifying." His eyes met mine for a brief moment, and the corners of his mouth tightened. "Once she was released, my mother was forced to become a child bride, because she had no money and no options. She gave birth to me at fifteen, and her husband left shortly after I was born. She did what she could to survive, but it haunted her that my grandparents had loved the vineyard to the bitter end. She met with your great-grandparents when I was quite young and begged for the right to work to buy back the winery. Your great-grandparents refused, and they died shortly after in a fire. My mother felt justice had been served."

"That's a terrible thing to say," I said. "If they had survived, they might have come around. Done the right thing."

Rogers chuckled. "Such as sell a burned-down, broken vineyard to a Jew? Perhaps they would have."

His words pained me.

"My mother had little opportunity in Germany," he continued, "but a rabbi helped her to immigrate to the United States. She came here with nothing, lived in a tiny apartment in Queens, and worked at a textile factory. Nearly every day of my life, she told me stories of the vineyard. I did quite well for myself, and one day, I took her back to Germany. When I saw it . . ." His steady tone faltered. "Abigail, I saw the legacy we had lost. It was so strange to see the life that could have been mine and my mother's. She talked about that vineyard until the day she died."

My throat was tight. "I'm sorry." When he didn't answer, I said, "How did you find us?"

"A private detective." Rogers looked out over the forest. "I promised my mother on her deathbed that I would get revenge. It took quite an expensive two years to locate your grandmother, but he did it. I applied to work at the hotel in Starlight Cove with the intent to learn what I could about the vineyard and the best way to destroy it. I never expected a chance meeting with your grandmother to bring me straight into the fold."

The sympathy I'd felt moments before switched to fury, especially to think of how many times my grandmother had happily told me the story of how the two had met. She'd been a target the whole time.

"You bastard."

"I'm sure it must seem that way to you." He adjusted the sleeves of his tracksuit. "However, I believe it is justice. I will take the vineyard in honor of my grandparents, my mother, and my family. The fascinating thing is that the two properties really are quite similar in size and scope. I would say you should consider a visit to Weingut Feierabend, but unfortunately, that's not in the cards."

I paused. "What do you mean?"

He didn't answer. My only focus when I'd confronted Rogers had been to express my outrage at his betrayal. Now, it hit me that no one knew where I was, not even Kelcee. My phone was in the car, resting on the console.

Rogers won't hurt you.

The logical part of my brain shot back: *Oh, yeah? Why not?*

Up until ten minutes ago, he would have been at the top of my list of friends and allies, but now he was trapped. Oma had paid out nearly a quarter of a million dollars to this guy. Why would he let me walk away?

I chewed the inside of my cheek. It had been a few hours since I'd texted Kelcee. There was a chance she would get worried, but she was also sworn to secrecy. She wouldn't ask for help unless it was absolutely necessary. The last time we'd texted, I'd mentioned I could be parked behind a tree all night, which meant she wouldn't worry for a while.

You have to trick him.

It was the only way to get out of the situation. I stared at Rogers for a long moment. What could I do? What could I say to convince him that I was on his side? Finally, I decided the best option was to play on his vanity.

I took in a deep breath. Then I gave a slow clap that echoed through the woods like gunfire.

"I have to admit it," I said. "I'm impressed."

He raised an eyebrow. "Sorry?"

"I thought I was the only one who'd figured it out. Yes, my grandmother ran away from home. She tricked Pappy into helping her, and I say, nice work. She got out of a shitty marriage, got new citizenship and a new life. She was never going to tell anyone until I found the box in the field that brought me to the safety-deposit box. I assume you dropped it? After stealing the ice wine?"

Rogers gave a slight smile. "So many questions."

Don't push him.

"It doesn't matter." I shrugged. "I'm just a little annoyed you got there first, but as always, you never fail to impress me."

Rogers leaned against his car. "I tend to impress myself, as well. If you must know, I had the box with me in the cab of the truck. It was the middle of the night, raining, and of course, the truck had engine trouble as I went down the hill. Isn't that just the way of things?"

"It wasn't raining the night of the party," I said.

"Correct. It was raining the night before the party."

My stomach twisted. Still, I chuckled and took a step toward him, like we were still friends. "Engine trouble? Not great timing. That's just our luck."

"Yes, you would have laughed. I got out and kicked the tires, which was the limit of my capability. However, it seemed to help. Either way, that must have been when the box fell out of the cab. What was in the safety-deposit box?"

"Papers," I lied. "That's how I discovered my grandmother lived another life." Fixing him with a frank gaze, I said, "So. You've got a sweet deal going with this. What's it going to take for me to join in?"

He blinked. "Say that again?"

"Rogers, you want the winery, and so do I. If Pappy dies, which he still could, we could cause serious complications coming out with this, now that I have those papers, which could serve as proof that my grandmother is not who she says she is. Look, we would have the power to tell my family how it's going to be. You and me, partners."

Rogers looked at me for a long moment. "That's putting quite a bit of stake in your grandfather's mortality."

Something about the tone in his voice made my stomach drop, and I remembered the faulty wire that caused the crash.

"You tampered with the plane." The realization made me feel sick. "You tried to kill him."

Rogers hesitated, but the look on his face said everything.

"Okay," I managed to say. "It doesn't matter."

You need to get out of here. Now.

"What if . . ." The fear pulsing through me switched everything into slow motion. My breath came in short, careful bursts, and my words were distant but distinct. "I don't want anyone else to get hurt, okay? They're still my family—they just have something we want. So, what if you keep doing what you're doing? Increase the financial demands in a big way, and I'll plant the seed that it's time to sell. You and I could make a private purchase as a corporation. No one would know until it was too late." Since he seemed to be considering the possibility, I added, "You'd be the primary owner. I'd handle the rest."

He picked a string off his velour tracksuit, wafting the scent of his aftershave my way. "Why ever would I want to share?"

I batted his arm. "Uh, no offense, but I practically run the place. You don't want to take over the vineyard and let it rot. We'd be a good team. I'm so sick of the bullshit patriarchy. Let me have a strong role, and I'll do it. Plus, I'm the one with the proof," I said, hoping the bluff sounded convincing. "You have no leverage without it and no way to get to it without me. Sure, you can keep going as you are now, digging through the trash for a bit at a time. Or we can team up and use the information I have to take the whole vineyard."

My heart pounded so loud I was afraid he could hear it. But I kept my gaze firmly fixed on his. If I could only convince him that I was on his side, I could get to the truck and call for help, and this would all be over.

"Rogers, you know how hard it's been for me," I said. "My grandfather has always favored my brothers. It doesn't matter how hard I work or how much I know. Pappy will never see me as a leader. You were right, saying what you did about the operations job. They could give it to me but still expect me to give precedence to them. But if I owned the vineyard with you, we could do whatever we want. I've waited my whole life for something like this."

The way Rogers rubbed his chin, I could tell he was conflicted. It was clear he'd never expected to get caught, especially not by me. I pressed on, squeezing my hands to keep them from shaking.

"Look, you've got a good system going." I forced a laugh. "I pretty much busted you stealing inventory. You should have seen your face when I walked up that night. I should have known then, but . . ."

I trusted you, you conniving, thieving monster.

"Your gifts for deception are pretty impressive."

Rogers smiled.

Ugh. There was nothing he loved more than a compliment. He was a vain, sad little man, and I couldn't believe I hadn't seen it before. I should have listened to my brother.

Dean.

My heart ached to think I had fought so hard to keep him so far away.

"Let's do it," I said. "Give me your word that we'll be in this together, and we'll be unstoppable. Eventually, we could even change the name. To Feierabend."

Rogers studied me for what felt like an eternity. I kept my thoughts on the laughs we'd shared, the moments we'd felt like best friends. Otherwise, I knew he'd see right through me.

"I have one question," he finally said.

"Do you have to drink ice wine?" I asked. "No, but I would like to keep producing it."

Rogers stretched his fingers. I'd always found the habit endearing, like the gesture of a pampered kitten. Now, it brought to mind a spider stalking its prey.

"Do you think I'm stupid?" His eyebrows pinched together, making him look cruel. "You would never betray your family. They're the only thing you've got."

A shiver started low in my stomach.

"Rogers, I—"

"Oh, Abigail. This was not my plan." His voice was anguished, and he started to nod, again and again, in a way that made him look unhinged. "I do hope you know that. However, you've left me with no choice."

He walked around to the passenger side of his car, reached into the glove box, and pulled out a gun.

I sucked in a sharp breath. "Now hold on."

"No, let's just get it over with!" He turned to me, dark eyes blazing. "Don't you realize what this will do to me? How this will hurt me?"

"Then don't do it," I whispered. "I'm telling you. I want to own the vineyard with you. Please."

He pressed his lips tightly together. Then he said, "I genuinely cared for you. In some ways, you reminded me of my mother. Sadly, you are not her, and this is the end."

My legs started to go numb with fear.

"Wait." I held up my hands. "I know my family would let this go if they heard your side of the story. Or I can keep it a secret. I—"

"There's no such thing as a secret." His hands shook as he checked the gun for bullets. "I think we both know that by now."

Images of my family ran through my mind. My grandmother and her quiet warmth. Pappy and his can-do spirit. Phillip, Kate, and their precious little girl. My mother and father, who I loved with every breath. Finally, Dean. The one who always believed in me, even when I refused to believe in him.

I watched in horror as Rogers walked toward me, the metal of the gun glinting in the low light. Desperately, I looked to the corners of the building for security cameras, but they only held cobwebs. I wanted to tell him he didn't want to do this, that he wouldn't get away with it, but the words stuck in my throat. Instead, a hot tear trickled out of my eye.

"I am sorry, Abigail." He gave me a searching look. "I do want you to know that I did care for you." Squaring his shoulders, he gestured at me with the gun. "Now let's go. Walk toward the woods, and we'll finish this."

I couldn't make a move, other than terrified tremors.

Rogers stalked up and glared at me. "Stop trying to make this hard," he demanded and hit me across the forehead with the barrel. The pain ripped through my brain, and my knees buckled. He grabbed me by the hair and yanked me to the edge of the forest, where it sloped down into darkness.

Run. Fight. Do something.

But there was no time.

Once he had me in position, he gave his familiar smile.

"Sweet dreams, sweetheart," he said and cocked the gun.

Chapter Thirty-Six

Tree branches crashed as a man barreled out of the woods and tackled Rogers, just as he pulled the trigger.

The sound exploded in my ears, and the smell of gunpowder lit the air. I dropped to the ground with a scream. Tree limbs and bushes cut my face and arms as I clawed my way down the incline, scrambling through the brush.

My only objective was to get as far away as possible.

Grunts and groans echoed through the woods, and I hid behind a tree. Peeking out, I gaped at the two figures in the moonlight. They were on the ground, wrestling.

The man who had jumped out of the woods was dressed in black. I watched, hand to mouth, as he drew back and landed two impressive uppercuts to Rogers's jaw. Police sirens screamed in the distance, and I gripped the tree, praying they would make it in time.

Rogers got away and drew back as if to fire. The man leapt forward like a panther, forced the gun out of his hand, and tossed it into the gravel drive. From the back pocket of his jeans, the man pulled out a pair of handcuffs, flipped Rogers, and snapped them on his wrists.

Blue and red lights illuminated the drive as three police cars roared up. I was not surprised to see Henry jump out of one of them, even though we were out of his district. But I could not have been more shocked when the dust cleared and the man who had saved my life got to his feet and turned toward the woods.

"Abby," he shouted, running to the incline.

"Dean!" I screamed.

I scaled the hill, losing my footing at least three times. My brother reached down and grabbed my hand, pulling me up and into his arms. He hugged me tight, and I burst into tears. Burying my face in his damp T-shirt, I breathed in the scent of sweat, gunpowder, and fear.

Pulling back, I realized Dean was wearing a holster with a gun.

"What is going on?" I cried. "Where did you get that?"

Henry led Rogers to his car and shoved him into the back. Through the window, Rogers glared at me, hate in his dark eyes.

"I'm older, so I get to ask questions first," Dean said. "So, let's start with this: What were you thinking? Why would you come out here alone like that?"

I locked eyes with Rogers. "I couldn't let him get away with it. Dean, he tried to kill Pappy. He tampered with the plane."

"I know." Dean looked grim. "I heard everything."

Henry walked up, an expression of thunder on his face. "You all right, Abby?" He squinted at my forehead and glowered. "That son of a bitch," he muttered, pulling out a handkerchief and dabbing it against my head. "We'll get you to the hospital as soon as possible."

"No, I'm fine," I tried to say, but Henry was already clapping Dean on the back.

"Nice work, kid. I knew it was only a matter of time."

Dean gave him some sort of a handshake. "We got him."

"What's this 'we'?" I asked, looking back and forth between the two of them. Suddenly, I got it, even though the handcuffs and the holster should have been my first clue. "Dean, you're a *cop*?"

He gave me a sheepish grin. "Guess the cat's out of the bag." Turning to me, he said, "I've been working undercover for a while now."

Henry clapped him on the back again. "We go a long way back, don't we, kid?"

I must have looked stunned, because my brother laughed. "I contacted Henry right around the time I was in rehab," Dean explained. "He had offered counsel and support back when I was a kid, starting to get into trouble. I was young and dumb and ignored him, but his advice stayed with me. Once I was clean, I decided to follow in his footsteps."

"Excellent choice," Henry said.

"So, I applied to be a police officer. I started working undercover about five years ago. I was up here on assignment."

"I knew it." I jabbed him in the chest with my finger, surprised that he felt made of muscle. "I knew there was more to your visit than you were letting on."

Of course, I hadn't had the first clue it was because Dean was an undercover *cop*, but still. I'd known something was off.

"What was the assignment? Can I ask?"

Dean ran his hand through his hair. "Right about when I was thinking it might be time for a change, Henry called. Pappy had come to him, worried someone was stealing money from the vineyard. Henry suggested I try something a little closer to home. The ice wine was a well-timed coincidence."

Henry spat on the ground. "That wasn't a coincidence. This guy was getting bolder every day. I wasn't too surprised when it happened."

"You knew it was Rogers the whole time?" I asked.

Henry and Dean looked at each other and laughed. Then Henry held up his hands. "I'm not going to tell her."

Dean gave me a sly look. "We had no clue. But you, dear sister, were under investigation." He grinned at my horrified expression. "Surprise. We looked at everyone, though. Don't tell Phillip he was the primary suspect."

I tried to imagine my straitlaced, bespectacled older brother as a criminal and laughed out loud.

"Do you think we'll be able to get the ice wine back?" I asked, glancing at the cop car. Rogers was sitting with his head down.

Henry nodded. "We've got a pretty good idea where it's stored. We just need to get a warrant or confession, whichever comes first."

In spite of everything, elation rushed through me. It was finally over.

The officer in charge of Rogers called Henry over to the squad car. Henry excused himself, his stride instantly official and furious.

Dean's voice went low. "I heard what you were saying about Oma and the vineyard. Is that true? She was paying him off for blackmail?"

Quickly, I briefed Dean on her history, and he whistled. "We'll get her a good immigration lawyer. It's going to be complicated, but we'll figure it out."

"That won't stop Rogers from spreading the rumor. Everyone will know."

Dean shook his head. "I'll set up some sort of a plea bargain to keep him quiet. Either way, he'll be behind bars for a long time."

I hugged my arms to my chest. It was a relief having Dean in on the secret, and given what he did for a living, I knew we could come up with a manageable solution for my grandmother. It didn't mean she wouldn't get into any trouble, but at least she wouldn't have to live in fear of being found out.

"I can't believe this is what you do." I studied him, noticing for the first time that my brother's arms were as thick as knotted rope. "That's why you snuck into my house, because you were investigating me." Dean nodded, and my heart sank. "And if you were working with Henry . . ." I ducked my head. "You knew I reported you."

He shoved his hands in his pockets. "Hey, I don't blame you. I wasn't exactly trying to look innocent."

Look innocent.

Something hit me. "Oh, wow. You're sober." I gave a vigorous nod, and the start of a major headache set in. "You were never really drinking, were you?"

Dean could not have looked more surprised if I'd told him I was working undercover too. "When did you figure that out?"

"Right now. But . . ." I thought over the past few weeks. "Every time you claimed to be drinking, you got it for yourself. If I poured you something, you had an excuse not to drink it."

He rubbed the stubble on his cheek. "Years of fooling some of the worst gangs in the city, and my own sister busted me."

Henry headed back toward us.

"When did you figure out it was Rogers?" I asked, brushing away mosquitoes. "Did he go back to the internet café? Your sleazy friend from high school works there, by the way."

"Jerry?" Dean grinned. "Yeah, he's cleaned up his act. No, Rogers never went back, but he called in the anonymous tip claiming I was trying to sell bottles. There happened to be traffic cameras outside the phone booth, which is how we spotted him. The fact that he wanted me out of the picture didn't make him guilty—it was still possible the dude just didn't like me—but Henry pretended to listen to the tip to give him a sense of confidence. I've been tailing him the past few days to see what he was up to. Imagine my surprise to see you flying at him like a banshee."

I touched my forehead. The blood was clotted, but the headache was worse than any hangover I'd ever had. "Pretty stupid."

"Yeah." Dean pulled me into a tight hug. "Still, I've never been more proud of you in my entire life."

"Why do you have me in a vise grip?" I asked, my face smashed against his shoulder.

"Because you're going to the hospital. Even if I have to drag you there."

I was about to tell him not a chance, but the words took too much effort. Looking up at him in the light of the moon, I registered the fact that my brother was watching over me once again. I gave him a big smile and then blacked out.

Chapter Thirty-Seven

The doctors kept me overnight for observation. I needed ten stitches and had a concussion, but considering all that was saved in our family, my injuries seemed like a small price to pay.

I fell asleep snuggled up under a pile of blankets in a sterile, freezing room, the stars twinkling outside my window.

The charms on my bracelet were the first things I saw when I woke. For a brief, terrifying second, it felt like I'd slipped back in time. Then I realized the stethoscope Braden had sent hung around my neck. At some point during the night, Dean must have gone back home and brought them both in.

Now, he was half-asleep on the chair in the corner. Once he noticed I was awake, he texted something, then hopped to his feet.

"How did you find my bracelet?" I asked, my voice still froggy with sleep.

"The pawnshop keeps records, going back years, in case any of the items were stolen." Dean gave me a sheepish look. "They gave me the contact information of the woman who bought it. It was a gift for her daughter, who had it tucked in a drawer and was more than happy to sell it. At a premium, I might add."

I burst out laughing and immediately grabbed my head. "Oh . . ."

"You okay?" Dean handed me a bottle of water sitting next to the bed. "It's going to hurt for a couple of days, but the doctors said you're going to be just fine."

I pulled the pillows behind my back and slowly sat up. "So, what happened with Rogers?"

The sound of his name made me grimace. The idea that Rogers was the one who had put me into the hospital was still hard to accept. He'd been like family for the past decade. So far, my mind refused to revisit the moment he'd pulled the trigger. I had a feeling it was going to take a lot longer to heal from that reality than from the gash on my head.

Dean must have noticed my discomfort, because he frowned. "You're going to need to talk to somebody to work through all this stuff, okay? It's not good to keep it bottled up."

I took a long drink of water. "Therapy was kind of on my to-do list anyway."

"Well, if this serves as any form of therapy, we recovered the ice wine."

"You did?" Gleefully, I clapped my hands. "How? Where?"

"Rogers had converted the back section of a pole barn to serve as a wine cellar. It was well hidden, with a false wall and everything. The ice wine was in there, along with half of the inventory he'd siphoned off from the bar."

A pole barn? That would be sweltering in the heat. The vintage bottles had probably turned on the first day.

"So, it's all ruined." The anger I'd felt came roaring back. "They rotted."

"No, it's fine. The place was temperature controlled and everything. It was pretty impressive, considering. The guy knows his wine."

"It's in his blood." I leaned back against the pillows, thinking of the anguish on his face as he'd explained his mother's attachment to Weingut Feierabend. It was so strange to think that terrible twist of fate had fueled our grandmother's passion for producing wine, which was then passed down to us. "Did you talk to Oma?"

"Yeah." Dean cracked his knuckles. "She's going to meet with an immigration lawyer and work through the legalities. As expected, Rogers is willing to keep his mouth shut in exchange for a lighter sentence, because he's facing quite a few charges, not to mention attempted murder."

I shivered. "Did she tell Pappy?"

Dean nodded. "He didn't miss a beat. He said, 'Oh, Greta. We all have our stories. Remember the carving in the cherry tree? That wasn't put there by the angels unless you think you're looking at one.'"

I clasped my hands. "Really?"

"Yeah. They kissed. Dad cleared his throat; Mom teared up . . . you know how it goes."

"Sounds about right." The air-conditioning whirred, and I pulled my blankets close. "I can't believe you didn't tell anyone you were a cop."

"Yeah, I know." He glanced at the bracelet. "There were times I wanted to say something, but I'd already put you guys through so much, you know? I didn't have the heart to tell Mom, 'Hey, I'm clean, but there's a good chance you're going to lose me anyway.' It seemed kinder to keep it to myself and let you guys think I was doing odd jobs. Especially once I decided to work undercover." He grinned. "Do you know Oma scolded me? Slapped my arm for not saying anything?"

"Good for her!" I said. "I should have done the same thing."

"Please," he scoffed. "You should have seen your face when Rogers pulled out a gun. 'Rogers, wait,'" he cried in a falsetto. "'Let's get a glass of wine and *talk* about this.' You would have been toast without me."

I giggled. Back when I was in the hospital, Dean used to make me laugh over the most inappropriate things. In spite of the splitting pain in my head, it felt good to have my brother back.

My cell phone buzzed. It was on the table next to the hospital bed, alongside a cup of water and a grape juice box.

"It's the chamber." I glanced at the number. "They probably want to follow up on our thoughts about the wine festival."

Dean waved his hand. "Nothing says commitment like working from a hospital bed."

"Hey, Dana." I picked up. "How are you?"

"Finally calling with some good news!" Her voice sounded bright and cheerful. "Not that you haven't had your own stretch of good news in the past twenty-four hours. I just saw on the news that the ice wine has been recovered, which is just wonderful. I was stunned to hear it was one of your employees."

"Yes, we're happy to have it back."

Dana waited. Once it was clear I wasn't going to volunteer anything additional, she said, "Well, I just wanted to let you know that after the incredible success of the wine festival—it had the highest attendance on record—we revisited the idea of the wine trail. We think it's a wonderful idea, and the city would like to do whatever is necessary to help."

My mouth dropped open. "Dana, that's great! Listen, the proposed list of vineyards has changed—"

"Don't even worry about that." Her voice was stern. "It's your project. You choose who gets to be involved."

"No." I looked at my brother. He was only half listening, reading something on his phone. "I want every vineyard to be a part of the wine trail, if they're interested. This project doesn't belong to me. It belongs to Starlight Cove."

Dana expressed the proper enthusiasm, and we hung up. Beaming, I explained the project to Dean. "You'll have to tell Pappy. He's on his—"

Just then, there was a knock at the door. My entire family waltzed in, our grandfather leading the charge. He looked thin and pale and still wore a hospital gown, but his mischievous grin was more than a little familiar.

"Well, Abby, aren't we two peas in a pod?" His voice boomed across the room. "I always said you were the one who was going to follow in my footsteps."

Instantly, my eyes filled with tears. "Pappy . . ." I pulled him in for a tight hug. Somehow, even in the starched hospital gown, he managed to smell like peppermints and red wine.

My grandmother put her hands on his shoulders. Leaning in, she said, "My dear Abigail, you were so brave. I want you to know I had a long talk with your grandfather and then the family last night. Once things settle down, we're going to work together to figure out what to do about this mess."

"It'll be fine," Dean told her. "I promise."

In a cloud of perfume and silk, my mother stepped forward and kissed me. "You are grounded for the rest of your life. I cannot believe you did that."

"I can." Phillip gave me a high five. "She's always been the tough one."

My father cleared his throat. "Since Pappy is still a little out of sorts," he began, "I've been asked to make an announcement."

"Oh, I've never been out of sorts a day in my life." My grandfather clapped his hand down on my father's shoulder. "Now, let's get to the good news. Abigail, you've impressed us beyond belief. A little birdie told me that job meant a lot to you. You can have it, if you still want it."

I fiddled with the bedsheets. "What job?"

My grandfather scrunched up his forehead. "You don't have amnesia, do you? I was in a coma, and I can still remember my first name. The job you wanted. The operations manager."

"Oh, right. No, I don't think I want that anymore."

My family looked at me in confusion.

"I want to be the director of operations," I told him.

My grandfather stared at me. Then he laughed so loud and long everyone else started in. "Done," he cried.

My family cheered, and I held up my hand. "For my first order of business, I would like to host an employee appreciation night using the missing inventory from the bar that was recovered. What's left of it, at least."

"That is a great idea." My mother gave an enthusiastic nod. "It's time we let them all know exactly how much they mean to us."

A nurse poked her head in the room. "Someone brought the party." She wheeled in a machine. "Let's take your vitals. Then I think we're going to make the moves to get you released."

For a second, the sight of the nurse and her machine almost sent me into a panic attack about the past. Instead, I focused on the present. I was alive and with the people I loved. That was all that mattered.

"It's been quite a journey, visiting this crazy place," Dean said.

"The hospital?" I asked.

"Starlight Cove."

My mother squeezed his hand. "So, you're going back to Chicago? There's not going to be enough crime in Starlight Cove to keep you happy."

"Oh, I don't know. I've been thinking it might be time to slow down a bit. The crime in this place seems a bit more my speed. Besides . . ." Dean looked at me. "I think I might miss a certain chef at a certain restaurant."

My heart leapt. "I am so glad to hear it."

"Speaking of, I texted her that you were awake," he said. "She's on her way."

Just then, there was a knock at the door. My grandmother peeked out and then grabbed Pappy's arm.

"Doctor's here," she said, steering him toward the door. "Everybody out."

My family filed out of the room at a suspiciously fast pace. Dean shot me a grin before leaving. Then a doctor in a white coat walked in.

I blinked. "I think you're on the wrong floor."

"I asked for a temporary transfer." Braden took a seat on the chair by the bed. A hint of a smile settled at the corner of his lips, and he touched the stethoscope. "Looks like this did the trick."

"So well that I ended up in a hospital bed."

"It must run in the family," he said. "So, how is your grandfather?"

"He smells like the vineyard. So, I think he's gonna be just fine."

Braden's eyes held mine. For a long moment, the buzz of the fluorescent lights, the pages on the intercom in the hallway, and the beep of my vitals went silent. The only thing I could see was him.

"I'm sorry I've been so distracted lately," I said.

He shrugged. "It happens."

"The doctor suggested I should slow down for a while, which means I'll have time for another tasting. If you're interested, I know this one winery with an incredible stash of ice wine . . ."

Leaning forward, he tucked a piece of hair behind my ear. "Nothing sounds sweeter," he said and pulled me in for a kiss.

ACKNOWLEDGMENTS

Thank you, first and foremost, to all of my fabulous readers. It was such a delight to learn that you enjoyed visiting Starlight Cove with *The Lighthouse Keeper*, and I am so incredibly grateful to Danielle Marshall and Lake Union Publishing for giving me the opportunity to tell additional stories about this town and its characters.

Lake Union is a dream, and I am consistently humbled by the immense talent of everyone on the team: editors, designers, marketers, and all of the other professionals so gifted at getting books into the hands of readers. Special thanks to Mikyla Bruder—talk about a marketing genius! Thank you for your boundless enthusiasm and hard work. Alicia Clancy, what an unbelievable treat it is to call you my editor. You are the best. One day, we will drink wine and eat Girl Scout cookies together as life intended. Lindsay Guzzardo, thank you so much for your excellent input. And of course, this book would not be on the shelf at all without the diligent and cheerful agenting of the one and only Brent Taylor. I will never forget the phone call where you told me that my dream of Starlight Cove was about to come true, and of course, I will never stop being thankful that you walked into that bookstore so many years ago. It is such an honor to work with you and the team at Triada US.

Writing a book is always an exciting challenge because there are so many things to learn and discover. A number of fine folks helped me along the way—but any and all mistakes are my own. Many thanks to Brian Hosmer, head winemaker at Chateau Chantal in Michigan; you were so awesome for answering the most mundane questions about wine. Cheers to you for helping this imaginary vineyard come to life. Mark Mackie, deputy sheriff in Springfield Township, Michigan, thank you so much for the work you do every day, as well as your generous knowledge. Much appreciation to Suzanne Shaffar, member of Embry Merritt Shaffar Womack, PLLC, for your legal expertise and that of your team as you answered a thousand random questions that typically started with "Okay, tell me if this scenario is even possible . . ." A million thanks to my extremely intelligent friend Dr. Karry Wilkes, for your insight into childhood illnesses. You have always been so helpful, and I feel blessed to have you in my life.

Finally, thank you, thank you, thank you to my family and friends. From the beginning, you have offered enthusiasm and support. To my writer's group—Frankie Finley, Jennifer Mattox, and Stephanie Parkin—your names have appeared in every book for a reason, and it is a delight to learn from your skill and friendship. Mom, thank you for always believing in me and pushing me to be my best. I am lucky to be your daughter. Finally, Ryan, you have given me the life of my dreams. Every single day, I am overjoyed for each second I get to spend with you and our precious family. I love you.

ABOUT THE AUTHOR

Photo © 2010 Brian McConkey

Cynthia Ellingsen is the author of three contemporary novels, *The Lighthouse Keeper* (a Starlight Cove novel), *The Whole Package*, and *Marriage Matters*, as well as a middle-grade novel, *The Girls of Firefly Cabin*. She is a Michigan native and lives in Lexington, Kentucky, with her family. Connect with her at www.cynthiaellingsen.com.